Praise for Louise Doughty's *Fires in the Dark*

'An epic novel . . . absorbing, shocking, hopeful' *Mail on Sunday*

'Compulsively readable . . . its triumph is the quiet authority of its telling,
an unblinking serenity of gaze' *Guardian*

'The reconstruction of Roma life has a loving and compelling vitality . . .
History can give us the facts; a novel such as this has the emotive power to
restore dignity to those who were so appallingly robbed of it . . . It delivers
truth in a knock-out blow, as only art can' *Independent*

'A book overflowing with newfound confidence and commitment . . .
without patronising her characters Doughty builds up a sympathetic
momentum which causes the horrors of the Holocaust to crash over the
reader in a bitterly personal way' *Time Out*

'Memorable and gripping. I have seldom before read sentences that evoke
so well the beauty of the landscape or the pain of hunger and cold' *New
Statesman*

'Louise Doughty's attempt to relate the plight of the Roma in a novel is
ambitious, but ultimately compelling . . . assumptions and inhibitions bind
each of us all too tightly into our own world, but fiction can release us into
another. *Fires in the Dark* does just this' *The Times*

'*Fires in the Dark* is undoubtedly both a topical and important book . . .
Combining a compelling human story with a necessary historical lesson,
Doughty's fourth novel is her best by far and nothing less than an essential
read' *Big Issue*

LOUISE DOUGHTY

STONE CRADLE

SIMON &
SCHUSTER

London · New York · Sydney · Toronto · New Delhi

A CBS COMPANY

First published in Great Britain in 2006 by Simon & Schuster UK Ltd
A CBS COMPANY

This paperback edition in 2014

1 3 5 7 9 10 8 6 4 2

Simon & Schuster UK Ltd
1st Floor
222 Gray's Inn Road
London
WC1X 8HB

www.simonandschuster.co.uk

Simon & Schuster Australia, Sydney

Simon & Schuster India, New Delhi

A CIP catalogue copy for this book is available
from the British Library.

Paperback ISBN: 978-1-47113-757-0

Printed and bound in Great Britain by CPI Group (UK) Ltd, Croydon, CR0 4YY

ACKNOWLEDGEMENTS

Thank you to Sharon Floate and all at the Romany & Travellers' Family History Society. Many of the RTFHS's publications were extremely useful, those by Robert Dawson in particular. Thanks also to Gordon and Margaret Boswell of the Romany Museum, Spalding. Thanks to the Banff Centre in Alberta, Canada (again) and to Jerome Weatherald (again). Thanks in particular to Thomas Acton, Jill Dawson, Jane Hodges and Jacqui Lofthouse for support and advice, to Suzanne Baboneau and Rochelle Venables, and to my agent Antony Harwood. I am indebted to Kevin Smullin Brown for the title and Toby the Sapient Pig for the poem.

The characters in this novel are invented but many of the incidents that occur are drawn from the memories and recollections of real-life sources, some of whom prefer to remain anonymous. My debt to them is immeasurable. *Paracrow tutis, my Petulengros, all Petulengros and jinimengro pals everywhere.*

The few words of Rummanus, or English Romanes, that I use in this book are drawn from a variety of personal and written sources. Where these did not agree, I favoured the personal as I interpreted it, thus any inaccuracies are entirely my responsibility. The only word which readers need to understand is *gorjer*, a pejorative for non-Romanies.

For Nathalie and Anna

CONTENTS

If foky ken jins bute,
Má sal at lende;
For sore mush jins chomany
That tute kek jins.

Whatever ignorance men may show,
From none disdainful turn;
For every one doth something know
Which you have yet to learn.

traditional rhyme
from *Romano Lavo-Lil*
by George Borrow

PROLOGUE

Peterborough – 1949

An autumn funeral, orange and black: it is November. Sunlight strikes the gas tower behind Wellington Street and makes the huge, corroded cylinder glow as if on fire. The iron walkway wrapped about it stands out in sharp relief, a stairway leading nowhere but around. Purgatory has come to Peterborough.

Lijah Smith, about to bury his mother, stares at the gas tower as the undertakers bring the small coffin from the house. He is standing on the pavement, next to the hearse, chewing tobacco and enjoying the twitching of the neighbours' curtains. Only Mrs Martin from number sixty-three has come out onto the pavement to stare honestly. Her husband worked at the Horse Repository before the war and Lijah knows them both. He nods to her. She nods back. He sees she has put on her best shoes and guesses by the way she is standing that they discomfort her.

There are four pallbearers but Lijah's mother is so tiny and light that one of them could have managed the coffin crossways in his arms. Two of the four place their end of the coffin onto the hearse, then step back to allow the others to slide it home. They turn their backs on Lijah and gather for a whispered conversation. Lijah guesses that the man in charge has decided he doesn't need them all.

Something changes hands between the men and two of them turn and bow, then stride off down the road. The chief undertaker steps forward and holds open the door for Lijah to climb into the rear seat of the hearse. Lijah turns and lifts the lid of his mother's dustbin, spits his tobacco into it and replaces the lid. He settles his cap on his head and shakes out the cuffs of his shirt. Before he gets in, he leans sideways on one foot. The coffin inside the hearse provides a surface so that he is able to see himself mirrored in the long window. He checks to see if the oiled kiss-curl that he plasters to his forehead each morning is still in place. He licks a finger and adjusts the curve of the curl, then turns back to the open door in time to see the two undertakers exchange a look.

'Righto, gentlemen,' Lijah says with pride, and steps into the hearse. For what he knows will be the first and last time in his life, he watches as a man – bought and paid for – bows and closes a car door after him.

It seems a shame to waste any of the plump black seating, so Lijah sits dead centre and leans back with his arms resting across the top of the banquette. As the hearse pulls away, he moves forward and taps on the sliding window. The undertaker in the passenger seat opens it. Lijah shuffles forward further and says, 'We are going up Eastfield, aren't we? We're not taking the back route?'

'Not unless you wish, sir.'

'Eastfield, right enough.'

'Of course, sir.'

The man has only just slid the window back into position when Lijah taps again.

'Yes, sir?' The man's voice has become exaggeratedly respectful.

'Nice and slow, like.'

'Of course, sir.'

'No, I mean, even slower than usual.'

'Yes, sir.' The man slides the window back and Lijah sees him mutter to the driver. Lijah had glue-ear for two years as a boy and has never lost his talent for lip reading. The man is saying, 'Bloody Norah, any slower, we'll be going backwards.'

Lijah sits back with a smile of satisfaction. They pass the Corporation Depot and turn into the main road.

The service is brief. Lijah is the sole mourner. Soon, they are outside again in the cold sunshine. The ochre-coloured tiles on the houses opposite the church look soft and textured in the light – two crows sit on a chimney pot. It is an autumn funeral, orange and black.

The hearse turns slowly into Eastfield Cemetery and proceeds along a wide path. Lijah knows this cemetery well. They are returning to the plot where his wife Rose was buried twenty years ago. The grave has been re-opened and Lijah is going to put his mother on top of his wife.

A new plot on the far side of the cemetery would have cost twelve pounds. Opening up an old one can be done for eight. The car was three pounds six shillings, counting petrol. Lijah offered to bring his own, but they weren't having it.

The vicar is no longer with them, which suits Lijah fine. His mother would not have wanted all that ashes to ashes nonsense. Lijah watches as the two undertakers slide the coffin out of the car and place it on top of the sheeting laid ready on the ground beside the open grave. You motored, Dei, Lijah says to himself, feeling a tickle of emotion inside him for the first time. You motored all the way up Eastfield Road, nice and slow, just like I promised you.

He steps up to the grave and looks down into it. He peers, trying to see what might be seeable after twenty years: the ant-riddled wood of the coffin lid? Rose's skull staring up at him, soil-filled sockets for eyes? The very image of death: he half fears and half desires it, for then he will be able to say to himself that he has seen it, and it is nothing.

All he sees is earth: dark earth. They mun't dig right down when they open it up again, he thinks. Well, I suppose that's just as well. Poor Rose. It was a very different funeral for her. No motor for his Rosie – they still used the horse-drawn bier twenty years ago, the crowd trailing behind on foot, led by Lijah and their three daughters sobbing fulsomely, and Dan all stiff and silent – but no Bartholomew, just a big hole in the air where Bartholomew should have been.

He broke his mother's heart that boy, Lijah thinks to himself. *What was left of it, that is.* Lijah scratches his right ear.

He realises that the undertakers and the gravedigger are waiting for him, so he gives the nod and the men lift the coffin up on the sheet and lower it down into the grave. They stand back with their heads bowed.

Lijah is suddenly angered by their solemnity. Have they not realised that this is a job to be done, without their foolish sentiment? He waves an arm to indicate they can go, for all he cares. He and the gravedigger can finish the job. He steps back onto the path and lifts a hand to his waistcoat pocket, fishing out his tobacco.

The head undertaker approaches tentatively and says, 'Would sir like to call in at the office later, to conclude arrangements?' Lijah still owes them six pounds.

'I'll settle here and now, thanks very much. Your job's done, young fella.' He unbuttons his jacket and waistcoat so that he can reach his second waistcoat, the one underneath, where he keeps his wallet.

The undertaker is clearly relieved. 'Oh, very good, sir . . . Cigarette?' He reaches into his trouser pocket and withdraws a packet of Capstan.

Lijah smiles. 'Right you are, then.'

When the undertaker has taken Lijah's money and lit his ciga-
rette, he lights one for himself, nods towards the grave and says,
'Don't normally get mother and daughter buried in the same grave.
Spouses, sometimes.'

'They weren't,' says Lijah. 'It's my wife in there, and it's *my*
mother is going in on top.'

The undertaker raises his eyebrows. 'Close, were they?'

'In a manner of speaking.'

There is a short pause, then the caretaker murmurs, 'Can't say
I'd like my mother-in-law on top of me.'

Lijah takes a sideways glance at the man and thinks, I daresay
she'd not be too keen on it neither.

The undertaker nods across the cemetery. 'Still, nice day for it.
You were lucky with a bit of sunshine.'

'Aye, I was that.'

Pleasantries concluded, the two men shake hands. The undertakers climb into the hearse and reverse with some alacrity. As they
pull away, they give Lijah a wave.

Lijah is suddenly tired. He sits down on the edge of the path to
watch the gravedigger fill in the grave. The gravedigger is an old
fella – perhaps even the same one who shovelled the earth on top of
Rosie twenty years ago. Is it really so long since she died? A picture
comes into his head, unbidden: the children traipsing up the stairs,
one by one, to say their goodbyes to their mother – the looks on
their faces as they came down. It was a painful death. Stomach
cancer. *Of the many things they blame me for, I'm surely not to blame for
that.*

No stomach cancer for his mum. She had stayed tough as old
boots until her nineties. Then she had dropped dead without warning in the street, on her way back from the tobacconists. She had
outlived her daughter-in-law by two decades.

Were they close? Lijah's features lift in a grimace at the thought.

His mother and his wife had hated each other for nigh-on thirty years.

The gravedigger pauses to withdraw a handkerchief from his pocket and wipe his face. Then he resumes. The earth is soft, his task noiseless.

Lijah stares across the cemetery. I'll be here one day. Well at least there'll be no room for me in there with those two, thank God. They'll have to dig another hole. Came into the world in a grave-yard; leave it in one. In between has been just passing time.

Beyond the grave there is a row of silver birches, their white trunks scarred with black, leaves mostly fallen. The oaks are still shedding slowly, unwilling to acknowledge the coming winter. The grave on the right of Rosie's is a beautiful piece of black marble. *Bet that cost a bob or two.* A scattering of orange leaves lies over it, look-ing just right.

The sun disappears. The cemetery is cold.

Dei, in my deari Duvvel's tan. Eh, mandi? The kitchema, that's all I'm good for, Dei. You always said as much. Ne ken, never has been. Lijah sniffs loudly and wipes his eyes with the back of his hand. The gravedigger glances up, then bends back to his work.

The gravestones that stretch to the left are all carved of stone. Peculiar how many are in the shape of books, Lijah thinks: open books – must have been fashionable once – all open in the middle. That's wrong for a start. They should be at the final page. The stone adjacent to Rosie's grave has a husband and wife in it. He can just make out the carved lettering. *Resting,* it says at the top, then underneath the names and dates. *Reunited,* it says at the bottom.

Resting. Reunited. There's a laugh.

An autumn funeral – right somehow. I'd like to go in the autumn, he thinks. He rises and brushes the seat of his trousers. The grass is damp. Lijah checks his watch. Time to raise a glass to his mother's memory at The Ghost Pig. He remembers what Rosie said she said to her, that time she turned up to live with them in

Cambridge. *You've married my son, and you'll sup sorrow by the spoonful 'til the day you die.*

Lijah tips the gravedigger and strides down the path. Over the nearby fence, he can see they are building another housing estate, across Newark Hill. New houses are springing up like crocuses these days. Peterborough is blooming. It will be one vast suburb, soon. Behind the bar at the pub, they have an unopened bottle of single malt. She was worth a large one, was his mother. Clementina. Lemmy. Lem.

PART 1

1875–1895

Clementina

CHAPTER 1

Elijah Smith was born in the graveyard of the church at Werrington, a village in the Soke of Peterborough. I can tell you this for certain, as I am his mother and so was there at the time.

It was a wild winter, dordy, yes. I've never forgot how bad it was. Me and my mother and father were staying in this cottage, for a bit, in the corner of the graveyard. Well, I call it a cottage – it was but one room with a little range and a dirt floor and an alcove for firewood, which was where I slept.

When my pains started, my mother wasn't there. She had gone to the Markestede and wasn't expected back 'til late – it was Wednesday and Werrington was the carrier-cart's last drop-off on a Wednesday. I had no idea when the baby might be due, being only a young 'un and not knowing much about those things. So there was no question as to my mother not going to market that day. It could've been another two months for all I knew.

At first I thought maybe I'd had too much fried bread at teatime. I had a wild hunger on me when I was carrying and would eat until I couldn't sit down any more. So there I was in the cottage, wiping down the little range, with my father sitting in the far corner, snoozing 'neath the lantern. It was dark outside. I'd been feeling peculiar ever since we'd ate and was swaying a little as I worked the cloth, rocking back and forth on my feet, which seemed to help. I didn't feel tired, though, not at all. I felt as though I could scrub that range 'til I could see my face in it.

I had just finished the surround of the hot-plate when it came, out of nowhere. It was as if the pain inside me had been like a few pebbles in the bottom of a washing bucket, swooshing around in lots of water, then suddenly all the pebbles gathered up into a rock which punched the side of the bucket, the inside of me, that is, and suddenly I knew there was a rock inside me and it was dragging down, down, on its way out.

There was no time to finish my cleaning. I dropped the cloth into the bucket next to the range and grabbed my shawl from the chair behind me. Thank God Dadus was asleep. I made it outside before I disgraced myself. I dropped on all fours and cried out.

I knew I had to get round the back, out of sight, in case my Dadus woke and came to look for me. I had a few minutes to crawl on all fours before it came again, *aieeee* . . . Luckily, it was windy and my Dadus was a sound sleeper. A few more yards. By the third time, I was only just behind the cottage but beyond caring who might hear or see me. The ground was damp, so I crawled to a flat gravestone and crouched down low over it, on all fours, gripping its sides. The pain came again, *uurrrr* . . . This time, a different sound. I was bellowing like a cow and pushing, inside. Then it eased.

In the short space it gave me before the next wave, I turned on my side and pulled my skirts up. I wasn't frightened. I wasn't anything but strong. I still remember that. The feeling of the pain goes away – nature's way of trying to fool you into doing it again – but

I have never forgot how determined I was. Every bit of me was up for doing one thing. My baby was coming.

He was trouble from the beginning, was Lijah. I know how people like to say how it was growing up without a father but he had fathers right enough, had them coming out his ears by the time I'd finished with him. No, he was a right bugger from the start.

We were not cottage-dwellers by nature at that time, oh no. When I fell pregnant with Lijah, we were living in our wagon on the green, alongside the others. There were four families altogether. There was my cousins, and some other Smiths they knew, and the Greys with the husband as fat as a pig who took the bed-box all to himself and made his wife sleep on the grass outside with her eight young 'uns. We weren't keen on them, the Greys, but Redeemus Grey was good at finding work and so we'd found it advantageous to stay with them. There's something ironic.

The villagers hadn't bothered us much, so we were quite surprised when the Constabulary came over. They took their hats off, all polite like, and said there'd been a vote or something at the Council and we had to go, and that's when my Dadus kicked up a bit of a fuss, pointing at me and my belly.

Eventually, the vicar showed up and said there was a cottage at the bottom of his cemetery we could have, just the one room like. Of course, what Dadus was most worried about was our *vardo*, but after a bit of talk, the vicar said, 'What if we say your wagon may be parked safely behind the vicarage?' There was even a field for the horse.

So for all the trouble that belly got me into, it got me and Dei and Dadus moved into a cottage in a graveyard.

The others went off, which was just as well. Things had been difficult since I'd started showing. Even before then, everyone knew certain things, and no one was saying anything, and in a little camp like ours there was no getting away from the badness of that.

I've seen girls in my kind of trouble put out to walk the highway on their own, but my mother and father stuck by me. Dadus was mad as a bear when Dei first told him, mind you, and called me every name under the sun. But I was his daughter, and he was damned if any other so-and-so was going to call me names as well. So they made it clear, without saying anything to anyone. Yes, their daughter was going to have a baby and, no, there was no husband within a hundred mile, but that was our problem and nobody else's and anyone who didn't like it could take it up with my Dadus.

My Dadus was like that, soft and hard at the same time. I think it's called being a good man.

I know rightly what you're wondering. It's what everyone wonders in a story like mine. *What was the fella what done it?* Who was Lijah's father? Well, you might ask . . .

When you have a babby yourself, you look at your own mother and father in a different light. My Dei was a small woman, even smaller than me, and I remember staring at her as I was nursing Lijah one day and thinking, I can't believe she did what I did – four times, in total. There was a boy who died firstly, then a girl who was an idiot and they had to give her to the asylum, then me, then another little boy who died when I was small. Four times my Dei did what I did on that gravestone, and only one child to show for it.

My Dei, she was the kind of woman who kept all her suffering locked up inside herself. I never heard her complain once about anything. She had very fine wrists, delicately boned they were, and well-kept hands like a lady. She used to keep a little brass tub with oil in it, which she perfumed with lavender and rubbed into her hands at night before she went to sleep. She took such good

care of her hands you might think she was a fine lady or something, instead of a Travelling woman who worked from dawn to
dusk her whole life: beautiful hands, but as strong as you like.

I lay on that gravestone after Lijah was born, with him tucked
inside my blouse for warmth and the mess that came with him all
around me – and I knew that for all the hardness of our stone
cradle, all I had to do was wait until my Dei got to me and everything would be all right, and it was.

Four times, my Dei did it and I knew she carried the ghosts of
her three lost babies around with her always, like shadows inside,
but she never mentioned them.

After Lijah I knew in my bones that whatever fell upon me in the
years to come, I'd never be doing it again. Taken from the outside,
then taken from the inside – that was enough for me. I wanted life
to be nicer than that.

The vicar must have said something in his church when Lijah was
born as for a short while his parishioners left meat pies on our
doorstep. I can tell you that was the first time such a thing had ever
happened to us, then or since. Dordy, it was a bitter winter. I stayed
inside nursing my new babby and it was like the world outside had
stopped and gone cold and dark because there was no point in it
being otherwise until my Lijah was ready to step into it.

But after a while, the pies had stopped coming and we ran out of
coal. We had all felt such a wild happiness, the first few weeks.
Then the realness of Lijah being with us and no pies and no coal
sank in and the tiredness which I hadn't minded 'til then started to
get a bit much and I thought how I had never been inside anywhere as much as I was then. It's a bad time to have a baby, that
time of year. Isn't natural. All else calves in the spring.

One morning, Dei said, 'It's Sunday, now Father why don't you
take me out on that horse round the villages? We need coal for that
babby.'

Dadus replied, 'It's a mean winter, Mother, no one'll give us so much as cup of water even it being a Sunday.'

And Dei said, 'We'll take the babby then they'll have to.'

I loved listening to them talking about my baby like that, arguing about what was best for him. I loved the fact that they loved him like I did, that he was parcelled up with love.

I did think my Dadus was right, though, so I said, 'No, Dei, it's too cold outside.'

'Give him a good feed,' she said, 'And I'll wrap him tight and he'll sleep the whole way round.'

I didn't like the thought of my Lijah going door-to-door so tiny but he'd been up half the night and I knew she was right about him sleeping if I gave him a bellyful. And I must admit I did think that I could crawl under the blankets and sleep a bit myself as I was still *mocadi*, you know, Unclean, and Dei wasn't letting me cook or tidy or anything.

'You stay wrapped up and we'll be back before you know it,' said Dei.

As soon as they were gone, I settled down on my straw mattress all ready to sleep the whole morning, thinking how, in fact, it was a lovely thing to have a few hours to myself for the first time since Lijah was born. I was going to sleep like a log, I told myself.

I should've known.

I couldn't get comfortable. I was so used to Lijah next to me, it seemed strange to be able to move around on the mattress how I liked. Then I started to think of Lijah and wonder if he was all right and think how maybe I shouldn't have let Dei take him after all and that was a mistake. There was no sleeping then. And even though I'd given him a big feed from both sides before they left, I felt full of milk for him straightaway, and sore, and one side of me seemed a bit hot and hard and Dei had said if you ever get hot and hard you've got to feed him until it's clear otherwise you get a fever. I started to sweat just thinking of it, and I leaked a little which made my blouse damp and I knew I'd never get to sleep then.

I started to imagine all sorts of things happening to Lijah. I thought of Dadus being careless and cantering and Dei falling from the horse. I thought of some *gorjer* housewife taking a stick to them and not realising there was a newborn babby in my Dei's arms. What if he needed a feed while they were out? *Be quiet, you fool, you fed 'im right enough. He'll sleep the whole way round the Soke.* I rolled over and pulled the eider round my ears, closing my eyes.

We'd had dogs set on us often enough. My son would make a tasty morsel for some old rangy hound.

Soon I was up and out of bed and wrapping a shawl around my shoulders. I knew I couldn't tarry in the cottage. I would go mad with it.

Well, it was far too cold to wander round the village like a bedlamite. So even though it wasn't wise, there was really only one place I could go.

It was back in the summer that I had first got into the habit of sneaking into the church services. I can't really say why I started doing it, except I was troubled in my head at that time, for obvious reasons, and it made me feel a bit better. Even before we got given the cottage, we had had some dealings with the vicar who had been good to us. He was a handsome man, tall and straight, white-haired he was, and a kind of peace came over me when I sat there. I suppose it was the only time when I was not with someone else or running errands or some such. It was the only time I could sit and think about things. It is not really done to just sit and think when you're a Traveller, especially a *biti chai* like me. Thinking doesn't get a fire built, nor catch a rabbit to stick on top of it.

I hadn't been inside the church since Lijah was born, so I felt a little strange as I crossed the cemetery, even though I could hear the service was well under way and knew how to get in without being spotted. I never used the main entrance – the iron door-latch clanged up and down like anything – but there was a little side door that pushed open right easy, so I could sneak down the side and sit at the back, where nobody could see me. From that position, I could watch the *gorjers* being holy.

I crept to my place, at the end of an empty pew, tucked away behind a pillar. Nobody paid any mind to me. They were all on their feet singing away and a right racket they were making.

> *Oh, the blood of Jesus,*
> *Oh, the blood of Jesus,*
> *Oh, the blood of Jesus*
> *Cleanses white as snow.*
>
> *Oh, the blood of Jesus,*
> *Oh, the blood of Jesus,*
> *Oh, the blood of Jesus,*
> *Yes, it cleanses white as snow.*

I closed my eyes and listened, and I thought how the hymns always seemed to be on about blood, and it made me think of the blood when Lijah was born and how it seemed clean blood in spite of all the other muck because this beautiful, new thing was coming through the middle of it. And I felt sad, all of a sudden, about how beautiful and new Lijah was, and me being so dirty and sinful, there in the church, and how he deserved a better mother than me. *The mud, the coin, the buckle pressed against my cheek.* And I found myself wishing things could be different for him, and perhaps he would have been better off if I'd left him on the vicar's doorstep, for what had he got to look forward to with the life we led? It must have been the lack of sleep made me think like that, for I'm not usually the type to fall to thinking on myself.

The vicar had started his sermon. I listened with my eyes closed, letting the words float about me. When I felt a bit better I opened them and sat up. It was a small church. I couldn't see the pulpit but I could hear him all right. He had a lovely voice, did that vicar. I've long forgot his name but I've remembered his voice: deep and soft, like he was going to be good to you.

'And so, good members of this parish,' he was saying, 'we must never forget that in our own lands we too have a heathen tribe among us . . .' It was something like that. 'Long may we dwell upon the vile hordes that afflict the Holy Land. For it is easier, is it not, to look at our neighbour's garden and see the weeds and bitter fruit therein than to contemplate our own dandelions?'

He's got a lovely voice but he doesn't half talk a load of blether, I thought to myself, giving a huge yawn and leaning against the pillar. The villagers were restless, too. I could hear them shuffling, up at the front. From where I sat, I could make out the Freemans. I could not see Thomas among them. I felt a sudden yearning for the life of a maiden, the life I had had before Lijah had befallen me, and left me a woman who would always be a mother of a bastard child whatever else happened. Thomas Freeman would sooner spit at me in the street than smile at me now, I thought. How smug his family would feel; how right in their judgement of me.

'And so I come to the matter in hand . . .' the vicar continued. How warm his voice is, I thought, and closed my eyes, '. . . our very own degraded heathens. I speak, of course, of the road-side Arabs, the *gipsies*.'

My eyes snapped open.

'As you will all know, I consider myself something of an expert on this unfortunate race, as we have in our very own churchyard here our own examples, among whom an innocent child has been born. As I was saying last week . . .'

Later, I decided that it was that particular phrase that hurt me more than anything. *As I was saying last week* . . . It was not just bad luck for me to have wandered in there that morning and hear him talk of us in such a way, oh no. He did it all the time.

'. . . it is the fate of these unfortunate children which most nearly concerns me, and the charitable trust I advise. Are we really prepared to cast them into the yawning jaws of hell?' And here, his voice rang like a bell. 'No, my good Christian fellows!' At this point, he must have leaned forward or pointed his finger or something, for there was a hush in the church that told me people were actually listening to him. I held my breath. I would have to wait until the next hymn before I crept out, for what should I do if anyone noticed me here?

His voice went back to normal. 'And so I come to the purpose of today's collection. You all know well, my friends, my abiding interest in the education of our youth. Before too long, I can report, I will be travelling to the Great Halls of Westminster to give evidence on the necessity of compulsion when it comes to the children of rogues and vagabonds. A truly evangelical mission to raise the monies necessary! As our good Lord himself said when he came upon . . .'

He was back to the Lord, but I did not need to hear any more. *As I was saying last week* . . . How long had he been making these plans? He was probably eyeing up my fat belly before Lijah even popped out of it. All the stories Dei and Dadus had told me about *gorjers* stealing our children – I'd always thought it was something grownups said just to frighten children into being good. *As I was saying last week* . . . How long had we got?

I was sweating. It happened when my dugs were full of milk. The back of my neck prickled with it, then felt cold. I was dizzy and leaned against the stone pillar, turning my face to it to cool it. Where had my mother and father taken Lijah? When would they be back? I wanted to be back inside the cottage, but my legs felt weak and I did not trust myself to stand. If I tried to leave now, and fell down, then I would be discovered. My only hope was to wait until they were singing like a bunch of crows and slip out the way

I had come. I wanted my son. I wanted to hold him and hold him and whisper to him that no matter how bad things got for us I would never, never give him over to the *gorjers*.

Dei said that by the time they got back to the cottage I was raving like a lunatic. I had our things all packed and bundled up. They'd only just got in the door when I was sobbing how the vicar was going to come and steal our babby and make him live with a *gorjer* family and go to school and be turned into a little *gorjer* boy. And that's how come we took to the road again, in the middle of the winter, all unprepared and with no proper plan in mind. We upped and left that very morning and I have never since ceased to blame myself for what happened as a consequence.

Lijah knew nothing of what was going on, of course. My innocent son was but a few weeks old.

Yes, well, like I said, he was trouble from the start.

CHAPTER 2

If there is one thing I have always been afraid of, it is being shut away. I am so afraid of it that thinking of it makes me go almost mad. And then I fall to reasoning how that's what madness is. It is like you're shutting *yourself* up, inside yourself, and the more frightened you get the madder you get and the madder you get the more afeared you are. And there is something round and round about this that makes me want to put my hands over my ears and shut my eyes – to shut myself away from the thought of being shut away. And then I see all too easy how a person could fall to screaming for no reason. It is like all the bad things in your life start spinning round and round you until they are like a wall you can't see past, and then you are finished, *oh dordy*, you are finished right enough. Not to think on't, is the only way.

My Lijah, when he was an old man and me even older and still around to see it, was fond of trapping wasps in jam jars and tapping the jar and shouting *garn wi'd yer*! and laughing and would never understand why it upset me so. We were living together then, in our little house in Peterborough, him an old widower, and me an even older widow. I could never sleep unless the door was propped open. I used a conch shell that I made shiny with shoe polish. And Lijah always said how it was all those years of Travelling made me not like closed doors and I never told him it was more than that.

I have thought on my fear of being shut away and happened across two reasons for it. (Living for as long as I have gives you the time to come up with the reasons for almost anything.) One is the thing that happened when we took to the road that winter. We would never have done such a foolish thing were it not for my ravings after I heard the vicar's sermon, and I have cursed for ever since that I had the bad luck to go into the church that day and listen when I was not quite of my right mind anyway, being a nursing girl and therefore sorry in the head. It was losing my wits that Sunday in Werrington that led to the awful thing that happened as we crossed the Fens, the thing that took Dei from us.

The other reason is, I met a madman once, a real one, and the meeting of him left such an impression on me that it is the thing I remember mostly from my childhood.

I am not sure how old I was, seven or eight or nine, thereabouts. The years of things are difficult for me to recall as I had no reading or writing and do not know even the year in which I was born.

Anyroad, when I was nobbut a little *chai*, Dadus sent me across the fields one day to see if I could find the tents where my cousins were camped. We were stopped at a big camp at Stibbington and were expecting them to join us, when we were all going down to Corby for the Onion Fair. After a day or two and they had not come, a cattle drover passed by that Dadus was friendly with and he told him there were bender tents over at Yarwell.

'Lemmy,' my Dadus says to me, 'Go over the fields and see if it's your cousins, and if it's not, asks them whereabouts they've been and if they've news of them.' He was thinking we might have to put the word out we had gone to Corby. The folk we were stopped with wouldn't tarry.

So I set off across the fields and I was happy as a little lark because it had got me out of butter.

We had the use of a milch cow at that time, a fine roan-coloured one, as I remember, and Dei was making butter that day. It took sixteen buckets of water for each churning and guess who had to fetch them sixteen buckets from the village well?

I was halfway there when I realised I had the carrot in my apron pocket. This was unfortunate.

We had finished off the carrots last night, when we had had dumplings and a bit of warmed-up gravy. As she dished up, Dei had passed me a piece of carrot and said, 'Put that in your pocket and keep it safe, it's for the butter.' You got a much better yellow with a bit of carrot added. I had forgotten all about it in my haste to get off and now I did not know what to do. Dei would be wanting that piece of carrot for the churning. I stopped and looked behind me. I had gone so far it was a bit late to turn back.

I was stood in the middle of the field. It was one of those fields that had a rise to it, as if the earth was breathing. I was right on the top of the rise and could see in all directions: the dip and lift of the world around me, distant trees looking grey and green and smoky and not a soul in sight. Before me, the ridges and furrows of the fallow earth tumbled and clambered. If I stopped still, then rocked on my heels, it looked as if the field was moving. It was a warm day, but with a breeze, a lovely day for walking to try and find your cousins. I looked up at the sky, closing my eyes to squint at the sun, as if there might be answers up there and something should happen to tell me whether to go on or go back.

I usually find that if you ask the sky to tell you something, it answers back, sharpish.

I had just dropped my gaze from the sky when I saw it. In the near distance, something was moving against the hedge. At first, I thought my sight was maybe a little squinty on account of the sun, so I closed my eyes and opened them again. I was right, something was moving to and fro in the hedge no more than thirty yards ahead of me.

At this I began to feel a little afraid, as I could tell it was an animal of some sort, yet it was too large for a dog, too small for a cow and too nimble for a sheep.

A terrible thought came to me. What if it was *Bafedo Bawlo*, the Ghost Pig? (That is the thing I am most afeared of next to being locked up and will tell you about some other time.)

Whatever it was, it was moving restlessly from side to side along the hedge, as if it was looking for something in the undergrowth. I thought maybe I should just turn and run but whatever it was must be able to see me plain as I was standing right there in the centre of an empty field and I reckoned most animals could probably catch me in a chase. I did not want to approach it, neither, so I took a middle course and started to walk to the corner of the field that was to its right. This way I was a-signalling that I was no threat to it but was not afraid of it neither.

Then a heart-stopping thing happened. It started to lollop alongside the hedge so that it would catch up with me at the corner. I stopped dead in my tracks and looked around but there was no help for miles around and I knew I must find out what this thing was. So I walked calmly, keeping my eyes on it, until after a few paces it became the shape of a man.

I say a man: it was as much beast as man. It was on all fours, but crouching on its haunches and using its knuckles to walk itself along. It was dressed in a shabby shirt and trousers of the same colour, which should have warned me of something. It had no shoes upon its feet and there was soil in its beard and on its hat. It was nothing but a tramp, a poor, filthy mumper come on hard times, and I did my best to take pity on it as I approached while wanting nothing to do with it if I could.

It was clear that the mumper was determined to speak with me, but then as I neared him he crouched down and flopped both arms over his head and shoulders, as if to protect himself from a beating. I stopped and stared at him. He raised his head suddenly, and I saw his face.

He was an old man. His eyes were big and watery – the lines on his face dark grooves. He had a few days' growth of beard that was grey. It was the face of someone in great pain.

We stared at each other for a while, then he threw his head back and gave a short bark of a laugh. This startled me and I went to continue on but he held out his hand and said pleadingly, 'No, child, child, stay a minute.'

I stopped and we stared at each other again. 'Pray, child, tell me,' he said, 'are you a member of the sooty crew?'

Who's he calling sooty? I thought indignantly. Has he looked in a puddle lately?

'I mean, are you part of the lawless clan? I think you have that look about you, and I cannot tell you what joy that is for me. Are you a child of Tyso, perhaps? You resemble him somewhat. Is he hereabouts?'

At this I began to wonder if he could be a *Romani chal*, but I could not believe that one of us could ever sink to such a state of degradation. I knew not what to do.

'I must be on my way, sir, I am expected,' I said gently, giving a little bob of a curtsey, Lord knows why.

He pointed across the field and said with pride, ''Twas in yonder brook I came across a sizeable gudgeon.' There was no brook anywhere nearby that I could see.

It was at this point I had the misfortune to notice that his trousers were unbuttoned. I gave a start, for I had never seen such a thing on a grown man. A sizeable gudgeon indeed. I was now becoming fearful again because my mother had always told me three things about mad people: they feel neither heat nor cold; they undress themselves at any moment; and they do not realise you are a person at all because they are mad and do not even know what people are.

I realised that the man in front of me was truly mad and so might do anything. He seemed to have forgotten my presence, for he was staring at the earth and muttering, 'Ah, the marshy fen . . . the marshy fen . . .' Then he fell to saying, 'Marshy, marshy, *marshy* . . .' as if there was something in the sound of the word that upset him.

There was nothing for it, I bobbed another curtsey, turned on my heel and began walking back the way I had come.

I only realised he was following me as he was almost upon me. I heard his breath close behind and turned on him. He had been running but at once dropped on all floors and bowed his head again.

'You can't come home with me, sir,' I said firmly, although my heart was knocking in my chest. 'My mother and father would not like it.' *Dei, I've come back with the carrot, oh, and I found a lunatic in a field and I've brought him back with me, too.* I had a sudden image of the lunatic spinning and bumping inside the butter churn.

Then he did something most alarming. He grabbed my hand. He kept his head bowed, though, and said, 'I am knocked up and foot foundered, Mary. I have walked from Essex. If you do not take me in, I will surely die.'

Well, he's not one of us, just a common vagrant, I thought, but I can't leave him in the field. I'll have to take him back to Dei and Dadus.

'Come back with me to the place where we are stopped,' I said, trying to sound as high and mighty as was possible. 'And you can speak to my father.'

I could think of nothing else to do. I could hardly turn up at my cousin's tents with a lunatic in tow.

He was good as gold after that, following behind me at a respectful distance, not speaking, only humming to himself now and then.

You should have seen the look on Dei's face when she saw me
walking back towards the camp, my very own lunatic following
close behind.

Later that day, the men held a meeting. There was a big clunch pit
on the edge of the camp and they would walk around it to the far
side and sit behind the bushes, so that they had their privateness
from the rest of the camp. I did something I had never dared to do
in my whole life before, or since. I followed my Dadus, at a safe distance, mind, then peeled off and went down into and up the other
side of the pit, so's I could hide behind the bushes and listen to
what they said.

It was a wicked thing to do, as I was naught but a girl, and I
knew'd if I was caught listening to the men talking the talk I would
be beaten to blazes. But I was passionate about the lunatic then, in
the same way that my cousin Elias was passionate about the mon-
grel puppy he had bought off the farmer the week before. The
lunatic was a *gorjer*, that much was certain, but he was my *gorjer*. I
think I had somehow got the idea that I could feed him bread
soaked in milk, like Elias did his puppy, and bring him back to
health. I think it was due to me not having had any little brothers or
sisters and not having enough things to look after. There were
plenty of babies in our camp – we were in a big camp then – but
there were lots of young girls as well and I only got jobs like cleaning and butter churning and I think I thought I was big enough for
more than that.

The meeting was a great disappointment, as they rambled on
about men's stuff – the horses and the metal-working – and I could-
n't for the life of me think why it was always such a big secret
when they went off to talk for it's not as if the rest of us would be
interested anyway.

Then it came to my lunatic. My Dadus said how he thought it might be useful to have the mumper around for a bit, as he could be put to work fetching and carrying and how we could leave him when we moved on to Corby. And one of the other men said how my Dadus would have to be responsible and Dadus agreed and that was the end of it.

And before they had finished talking I slithered back down into the clunch pit and scrambled up the other side and got my clothes all chalky but I didn't care as I ran back to our camp across the fields because I couldn't wait to see my lunatic.

And so it was, the very next day, I had him carrying sixteen buckets of water to and from the well, while I walked behind him. And he was as quiet and biddable as a lamb, and the other girls crowded round me asking me how I had tamed him so quick and I could see in their eyes that they were right jealous and wanted to go out in the fields and get their own lunatic.

I was only a *biti chai*, otherwise I would have realised that someone in the village would have seen him going to and from the well with me and said something to someone else.

That evening, I took my lunatic a plate of potatoes and a cup of buttermilk. He was sitting on the edge of the camp, cross-legged, seeming to understand how he mustn't go too close to anyone's *vardo* or interfere with anything. I carried the tin plate over, heaped with potatoes and onions all fried up nice and brown, and a spoon to go with and the cup in the other hand, and he looked up at me with shining eyes as he took it all from me.

I sat down next to him, at a little distance, and watched him feast. He ate and drank with great purpose, like a man who could not think of anything else until it was done.

When he had finished, he put his plate on the grass and looked up at the sky. It was a warm evening. The last of the sun was on his face. He belched, then stared at me. His look made me uncomfortable, so I turned away. When I glanced back at him, he was staring at our camp. The women were all cooking, and smoke rose from the fires and drifted around, hazing everything: evening light, golden. It suddenly came to me, all at once, how good my life was, for I was seeing it through his eyes.

My lunatic gave a sigh. 'I wish I could die, here and now,' he said, his voice quite level and normal. 'For I think there can be no contentment greater than this, the open sky. What is it about potatoes cooked under the sky, do you think? Can it be the summer air gets into them?'

'My mother used a bit of the fresh butter,' I said.

'Ah . . .' he said.

I was enjoying this small, normal conversation, and was thinking about asking him some questions about his life and how he came to be a lunatic. Then, suddenly, he started smacking the side of his head with the flat of his hand, as if there was something in the other ear he was trying to dislodge. 'Gone! Gone! Gone!' he groaned. I felt a rush of disappointment, for I had persuaded myself that with enough fresh air and potatoes, he might be brought sane, then I would have the pleasure of telling people I had cured a madman once. But I saw my own folly at once.

He muttered into the ground, as if he had forgotten me. Then he lifted his head and glared at me. 'That blackguard Taylor! I'd like to take a stick and knock his hat off!' His shook his fist at me, and I rose without a word and ran back to the safety of the camp, leaving his empty plate and spoon on the ground.

The men came two days later. They entered the camp as *gorjers* do, marching around like they own the earth and can go anywhere whenever they like. As they strode up to our *vardo*, the men and boys gathered round, at a discreet distance but watching carefully, in case they had come for one of us. My Dadus raised his hand in a signal that it was naught to bother about, for he knew why they'd come right enough.

The lunatic was sitting cross-legged by our *vardo*, and my Dadus pointed him out. I thought the men would go and speak to him, but they said not a word. They went over and grabbed him, one arm each, and hauled him to his feet, then dragged him across the camp, to the edge of the common. I ran after them, and Dei and Dadus followed behind.

The lunatic had begun to struggle and whimper like a baby. It wasn't mad crying out, it was moaning in fear. It was horrible how not-mad it was. As they reached the edge of the common, he broke one arm free and began to flail it about. At this, the men lost their tempers and pushed him face down in the dirt. One sat astride the lunatic's back and pulled his arms behind him. He cried out in pain, his face pressed to the dirt. The other had a bit of rope and he began to wind it round the lunatic's wrists to bind them, cursing as he did.

I tugged at Dadus's sleeve and he understood me right enough. 'I think you may be gentle with the old fella,' he said to the men, 'he was ill when my daughter found him and has not fully recovered. He told her he had walked from Essex.'

One of the men gave an unpleasant, disbelieving sound. 'Essex, my arse. He's escaped from Northampton General Lunatic Asylum.' He stood and hauled my lunatic to his feet. 'Come on, John,' he said, 'that's the last you'll be bothering folk for a while.' His tone was not unkind, more casual, which somehow upset me all the more.

I followed to the start of the lane. Parked by the verge was a small wagon with a flat roof. It was so tiny that the whole of the back of it was the door, and they lifted my lunatic up and into it and it was then he began to cry. They slammed the door shut behind him and bolted it and there was a small barred window in the back and he stared at me through it.

The look he gave me as they pulled the wagon away will stay with me until the day I die.

My Dadus came and rested his hand on my shoulder. 'It's what they do with folks that lose their wits,' he said gently. 'They are chained up and beaten like dogs and the more they howl the more witless they are thought to be.' He shook his head and then turned back to the camp.

I realised I was crying too and wiped my face with the back of my sleeve. My mother came and gave me a gentle cuff about the head. 'Here,' she said, and thrust a handkerchief at me to wipe my face. 'That's how it begins,' she said, 'You lose your dignity and next thing, you're sliding down into the mud.'

I knew she didn't really mean it, that wiping your face on your sleeve was the beginning of losing yourself and going mad, but I took the point all the same. It didn't matter what happened to you, how much you were hurt by the world, you must never break down in front of others and let them see, because once you lost your dignity other people thought they owned you. They thought they could push you into a tiny wagon no bigger than a dog kennel and you had no right to mind. I've never forgotten that, although I know that my lunatic had probably forgotten me by the time his little wagon had turned the corner at the bottom of the lane.

When we left Werrington, that winter when Lijah was just a new babby, we headed straight off Whittlesey way. I felt bad because I knew Dei had liked the cottage in the cemetery, liked being able to cook and clean more easily for a while. Dadus had never been happy there, mind you, and was glad of an excuse to get out. There were ghosts in the ground, he said. Evil spirits.

We took it slow, a few miles a day, as we'd not used the *vardo* for a while. We were as far as Prior's Fen when Dadus stopped and said there was a problem with the back axle so we all had to get down. The wind blew down the road and Dei and me huddled round tiny Elijah. Then it began to rain, that freezing, stinging rain which feels as though someone is sticking needles in your face.

Dadus told us to go and shelter beneath the oak by the crossroads for we couldn't go further until he'd moved everything about in the *vardo*. The weight inside needed shifting, he said. So Dei and me hurried off down the road and the rain came down and down and by the time we got to the oak we were both soaked through and my feet were wet and slipping in their clogs.

We huddled down against the trunk of the oak. It was rough against our backs but the rain made the earth smell warm and at least we were sheltered which was more than Dadus was bending over the *vardo*'s back axle. Dei was shivering, and I felt worried for her, for I knew she was thinking how we could have all been back in the cottage. It would be dark soon, then we'd have to pull the *vardo* onto a verge, which is the thing most likely to get you in trouble with the gavvers.

I said, 'Should we go back to Eye Green, d'you think, Dei?'

Dei said, 'I'm not keen on the folk at Eye.'

After a while, a farmer rode past on his horse, leather cape over his shoulders. He slowed as he passed by, looked down at us huddled beneath the tree, and spat at our feet. Then he trotted on.

It was near dark by the time Dadus trotted up to us and still raining. 'I've fixed it up enough so's we can make it to that row of oaks,' he said, 'but Dei will have to walk.'

'I'll walk,' I said.

'Don't be foolish now,' said Dei, as she struggled to her feet.

In the end, we all walked, all but Lijah of course, who lay swaddled in a basket inside the *vardo*, and as I put him in I thought how wonderful to be a little babby and to be wrapped up warm all the time and have nothing to think of. Dadus led the horse, which was starting to shiver, and Dei and I guided the *vardo* by pushing either side, but it was all we could do to get it round the corner and in the dark we could hardly see the lay-by and we were all soaked to the bone. Dei and I went in first and lit the lantern and took our wet things off and stowed them, then hung the curtain for Dadus. He wasn't speaking when he finally came in, he was that soaked and cold. And we were all hungry and there was nothing but Dei gave me a last bit of bread and said a nursing girl had to have something inside her. And I must say as Lijah woke and cried to be fed I felt right sorry for myself, for I felt as though everything was wrong but I didn't know yet how much wronger it was going to be.

We were low on oil, so we shut the lantern as soon as I'd finished feeding His Lordship. There was nothing for it but to bed down and wait until the morning. Dei took down the curtain and hung up our wet things so that the warmth of us would help to dry them in the night. I went to sleep on the floor of the *vardo*, with Lijah next to me, hearing the clatter of the rain on the roof, which is a sound that has always helped me go to sleep. But there was also the not-so-nice tap-tapping of the drips from our wet clothes that smacked and busted against the polished floorboards, right close to my head. And these two sounds didn't get along, for all they were both water, and they argued in my head until I went to sleep.

Lijah woke me at first light, and I fed him. I could tell from the movement of him that he'd dirtied his swaddling things and I had better change him. Dadus and Dei were still unmoving on the bed-box, so I levered myself up gently, with Lijah in the crook of my arm. The box where I kept his clean cloths was in the cabinet beneath where they slept, and it was hard to lift it out one-handed without disturbing them. When I opened the door to go outside, the cold, white light flooded the *vardo*'s shuttered darkness and I stepped out as quickly and carefully as I could, pulling it to behind me.

The rain had stopped during the night and, although it was chilly, the air was light, and there was that nice feeling you get when a horrible night has ended – like, whatever's going to happen today'll be better than yesterday, for certain. The grass was soaking, so I sat on the step and laid Lijah across my knees and unwrapped his swaddling and cleaned him as best and quickly as I could. His little barrel body went blue with the cold and his arms and legs were flung wide and flailing against it. Then I wrapped him up again, hoisted him and tied him to me with my shawl.

I stood holding his dirty things, wondering what to do. I could just go back inside and stow them, but I didn't know when Dei and me would next have the opportunity to boil some water and wash them out. There are some parts of Travelling with a babby that are not right easy. So's I thought to myself, I'll take a walk down the lane and see if there's a stream nearby.

I had my heavy shawl on, but even so I went quickly. Lijah was awake, and looked up at me with those black eyes of his, as if he was wondering what I had just put him through and what I would do to him next. I talked to him as I walked. 'You've nobbut yourself to blame, *amaro chavo*. *Akai, adoi, atchin tan or duva in the biti drom in a brishenesky cheerus*, you've to be wiped . . .' He gave a squirm, and screwed up his face, as if he wanted to cry but couldn't quite decide if it was worth the effort. '*Kushti tikner mush* . . .' I soothed him.

We'd been down this way before and I had a memory of a ditch with a stream beyond the crossroads. The Fens is like that. You get water almost anywhere. I found it right enough, no more than a trickle, but enough to unfold the swaddlings and lay them flat on the stones beneath the water, weighted down. Dei said how she'd seen babies die of not having their swaddlings changed enough, of how the skin got reddened until it swelled and cracked and the babies got a fever. She thought it dreadful some mothers didn't realise that – although I have to say my Dei was hard on other mothers as only a woman who has lost three children can be.

I can still remember squatting by that stream, Lijah strapped to my chest, looking up at me with his eyes wide, while I watched the clear water run over the yellow staining of the swaddling clothes. I can remember thinking how it was good to have a mother who told you what was what. How would I have managed Lijah without her there to tell me?

It was the last time I was happy and ignorant like that. Happy, despite the cold. Clear water running. My baby on my chest, dark eyed and knowing everything.

As I was walking back to the lay-by, I saw them, standing by the *vardo*. There was two of them, one of them holding their horses' harnesses, the other a-banging on the side of our wagon. 'Dei! Dadus!' I shouted in warning. The men heard me and looked round.

I began to run towards them, but I couldn't go so fast with Lijah strapped to me and the wet swaddling in the crook of one arm. While I was still some yards away, Dadus came down the step, pulling his braces over his shirt. The men turned to him.

I reached them as they were showing Dadus a piece of paper. As I ran up, Dadus glanced at me and said, all cross-sounding. 'Lem, go inside.'

'Is it all right, Dadus?' I whispered.

'Go inside,' he said.

Inside our *vardo*, Dei was pulling on her outer things. Her face was set.

'Dei, it's the gavvers . . .' I said. 'What do they want?'

'Same thing they always want,' said Dei, and I could hear in her voice that, though she was trying to sound casual, she didn't feel that way at all.

'Pack stuff up,' she said, and together we began to roll blankets and stow the eider. Having Lijah strapped to me made me slow and clumsy but he had gone back to sleep and I didn't want to shift him.

The door opened, and Dadus came in. He stood there for a minute, looking at us.

'They want my hawking licence,' he said.

I looked at him, and at Dei, and I knew in that minute that we all had the same stricken look on our faces. Dadus had let his licence run out before Christmas. *Joseph Smith, Hawker of licensed goods, Knives, Kettles and Sundry Kitchenware*. It cost two pound to renew it, and he said he'd get another when he'd been to the wholesalers at Whittlesey as there was no point 'til then. But *Licensed Hawker* is what he called himself, and the gavvers wanted the proof.

'Show them the old one,' said Dei. She lifted the lid to the high chest.

'I'll ask them if you can stay here, at least,' he said, and went out again.

I looked at Dei. At least?

Turned out it was more trouble than it was worth, apprehending us. I heard one say it to the other, as they hitched our *vardo* to the horse. They had to send for a cart from Eye for us and all our things, on account of the back axle. Then they took us to Whittlesey and we spent the night in the *vardo* in the yard and they fed us quite well with a sort of stew. In the morning, they said we were going down to Ramsey but they wouldn't say why. Well, they weren't going to bother with the *vardo* all that way, so they put us in a huge wagon with a load of others.

I don't think I understood even then how bad it was, on account of how Dei and Dadus kept saying to me I wasn't to worry. I should have realised, they said it so often, that worry was exactly what I should have done. But looking back on it, even though I had a baby, I was still something of a child. Dadus told me he had been *apprehended* four or five times and nothing had ever come of it. Quite cheerily, he said it.

The others in the big wagon were mostly loose women and tramps from round about, so we wouldn't lower ourselves to speak to them. We went the back route, across Glass Moor, and they stopped at another village and picked up a Travelling family like us. We rokkered to them right enough and they said something

about how there'd been a load of trouble down at Pondersbridge
and across the Fens on account of it being such a bad winter, and
how the gavvers were going around picking up Travelling people
all abouts. They said how they had been part of a big camp, and
their horses were all tethered in the next field and a whole gang of
local men had come and untied the horses and flapped umbrellas
at them to frighten them away. And some of them had run away on
foot but they hadn't as they had old folk with them who were
poorly.

We were in Ramsey a week, kept all together in a lock-up, a
filthy, low place. I don't care to describe it. I suppose it was then I
began to realise this might be bad. There wasn't a proper court-
house, so the magistrate held our hearing in the local pub one
morning, in the top room. It's all a bit strange to me now. A woman
came and said how a *gipsy* had come to her door and she'd turned
her away, and later her chickens had gone poorly and started stag-
gering about, then another pair had come and offered to buy them
off her cheap. I was only half listening. Then she said the second
two was a young 'un and an old 'un and they had a baby with
them, and she pointed at me and Dei. I wanted to laugh out loud,
it was that foolish. I had never seen the woman in my life.

The magistrates called her the *prosecutrix*. When she went to the
back of the room, she stood next to a big fella, and I saw he was the
farmer that had spat at us as we sheltered underneath the oak tree.

There were so many other people in the room saying things that
I lost track. I just held my Lijah. But I could feel Dei and Dadus
either side of me getting stiffer on the bench in a way that meant
they were upset. Then we were all standing, and the magistrate in
the middle, a white-haired fella, was saying, 'One week hard
labour followed by five years in a reformatory,' and Dadus was
stepping forward with his hat clutched in his hands and tears were
running down his face and he was talking about Lijah and saying
how I was still a nursing mother and so young and all – and it was

only then I realised they were talking about me. I looked at Dei, and she was crying too, with her eyes closed and lips a-flutter, which meant she was praying.

We all sat down again, and the white-haired fella goes into a huddle with the others.

There is a way to get through being told something terrible, and that is not to believe it until it is proved to be true. At least, I thought so's at the time, although I have since changed my mind and am more into plain speaking.

I think we were let out the room for a bit. I can't rightly remember. I know that, some time that day, the lady who ran the public house came up to me with some bread and cheese and said I was nobbut a child myself and had not a scrap of flesh on me and if I was to look after that babby I needed feeding up. I gave some to Dei and Dadus but they wouldn't take it.

We were back in the room then. It had a lot of windows and a low ceiling. They probably had wedding parties and such when it wasn't for the magistrates. The white-haired fella said how he had been moved by what my Dadus had said and the fact as how Dadus had been a licensed hawker and had not been in trouble before spoke something. But he could not let people like us think it was all right to go around poisoning people's chickens just whenever we felt like it. But he was mindful of how to take an infant from a nursing mother was not right. As such, I was getting a fine. Our *vardo* and things would be sold to pay for it if we did not have no money. But he had to make an example of all miscreants and because of that Dei would get four weeks' hard labour, not two, and I understood she was doing my hard labour for me and I started to cry but Dei and Dadus were quite calm by then because I wasn't going to the reformatory neither. Dadus got a fine for not being licensed.

All I understood was that I wasn't going to be put away and Lijah would not be taken from me. I didn't really understand about

Dei. She was being sent to the House of Correction in Huntingdon, they said. Dadus and I would have to stay in Ramsey to sort out our fines.

When we got outside, it was cold and sunny. There was the same wagon waiting. Dei went forward and I went to go with her, but Dadus put his hand on my arm and said, 'No, Lem, you and me are staying. It's just Mother is going.' And I stood holding Lijah and staring at her as she climbed up. There were windows in the wagons, and I waited for her face to appear at one, but it didn't, which was perhaps for the best.

'When we've sorted out the fines we'll go down to Huntingdon and find somewhere to stop until she gets out,' Dad said.

Hard labour, our Dei? 'They won't make her lift rocks or anything, will they?' I asked Dadus but he wouldn't reply.

CHAPTER 3

Cannon balls. It wasn't rocks, we found out, it was cannon balls.

We were lucky, and managed to get the fine paid up in a fortnight. Dadus found some local Lees who helped us out a bit, and we stopped with them while we came to an arrangement. They paid our fine and then kept our *vardo*, which was a beautiful bowtop, while we set off on the horse for Huntingdon. They would keep the *vardo* for us until we returned with Dei and paid them back. We were that relieved, as to have sold it outright would have been the end of us.

We had a little money left over after we'd paid the fine, so when we got to Huntingdon, we tried to get a room at an inn called The Sun. I could tell the inn was called The Sun, as I could see the sign swinging in the wind and the bright yellow sun a-painted on it, with pointy rays. There was sleet falling, at the time.

They turned us away, even though we could see there were no horses in their stable, but the woman came out after us and said there was another place at the bottom of St Peter's Hill that took what she called *all sorts*. It was worth us trying, she said, on account of it being close to the House of Correction. She didn't like to think of the baby having nowhere to lay its head what with the sleet coming down an' all. We thanked her right enough.

The other place had a sign that was a dog raised on its hind legs snarling at a bone that was flying past in the beak of a big black bird. The downstairs bar was dark and crowded and there was a terrible noise of shouting coming from upstairs, and the young man who spoke to us said there were eight to a room but only six in one of them so we could have that. At this, Dadus told some story of how Lijah was awake all night and the young man would get complaints in the morning and wasn't there a shed or something out back, next to the stables? He looked at us a bit funny but of course we could have told him that we would rather stop by the horses than with a bunch of stinking, drunken *gorjers* any day. We didn't like paying for it when there were any number of stables in the town we could have slept in for free if we'd left the sneaking in until dark, but considering the position we was in we could not risk getting into trouble. Dei would be depending on us.

As it turned out, there was a shed with a hayrick behind the stables which was as cosy as anything and we saw to the horse first and then the young man gave us some blankets and a talking-to about not lighting a fire, as if we were stupid. Dad went off and came back with the good news of having found a baker's shop where they would give us bread each day if he was there two hours before dawn to help unload the furnaces. And this piece of luck was so large that I felt almost cheerful as we settled down at the bottom of the hayrick and ate fresh rolls, and talked about how the next day we would queue at the prison with the other relatives and send a parcel of rolls in to Dei. We talked about how pleased she'd be to get them.

*

The next day, after Dadus had done his shift at the baker's, we set off for the prison.

There was a right old crew queuing at the gate of the House of Correction. You've never seen such a bunch in your lives. There was the bony women with their bony children waiting to see the Debtors, and the loose women with their faces painted and even some gentlefolk, standing to one side, who were let in first, of course. Dadus said how he heard one say his brother was in there for *sedition*.

'What's that?' I asked quietly.

'Talking about not liking high-up folk,' Dadus replied.

I had never been near such a place before, and it felt strange to see the whole world there, and to think that such calamity could happen to anyone. It made me feel a bit better, I suppose, like even high-up folk had their bad luck sometimes. Maybe that was one of the reasons why I stayed hopeful, even then; why I was not on my knees in fear.

After a while, we were let into a yard. It was rutted and muddy but the mud was frozen so at least we weren't ankle deep. Some of the people who were waiting were squatted against the wall but it was so cold I had to keep moving, up and down, bouncing Lijah on my arm. One of the loose women came over and started pulling faces at my Lijah over my shoulder, to play with him. I was for putting up with it, but then she lifted a finger to touch his cheek with her long scratchy nail. I turned away, for I would not have my child touched by such a woman. She cursed me under her breath and went back to squat against the wall.

I cradled Lijah's head with my hand, and kissed him, and whispered to him, 'Well, at least we're out of the wind now, aren't we *chavo*?'

We waited and waited and Lijah began to cry on account of wanting feeding. I didn't want to leave Dadus but I couldn't feed Lijah in the yard with all the hungry eyes that would stare at me.

Eventually, he'd had my knuckle to chew and all the dandle I could manage and I said to Dadus, 'Dadus, I'll have to go off and feed him,' and he said, 'Right you are, Lemmy.'

So I left Dadus in the yard and slipped out the door past the others still waiting in the wind and went and found a lane and a fence with a gap. It was freezing, but for all that it was nice to be out of that yard for a few minutes. It was just me and Lijah, and the good feeling of making him completely happy, his little mouth a-pulling at me, and his fist a-clenching 'round my finger. *Biti*. Little. It was all I could think, looking down at him. You are so *biti*. I let the shawl around his head drop back so's I could stroke his fine baby hair while he fed.

I winded him, then he was asleep on my shoulder for a bit, and I think I must've dozed a bit myself with my back against the wooden fence, for I started awake and the light felt different, so I sorted myself out then hurried back to the yard.

There was no sign of Dadus, and it was only by asking that I found out he had gone in. I thought the warder might not let me past but he took pity on me and I found Dadus was still queuing but in a stone corridor now.

Came our turn, right enough, and we went into a room with a faraway ceiling, where the windows were so high up too you couldn't see out of them even if you stood on a table and jumped. There was a man with a big book behind a desk and when we told him who we were there to see he frowned, still looking down at the book. He asked us to repeat the name. Without saying anything, he got up, slammed the book shut and left the room by another door.

Dadus and I glanced at one another.

Eventually he came back and said we're to go away again, but that we're to come back the next day, only not to join the big queue in the yard but to go to a side door. After that he wouldn't say nothing, only opened his book again and made it clear he wanted us to tell the next one to come in.

'What d'you think's happened to Dei?' I asked Dadus, as we walked away from the prison, and I knew he thought it bad for he snarled, 'Leave it, Lemmy,' then strode off down the dirt road that led to our lodgings, leaving me to hurry after, clutching Lijah to me.

I tried not to think on't, but that night I lay awake, and heard by the silence next to me that Dadus was awake too, there on the straw. In the gloom, I could see the shape of his broad back. He was turned away from me, and I felt frightened then, frightened of everything.

The next morning, soon as Dadus was back from the baker's, we went back to the House of Correction and found the side door and rang the bell, and at the little tinkle of it my Lijah jerked his head.

The warder who opened the door to us was a cheery sort of fella. He had a beard that ran from one ear, down to the chin, then up to the next ear, just on the edge of the face like, with no moustache, so's it looked like his beard was a strap that was holding the rest of his hair atop his head. He took us down a narrow corridor and into a little room that was the warders' room. One wall of it was shelved and on the shelves was jars of beer. In the other corner was a barrel, with two other warders sat either side.

The two other warders were reading a newspaper and looked up at us, unfriendly like. Normally, I would've stared back, but I dropped my gaze, as I knew how important it was that we were on good terms with them so that we could find out what had happened to Dei.

Dadus was staring at the jars, and said to the bearded one, 'D'you not lay your jars on the side, on account of the sediment?' I realised he was being friendly too, for the same reason.

'The shelves are not deep enough,' the warder replied.

'That's a fine load of beer, anyroad,' Dadus said, 'You fellas must have a fine time in here,' and the seated men's faces cracked into smiles.

The one with the beard explained how's they were allowed to brew the beer that got sold to the prisoners, and how it was only the most trustworthy of them did such a thing. He made it sound like an honour, but one of the seated ones gave the game away by saying, 'We wouldn't be able to keep our rent up, otherwise, not on what the County give us, you know. You'd be amazed if we told you how little it was.' Later, Dadus explained to me how the men were paid very bad and that was accounting for how they were often the lowest sort and behaved in an evil way towards the prisoners sometimes, but I still don't think it makes it right.

Then, the two seated fellas stood up and put on their top hats and buttoned their jackets as to leave, and the bearded one said, 'Bateman, should I get the nurse to take these two down?' and the other said, 'She'll not be allowed to leave the sickroom, you'd best do it yourself, but not just yet as she'll still be attending to them.'

Third one said, 'Best leave it 'til she's done.' And two of them went out.

At the mention of a nurse, I saw Dadus go pale and I felt myself start to sweat and I took the liberty of sitting down where one of the other wardens had been sitting – luckily the bearded fella didn't seem to mind.

'Can you tell me what has happened to my wife?' Dadus asked the question as casual as if he was asking the hour of day.

Bearded fella looks surprised. 'Did they not say?'

Dadus shakes his head.

I was glad I was sitting down then, for what the fella said was so horrible I think my knees would have given had I been standing.

There had been an accident. Both her legs were broken. It happened on the tread-wheel, the second week she was here. The first week of hard labour was always shot drill, the fella said. There was never enough room for all the hard labourers on the tread-wheel, so everyone got put on shot drill for a bit when they first arrived.

'What is shot drill?' my Dadus asked, and I could hardly believe
how he could keep his voice so steady.

So the bearded fella told us and afterwards I wished he hadn't.

Shot drill was where you took a cannon ball from a pile in the
yard, stacked up against a wall, and you carried it over to make
another pile, and it was a pyramid, and there had to be ninety-one
cannon balls in each pyramid. And if there weren't you did it
again.

I imagined my tiny, little Dei counting as she staggered across
the yard in the bitter cold, '*Axis . . . nevis . . . tay . . . enin . . .*' I
imagined her counting to stop herself from thinking of the pain of
it.

I thought of how she must have been relieved when they told
her a place was found for her on the tread-wheel.

It was on account of the water, the warder told us, that the accident had happened. He didn't agree with the use of water on
tread-wheels. He had been a warder up at Kirkdale where they
had the biggest tread-wheel in the country and they used it to grind
wheat and some others used theirs for weaving. But ours is used to
turn water, he said, and that makes the steps a-slippery and accidents are not uncommon, I'm afraid.

It was only later that I thought, I never asked him what the turning of water was for. I had these strange thoughts of rivers and
streams being turned over and over, in the way you might air an
eider, but for no good reason – and my Dei having been crippled on
account of this turning of water for no good reason. And that, of
course, was even worse than her being crippled for the milling of
wheat.

I think he must have realised what bad news this was for us,
because he said then, 'I'll just leave you for a minute and go and see
if the nurse will have you,' and went outside.

Dadus came and sat next to me and we couldn't even look at
each other. He put his hands over his face, and I knew he was

struggling with himself for my sake. And I felt our lives fall away from us, like water through my fingers, for whatever happened after this we would never be the same as before.

After a while, one of the ones with a top hat came back in. He took six of the beer jars down from the shelves, one by one, and stacked them by the door.

Dadus said to him, lightly like, 'So how do accidents happen on the tread-wheel, then?'

'Folk slip, go under,' was all his reply, then he started saying how we shouldn't believe everything the first fella had said on account of him having once been a felon himself and that was how he thought himself an expert on the tread-wheel. He claimed to have been a warder elsewhere but it was well known that he had served three months for bastardy up at Kirkdale and only got out when he had paid the four pound fine to the workhouse for the upkeep of the child.

This took my mind off our current anxiety, for a bit, as it astounded me to think that a man could go to prison for the getting of a child and I couldn't help thinking how much I would have given all the gold in the world to have taken my Dei off that tread-wheel and put there a certain man who shall remain nameless.

Top-hat fella went out again, with two of the jars of beer, and we sat some more for what seemed like a long while. Lijah was asleep the whole time. Eventually, Dadus got up and went over to the small, square window in the wall next to the shelves of jars. He stared out of it for a while, and the light on his face showed me how old he was, and I thought, *he looks an age older than he did this morning*.

The bearded fella never came back. A different one, one we hadn't met before, came in and took us to the door of the sick-room, and I knew'd we were getting near it still some feet away from the stench that came from the open door. We knew the stink of sewerage right enough, but this was something different, something deep and coloured. 'What is that smell?' I whispered to Dadus, as I tucked Lijah tighter into my shoulder.

The warder accompanying us heard me and leaned towards me staying sternly, 'It is the stink of corruption, young lady, and let that be a lesson to you.'

As we reached the door, he said, more normal like, 'Gangrene. We've a few cases at the moment.'

The room was another high-ceilinged one but the windows were smaller and didn't admit much in the way of light. There were about a dozen beds in there, made of boards. I looked quickly down one row. The two women in it nearest to me were both sitting up and knitting. They both had triangles of cloth over their noses, held around their ears with bits of ribbon. The rest of their faces was red and pockmarked and Dadus told me later they had an evil *gorjer* disease that was eating off their faces bit by bit.

It was a soft sighing sound made me look the other way, and it was then I saw Dei. She was flat on her back, with her legs slightly raised. She was turned towards us – her face was pale and her gaze misty with pain. She lifted a hand.

A nurse in a grey uniform got in front of us as we went to her. 'I can allow you a few minutes only,' she said, 'and then we have to lock this room as I must attend elsewhere.' She turned away and left us to it.

Dadus reached out to Dei and took her raised hand. I went around the other side, turning Lijah towards her so she could see his sleeping face. Her head was bare and her hair white at the temples. Her skin was as grey as the nurse's uniform and seemed to hang on her face like it was too loose for the bones beneath. I could not believe the change in her. She was an old woman, suddenly, and I felt this thick load of panic inside but I did not want her to see it, so I smiled. She smiled, and tried to speak, but it was clear the pain was too great, so we talked to her and told her how we'd quit

our fines and had found lodgings nearby until they let her out. I
bent and put Lijah down on the boards, next to her, and she managed to turn her head a little and look at him.

After a short while, the nurse came over and fussed us out. It
broke my heart to be leaving Dei there but we made sure she knew
we would be back just as soon as they'd let us.

As the nurse locked the door behind her, Dadus said,
'Whereabouts in the town can we purchase laudanum for her?'
and the nurse told him the name of the chemist's, and said how we
was not to worry about her being sent back to the cells but as soon
as she could sit she would have to quit her sentence with light
labour, like the others. She saw what we thought of this by the
looks on our faces and said that in most other prisons a hard
labourer with broken legs would have been tossed back in the cells
to take their chances with the rest. It was only on account of
Huntingdon being so progressive that there was any such thing as
a room for the sick and injured.

All the way back to our lodgings, my father said nothing, but his
fists were clenched and he strode at such speed that I ran to keep
up.

We got Dei back when her time was done. She hadn't had to do the
light labour after all, on account of being in too much pain to sit.
Dadus used the last of our money to hire a cart so that we could get
Dei back up to Ramsey and get our *vardo* back from the Lees. It was
a big problem how we'd get the wherewithal to pay them back, and
to keep buying laudanum for Dei, but all I could think of was how
once we got Dei back then it would all be sorted. I realised how,
though she had always been the quietest one of all of us, she had
always done the most and held it all together.

We took Dei on the cart across the bridge. There was a big
common on the other side of the river where some of our Travelling
folk camped sometimes and Dadus was thinking how we might be

able to stop with them for a few days while we worked out whether Dei could make it up to Ramsey.

It was the coldest day of all. We piled blankets on Dei but she was shivering and sweating in turn. Dadus had talked a pie out of the baker, to give to Dei, to celebrate the getting-of-her-back. She took a nibble at the crust then said she couldn't manage the rest, and this worried me more than anything for after four weeks of gaol fare she should've fall'd on it.

As we crossed the bridge, with Dei on the cart and Dadus leading the horse and me carrying Lijah, I looked down. The river had frozen over. The *gorjers* were out skating. I could see a group of women just past the arch, about six of them. They were skating in a circle, slowly, with their hands tucked into fur muffs and their long coats flying out behind them. One of them slipped and wheeled her arms and then fell, and they all burst out laughing.

I looked back as we left the river behind, at the dark figures skating on the grey ice, flying around like big birds, as free as you please.

The Travellers on the common took us in. They were a small group and it turned out they were related to the others we had been in the wagon with on our way across the Fens. They were eager for news of them, and we were sorry as our trial had been before theirs so we knew not what their sentences had been. But Dadus promised he would find out when we got back to Ramsey, and get word down to them.

They were mostly Smiths, and Greys, but none of the Greys were related to Redeemus Grey and his lot that we'd been with in Werrington, although of course they knew of them. There was a cousin of Dei's, from the Kent Marsh Smiths, and when she saw the state Dei was in she fell to a-wailing and a-weeping and swore to us she would nurse Dei like her own daughter, and though I was grateful I couldn't help feeling that what Dei needed most was quietness, and me. They weren't well-off folk, otherwise they would never have been stuck on the common with the weather so bad, but they were better off than us and took us in.

Dei died four days later. I was with her, holding her hand. Dadus had gone out with some of the other Smith men. The other women had taken over the caring of Lijah and I just had him for feeds. I sat next to Dei the whole time, in the bender tent the folk had, with an extra layer they built over to try and help. It was bitter cold, but she didn't seem to notice. I stroked her fine-boned hand and I talked to her softly of what trouble Lijah was going to give me and how she'd better get well soon as I'd be needing help of her. At that, she gave a small smile, though she was long past speaking by then.

When she was gone, I couldn't bear her cousin, a-weeping and a-wailing. I felt like she was trying to take my grief, for who was she, after all? It was an uncharitable thought. I would have cried myself, I think, but for the wailing cousin. She made my face stony, for I wanted to be different from her to show her how much less my Dei was to her than me. You wouldn't think such things should matter at a time like that, but they do.

I let the cousin's wailing tell Dadus what had happened. He would have heard it as he came back towards the camp. I hope he let himself stop for a minute and take a breath, a deep breath, as it would have been the last breath he took before he knew for certain that our Dei was gone.

We burned her, that very night. We put her on the cart, with her few things, her shawl and her sewing things, and took her to the far side of the common and laid her down and piled wood on her.

Dadus and me stood by and we were getting through it, just watching the flames alongside the others gathered round who were our new family now. Then, all at once, there was a loud bang, and an orange flame shot skywards, and the branches we had piled on collapsed inwards. A shower of sparks flew up into the night air, and it was like Dei was escaping into the black sky. And Dadus next to me fell on his knees and bent over with both arms across his stomach as if he was going to be sick. He opened his mouth wide, and there was an awful, long moment when no noise came, but then he let out his howl, and it filled the sky. I dropped to my knees as well and put my arm around his shoulders, and tears were running down my face; but I realised I was frightened by Dadus collapsing down more than wanting to comfort him. I thought, after this he will be broke, just like Dei's legs were broke, and I will have to take care of him just like I do Lijah, and I already saw me making the decision about getting the cart back to the farrier and how we would pay back the Lees up at Ramsey and the whole future was falling on me, and I was foreseeing it – and I had never really thought on Travellers who tell the *gorjers* they see such things, but I saw my life there, going up in flames.

And then I could not forgive myself for thinking of myself and not of Dei.

Dadus stayed to see the fire out, but I could not, and, as it died down, I took my leave and said I would go back to the camp for Lijah. I was wept out and spent by then, and was full of air and nothingness, and this hollow feeling hurt so much inside that I had my hands pressed to my chest as I crossed the common in the dark. And so it was I came to the camp where some of the women were seated round a fire and the Marsh cousin took one look at me and handed me a bundle and I was in that much of a state it took me a moment or two to realise she was handing me my son.

I took him, and I thought how he seemed heavier since Dei had died. He was quiet for once, and I put his arm around my neck, and I felt myself begin to weep, and I did not want to frighten him so's I tried to do it quietly but he must have felt my body shake, for he did something he had never done before. He clutched at me. He was so little, he was only just able to move his arms and do such a thing. But as I held him, he held me back, and it was the sweetest feeling I had ever had. And I loved the weight of him, my son. And I thought how my Dei must have held me like this once, and how these things continued, and how my Lijah was now all to me, *all*, and as long as there was breath in my body, nothing nor nobody would ever take him from me, and if I close my eyes I can still see the loud orange flames against the blue-black sky and the shower of sparks and hear my Dadus howling and feel my soft, heavy son in my arms, even now.

CHAPTER 4

The time has come to talk of Lijah grow'd, for that is the marrow and fatness of my story.

I sometimes think on't, that Lijah is my story. Until you have a child, you believe the story is yourself, for your small mind cannot stretch beyond that, and why should it? You have no other way of thinking. It is when you have a babby that you realise the world goes on and on, and you are not the story any more, you are just a small part of someone else's story. A bit like us going round the sun 'stead of the other way round. I had my son, and then I went around him, and when he was not there it was dark – and I'm not saying we don't all need a bit of night-time too, for we do, but there was no daybreak until I knew where my Lijah was and what he was about.

When he was small, I thought it might stop when he was grow'd, but if anything my feelings for him grow'd as well. It was because he had naught else but me, so I had to be enough to make up for that, and I reckon it became a habit I could not stop.

No girl would ever have been good enough for my Lijah. I'm not so stupid as to think that. But of all the lasses in the Fens, the flat old Fens where you can see as far as you like and know the world is big enough for anything, he had to pick *her*, the *grasni*, all clouds of gingery hair and great huge cheeks and hips and all bigness and softness like an eider you could lose yourself in. Oh, I'm not saying I couldn't see the attraction.

The thing is, about redheaded people, they smell a bit high.

We went fruit picking every summer when Lijah was a boy. The travelling was all a-slowing down by then, for they had made a new law, the *gorjers*, that said we should not camp on the commons no more and this made it very hard as we were not allowed to stop on roadsides or farmers' lands neither. The only way we could stop anywhere when we needed to was by breaking the law – and as we were breaking the law we only did it for a short bit before moving on to break the law somewhere else. So their new law meant we had to break the law a lot more often than what we had before.

The only time the farmers wanted us was when it was a harvest, of course, and then we had fine times for it was like the old days with folk showing up from all over. That and the horse fairs was the only times it was like it was.

It was by the cherry orchards of a farmer named Childer that the part of my life as it was ended. I was married by then, to Adolphus Lee, and then widowed within half a year of Lijah being married himself, but I am getting ahead of myself and getting things in not-the-right-order again, so I will go back awhile.

Dadus and I made out all right for some years after we lost Dei but I can't say as I remember it as a good time. Dadus hawked his kitchen goods but without the talent he had had for it before, for Dei had been behind him, suggesting all the time. And I remember things being hard, going from place to place. And our only joy in all this time was Lijah.

We even went so far as to try and settle once, on Lijah's account. We found a site over at Paston, where a large group of Lees had managed to buy a bit of land off a farmer, Lord knows how. So they were making their own little kingdom, these Lees, and they were a bit high and mighty with it but we thought we'd give it a go on account of trying to get some schooling for Lijah. I had never forgiven the vicar at Werrington for killing my mother, but I had come to the conclusion that if Lijah was going to get ahead in life when he was grow'd then a bit of *heducation*, as Dadus called it, was maybe no bad thing.

We asked around a bit and found what looked like the perfect place for him. I didn't know a right lot about schools, having never set foot in one in my life, but I was rather taken by this big old building in the middle of a field, with a church attached, just a couple of miles from the site. It was organised by nuns and I had to go and speak to them first. They were like big crows – big crows who had starch for breakfast every morning. I liked the look of them. *They'll put 'im right*, I thought.

First morning, I had him up nice and early and into the clothes I'd pressed the night before. He wasn't going to let me down, I told him, or he'd catch it from me, good and proper. He was small for his age, was Lijah, with black hair and heavy brows. He often had a fierce look, for he was not the sort of child who was inclined to smile unless he knew there was something in it for him. I saw the way that people looked at him sometimes, wary like, as if he was a terrier, and I always wanted to say to them, *but you should see him when he's sleepy, when he clamps his arm around my neck like a vice and won't leave go, and I have to lie beside him until he's sound asleep and if I try and move too early he cries out and pulls me closer.*

I knew nobody else saw what I saw in my Lijah, the small boy who cried out, so I worked hard to make him look as sweet as possible that morning, so that the nuns might find him appealing and not be hard on him. I brushed and oiled his hair, and for good measure I took a comb and gave him a kiss-curl in the middle of his forehead. I do swear it was the first time in his life that boy had looked angelic.

Before we left, I gave him a sugar sandwich wrapped in brown paper for his dinner, and a lovely little *lolli pobble*, a red apple, which I'd polished to a shine. The apple was for break time, I told him, and he was to go into a quiet corner to eat it. He wasn't to show it to none of the other children he'd be associating with. They were only the children of the local peasants round here and they'd probably never seen such a lovely little apple and would have it off 'im soon as look at it. I was proud of that red apple, as you can probably tell, which was my undoing as it turned out.

Anyroad, we walked over there at a brisk pace, him holding my hand and trotting to keep up, and I was that keen not to be late that we were early and had to hang around and he kept getting the apple out and looking at it and I said put it in your pocket and leave it there. Eventually, one of the nuns came to open the place up, a tall woman with a long nose, not one of the ones I'd met. She looked down the length of the nose at us and smiled. 'My, we are punctual,' she said, and I didn't much like the tone in which she said it, to be frank.

Lijah was looking at the ground, so I poked him on the shoulder and he lifted his head and said, 'Morning, Miss.'

'Sister!' I hissed at him.

'Morning, Sister.'

She gave another of those smiles, and I still didn't like it.

Before I turned to go, I bent down to him and said, 'You show me up today young man and I'll tan your hide so hard you won't sit down for a week. And don't let nobody touch that apple.'

He turned without a word.

*

I got the full story later, of course. They always like to make sure you get the full story, don't they? What I think happened, more or less, was this.

My Lijah gets into the classroom and to start off with he behaves himself right enough, even though he hasn't a clue what's going on. He knows enough to watch the other children and to copy them, and the lesson begins, and there's a nun at the thing on the wall they call a Black Board and she's writing on it with chalk and they all have their slates and chalks and they're copying her. And maybe the other children aren't quite as common as I thought as I'd stood behind a bush and watched them arrive after Lijah had gone in: the girls all had pressed pinnies and aprons and the boys had cleaned shoes and oiled hair, although none of them had a kiss-curl as smart as my Lijah's.

What I heard is something like this. While one nun is writing on the Black Board, another nun is walking up and down between the rows of desks to keep an eye on the children. Maybe she's flexing a ruler, just to make sure they knows what's what. She gets to the point where she's passing Lijah, and she stops and she sees a bulge in his pocket. 'Elijah Smith!' she says, and heads lift. 'What is that in your pocket?'

'It's my apple, Sister,' Lijah says.

The nun sticks out her hand. 'No food allowed in the classroom, boy, you should know that.'

At this point, I reckon my Lijah is faced with what you might call a bit of a dilemma. And the dilemma is this: what is he more scared of, the ruler in the nun's hand, or the leather strap that I keep in the *vardo* which I take out each morning and hang from a nail in the porch? Well, there's no contest, the strap wins hands down.

'I'm not to give the apple to nobody, Sister.'

At this, the nun might've got nasty, of course, but some of them looked quite nice so she might have just as easily been understanding and kind being as it was my Lijah's first day and he was

only a poor, ignorant *gipsy* boy. 'It's all right, Elijah,' she might
have said. 'You can give the apple to me, and I will keep it nice and
safe for you and give it back to you at break time.'

Well, my Lijah wouldn't have been fooled by that. Oh no, the
kindness would have tipped him off. This nun wants that apple for
herself, he would have thought. She's heard tell of how red and
shiny it is, how it is hard as a conker and will burst with juice as
soon as you bite into it. The very thought of it is making her mouth
water. She's feeling peckish. She's thinking, if I've got to walk up
and down this class half the morning flexing this ruler, I reckon I
need a little something to keep me going.

He always went a little red himself when he was angry, did
Lijah. 'You can't have my apple, Sister.'

At this, the kindness would have disappeared, I reckon. The nun
would have held her hand out and lifted the ruler. Meanwhile, the
other children would be staring open-mouthed – little slugs would
never have seen such defiance.

Well, at some point, my Lijah decides to bolt for it. The nuns told
me he did it of his own accord but I reckon one of them tried to
grab him because suddenly he's up and running rings round them.
They chase him round and round the classroom and when one of
them nearly catches hold of him, he leaps up on a desk and the next
thing he's leaping from desk to desk over the heads of all the other
children who are squeaking like mice and cowering and the nuns
are shouting for help and it all ends up with Lijah standing on the
nun's table in front of the Black Board where she has foolishly left
a pile of spare slates and he picks up the slates and as a nun rushes
towards him he spins it at her and, BANG! Right on the forehead!
Down goes the nun.

And he doesn't stop there because by now he's enjoying himself
so spin goes slate after slate, in all different directions. The other
children duck so they won't get beheaded and crash go the slates
through the big, long windows that look out of the field. (This bit I

know is true as I saw the windows for myself when the nuns took me on a tour of the damage Lijah did, and the postman stopped us to say how he'd never been so surprised in all his life when he came up the lane and saw slates come crashing through them windows and flying towards him.)

Eventually, Lijah runs out of ammunition and the last remaining nun is closing in on him, so he jumps down from the table and belts for it, but he sees the postman in the drive so he swerves and runs to the church. The side door is open and somehow he gets in the tower and bolts the door behind him and he's up those stone steps quick as a squirrel and he finds the bell-pull and by then he's probably shouting, 'Dei! Dei!' having quite forgotten the leather strap and thinking only of how he's saved his apple so far and wants me to come and get him before the mad *gorjers* do him in.

So he does the only sensible thing he can think of doing. He grabs one of the bell-pulls, and swings on it.

Now, those bells had not been used in living memory, I got told, so the tolling which rang out across the fields and the surrounding district would only mean one thing to the dozy inhabitants: imminent Napoleonic invasion.

By the time I got there, the whole village was out.

There was nothing for it. I stood at the bottom of that tower, and I lifted my finger to my Lijah, who stared down at the vast crowd beneath. I rokkered to him straight, in Rummanus like, as I wasn't going to have the whole village understanding me. Roughly translated, it meant, *if you don't come down right this minute, I'll kill you.*

That was the start and the finish of Lijah's *heducation*. Aye, the kiss-curl was the only good thing came out of that *hexperiment*.

We moved on from Paston after that. For a while, we were over in Northamptonshire. I made baskets for a shopkeeper and taught Lijah how to wet and weave and he was talented at it, as I knew he would be. I taught him his coins as well, and all the other things he needed to know to do business in the world, and I reckon by the time he was ten or twelve he knew enough from me and Dadus for a good enough life and never mind the nuns. Those smart children in their pinnies and shirts might be able to write on Black Boards but could they coax milk out of a goat what didn't want to give it? No, I don't reckon they could.

There were many times he didn't get fed proper, of course, and he stayed a small fella. As a consequence, he developed the habit of looking after himself, so's he wouldn't get picked on. That's the thing about camp life. You have to let the *chavos* go off being hectic when there isn't a job to keep them busy, and then they fall to arguing and before you know it you've another mother standing outside your *vardo* rolling her sleeves up and calling you out. My Lijah learned to look after himself pretty sharpish, on account of him being small and also on account of being got at sometimes.

I suppose it's when boys are nearly men that they feel they have to start really getting at each other, for without knowing they are already strutting about like cocks in the farmyard in preparation for the competing they've to do later in life. We were back on the Fens when Lijah reached that age, on another big site with a whole load of Smiths and Herons and Lees.

'Dei,' he said to me one afternoon, thoughtful like. We was sitting next to each other on upturned boxes, by the fire. It was one of those times when there was no money for tea, so he was burning some old bread on a spike, then I was going to scrape the burnt off, into the water I was cooking. I laugh to think we had to do that, now, but it wasn't bad if you got it right.

He didn't normally talk to me thoughtful like, so I knew there was a question coming. I looked at him. There was light shining on his hair, which was soft and shiny, and I thought how hard it must be for a boy his age: a boy no longer, nor not yet a man. What a strange, in-between creature that is. What was he? He must've wondered that, and I couldn't help him, of course, having been a girl at that age myself.

Not for the first time, I felt a small ache inside, seeing him sitting there. It was his shoulders. He had bony shoulders that made him look fragile, like a bird, and I wanted to just hold him when I looked at his shoulders and keep the whole small, tough-little body of him wrapped up inside myself, all safe.

'Yes, Chicken . . .' I said.

'Dei . . .' He scratched his head, then held the toast up, turning the spike round to see it was done enough both sides. 'Was my Dadus a *gorjer*?'

Looking back, it was something amazing he'd not asked before. 'Why are you asking that, Chicken?'

He decided the bread was blackened right enough and went to pull it off the spike, but it was too hot and burned his fingers. He gasped with annoyance, shook his hand in the air, then put the fingers in his mouth.

That kept him quiet for a moment or two. Long enough.

'I had a fight with Zephyrus and his brothers . . .' he said.

'I know, I heard about it.' There isn't a thing can be done in a group of Travellers but the whole camp doesn't get to hear about it.

'Well it was 'cause they were a-calling me a half 'n' half.'

I knew'd that too, but it saddened me to hear him say it, for I could not bear he was getting into fights on my account.

I leaned forward to him, so's he knew I was serious. 'You listen to me, Lijah Smith,' I said. 'You are going to be as much a *Romani chal* as any *chavo* in this camp, in the whole district, in fact. Don't you let nobody ever tell you you're a half 'n' half. No one in the world has the right to call you that, for it ain't true.'

He paid attention to the toast, but I could tell he was pleased. I thought perhaps that was the end of our little talk but then he caught me out by saying, 'So who was my Dadus, then?'

'Your Dadus . . .' I said, as I took the cooled-off toast from him

and picked up a blunt knife to scrape it into the saucepan, 'Well,
you might ask . . .' I could see from the corner of my eye that he
was watching me carefully.

Tshk, tshk, tshk went the knife against the toast and the tiny black
crumbs fell into the water. 'Your Dadus was a Romany King, that's
why we had to keep the love between us a big secret, as the whole of
his kingdom would have fall'd apart if word of it had ever got out.'

I glanced at him. His eyes were big as teacups and dark as down-
a-well. 'He had a *kingdom* . . .' he said.

'Aye, Chicken, he did. He came from the Kingdom of Russia,
where the Russians live. He was just King of the Romany bit of it,
mind, and as well as being a King he owned a thousand horses,
and it was part of his job to bring the horses to this country and sell
them, and that's how come he passed through Werrington one day,
with the horses, and that's how come you were got. And he made
me promise on my life never to tell a soul, for he was bound to go
back to the Kingdom of Russia and marry some cold princess that
he did not love, but he said he would remember me for ever.'

'And did he know you had a babby by him?'

I thought I could detect a note of not-quite-believing in his voice.
Tshk, tshk, tshk went the knife against the toast.

'He did not, my poor child,' I said sombrely, 'for I had no way of
getting word to him, nor will we ever have, for he is on the other
side of the world being the King of Russia, but I know he thinks on
us from time to time, when it's all snowy there, as we talked of the
fine son we might have together one day. And I think in his heart
he knows that son is out there somewhere and longs for him, for
the cold princess will have got him nothing but girls.'

I had taken the crumbs from the toast and it was enough. There
was only a crust left but I handed it to Lijah and said, 'Chew on't,
if you like.'

He took the toast. 'So, are we rich then?' he said thoughtfully.

'Aye,' I said, stirring the tea we had made together. 'In our hearts, *amoro chavo*, you and me is richer than this whole camp put together.'

It was that very next day that I first set eyes on Adolphus Lee. I was with a group of the older women, and we had been out dukkering, which was mostly older women's business but as I am small and dark they let me along. I was what the *gorjers* expected, I suppose. I didn't like it much as it was a daft business and I wouldn't do it if there was anything else going. I'm not saying I couldn't see things when I looked at a person. Especially the young women. It was the young married women who wanted their fortunes told most as they were the ones most hungry to know if there was still something to look forward to. I looked at some of them and saw their whole lives before them. But I never told them what I saw. That would be demeaning to what I was able to do. I told them what they wanted to hear, which was quite a different thing altogether.

So me and the old 'uns was walking back through the camp when we passed a new group just joined up, and there was a big fella standing by a tin tub atop a tree stump. He was washing himself, passing the cloth up his forearms, and splashing water over himself. He was big in a not-handsome sort of way, to my eye, as if he had grow'd a bit wrong, clumsy-like. But a big fella is a useful thing in our sort of life and so we all gave him the eye as we passed, which is a thing none of us would have dared on our own, but as we were all together and the others were all old and well past the age of meaning it, it was sort of jesting with him.

And he seemed to take it in good part, for he looked up at us, a little bit smiling but only a bit, and straightened himself, flexing his arms as if to show off, and we all obliged him by giggling like girls. And then his gaze fell upon me.

He was not to know, at the time, that I already had a child who was a strapping lad, for I always looked younger than I was at that time, and I suppose I wasn't quite worn'd out with it yet.

And I stared right back at him, a thing I would never have done were I not with the old 'uns.

The way it went in those days, you saw someone you liked the look of and you did a bit of asking round. But it was up to the boy to go a-asking – wasn't seemly for the girl to do it. Anyway, I wasn't a girl no more and Adolphus wasn't hardly a boy, neither. I found out later that his family had been on at him to find a girl for years.

Anyroad, for all I thought my life was sorted at that time, I couldn't help myself from wondering about the big fella I see'd washing himself, and each evening when Dadus came back we would sit together and I would wait for him to broach the subject with me, for it would be my Dadus anyone spoke to first. But nothing happened, so I thought no more on't, and I didn't see the big fella again for a while, although I happened to walk past the spot where the new lot were pulled up perhaps one or two times more than was strictly necessary.

I found out, though, as you can always find out eventually as long as you are sly about it. His name was Adolphus Lee, of the Derbyshire Lees, who were well thought of as wagon makers. And they had settled for a bit so's Adolphus could finish his own *vardo* for he was right set on that before he took a wife. It was not really usual for a man from a family like that to make his own, but rumour had it he was so proud he would not accept help from even his own cousins. And proud he must have been, for it was something of a mystery as to why he was not wed yet. No one good enough for him, they said, which made him something of a challenge. As a result, every marriageable girl in the camp was finding an excuse to wander past and take a look at the fine catch who insisted on doing his own sawing and planing.

It takes a long time to build a *vardo* on your own, I thought, and most girls round here don't have the patience to hang around that long, for they're too scared of losing a chance elsewhere. Young people nowadays like things settled quick, to allow themselves more time for repenting, I s'pose.

But the other part of me knew it was foolish to even think on Adolphus Lee. They were quite a grand family, those Derbyshire Lees, and we may have been a grand family once too but now we were shrunken and what were we but a broke old man and a small boy and soiled goods between?

It was because I had no hopes in that direction made me bold. I was interested in Adolphus Lee and his *vardo* and felt I could show an interest without anyone thinking on't too much. And so it was, one spring morning, I found myself going past the edge of the camp where he was a-building.

The frame was already in place – he'd had help with that of course – but now he was on the smaller jobs and working alone. I had taken my Dadus along with me, although he was under the impression that he had taken me along with him. Lijah was off somewhere, being hectic.

Adolphus Lee looked up as we approached, nodded to Dadus, then bent his head back to his work. We stood and watched and it seemed he understood that we didn't want him to stop. But after a while, he did, pushed his hat up from his forehead and said to my Dadus, 'I'll be starting on the porch floor tomorrow, I reckon.'

My Dadus says, 'It's the sealing of it is the thing. Folk forget how a porch floor gets the rain when it slants in and they go rotten something easy.'

Adolphus nodded.

They carried on a bit more like this, then Dadus said, 'Well, we'll not keep you from your work, young man.'

'Aye.' He nodded. 'Good day to you.'

We turned, but not before he took the trouble to look at me and give me my own nod, separate from my Dadus's. And that was when I first got the idea I could have him if I wanted him.

This thought threw me somewhat, for up until then I thought I knew'd the whole shape and colour of my life to come. I wanted no husband, nor any more children, and had seen myself getting old and Dadus dying and it being just me and Lijah and him grow'd and taking care of us. But Dadus was slowing down fast now, and it was coming to me that we might be losing him sooner rather than later, and I had to start thinking on what would happen to me and Lijah then. And here was Adolphus Lee, in front of me, and I still didn't want no husband or children but I found myself a-thinking as we walked back to the camp, *I hope he's planning rails for the shelving*. It's the kind of thing a man forgets until a woman points it out to him, for ornaments and china need a rail to keep them in place, in case you ever have to move off sharpish and don't have time to stow them all.

And so it was that me and Dadus and sometimes Lijah got in the habit of visiting Adolphus Lee as he worked, once in a while, to see how the *vardo* was taking shape. And sometimes, when we got there, there would be young girls there with their brothers or fathers a-giggling and offering him tea, but I never saw him nod to one of them the way he nodded to me that first time we went.

And the fact that I had no hope of him helped me be cool, and not a-giggling like the other girls, and often I had Lijah round my feet anyhow. Adolphus was right good with Lijah. It was Lijah helped him plane the roof ribs out of ash. I was standing by them and heard him tell Lijah how the best flooring you could get was sailcloth like they used in sailing ships, and how you could paint it your own way with oil paints but that it was right expensive and a lot of work. Then, without looking up at me, he added, 'But then anything worth the having of is a lot of work, Lijah, I 'spect you know that now. I wouldn't value anything that came easy.'

That night, I could not sleep for thinking of Adolphus Lee.

Then, I did not go there for a while, because of the unfortunate thing that happened.

I was on an errand to find dandelion roots. There was a long hedgerow ran along the camp that was thick with them, but they had mostly been picked, so one day, early evening, I found myself walking a long way along it and thinking how it was nice to be a bit away from the camp for a while. So I decided to go a bit further. And then I came across them.

I saw her face but not his, as he was atop her and had his back to me. I recognised them as a man and wife from our camp. I don't think she saw me as she had her eyes closed and was holding his hair in her two fists. Her head was thrown back, her bare knees raised either side of him. *The mud, the dirt of it . . .* Horrible noises, they were making, both of them, like animals. And I turned and fled back to the camp full of disgust trying to shake the sight and sound of it from my head. And that night I could not sleep again for thinking, *that is what he will expect of you, you fool. That's what being married is.*

The next day, Lijah comes a-running up and says, 'Shall we go and see Mr Lee's wagon, Dei?' and I replied, 'You go if you like. I'm going to be too busy for a while.'

I knew this would be repeated, and I knew he'd get the message right enough.

I thought I would see no more of Adolphus Lee, and was getting used to the idea, when he turned up at our *vardo* about a fortnight later to speak to my father. He was walking into the village, he said, and was going to buy some pitch for the porch floor, which was finished, and which sort did he think he should get?

Well, he was making himself pretty obvious, but I was resolved by then.

It didn't help when Dadus said. 'Go to the blacksmith at the end of the village, not the first one, he's a *bafedo mush*. I've done business with the other and he's *kushti*. Take our Lemmy, he'll remember her.'

To this day, I'll never know if my Dadus knew what he was doing. He was getting on a bit by then, but even a man who's going a bit strange in his head knows what he's doing when he tells another man it's all right to walk his daughter down the lane.

Well, we had to take Lijah with us, otherwise there would have been an almighty scandal, but of course we were only just beyond the camp when Lijah ran on ahead and had soon disappeared round several corners, and there was a mighty silence between us then as it was the first time we had been alone together.

Eventually, we talked a bit about the *vardo*, and he said, 'Of course, you'll see when you come next, as I've done quite a lot since you last came by.' That was a bit pointed, and led to a little more silence between us.

I thought to myself as we walked, I must be honest with this man, for he deserves a pretty young girl who will be a full wife to him and give him a dozen children. There is score of them at least back in that camp who would be happy to do it. I knew that I could not allow him to have any hopes of me, but in truth it broke my heart, for I knew then he would leave off thinking of me and it had been a nice feeling, the past few weeks; to be a-walking round thinking on someone else who was maybe thinking on me. There were plenty of girls waiting for him. Word had got round the camp about our visits to him and I'd seen the way they looked at me and thought me fortunate to have his attentions when I already had another man's child like a millstone around my neck. But it was not fair on the man to lead him a dance, so as we walked along that lane, I said to him, casual like, 'I do feel right sorry for Delilah with those sixteen children round her neck and it makes me more than ever certain that one of them is enough for me.' I was talking of a Heron woman we both knew of who was in the habit of having twins and had three sets of them as well as a load of others. She was something famous in that camp, for not only had she had so many, they had all stayed alive.

There was yet more silence between us for a few paces after that, and in that silence I thought I could hear the heavy tread of his boots on the path a little heavier, for you know how it is when a quietness gives one sound a certain weight.

I knew he would not speak, for I could sense he was a little flummoxed. So, I continued. 'Not that I am saying I do not love my Lijah, he is everything to me, for all the trouble that he causes. He is all the man I shall ever be in need of.' All I needed from Adolphus was one sign or word to say that he had understood me, but he refused to be provoked.

I saw there was nothing for it but plain speaking, for I could not conclude this walk until I was certain I had released him from any obligation to me. He would be on my conscience else. 'Which is why I have always thought it best not to marry.'

At this, as if to prevent further declarations, he burst out, 'But a child is not the same as a husband, Clementina!'

I kept looking straight ahead as we walked, for I knew he would be bright red in the face and be trying not to be, and I thought of how my Lijah always goes red at certain times as well, and I ached inside at the thought of losing Adolphus Lee and all the goodness inside him. He could be Lijah's father, I thought. Why should he not be? *And what when he asks of you what a husband always asks of his wife?*

'Aye, you be right there,' I said bitterly. 'A husband asks for a certain thing a child would not, and a child grows up and leaves you and stops asking but a husband is always there and always asking.' I could not have been more plain if I had stopped in the middle of the path, taken up a stick and drawn a picture in the dirt.

Again a silence between us and again the tramping of his boots. Even the birds seemed to have stopped singing in honour of the business being decided between Clementina Smith and Adolphus Lee.

'What if you were to have a husband who never asked?'

There was no silence then, for I could not hold back from letting out a little, scornful yelp. 'No such man exists upon this earth. Any girl will tell you that.'

And at that Adolphus Lee stopped dead in the path. And I had to stop too, a few paces on, but I could not bring myself to turn and look at him, for I was allowing love for him to creep into my heart and it was hurting me. It was hurting like the pain you get in your side when you have been running too fast, and I even pressed one hand against my ribcage to prevent it, breathing hard. I did not want him to see my face. He would guess at it.

He spoke to my back. 'He does, Clementina.' Then his voice became a whisper. 'I swear, he does.'

It was too much for me. I could not stand that happiness was being offered to me, for I was so used to the lack of it. Without looking back, I gathered my skirts and ran off, calling out for Lijah.

That evening, the folk in the next *vardo* called us over as they had some boiled bacon. Way it was back then, all us Smiths tended to pull up together, as if we were our own a-little-bit-separate camp. We was close to the Herons but not so much to the Lees and the Boswells as to be honest I think they thought not-so-much of us. Sabina Smith had said would I do the leeks to go-with, and of course I said yes, so I had a pile of leek rings in a great skillet, the green mixed in with the white, all soft and slippery with butter, and I took them over, and everyone was in a right good mood. Things had not been so good lately but here we all were with some boiled bacon and leeks and fried bread to go with, and soon the men were full as anything and the children were running round.

This was the best bit of life back then, when the men and children were happy and fed, and you got to sit down and light a clay pipe with the other women knowing that just for a few moments nobody expected you to do anything.

Sabina Smith and myself were quite close at that time and we had shared a pipe of an evening often enough. She piled up the tin plates and gave them to her three girls to take down to the stream and settled herself down on a tree stump with her skirts spread around her.

I squatted next to her, poking the fire with a stick.

Sabina nodded after her girls. 'Jeppy's a woman now, just this morning.'

All at once, I felt I could not bear Sabina, or her Jeppy, and I thought how I would like to take the hot stick and poke it in her ear.

'Aye?' I said.

'When it happened to me, my mother gave me a slap, and when I said why did you hit me she said, you're a woman now and you've got to get used to what a woman's life is like.'

Sabina was like this, always wanting to talk about what it was like being a woman.

She must've expected me to join in with some such story but I wasn't in the mood to talk about things like that and I thought why is it some people need to be a-talking all the time, and what is it with us folk? Here's Sabina telling me her secrets, and Jeppy's into the bargain, and she's telling me like no one else is listening, but she knows that anything said will be known by all the women in the camp tomorrow, as that's the way it is.

I suddenly felt how I was not-liking our sort of life so much. Do *gorjer* women do this, I thought? Probably not, as they have a wall and some air and then another wall between them. And I fell to thinking how there might be times when it was nice to have walls to shut out other people.

I had not often thought like this before and it was strange I should think such thoughts that evening, with boiled bacon inside me. The men happy and fiddling, dinner done – this was usually the best of it. And I felt sad thinking how nothing was right for me at that moment. All I wanted was to be away from it all, and Sabina and her gossiping. I wanted to be on my own.

It was a bad thing in our life, to want to be on your own, for we had only got along by helping each other – and fighting each other as well, if the moment came. But to want to be away from other people, well that was thought of as something not right. And I thought wistful-like of Adolphus and how often he was working alone on his *vardo*.

And it came to me. The *vardo* was an excuse. He could have married years ago – many a man does before he has his own wagon. He hadn't married because he didn't want to be married, no more than I did.

Sabina's sister Evadina joined us and that got me off the hook a bit. She had pickled some nasturtiums but I hadn't had them with the bacon as I like them best in a sauce.

It rained overnight. The next day, I gathered my skirts in both hands and picked my way clear of the puddles and walked to the far side of the camp, right through it rather than round it, so as many people as liked could see which way I was going.

Adolphus Lee had pulled the covers from his *vardo* and hung them from a bit of rope strung between two trees. He had a fire lit. He glanced at me as I approached but I couldn't tell if his look meant anything.

'Did the damp get in, then?' I asked him, nodding at the covers.
'No, they held.'

As he said it, one of the ropes loosed from where he had tied it and one of the covers slipped with a sighing noise to the ground. Together, we went over and lifted it, one side each.

'This one's dry already,' I said. 'We might as well fold it.'

We held a side each, arms wide, and walked together.

When it was folded, Adolphus turned to the *vardo* and said, 'I've to decide on the windows.'

'I like sash,' I said.

I saw him hesitate. Sash windows are a wee bit heavier than

other sorts and every ounce counts when you're going uphill. He was the kind of man to weigh such a thing.

He looked at me. 'Sash it is, then,' he said.

And things between us were agreed.

We had twelve years together, myself and Adolphus Lee. He was as good as a father to Lijah, as good as my Dadus had been before he came along.

Dadus passed away during that time, and I don't know how I would've managed that without Adolphus or what would have become of me and Lijah. Dadus had been a broken fella ever since we lost Dei but it still hurt me terrible when he went. I think perhaps I am not so good at the letting-go of people.

I let go of my Adolphus easiest of all. I think the truth was, he always loved me more than I loved him, and that gave me a nice safe feeling, and he bequeathed that to me after he was gone. He clutched his chest one evening and went to bed early.

But I am getting things out of order. I said yes to Adolphus Lee, and in the twelve years we were together he never gave me cause to regret it. Twelve years – how many nights is that? He kept his promise for every one. We never talked about it. You didn't talk about things back then. Nowadays, people go on about it all the time, as if it's the only thing that matters. That side of life is over-thought-of, in my opinion. People talk as if it is all, and it is not.

CHAPTER 5

Let me tell you a small story about dead people. Us Travelling folk do not like to talk about them much. Some people think that a dead person cannot help but think ill of the living and that is how a ghost is always evil. Some think it is bad luck even to say someone's name once they're dead. But I have not altogether agreed with that. I like to think on the dead.

There would be many of our type who would never have taken up the vicar's offer of the cottage in the graveyard at Werrington. There would be many who would rather have slept in a bed of nettles. But I am thinking that it is one thing to be prejudiced against the dead for a good reason, a-Travelling, and another when you are settled and a dead person is not such a problem. Let the *gorjers* have their *mulladipovs*, with their holes in the ground full of ghosts, good and bad. Is that any worse than to be a soul a-wandering all the time?

You can tell I am a little unusual for my type and of course I did end up in a house by the Corporation Depot, but let me tell you there are plenty of worse places to end.

Lijah was born at a time when little children died often. Rich or poor, Traveller or *gorjer*, made no difference. If there was sickness in a village it could come a-knocking any time. Of course, it stood a better chance of getting in if you were poor.

That whole time I was carrying Lijah and we were living in the cottage in the graveyard, we would see them, the secret burials. They always happened at night. We would hear the creak of the cemetery gate, the turning of the handcart wheels on the gravel path. We would go to the door to watch. Past our cottage they would come, the vicar leading, praying as he came. Behind him would be a poor family, sobbing and sobbing, pushing the handcart with a little dead child wrapped in cloth and lying on it.

They were the worst off of the parish, folk who could not afford a plot or a gravestone of their own. They must have begged the vicar to put their little one in Holy Ground and he had found a way to do it. Him and his sexton together, they opened up a grave, in the dark, and put the little child on top and closed it up again. They opened up the graves in no particular order, as far as I could see, whoever they belonged to. They just worked their way along the rows.

After the first time we saw it happen, the vicar came over to us afterwards and gave us a coin not to say a word to anyone. We took the coin, of course, but it upset my Dadus. When they were gone and we were back inside, he said, didn't they realise that if they kept opening up the ground then the *mullas*, the ghosts, would be getting up and walking abroad? He thought it wasn't good for me to see it in my condition. My unborn child would be cursed.

But the next time we heard the creak of the gate and the turn of the wheels on the gravel, we still went to the door to watch, peering in the dark. I know it sounds peculiar, but I found something comforting in it. I thought it was good that these poor little children should not be put in the cold earth by themselves but should rest in the arms of someone, even if it was a stranger. And maybe it was nice for the folk already in their graves, lying there alone for all eternity, to be joined by a little girl or boy who would keep them company. I thought it a nice thing.

I can't rightly think what it was made me think of that story. I was about to start telling you of her.

We were picking sour cherries. It was fine work. It was a huge estate we were on, owned by a farmer who went by the name of Childer. He always used Travellers to pick his cherries so we saw the same folk year in year out and whole families would go out together. You would go and take your basket from the shed with a strap to put over and then when it was filled you would go and get it weighed. Some people would complain about the cherry picking, about what hot work it was and how the strap across your shoulders would chafe and your hip would ache once the basket started getting full. But I liked it. I liked the freshness of it. I liked the staining of the fingers and the testing of a fruit, a small tug to see if it was ripe enough. Even the darkest ones were not ready sometimes and resisted, and I liked the way that everyone knew to leave a not-ready fruit undamaged so that in a day or two someone else would get the benefit of it.

And, of course, there was no danger that sour cherries would get eaten up the way sometimes happened with apples or strawberries. It would be a man and a half ate more than a fistful of sour cherries. The most I ever managed was one, at dawn. The picking started at first light and a single sour cherry would always wake me up. You could eat a box of lemons easier.

Sour cherries. That is how came she came into our lives.

Rose Childer. She was the farmer's stepdaughter. I found out she was only a stepdaughter later on, of course. At the time, all we knew'd is that every Friday evening the farmer's daughter came around the wagons collecting the rent. She did it then as we had all just been paid. She had a leather bag slung over her shoulder, and everyone knew this big farmer's girl as she had bright red hair like a cloud about her head. She tied it back in a velvet ribbon, but it was that soft, frizzing sort of hair that would not stay tied and floated round her.

We was all right nice to her, of course. We knew'd which side our bread was buttered. She would come along of a summer evening and go from *vardo* to *vardo* and it was always the women who would deal with her, straightening from their fires and wiping their hands on their aprons. 'Why it's young Miss Rose . . .' they would say with great, beamy smiles. 'Will you stop and have a cup of tea with us?'

Mostly she would say, 'Thank you kindly, but no, I must get round,' or some such, but once in a while someone would persuade her to stop and then out would come the china teacup which would only be given to a *gorjer* guest and the children would come and stand around with fingers in their mouths. Once, I even saw her pull a Boswell boy onto her lap and tickle him until he ran off. And most of the other women fell for it right enough and said, 'That farmer's daughter is decent enough for a *gorjer* girl.' As if they were forgetting we were all so nice to her because we wanted to stay the right side of Childer.

The men would always make themselves scarce, of course. No man who ever stared at a *gorjer* girl would find himself forgiven by his wife, so they took their hungry looks off elsewhere and it was us women dealt with young Miss Rose. She wasn't so young, in fact. She must have been past twenty and should have been long wed, in my opinion. She wore white blouses with lots of pleats in them that blossomed round her. Her skirts were wide too. The ribbons in her hair were always smart looking but she had great big open boots, farm girl's boots, fit for striding round a *gipsy* camp.

I have always had dainty little feet myself and whenever I could

I made a show of them in pointy lace-ups, even if the weather was not quite fit for it.

My Lijah was gifted at many things but fruit picking was not one of them. He was magical with the horses, mind, and made a tidy living out of the buying and fixing and selling of them when he was older. And he could fashion anything out of wood or metal. He had not been with Adolphus and myself for the first part of the summer as he had been down at Stow. Then he joined us back up at the Fens and set to making pegs and cutting boards. He had an idea to carve patterns around the edges of the boards as he said it was a thing a *gorjer* housewife used several times a day in her kitchen and a nice-looking one would fly out of a hawker's basket. I said to him it was no use if he was going to be a pack-man that summer as they would be too heavy to carry in any number. And he said how he was a planning on getting hold of a knife-grinding barrow and would build a special basket on the side to keep the boards in and would sell the boards when he'd sharpened the knives. I could tell he was pleased with the poetry in this.

Anyroad, it was because of his plans to sell the cutting boards that he was by the *vardo* that evening. He had come back with some blocks of wood a little earlier and set them down by the step. I had taken the horse from him and said I would rub it down. We had a nice little bay at that time, quiet and cobbish, with a fine amount of feather. I was fond of it. We called him Kit.

I had taken Kit over to the shade beneath the trees for tethering, watered him and stroked his nose. I liked to feel the bone beneath. I was walking back towards the *vardo* with the bucket, when I heard voices.

As I came around the front, they fell silent. She was standing in front of him, looking down. The sun was behind her. He was looking up, and he had a look on his face that I had never seen before. He was holding a knife in one hand and a block of wood in the other.

I waited for them both to start at the sight of me, but instead, the farmer's daughter looked at me calmly, gave a half-smile, then reached into her leather bag and got out her pencil and notebook.

Lijah went back to his carving.

I gave her the money and finished with the bucket and did a few other things and then I came and tended the fire. Miss Rose moved on to the next *vardo*. Lijah was intent on his cutting board.

I took an iron and turned the logs. 'You might've turned this before,' I said. 'We'll need it high if we're to eat before nightfall.'

He did not look at me, just carried on, which was a thing he commonly did as a boy and young man and it always made me mad as anything.

'That's if you can bring yourself to think of anything as ordinary as supper.' I said, rising.

After we'd ate that evening, Adolphus said how he was going to lie down a bit. He'd been doing that a lot lately, feeling slow and poorly of an evening. His bigness had turned to fatness and he often looked bad around the stomach, as if the insides of him was bursting to get out and his skin was tight with it. I was a little worried about him, for to my mind he was not yet old enough to be getting slow and pained in that way.

Lijah rose as well and said, 'I'm off to take Kit into town, Dei.'

Well, that was like a red rag to a bull. I knew'd what he was up to. All the young lads had taken to it recently, visiting the public houses in the town a few miles off where they weren't known and coming back all hours even when most of them had to be up before sunrise. Lijah was the worst of it, for a hawker keeps his own hours. I could not stand the thought that he liked a drink from time to time. Neither my Dadus or my Adolphus ever drank and I knew'd not how it had begun, this habit of his.

'That horse has done enough work for one day and you've enough to keep you busy round here,' I said sharply.

He turned and snarled, 'Leave it, Dei!' before snatching his coat and hat from the peg and striding off.

I was ashamed that he should talk to me like that in front of Adolphus.

Adolphus did his best. 'Shall I go after him?' he asked, knowing what I would say.

'You're not well,' I snapped, and turned away, and then felt bad that I had been unpleasant to Adolphus only on account of Lijah being unpleasant to me.

I heard him come back later. He was bumping around beneath the *vardo*, where he always slept in summer. It was black as black outside, so I knew'd it was late. Once, he had come back so lathered he had forgot to tether Kit but that horse never wandered off. It had more sense than the lot of us. I turned beneath the eider, enough to make the *vardo*'s boards creak so Lijah below would hear me and know I was awake. Next to me, Adolphus was breathing softly.

In the morning, at first light, I was woked up by Lijah whistling to himself. By the time I had got down from the wagon, he had blow'd on the embers of the fire and got it flaring up and was heating the kettle. He grinned at me and clapped his hands together. 'I reckon you'd like a cup of tea before you're off to strip another of those cherry trees, wouldn't you, Dei?'

Perhaps he isn't such a bad lad after all, I thought to myself.

He stayed cheerful all the rest of that month. And though he went off to town drinking a lot he was never sore and silent in the mornings like he had been before. He made a whole pile of cutting boards and they were stacking up but he said he had a few other things to be getting on with before he hired the knife-grinding barrow. We started to talk about where we should move on to once the harvest was done. In years before, we had stuck around that site for a while and just earned the rent by other means, but some of us weren't so sure that Childer would be on for letting us do that again, so the talk was all of whether we could persuade him round or not.

That was how come Delender Lee said to me one day by the stream, in front of a whole bunch of other women, 'Course, Clementina, what we need is for your Lijah to put in a good word for us in high places and we'll all be fine, won't we?'

I looked at her. One of the other women muttered, 'Low places, more like . . .' and there was a whole load of smirking and looking down went on.

That was the worst of it. If they had all burst out laughing out loud I could have laughed too and pretended I knew all about it. But the fact that they looked down and just glanced at each other meant not only did they know, they knew that I didn't.

I gathered up my wet things and threw them into the tub even though I was only halfway through. I picked up the tub and left without a word. I suppose I should have just ignored it but I couldn't carry on washing clothes with them after that. I felt their gazes on my back, and their exchanged looks as I climbed back up the rise to walk back to the camp, and as I crossed the field I had to bite my lip to stop my eyes watering with shame.

I knew I had to tackle Lijah. For what sort of mother would I have been if I had just ignored it and let him make himself a laughing stock? I must do it right away, I thought, before I lose my nerve.

I dumped the tub down behind the *vardo* and found him where I knew'd he'd be, a-sitting on the step. Afterwards I thought, he knew before I spoke to him what it was about on account of how he didn't greet me. He had probably been expecting it.

I stood over him for a moment, but he did not look up. Instead, he continued cutting at a new block, and I stupidly watched the pile of shavings grow between his feet, all the while waiting for him to give me my cue. And all the while I felt my blood boiling up as I thought of how the whole camp knew more about my son than I did. There he sat on that step, the person who'd been everything to me these last twenty years, even though it killed my Dei and kept us moving and gave me more trouble than a dozen other children could have done. And I had poured everything into him. Everything he was; his neat shirts that I stitched, his fancy waistcoat – the kiss-curl on his forehead. It was all me. I thought I would burst with it, with him not realising.

Eventually, he knew'd I would stand there all day unless he spoke first. Do you know what he said?

'Say your piece, Dei.'

That was it. He didn't even look up. *Get it over with, makes no difference to me.*

So I let him have it straight. 'I don't know what you think there is to be so not-worried about,' I said, and I was surprised at how calm my voice sounded. 'It may not bother you to have the whole camp talking about us behind our backs but it bothers me and I think you might do a bit of respecting of that. You've always gone your own way. You've always done whatever you've wanted to do without so much as a thought for me or Adolphus. I suppose I should've got used to it after all this time . . .' He stopped shaving the block, although he still did not look up.

'Dei . . .' he said, but I was under way by then.

'Ever since you was a boy you've done exactly as you please with never one thought for what folk might say. You've larked about and disrespected, never mind the drinking you've been doing recently. But in all my born years, with everything that's happened to us, I never, *never* thought that you would sink so low as to be seen mooning over a *gorjer* girl. I would have thought you'd have more pride than that.'

That stung him. He looked up then. His eyes narrowed. 'You can talk, can't you?'

I gasped out loud. 'Don't you dare bring that up. That's years ago. I've told you, you ain't no half 'n' half, whatever they say, don't you dare say that to me.' He must have seen the fierce look on my face for he dropped his gaze again. There was a silence between us. *He's slipping away from me,* I thought, full of misery, *my only child.*

Then he said, 'I likes the way her hair looks in the sun, Dei.'

That was it? For that, he was prepared to tear everything apart, to leave me and lose his work and be always looked down upon by all the people around us and have his children sniggered at? *Rose.* A farmer's daughter, with her cloud of hair and her broad hips and shoulders and that great body of hers that said, look how large and soft I am – and what more did any man want? And suddenly I thought of my poor, tiny little Dei, as small as a bird, who was broke so easily on the tread-wheel all those years ago, snapped like a twig, and I thought that big, soft Rose looks at me and she thinks I'm like a little bird as well, but I've got news for her. I'm tougher than my Dei was. I won't break nearly so easy.

I likes the way her hair looks in the sun.

It doesn't matter how much you love a child. It counts for nothing, not when he gets grow'd, and sees a girl's hair in the sun.

I was sore after our argument, right enough, but we had argued plenty before and the thing about me and Lijah is we fought like anything but then we cleared the air and the next day we just got on with it. Adolphus always found that hard to understand. He would hear us a-shouting at each other and off he would go on some errand or other, shaking his head. Then he would come back and Lijah and I would be chatting all peaceable, and he would shake his head again. I think he felt a bit left out, in truth, for he and I never shared a cross word in the whole twelve years we were together.

Lijah had gone off somewhere after we spoke and was not back before we went to bed but I didn't think on't and the next day I got

up at first light as usual and stepped down. I took the clods off the
fire and blew on it, and smoked it up into life. I put the tripod over
and hung the kettle, which I had filled the night before, and only
then did I turn around to stir Lijah.

The ground was damp with dew. The early morning air had that
fine freshness that summer mornings have, when you know it will
be hot later so you don't mind the little chill of it. Just breathing that
air was like quenching a thirst. A thrush was hopping in the grass.
As I turned it took fright, fled.

Lijah wasn't there.

That was it. I knew it. He'd gone for good. His blanket roll was
gone too, and his pack that he normally put his head on and I
didn't need to go round to the back to know his box of small tools
and his blocks would be gone too.

I drew breath, great large gulps of that fresh, dew-laden air. Then
I clamped my hand over my mouth to stop myself from crying
out.

It was three months before I got word of them. They had married in
Cambridge, in a church. Apparently, she had said how if she was
giving up her family and everything then the least he could do
was wed her proper, so they did it just like a pair of *gorjers* with a
vicar and everything.

I only heard all this because once they were settled in
Cambridge, Lijah got to know the local hostelries, of course, and a
man he drank with there was a Heron, a nephew of Manabel
Heron, who was married to a fella in our camp. It wasn't Lijah sent
word to me or anything. I found out just like anyone might find out
when word gets round about what so-and-so is up to, and of course
the whole of our camp was agog with the news that Lijah Smith
had run off with the farmer's daughter. They were talking about
that one for months. Yes, you can imagine how much I enjoyed
walking around the camp after word of that got out.

Tale was, after Rose Childer's father had found out she was consorting with *gipsies*, he horse-whipped her and locked her in her room, but she got out and shinnied down the drainpipe and came to Lijah in the night. I can't rightly credit it, as I can't see her shinnying down anything myself but that was how the story went. In the morning, her father and her brothers went after them on horseback but they couldn't find them, which was a good thing for my Lijah.

I don't know how long after that they was married. But this nephew of Manabel's said Lijah told him that none of her family showed up, even though she sent word of the where and the when, hoping they might forgive her as she was getting properly wed in a church an' all. Not one of them showed, but the church bells was rang as they came out, and later we found out her father had paid for them to be rung, though he would not show his face.

No one sent word to me, of the where, and the when. No one asked for my forgiveness. Perhaps they thought there was no need.

Anyroad, about ten years later, Rose said to me how it would've been better if one of those church bells had fallen off and killed her stone dead, such a life she had with Lijah.

It was later that same summer that I lost my Adolphus. And by the time it had happened I had sort of thought it was coming soon on account of how he was getting short of breath all the time and had pains in his chest a lot.

There was nothing I could do for him when he was poorly, but there was something I could do once he was gone. No one was ever going to pull that fine *vardo* of ours but him. I had promised him that much, and it went up in smoke with him. I could've sold it for a pretty penny, and nobody would have held it against me on account of how I was left with no one and would have to be looked after by the camp and have people pretending they respected me when they pitied me, in fact. But it had to go with him, his *vardo*.

He had planed and painted every inch himself. Even the sailcloth flooring with the swirls that meant something to us alone but no one else could ever read them. Unusual it was, with its sash windows. I saw a few men shake their heads with sorrow as they piled the branches on.

I had been into town the day before and gone to the dressmakers, and do you know what? I had to buy a child's mourning dress. They said they had nothing small enough for me and it would have to be made to order and of course there was no time for that so I bought a child's dress and did a few adjustments. It had pleats down the front. At the neck, I wore a broach, and Manabel Heron said to me that when I walked back in the camp they thought a fine lady had come to visit.

I bought some pointy lace-up boots, as well, but I did not wear those in the camp as I did not want to ruin them. They were for my journey. Those, and the new carpet-bag I bought for my things, the buying of them took most of what I had kept by.

I had nothing after that: no son, no husband, no *vardo* to live in and no way of living in it even if I had. When I burned Adolphus I burned up my whole life until that moment, all the miles I'd Travelled and everything that went with it. Lijah had taken Kit with him when he went. I had given my china to Manabel and sold my few bits of jewellery to buy my dress and boots and bag. There was only just enough left over to pay someone to take me down to Cambridge.

PART 2

1877–1901

Rose

CHAPTER 6

My name is Rose Smith and I was born on Paradise Street, in East Cambridge. I wasn't a Smith when I was born, of course. I was Rose Blumson. My mother was Emmeline Blumson, laundry maid, and my father was nowhere in sight.

I became a Smith when I married my husband, Elijah Smith, who I met when he came fruit picking at the orchards that belonged to my stepfather. That was later, of course.

East Cambridge. The Garden of Eden, they called it. Lots of those streets south of Maids Causeway had their own allotments back then, and the grocers and fruiterers had shops and warehouses nearby. Fruit 'n' veg was big in that district. The traders round there supplied the colleges and all the posh folk. That was how that area got its name.

The houses on Paradise Street didn't have anything fancy out back like allotments, just a yard and a privvy. Paradise was south of Fitzroy Street, one of the new terraces that they built not long before I was born, on account of all the railway workers coming to town. The houses were neat enough but they hadn't got the roads or pavements sorted out and when I was a baby my mother had to take me to lodgings on Prospect Row, on account of the flooding and the sewerage problem. Great lumps of it would float down the road, apparently. We had a spell on Adam and Eve Street, then back to Paradise.

My mother called me Rose because I was born in the Garden of Eden. She might as well have called me Carrot, or Swede, to be perfectly honest, but as a child I liked to tell myself that I was born beautiful and perfect, like a flower in a garden. My mother was a simple woman, loving but simple. She was sixteen years old when she had me, and unwed. It's a common enough story – so common, in fact, that I was inclined to embroider it when I was little. She was a college laundry maid and I used to have lots of fancy thoughts about how my father was probably a lord or something. The young gentlemen at the colleges thought nothing of getting a handful of bastards along with their learning, after all. There's plenty a child runs along the poor, narrow backstreets of East Cambridge with blue blood in its veins. Perhaps my father had a great mind to go with his great fortune, I used to think, and I would one day come across him on Jesus Lane with a book in his hand and a frown upon his brow. I imagined him as a noble young man, with a head of fair curls. Maybe, one day, he would be out punting on the Cam and I would fall in from the bank and he would rescue me, and after one look at my face he would embrace me as his own dear child. I would never have to turn a mangle handle again.

I nagged my mother terribly to know who my father was and my ideas were so fancy that I daresay she thought she had better disabuse me as soon as I was old enough to believe her. When I was about six or seven, she took me by the hand and marched me round the corner to Fitzroy Street, where there was a whole load of big shops – a fishmonger's, and the shellfish shop, and a grocer's by the name of Rawson's. The Rawsons were a significant family round our way, owning quite a few places and renting out allotments in return for produce.

We stood across the road, my mother and I, holding hands. It was a busy morning and there was a lot of pony and cart traffic going to and fro but we could see Rawson's well enough. Boxes were stacked up high upon the slope outside. They had just had in a load of new cabbages, the pretty ones with dark, crumply leaves, and they had been arranged nicely in the boxes so they blossomed out, as if begging you to buy them. Apples gleamed in piles on the other side. I can still picture it. It was riches to me, then.

Through the window I could see Mr Rawson, a large fella with a belly to match, a drooping moustache and no hair on his head. He was patting butter on a slab. One of his sons was helping out behind the counter, holding a fold of blue paper and flipping it over to make a bag.

'That's your father. So, are you happy now?' my mother said.

'What, the young fella?' I said, a little confused, as he was married not the week before and we had all gone out onto the street to see him bring his wife back on the cart belonging to the Orchard Tavern pulled by two beautiful greys.

'No,' she said, 'not him, the old fella. Mr George Rawson. He got me with you and hasn't spoken to me since, nor will he ever. And if you were to go in there right now and call him Dad, he'd chase you out of his shop with a big stick. But I reckon most folk round here know it, and you should know it too.'

Well, this was something large to squeeze into my small head. George Rawson, my father? But he was big and fat, with four grown-up sons, and his wife still living. And they all had houses in the streets round ours and we must pass one or other of them in the street every day, although we had no need to go in their shop as there was a little fruiterers just at the end of Paradise owned by a man called Empers.

When you're that age you just accept what you're told, and although in truth I was mightily disappointed that my father was not a lord with a noble brain, I can't remember feeling much about it except just an oddness in my stomach if I saw one of the Rawson family around.

You could say that fruit and vegetables played an overly significant part in my early days. Apples, potatoes, cherries and the like. That was how I ended up with a stepfather.

When I was ten years old, my mother stopped being a laundry maid and got a job helping out at the shop at the end of our road. It was owned by our neighbours, Lilly and Samuel Empers, who became like my aunt and uncle. After she went to work for them, my mother and Lilly Empers got as thick as thieves.

Lilly had worked the shop-front all her life but she was somewhat older than my mother and had an inflammation of the spine that meant she could not stand for long. So, when their shop expanded and business increased, they asked my mother to give up her laundering and help them out. One of their regular suppliers was a farmer named Childer, who had his farm up near Cottenham, on Smythey Fen. River Farm, it was called, on account of the closeness of the Old West, part of the Great Ouse. Muddy river, the Ouse.

Farmer Childer must have come into the shop when I was there, as I helped out often enough, every day after school, but I don't recall being introduced to him. I can't help feeling that if I'd only seen him, I might have also seen through him, in the way that children can. I might have been able to warn my mother not to marry him. But perhaps that is no more than wishful fancy on my part.

In truth, what can a ten-year-old girl do with her life? What power has she? None, I soon discovered. You are no more than chaff.

No, I do not remember meeting Farmer Childer in the shop, nor do I recall being told when he first took an interest in my mother. The first I knew of it was when my mother went away for one night and I stayed with Aunt Lilly, and Aunt Lilly said when my mother returned, she might have some news for me.

She had news all right. She was married. I had a father. He was a Fenman, an important farmer, she said, and we were going to live together on his farm. Oh, and I had a set of new brothers into the bargain.

She told me this in the shop, as I sat on the stool, eating the sugar twist she had brought back for me as a gift. Her eyes were shining as she knelt before me and looked up at me, hopefully.

'Rose,' she said, 'Guess what I had for breakfast this morning?'

I sucked on the twist, staring down at her.

'Toast and chocolate.'

Later that day, I overheard a conversation between my mother and Aunt Lilly. Aunt Lilly was saying, 'Are you sure you want to take her? Are you sure he doesn't mind?'

'Lilly, no, I said, didn't I?'

'Well I just wanted to say again, just so's you knew.'

They were in the back of the shop. I was behind the counter, stacking the weights in the right order next to the scales. We were due to close soon. There was a thick curtain across the doorway that led through to the back: not thick enough, mind. They were trying not to be heard, but only in that half-hearted way that adults do when they think a child won't understand anyway.

'Part of why I'm doing this is to get her out of East Cambridge.'

'It's not that bad.'

'It is, Lilly, and you know it. At least there's no soap works on the Fens. You know my Rose's chest has always been bad.'

'Well, it was good enough for you, wasn't it?' I could tell by Aunt Lilly's voice she getting stiff and upright in the way she sometimes did.

My mother lowered her voice. 'It wasn't, Lilly, you know it wasn't. I was near taken for the Spinning House. And my Rose, who knows but she might end up like I did.'

'Emmeline!'

'Well, I'm sorry but it's true. Facts is facts. I don't want Rose being like me when she's grown. I want to see her a proper married missus, with a husband to look after her.'

I remember the day we left East Cambridge. That I do remember. A young man came to fetch us on a cart, and my mother said he was one of my new brothers, Horace. I took one look at Horace and gathered he was none too happy about the arrangement either but my mother seemed oblivious to any of it, loading up our few things and cheeping like a canary.

The neighbours gathered round. People who had scarcely been on nodding terms with us helped my mother with her trunk and hugged her and wished her luck.

Mrs Chadwell from number eleven came up to me and bent to give me an embrace. 'Now, Rose,' she whispered in my ear. 'This is your mother's big chance in life so you be a good girl and don't go messing it up. You're very lucky that a man like that is prepared to take you on, all things considered.' I understood her right enough. Funny, but I never felt like a bastard until my mother married.

Farmer Childer was a deal older than my mother. He had three sons. The first was the grown-up Horace whose coldness had a very simple history, I soon discovered. His mother had died in childbirth and he had known nothing but his father as a boy. The next two were William and Henry, by the farmer's second wife, Agnes. She had died of the Fen ague not six months before the farmer met my mother.

At least William and Henry had been raised by a mother. William was a soft, pale thing, who wore his grief like a child who is playing ghosties wears a bed-sheet. It covered the whole of him. Henry was a terror, for ever neglecting his farm duties and running off. They were both older than me and had finished their schooling and worked all their daylight hours on the farm. Three sons meant no hired help for Farmer Childer, except when a harvest was due in. But he still needed a wife for keeping house and book-reckoning.

The fact that Farmer Childer had got through two wives already was a disadvantage when it came to finding himself another in the immediate locality – and he needed another in a hurry. Being an unsociable sort of man, I don't think Farmer Childer came across women in his daily business. And anyway, his needs were quite specific. Jobs around the farm were already allocated. He didn't want a woman who was going to march in and run things her own way. No, he needed a woman like my mother who knew her place and would roll up her sleeves and work like a beetle from dawn 'til dusk. He wanted a woman who would be nice and grateful. And she was, my poor mother, oh she was, even though the cup of chocolate she had tasted on her wedding morning was the only one that ever passed her lips in the whole of her brief married life.

It is hard for me to go into what happened next, for my mother's death was as sudden and unexpected to me as her marriage had been. We had been living on the farm for less than two years. They had not been happy ones. Horace, the eldest son, was as mean as his father and did his best to make our lives a misery from the start. My mother worked in the kitchen all hours, when she wasn't looking after chickens or the vegetable patch or the goats, and seeing as she was a thin young woman who had not been raised for farm life she acquitted herself very creditably, I think.

I wish I could say it was the work that wore her out but I know it was more than that. It was disappointment. She must have been wondering, the whole of my childhood, what it would be like to have a husband, and I suppose she had gilded her imaginings somewhat, considering how hard it was without one. Then she got one, and he was the kind of man whose sole comment at the supper table was, 'Mrs Childer, I believe I have noted before how a stew must be well salted, have I not?' with an air of such disdain you would have thought he was addressing the lowliest of serving girls.

Mrs Childer. I hated that he called her that. She had a name but he never used it, not in front of me, anyway. He probably called all his wives *Mrs Childer*, to save him the trouble of learning a new name when one died on him. He killed my mother, did Farmer Childer, as sure as if he cut her throat with his own razor.

It was a damp, cold March. She had had a cough and a fever for a week, and was losing her food both ends, although he did not know that bit of course as it was me that tended to her.

One evening, he came and stood at the door to her room while I was mixing beeswax and tar for a poultice. I was doing it in a small metal dish held above a candle. The smell was deep and warm and the yellowy beeswax was goldening amidst the tar. Tiny bubbles surfaced as I stirred.

I was not frightened at that time, for what child can imagine that their mother is about to leave them for ever?

Farmer Childer – Father, as I had been told to call him – stood at the door and said, 'Mrs Childer, must I get help from Cottenham tomorrow? The vegetable patch wants attending and if we need help in the morning then I must send Horace now, I think.' He could have told me to do it, of course, or one of the boys. He was making a point. She had been ill quite long enough, in his opinion.

And she replied, in her weak, chirrupy voice, 'Oh no, Mr Childer, there is no need of that. Another night and I shall be right as anything.'

After he had gone, I brought the poultice dish over to her and said crossly, 'What did you say that for, Mum? You know you need more rest.'

She did not reply, but lowered the sheet and unbuttoned her nightgown so that I could spread the poultice on her chest.

I blew across the top of the dish. It is a tricky thing to apply a beeswax poultice. It must be cool enough not to scald a person but not so cold as to thicken before it is spread.

She closed her eyes. I spread it on her with the wooden spatula, then laid brown paper over the top so she could button her nightdress over it.

'This will do the trick, I'm sure,' she said.

I sat by her for a while, holding her hand. I thought perhaps she was falling asleep. Then, without opening her eyes, she said, 'Why do you never speak when Mr Childer is in the room? I don't think I've ever heard you speak when he is nearby.'

I was twelve. I did not know how to answer. Now, I know the reason. I know it was because I hated him for looking down on my mother, for accepting her gratitude as his due – for looking at her and seeing no more than his third wife, when she was everything to me.

And I hated her a little bit too, sometimes, because I could not understand why she seemed to think so little of herself. Girls of twelve can't understand that of their mothers. They only learn that women should think little of themselves when they are older.

My mother fell asleep shortly, and I watched her face in the candlelight and saw how much older and more lined it seemed – and still I did not have the sense to be afraid.

She got up the next morning, of course. The poultice hadn't made the slightest bit of difference and her thin body shook with the coughing as I helped her dress. She went out in the cold and damp and weeded the vegetable patch. That afternoon, she took to her bed again and two days later it was obvious even to my stepfather that a doctor must be sent for and he came and gave her pills and they made no difference either.

She was in bed another three days before she went.

And that's how come I ended up living on a farm far from where I grew up, with a stepfather I hated and stepbrothers who hated me. Well, two of them hated me: Horace because he hated everybody, and the youngest, Henry, because my mother had replaced his. The middle one, William was kind enough. When he saw how grief stricken I was, I think it eased his own sorrow a little. He gave me a handkerchief at her funeral. The next day I laundered it, and when I returned it to him, pressed and folded, he said he would like me to keep it as a sign of how sorry he was.

Farmer Childer did not marry again after my mother's death. I would like to be charitable and say he could not bring himself to – but I think the truth was, he didn't need to. I was twelve, old enough to take over the cooking and cleaning and the hens and the vegetable patch. What did he need another wife for, after all, with an almost-grown stepdaughter in the house?

CHAPTER 7

The Travellers came every year. Funny now to think Elijah and I might have passed each other on the way to the water pump when we were children and not known each other.

I don't remember first seeing them or thinking them strange – on the contrary. It was a little bit of the outside world coming to our farm. Suddenly, there was noise in the fields, and other children my own age, although I was not allowed to play with them, of course.

I finished my schooling the year my mother died. There was too much for me to do on the farm for my stepfather to allow me to continue. One of my duties was to go collecting the rent from the wagons, at the summer and autumn harvests. They rented the field from us, whether they were working our harvest or not, and sometimes some of them stayed on after harvest was done. There was often other work locally, which suited them and suited us as we rotated their campsite each year so the fallow fields brought in a little income, which was always welcome.

I was thirteen the first time I went rent collecting, and I can still remember how important it made me feel, with my little notebook in my hand and big leather satchel slung across my chest. The children of the camp would stop and stare at me as I passed and I did not mind the hostility in their gazes for their mothers were most polite to me and treated me like a little queen. The only time I felt bad was once when I was leaving the camp and a boy halfway up a tree called down to me. He was pulling faces at me. Come to think of it, it was probably Elijah.

One day, when I was about fourteen, a piglet got out of our pen behind the farmhouse. It was my fault. I had been pouring feed in the trough and was leaning over and my leg had nudged the gate, which was not properly latched. Out shot the little so-and-so, like a bullet. I saw it happen and would have had him but as I turned I slipped on some damp straw and ended up on my knees in the yard while the piglet disappeared behind the cart shed. I knew there was no time to be lost, so I jumped to my feet, pulled the pigsty gate firmly closed and ran after, scattering hens like nobody's business as I ran.

As I rounded the cart shed, I saw the piglet scoot across the field. I scrambled over the fence and headed after him but I reckon that piglet was bewitched as it ran pell-mell across the field, into the next and across it too, and straight into the Traveller camp. It disappeared in there and I stopped and burst into tears. I knew how much trouble I would be in if I could not find it and for all I knew it had been kidnapped already and would be roasted that very night if I did not save it.

One of the men was striding out of the camp on his way somewhere. He saw me wiping my face with my apron and asked me what was up. When I told him he said, not to worry, he would find the piglet for me, and off he went back into the camp.

While I waited for him, two girls around my age came past.

They were both carrying babies, and I smiled at the babies. They stopped and came over and gave me the babies to hold. I didn't know if they were boy babies or girl babies but they were such sweet, swaddled dumplings that I forgot about the piglet for a bit. One started to cry, and I jiggled it up and down a bit. The girls laughed at me when they saw I didn't know how to hold it properly but they weren't unkind about it. They showed me how to put the baby in the crook of my neck and let it nestle there and were astonished when I said it was the first time I had done it. When I told them I was only fourteen they declared it was time I got a move on and had some of my own.

After they left, I hung around a bit more, but the afternoon was getting late. I gave up on the man who said he would find my piglet and went back to the farmhouse with my head down, hoping that at least nobody would notice the piglet was missing that day and I might have time to go looking for it the following morning.

My stepfather was waiting for me in the kitchen. Where had I been? he wanted to know. I told him I had been collecting worms for the chickens. Where were the worms? He wanted to know that too. I burst into tears, such a poor liar was I. He gave me three strokes on my arm for lying to him and six strokes for losing a piglet; then another six for wasting time talking to *gipos* and another three to remind me never to do it again. Each stroke was weighed and measured. He never beat me in a temper, I'll say that for him.

I went outside afterwards, to cry and find a dock leaf to rub on my sore arm. William came over and said the piglet was safe and sound. The man had found it while I was talking to the girls and, thinking I would have returned to the farmhouse by then, had brought it back directly, swaddled in a blanket and tucked under his arm. Father had given him a shilling for his trouble.

I took care not to befriend any of the Traveller children after that, although I looked out for the girls my age and their babies and was pleased each year when they came back. The children grew, and more babies were added, and depending on which field they were camped in and the direction of the wind, I could sometimes lean out of my window in the evening and hear the shouts and cries from the camp, the playing and running around.

Was Elijah the boy who sneered at me from the tree? I have sometimes wondered. It doesn't seem important now.

Elijah Smith was firmly on the ground the first time I remember setting eyes on him. It was several summers later. We were both full grown.

It was a pleasant evening, warm and sunny. We had had a lot of rain that month but that day had been fine and things were drying out nicely. We were midway through a goodly cherry harvest and the camp was large that year. I enjoyed my Friday evening walks over there – as I approached, the smells would float toward me: wood smoke, the cooking of onions and potatoes, tobacco from their pipes.

As I neared that evening, I saw that a new wagon had pulled up on the edge of the camp, an elaborate green and gold one with gilt porch lamps. I pulled my notebook and pencil from my satchel and turned to the last page, to make a note of it. I saw that a young man was sitting on the step, and had time to think it unusual that I was about to speak to him, as it was normally the wives I dealt with.

I stopped in front of him.

He looked up at me.

The sun was full on his face, which was wrinkled for a youngish man – weather beaten, I suppose. His eyes had a look in them, both childish and knowing. His teeth were crooked. He looked like a friendly dog, sitting there, a dog looking for someone to adore. He was dressed in a leather waistcoat with fancy buttons, I remember noticing that, and on his head he had a brown felt hat. Just showing beneath the brim of the hat was an oiled kiss-curl that curved across his forehead. There was something in the vanity of that kiss-curl that pleased me, for I lived with four men who never looked in a mirror from one week to the next. He was working at a piece of wood with a knife and, as I glanced down at it, I noticed how clean his hands were. I looked at his face again and saw he was smiling at me.

We did not speak.

We smiled at each other.

What was strange was that it was just as if we were having a conversation, all the things that were said with our smiles. We held each other's gazes for so long that there could be no mistaking our smiles for mere politeness. I felt a feeling I had never felt before, as if the solid core of me had melted away and inside there was nothing but air. I was eighteen years old and a great lummox of a girl by then, but I felt suddenly as if I was light enough to float up in the sky, if I wanted, to rise above the field and the wagons and the farm and the muddy old Ouse and everything that kept me tethered to the Fens.

Then I noticed a tiny, dark-skinned woman who was standing next to the wagon. Her hair was drawn back into a headscarf and her apron reached almost to the ground, making her seem quite doll-like, although the expression on her face was not at all the friendly, open gaze of a child's toy. Quite the contrary. Her brow was furrowed and her mouth tightly pursed. She stared at me with pin-prick eyes. She reached into her apron pocket and drew out a small cloth purse, then stepped forward and handed me some coins.

I took them and opened my hand.

She said, sharply, 'You'll find it is the exact amount.'

I did not like the insolence of her tone and made a point of continuing to stare at the coins as if I was counting them, although I had seen at once that the money was indeed correct.

The young man sitting on the step watched the two of us.

I put the money away, opened my notebook and ticked next to where I had written: *Green and gold wagon, gilt porch lamps*. Rent was due by the wagon, as we never knew who or how many stayed in each one from one night to the next. I would always write little descriptions of each wagon in my notebook so's I knew who had paid up, although sometimes when I arrived they would have been moved around, to confuse me, I think, in the hope I would not bother to count up and maybe miss one. I have a good memory for colours and patterns, however, and I don't believe I was ever fooled.

I hesitated for a moment. I wanted to speak, to assert myself somehow, but I could think of nothing to say. I nodded, without really looking at either of them, and turned away.

As I walked off towards the other wagons, I was dying to look round to see if he was watching me go but knew I must not, for fear of the humiliation if he wasn't.

On my way back to the farmhouse, I fiddled with my hair ribbon and inwardly bemoaned the unruliness of my dry locks. George Rawson the greengrocer might not have given me his name or any acknowledgement, but he must have had red hair somewhere in his family as I had inherited my horrid frizz from somewhere. My mother's hair was sleek and dark. I cursed the father I had never known, that day, and wondered a little desperately whether, if I oiled my hair every night between now and the following Friday, I might be able to fashion proper ringlets.

When I got back, I pulled my notebook and money-bag out of my satchel immediately and sat down at the kitchen table. Horace was at the other end, slumped back in his chair and drinking tea. Father must be out, I thought, otherwise Horace wouldn't be drinking tea when he should be checking the irrigation ditches.

As I took out my pencil and turned the pages of my notebook, I thought of how thirsty I was. I promised myself a drink of water as soon as I had added the first column. Horace would have gone by then, hopefully.

William came and stood in the doorway with his boots still on and said, 'Rose, have you seen Henry? He said he'd help me with the sow. He said he'd be back by now.' We had a bad sow at that time. She bit when you tried to pen her.

Before I could reply, Horace snarled at William, 'She's just this minute come in and she's got to add up before Father gets back.'

William left without a word.

I glanced at Horace, surprised. He had never shown concern about me finishing my duties before now, not if he wanted something to eat or a collar starching. Everything had to be done straightaway for Horace. I looked after William, frowning slightly, and wondered whether to go and help him with the sow myself, for I knew he was afraid of her and I was not. Sows are like dogs, only more so. They can smell fear.

When I looked back, I saw that Horace was leaning forward on his elbows and staring at me. He was a bulky man, like his father, dark haired and red faced, with lumpen features. There was no kindness in him, not a drop – that much I knew after eight years on the farm.

'Have you ever given thought . . .' he said, as if we had been in the middle of a conversation when William had interrupted us, '. . . as to what might happen when Father passes on?'

It was such an extraordinary remark that I made no reply.

He rose, swaying slightly, to his feet. I wondered if he had been drinking. He walked casually round to my end of the table. He stood next to me, and looked down at me.

'No?' he said. He was standing very close to me. I was aware of the strain on his belt buckle. He was on the last hole of the belt and the leather was giving. His stomach moved in and out a little with each breath and for some reason he seemed to be breathing hard.

He smelled of turned earth and dried sweat, of River Farm and the brown Great Ouse.

He put a hand on my shoulder and leaned his weight on me. He lowered his face to mine and murmured, 'Perhaps it is time that you did.' He squeezed my shoulder once, hard, then turned and strode outside.

I returned to my column of figures but as I looked up and down I was unable to add one digit to the next, for too many other things were adding up inside my head: my stepfather's age; the way Horace was more and more in charge these days; the growing antagonism between him and William. When I put these thoughts together, the sum total was large and unpleasant.

I had always assumed I would leave the farm one day, when I was fully of age. It was not my home, after all, and never had been. I was little more than a servant. I had not thought of what I would do or where I would go to, but I had never once seen myself slaving away and growing old there.

Now I saw that, in the absence of my making any firm plans for my future, plans were being made by others, on my behalf.

Friday evenings were my favourite part of the week. I saved my sewing until then, which meant a whole evening sitting down. Once I had cleared away the supper table, I would go up to the linen cupboard outside my room and take down the mending that had piled up since the previous Friday. There was always a great deal of it, as farm working men collect a fair amount of wear and tear on their things. I should have really done a little of it every evening but I liked to save it all up. It would not have been acceptable for me to sit down for two or three hours at a stretch for any other reason, but even my stepfather knew that sewing had to be done.

The summer evenings were best of all, for I did not have to do it by candlelight. I would take my favourite seat in the kitchen, by the open door, and sew until dusk fell and I was forced to move inside. Lately, William had taken to joining me with a book. His father asked him once what he was reading and he said, 'An analysis of Fen drainage patterns, Father,' although I do believe I once caught him reading a novel.

That evening, William was seated next to me with his book, and Horace and his father were in the kitchen with their pipes. Henry was in disgrace for his absence earlier in the day and so had been given the entire list of evening duties to perform on his own, which would take him until well after dark. The dog, Eddy we called him, was asleep on the step. I was sitting right by the open door and was weaving a length of cotton in and out of a tear by a shoulder seam on one of Henry's shirts. He did the least work but damaged his clothing most greatly, which was a thing I never fathomed.

Horace was brooding and silent, but that was more or less as normal.

When he had finished his pipe, Father rose. 'I shall retire early,' he said, to the room in general.

I put down my sewing. Father liked to take a cup of hot milk up to bed with him.

He lifted a hand, 'No milk for me tonight. I am still bloated from supper.'

He was rising at three in the morning to go to visit another farmer at Chatteris Fen who had a disc harrow for sale. Believe it or not, Farmer Childer was still using a bush harrow in those days, so unwilling was he to pay hard cash for anything. The stubble we had, he should have invested in a disc harrow years before.

'Shall I leave bread out or pack a breakfast for you, Father?' I asked.

'Pack it,' he said. 'I won't eat before I set off.'

After he had gone upstairs, Horace, who had been staring gloomily ahead, looked at me and said. 'You can make *me* some hot milk. I'd like some honey in it.'

I had just picked up my needle. 'I'll finish this seam if you don't mind, Horace.' I was tired and irritated by his strange behaviour and I suppose some of my annoyance must have showed in my voice. My thread had ended and I was raising the garment to bite it off the needle, otherwise I might have seen him rise and come towards me.

I looked up as he reached me. He raised one hand and struck me with the flat of it, soundly, across my face.

The room blurred and blackened. He did not knock me off my chair, not quite, but my head reeled as I righted myself.

William had jumped to his feet and let his book drop to the floor.

Horace was standing before me, panting, as if he had surprised himself by his action as much as he had surprised me. Then he looked round. I followed his gaze and saw my stepfather standing at the bottom of the stairs, staring at us. I don't believe there was ever any other occasion when I was grateful for his appearance.

We all waited for him to speak. He did not move, his gaze flicking from me to Horace, then back again. After a pause he said, 'I have changed my mind. You may leave my breakfast out.'

He turned and went back upstairs.

We all remained motionless for a moment, listening to the creak of the stairs beneath Father's heavy tread. Then I was unable to prevent myself exhaling in shock.

Horace was still standing in front of me, looking pleased with himself. His look said, *See, I am in charge now. Now do you understand?*

I put down the sewing on the windowsill and rose from my seat, my legs trembling slightly. William was still standing next to us. I could not look at him. I turned and walked across the kitchen to the larder, where there was a full churn of milk.

Had I been thinking straight that evening, as I lay in bed turning the events of the day over in my mind, then I could have written the rest of my life story right there and then. Horace's slap had sealed my fate. But all I could do was stare at the blackness of the air above me, where I knew the ceiling was, and wonder if the roof was still up there, in the dark, for I no longer felt certain of anything.

It rained heavily overnight, as it had done most nights that month. Sun and rain: what every farmer wants. The next morning, I rose at dawn as usual, my head full of thoughts and clouded-feeling. I tiptoed downstairs. My stepfather had already left. I had put his breakfast out the night before – bread and a piece of cold mutton on his pewter plate in the larder, covered with a dampened cloth to prevent the bread from drying overnight. I checked to see if he had eaten it but he had not. I lowered the cloth gently, as if I had been peeping at a corpse. *I must be careful how I tread now*, I thought.

I was keen to be out of the house by the time the others rose. In winter, there are the fireplaces to be cleaned and laid first thing but without that to hold me up, I was able to slip out with my wicker basket, to go and look for eggs. The brothers often went out and did an hour or two around the farm before returning for breakfast, so I reckoned if I timed it right I would be able to avoid Horace until mid-morning.

Once the eggs were collected and the goat had been milked, I was a little stuck. I knew I should really return to the farmhouse and get on with my chores there but I could not bear it just yet, so I racked my brains for an excuse to go over to the Travellers' camp. It came to me quick enough. I owed Mrs Boswell four shillings. I had not had the right change on me when I saw her the night before and had said I would knock it off the following week's rent. She had seemed happy enough with the arrangement but, I thought, I could always pretend I was passing that way this morn-ing and thought I would drop by. Perhaps I would go past the

green and gold wagon on my way. I wondered how early the smiling young man liked to rise.

I grimaced as I set off, thinking that in my haste to put the
eggs and goat's milk in the larder, find four shillings and get out of
the farmhouse, I had not even brushed my hair – my wretched
hair. As I walked, I pinched my cheeks to bring some colour to
them.

The field they used as the campsite got muddy very quickly, as you
may imagine, for the soil was already broken up so well that even
in summer a light rain could make it boggy in an hour or two.
When I walked over from the farmhouse, I always tucked my skirt
into my waistband to stop it getting dirty, but that hitched it rather
high and showed an unseemly amount of petticoat. As soon as I
was near enough that anyone might see me, I would pull the folds
of my skirt out from the waistband and hold it up, but not too
much, as I picked my way towards the wagons.

It was still early but as I approached I saw the camp was up.
Some of the older women were tending fires, as usual. I supposed
the younger women and the men had already gone over to the
orchards for the day. I wondered whether William would remember to check that the Orchard Manager had showed up. We had a
man come from Rampton to weigh and grade the fruit but he drank
and was unreliable. It was William's job to go over each morning
and make sure he was there.

The green and gold wagon was shuttered and no one was
about. I felt both disappointed and relieved. I wanted to see the
young man again but did not feel at my best that morning.

A little separate from the camp was a group of five caravans
that all belonged to the same family, a large group with many
children, always nicely dressed. I gathered that they were perhaps
a leading family in some way by the way I saw the other
Travellers speak to them. The woman in charge was large and

fair skinned. She always plaited her hair with ribbon and wore long earrings and many bangles. When I first visited her, I could not stop myself from staring beyond her into her wagon, for you have never seen so much fine china and engraved glass as was in their home. I could not imagine how even a pair of geldings could pull their wagon with all the grandeur it contained. How she managed to keep it all, and herself and her children, so smart and tidy with a life on the road is a thing I have never been able to fathom.

The family was down in my book as Boswell. Most of the others on the site called themselves Smith or Price, although I had learned that names were a somewhat fluid concept in the encampment and I never set much store by what they told me. I liked Mrs Boswell, and realised as I approached her wagon that I was hoping she would be there and the others not around. She usually offered me a cup of tea, although it had taken me a couple of visits before I got over my shyness enough to accept it. She offered it as though she meant it, as though she was truly concerned that I might need one. She would never take a cup with me but sit and watch me with great care while I sipped my own. She liked to ask me questions, showing a great interest in the life of the farmhouse and in the domestic habits of our family. She seemed to think there was something strange about the way we lived. For instance, I once told her about how one of my morning tasks was to go from room to room and empty everybody's washing bowl. She looked most shocked and said, 'You mean you take the men's washing water that they have put their hands in and just tip it outside the back door?'

'I usually water the parsley with it,' I replied.

She explained to me that each member of her family had their own washing bowl, which was never used for any other purpose. Everyone disposed of their own water with the utmost care, for it was like getting rid of a little part of yourself, and to allow someone else to just tip it away was like scattering your secrets. When she told me this, she was most hesitant. I had to encourage her with looks. 'And the idea that you should put your dirty water on something that might be *eaten* . . .' Her voice had become a whisper and she was unable to finish the sentence, as if we were discussing something too foul for words.

That morning, I found myself hoping hard she would offer me tea, so we could have one of our little chats. I would talk to her about almost anything, I thought, as long as I could sit down for a while and not go back to the farmhouse.

She was there all right, boiling water and chiding one of her children, but I saw as I approached that she was busy and would not be inclined to indulge my unexpected visit.

I stopped in front of her, feeling foolish. 'Mrs Boswell,' I said, reaching into my apron pocket, 'I was passing and thought I should return your change to you. I am sorry I did not have it on me last night.'

She looked a little puzzled and said, 'You did not need to come this way for that. Friday would have been fine to settle up, Miss Rose.' We had agreed as much the night before.

I wondered if there was an implied insult in my returning the money early, as if I thought she might be in need of it. 'I was passing,' I repeated, which was a silly thing to say when the encampment was stuck out in the field and not on the way to anywhere.

I handed her the money, then said hopefully, 'Well, I won't keep you . . .'

She did not take the hint. She dropped the coins into her apron pocket and looked back at her child.

I was sorry I had come. I turned to go.

She said, 'Miss Rose.'

I turned back. She was regarding me in a kindly fashion. 'You need a porte-jupe, do you, Miss Rose. The bottom of your skirt is muddy. Are you telling me a fine young lady such as yourself does not have a whole drawer of them?'

I had not the faintest idea what she was talking about.

'A porte-jupe, a skirt grip.' She glanced down at her own skirts, that were held elegantly in place by a series of grips attached to long ribbons which hung from her waistband, lifting her skirt slightly at pretty intervals so it was clear of the mud. The front ones were invisible beneath her long apron.

Well, of course I knew what a skirt grip was, although I had never heard it called by such a fancy name.

I knew it was overly familiar of her to comment on my dress but I was in need of sympathy that morning and could not help myself from saying, 'I live with four farm-working men, Mrs Boswell.' She knew my mother had passed on. 'I am afraid the feminine aspects of life are not really catered for in our household.' At this, and with current events to the front of my mind, I felt tears come to my eyes and I bit my lip.

She turned away without comment. I felt rebuked and trudged slowly back to the farmhouse, awash with self-pity.

Horace, William and Henry returned to the farmhouse mid-morning for their breakfast. I had made eggs with dill and parsley, a favourite of theirs. I served it in silence, allowing myself a moment of grim satisfaction at the thought of how – according to Mrs Boswell's philosophy – I was giving them herbs coated in their own filth.

They didn't talk between themselves and none of them spoke to me. The four of us didn't even look each other. I realised that, despite the strange events of the previous evening, our day would continue as normal – silent, weighted with routine, and I felt as though my life was like a huge eiderdown smothering me, as if I could hardly breathe or move.

They left. I stacked their plates at the table. As I was walking to the scullery holding them, I stopped in the middle of the room and just stood there for a minute, looking at nothing, just breathing. I closed my eyes.

The following day was a Sunday. We did not even attend church in that household, so removed were we from the outside world. Cows still had to be milked and vegetables dug, earth turned, sows and piglets fed. With a harvest in progress the men were busy all day and my own duties trebled. I forked over the stinking straw in the pig's pen with renewed vigour that morning, turning and turning the damp, blackened straw, staring at our vicious sow with hatred. She made no move to nip me. My misery had made me invincible.

Monday came, and Tuesday – the week progressed, and I realised that the only thing keeping me on my feet was the thought of Friday teatime, when I would go to the Traveller camp and collect the rent. I needed his smile. I needed it more than bread or salt. I dreamed of his smile all day long. I thought of it so often I felt I was wearing out the image in my head and it was becoming bled of colour, faded.

It was only as I walked towards the camp on Friday afternoon that it occurred to me that I was, perhaps . . . deluded. I had not exchanged so much as one word with the young man with the crinkly eyes. A smile, a look – small stuff to hold on to. Was I going mad, in my unhappiness, to wonder if he had been thinking of me that week, as I had been thinking of him? Foolish girl, I chided myself, as I strode over. He probably looks at a hundred girls a day – you've seen yourself how that camp is full of slim, pretty things with plaited hair. What makes you think he'll have thought of you, a big hulking farm girl with red frizz on your head? That hair alone is an embarrassment.

My attempts to fashion ringlets had come to naught and I had tied my hair up with my usual velvet ribbon, but it was a windy summer's day and already strands were escaping and sticking to my face.

As soon as I see him, I'll know, I thought, as I approached his wagon. I'll know, from the look on his face, whether he feels the same as me.

There was no one by the green and gold wagon. The door and shutters were firmly fastened. I glanced about but could not see him. Disappointment washed over me like cold, dirty water. If his smile had meant something, then he would have been there the following week, surely, to see me again.

I hovered around longer than was decent and soon noticed a group of three women at the neighbouring wagon, staring at me. Was I imagining it, or were they laughing at my expense?

I went over. One of them I recognised. She gave me her rent and then some extra, nodding at the green and gold wagon. 'This is from them. They've gone to Long Stanton.'

Long Stanton. Never had Long Stanton sounded so far away. I took the money and turned.

The last wagon I visited was that of Mrs Boswell. She gave me the rent and watched me tick my book, then handed me a small parcel, wrapped carefully in brown paper and tied with ribbon. 'This is for you, Miss Rose,' she said, 'to be opened in the privacy of your own room.'

I looked at it, then back at her. She had already turned away.

When I got back to the house, I was burning to run up to my bedroom and open the parcel. Could it be a message or a gift from him? But why would he leave it with the Boswells? I knew I had to do the books immediately and take the reckoning to my stepfather, then get on with making supper. Then there was an evening of silent sewing to endure.

It was not until bedtime that I was in my own little room with the door locked behind me. I took the small parcel from my pocket and held it up to the candle on my windowsill, to regard it properly in the soft, yellow light.

I could hardly bear to open it. When it was opened, I would know what was inside and was bound to be disappointed. A gift. I bit my lip as I looked at it, for I was realising that, since my mother had died, nobody had given me a gift. Not one. Birthdays were not acknowledged in our house, and even Christmas was marked only by a dinner of goose, cooked and served by me, as all the farm duties still had to be done and Father did not believe in excessive celebration. I think one year I had an orange from William.

Eventually, I slipped off the narrow blue ribbon and unfolded the brown paper.

Inside my little parcel was a brooch of some cheapish metal in the shape of a sunflower, with a boxed clasp, and a long, fine chain attached. At the other end of the chain was a slender grip, fastened by a clasp, which you slipped along its length. It was a tawdry thing, somewhat worn and old-fashioned, but practical, and it brought a lump to my throat. Even if it was Mrs Boswell's own and not bought, she had folded it and wrapped it and tied it with ribbon. She had told me to open it in my room because it was a woman's thing, a thing a man could not know about or understand. I sat holding the skirt grip beneath the candlelight and wept for my mother and for all the things she might have said or given to me as I became a woman myself, if she had been given the chance. I wept for her as I had never wept before.

It was that night, in the dead darkness before dawn, when I was sound asleep and wallowing in dreams, that Elijah Smith threw little sticks against my windowpane.

The sticks themselves did not awaken me – I only knew what he'd thrown when I found some of them on the windowsill. I was woken by the barking of the dog, Eddie, in the yard. By the time I got to the window and raised it, Eddie's racket had frighted him off. I was just in time to see Elijah leap the fence – no more than a glimpse in the moonlight, but enough to recognise him by.

I watched the shape of him be swallowed by the darkness. So I was not deluded, after all.

CHAPTER 8

It wasn't much of a wedding – I have to own that now, although at the time I was so cheerful that we had pulled it off that what was missing hardly mattered. I told Elijah I wanted it done properly in St Matthew's Church, so we had to wait for the banns to be read. We went to church for each of those Sundays, and my heart sang as the vicar announced our names for the whole wide world to hear – oh, I wanted every man, woman and child in the country to know I was to be wed.

Elijah proposed to me exactly three weeks after he threw sticks at my window. We were lying on the bank behind the Traveller encampment. It was the fifth time we had managed to be alone together.

It was early evening. The sky had already lost its goldenness and was taking on the purplish, slightly sickly hues of dusk. It was making me sad. I dreaded having to return to the farmhouse and was telling him so. By then, he knew everything about my stepfather and brothers, about the strange behaviour of Horace.

'Sometimes I think I will go mad if I spend one more night there,' I was sighing.

'Come away with me, then.'

I looked at him. He was lying on his back with his hands behind his head, chewing on a piece of long grass and looking at the sky.

There had been no pause before he said it, and it was lightly said. You might have thought he was suggesting, *How about a cup of tea?* I sat up and looked down at his face, searching for some sign of the weight behind his words, but his eyes were shut and the rest of his face remained closed too. After staring at him for a moment or two, I was none the wiser.

When I did not answer him, he opened his eyes, looked up at me squintingly, and repeated the suggestion. 'Come *away* with me, and when you're mine, there won't be a man in this world but me has a right to lay a finger on you.' He put one hand on my sleeve. 'You'll be my Rosie, for good. And that will be it, my girl.'

Within a space no longer than a few tickings of a clock, I moved from thinking, *how absurd* to thinking, *yes*.

How could I possibly run away with Elijah Smith and just leave everything?

Well, what, precisely, would I be leaving? I had very few possessions and no money, my stepfather had seen to that. The only thing I valued was a gold chain my mother left me which I wore round my neck day and night, so that was easy enough to take along with me. I only had that because she had given it to me herself when she became ill. She must have known by then I would get nothing from the farmer. That and the skirt grip Mrs Boswell had given me were the only possessions I valued in the whole wide world.

The farmer. My stepfather. I thought of his fury when my departure was discovered, and that of the dreaded Horace. And then I thought – and I must confess this gave me no little pleasure – of how affronted my stepfather would be to have a Travelling man for a son-in-law, of how he would have to lie about it to his Alderman friends and always wonder if his lies would be discovered. We might not mix much with the local people but that didn't mean we wouldn't be worth gossiping about. *Have you heard about what the Childer girl has gone and done? She's run off with a Gypsy!* Oh my, how it would wound him and Horace to have that whispered. That wouldn't do much for their marriage prospects.

I looked at Elijah. He was a handsome man, with his crooked teeth and smile that made me dizzy. I thought about him all day long. If I saw him talking to somebody else, man or woman, I felt ill because he was attending to them, not me. We had kissed three times and each time it was like drowning. When he had his mouth on mine, I forgot the rest of the whole world. I forgot I needed air to breathe. *Put your hands on me*, I wanted to say. He had been quite polite so far. He had held my head, and stroked my face, that was all.

I had never been touched tenderly by a man before and it was as though I had discovered some extraordinary secret. I burned with it, in places where I had not realised it was possible to burn.

I loved him, but I knew nothing of him, really. He might abandon me, for all I knew.

'I'll not give myself to you until we're legally wed, you know that, don't you?' I said boldly to him, and he replied with a broad grin, for he knew that meant I was going to agree.

'I know that, girl.'

'But where shall we go to?' I already had a feeling that the practicalities of this matter would be down to me.

'Let's go to a town,' he said, 'for I've had enough of fields and mud for the time being.'

'We can go to Cambridge,' I replied. 'I have an old friend of my mother's there and we can stay with her while we find our own little house.'

He frowned and stroked his chin. 'A house? So you're going to make a proper *gorjer* of me, are yer?' Then he smiled again. 'You had better make me some fancy clothes if I'm going up in the world, my girl.'

'I can sew well enough.'

He stood. 'Better go and pack your things then, girl.'

I must confess I felt a little dissatisfied as I crept back to the house, for in truth I had always imagined that when a man proposed to me it would be with great protestations of love; but I already knew that Elijah was not a man for great protestations of any sort, and that was something I would just have to get used to.

I may not have had the romantic side of a proposal but I had something just as good – the excitement of running off. I hugged it to me. I was going to pack my things and run off in the dead of night and my stepfather and stepbrothers who thought they owned me were going to wake in the morning and find I had slipped from their grasp.

I should have left them a vicious little note, something about how they would have to boil their own milk from now on – but in truth I was too afraid to do it, and reckoned the empty bed they would discover in the morning would speak for itself.

Our arrival in Paradise Street must have caused a small stir, I think; given folk something to talk about. There had been no means of warning Aunt Lilly we were about to show up on her doorstep, and I had not had any contact with her for years. We just showed up one afternoon. Standing on her doorstep, waiting for her to answer the door, was almost more frightening than running away from River Farm in the dark, wondering what on earth I would do if Elijah and his horse were not waiting for me at the end of the lane.

The door opened, and there was Aunt Lilly, scarcely changed from when I had last seen her eight years previous – apart from the fact that she had taken to dying her hair orange. A look of puzzlement, then curiosity, crossed her face. Then her hand went to her mouth and she gave a cry of recognition. She stared at my cloth bag, and Elijah standing beside me, then she shook her head and pulled a face both tragical and comic, lips pressed together and mouth wide, like a duck. I couldn't work out if she was pleased or not.

She stepped back from the door, turned her head slightly and called out, 'Samuel, Samuel, come here directly.'

Samuel Empers came to the front door slowly. He had aged much more than Lilly.

Lilly turned back to me. 'It's Emmeline's girl. Our Rose,' she said, as if I might be the one in need of reminding who I was. She opened her arms.

They gave us tea and we discussed where Elijah might lodge. She had a nephew over at Old Gas Lane who owed her a favour or two – and there was a small stables and yard behind his place where we could put the horse and Elijah would be handy to care for it. We told her Elijah was a horse-dealer and general trader, and she knew well enough what that meant. I saw her looking a little askance at him but thought, ah well, she'll get used to the idea.

Elijah didn't say much during this first encounter. It was strange to see him quiet and unsure of himself. He did not know whether to sit or stand and clutched his cup of tea like someone drowning. He kept glancing over at Samuel Empers, as if he thought the man of the household might help him out, but Samuel Empers was always entirely ruled by his wife so Elijah had no assistance from that quarter. When it was decided that Samuel should walk him over to Gas Lane, Elijah leaped to his feet in gratitude and gave me no more than a nod before he was out of the door.

We all retired as soon as Samuel returned from safely stowing Elijah. It was agreed that I was to sleep in their bed, with Aunt Lilly, and poor Samuel deposit himself on the settee downstairs. There was nowhere else in those little houses. I had gone out of my way to ensure they knew Elijah and I would not be a burden to them – we would wed as soon as we could, and find our own little house to rent. Exactly how we were going to support ourselves was a matter we did not discuss.

The only awkwardness came as Lilly and I were in the bedroom, preparing for sleep. We had performed our ablutions. I was sitting up in bed, beneath the quilt, and Lilly was wrapping papers around locks of her orange hair, one by one, and pinning them to her skull.

We were talking of my mother.

'And where is she buried?' Aunt Lilly asked, as she licked her comb and pulled it gently through a section of hair.

'Cottenham,' I replied. I hesitated. 'It was a small funeral. Just the family.'

Aunt Lilly stopped what she was doing and looked at me. 'I only heard of your mother's death from another farmer. Mr Cooper at Chatteris Fen Farm.' She looked down at her lap. 'He was bringing in radishes that year, although I think he's now moved over to sugar beet.'

'Mr Childer did not write to you?' I had always wondered why I had never heard from Aunt Lilly after my mother died.

Her face grew grave. 'He did not, my dear. I wrote to him, however, after my conversation with Mr Cooper. I offered to have you. We should have – well, Samuel and I not having our own.'

I stared at her.

She lifted her arms to apply another paper to her hair, then let them drop. 'Perhaps I was clumsy in my letter – I am not good with words. He stopped supplying us after that.'

We lay next to each other in the darkness, Aunt Lilly and I, but for a long time after she began to snore, I could not sleep. I was turning over in my mind my stepfather's wickedness. Of course he did not want to send me back to East Cambridge. He did not want to lose an unpaid servant. No wonder he stopped supplying Aunt Lilly. He wanted nothing more to do with her.

After I knew this, I began to regret my cowardice in having run off from River Farm without giving my stepfather a piece of my mind. I wanted to hurt him back for all the hurt he had caused me. I should have liked to have written him a letter in which I told him exactly what I thought of him, but in truth, I was still too afraid of him to do it – I was not fully of age, after all. What if he came after me and tried to take me back to the farm?

After a week or so in Paradise Street, I thought more calmly and realised that if he and Horace were going to try and get me back they would have done it by now. No, he had washed his hands of me, probably assumed I had lain beneath a hedge with Elijah and become a *gipo* on the spot. The more I thought about it, the more wounded I felt that they were not even bothering to enquire after me. I bet he's already forbidden his sons to mention my name, I thought bitterly, as if I never existed.

So I wrote to William instead. William was the only person I regretted leaving behind at River Farm. I knew he would find it hard without me. Without a woman to bully, the men in that house would turn upon the weakest among them. And pride came into it, a little. I wanted William to know that I wasn't sleeping in a gutter somewhere, that I was going to be a decent married woman. I didn't want him to think badly of me, and I suppose if I'm honest I was hoping the information would leak out to the rest of the family, then, whatever else they thought of me, there was at least one bad thing they would not be able to think.

So, soon as we had a date fixed for the wedding, I wrote to William, telling him the where and the when. I said he was welcome to come and give me away if he liked, as I regarded him as my nearest male relation. I don't know whether he ever got the letter safely – perhaps my stepfather intercepted it – but either way he never showed up at the church. Elijah and I were married in front of Aunt Lilly and her Samuel, and two new friends of Elijah's. More of them later.

At least the sun came out, as bright and cheery as a blessing from the whole wide world, as if to make up for the fact that Elijah and I had not a single relative between us to see us intertwine our lives. As we walked out of the gloom of St Matthew's Church, it was as if the whole street was bathed in light. We all stopped on the steps and beamed at each other.

We were doing the whole thing on the cheap, of course. We had to borrow for the marriage licence, which was a lot more than either of us had expected and there was no chance of a gold ring or anything like that – we used a cheap dress ring of Lilly's – but honestly I didn't care. It was in a church and it was legal, just like my mother would have wanted for me.

Then, as we made our first move down the steps, the church bells began to ring. We all looked up at the blue sky, amazed, as if the peals were coming from heaven itself. Lilly cried out, 'Now, isn't that lovely!'

I hadn't expected any extras like that. I turned to Elijah and said, all happy about it, 'Where did you get the money for them to ring the bells? I didn't know I was getting that!'

If he had had any sense, he would have just smiled and got the credit but instead he shrugged and said, 'I didn't know they would be rung.' I could see he was as surprised as me.

'Aunt Lilly?'

'Don't be daft!' she laughed.

We all stood around for a minute, smiling and listening. When the peals stopped, Lilly said to Samuel, 'Sam, go on in and ask the vicar. Ask him who paid for the church bells to be rung.' She was nodding at Elijah. I think she still thought he had done it but wouldn't own up to it.

Samuel caught up with us as we were walking down the road. We were all off to the Old Norfolk for a celebration of wine and little cakes. 'A gentleman who wishes not to be named,' he said, as he drew alongside us, tapping the side of his nose.

William, I thought to myself, for there was no chance my stepfather would ever do such a thing. And even though I was happy as anything to have my handsome new husband by my side, I felt a tiny twist of pain inside me, like a stitch but only momentary, at the thought of William's sad, pale face, and what would become of him now I had left.

It's funny how you can make yourself joyful when you put your mind to it. My wedding was nothing like I had fantasised about when I was a girl. I had always seen myself in a gown with a long train. I had always thought I would have months to plan it, to make favours and embroider my underthings with bluebirds. And somehow, Lord knows why, I had always pictured the church full to the rafters. But even though I had married with not a single relative to witness it, in a brown wool dress and a bonnet rented from the pawnbrokers, I was happy, yes happy, as we strode along Gas Lane and up past the Victoria Soap and Candle Works. We were a tiny party – and me hardly a beauty after all – but I was young and strong and smiling, and I paraded in front, arm in arm with Elijah, holding a posy. And people came to their doorsteps to smile back at us because everybody loves a wedding, however meagre.

I had made my own decision to run away from my stepfather and make a new life with Elijah Smith, and, for the first time in my life, I had done something for myself instead of being done to. It was a grand feeling. It was a blue-sky day, and cloudless. My feet hurt in my borrowed shoes but I didn't care. I was a properly married lady and the church bells had rung as I came out into the sun.

I won't pretend that first year was all plain sailing. I sometimes find myself thinking that everything was fine and dandy between me and Elijah before she showed up but I know that is no more than a comforting falsehood and it does me no credit to rely on it. No, there were many things about Elijah that would have been difficult however it had gone between us.

I had no illusions about our lives together, how difficult it would be for us to support ourselves. Some might have thought me mad to leave a well-off farm and go back to the town – for whatever else was wrong in that sad house, there was always enough food on the table. I ate meat every week I lived there. I was a strong girl, as a result, and would have happily rolled my sleeves up and got work but as I was soon to be a married woman that was going to be difficult.

And the minute I *was* a married woman, I started wanting things in a way I never had before. On the farm, where I had scarcely owned the clothes I stood up in, it had never occurred to me to desire objects – well, I never came across any objects I desired. But once I was back in Paradise Street, in a city full of shops, well, I couldn't help noticing that other people had things that I hadn't.

Somewhere to live, for a start – and things to put in the somewhere. Even before we had our own little parlour, I started dreaming of a proper hair couch to put in it – forty shillings it would be, I said to Elijah, but if we settled for cloth it would only be twenty-five. A marble-top washstand for the corner of our bedroom – now that was my idea of luxury, to have a grand thing like that that was not even on display for visitors, but just for me and him. That was my idea of wealth, that was, to be able to afford something like that.

Oh, I did want a marble-top washstand. I think I thought my whole life would be complete if I had one of those. When I told Elijah, he rubbed his chin.

I couldn't quite work out exactly what it was my new husband did for a living. Sometimes he had a bit of money on him and sometimes nothing at all. Either way, he had a confidence about him that reassured me we would get by somehow. He had told me he dealt in horses sometimes and that he did some hawking. He was certainly very good at fixing things and could turn on the charm all right when he needed to.

There was one small incident, not long after we arrived in Paradise Street, which tells you all you need to know about Elijah. We were having a light supper with Lilly and Samuel, and they had gone to some effort for us even though it was a small meal, putting out the best tablecloth and cutlery and all. Lilly had dished up in the kitchen and brought the plates into the parlour laden. As she entered, she said, 'Sit down, the lot of you, let's eat while it's hot. I can't abide a cold supper.'

We sat and she put plates down before Elijah and myself – corned beef fritters and cabbage in gravy. I saw Elijah frown, lift his hands to the edge of the table, and move it a little.

'You've got a wobbly table leg, here, Mr Empers,' he said to Samuel.

Samuel was unperturbed. 'I have that, young man. I'll get around to fixing it one of these days.'

Lilly had gone back into the kitchen to get the other two plates and overheard this as she returned. 'I wish you would, Samuel. I've been on at you about it long enough.'

Elijah jumped to his feet. 'I'll sort this out soon enough!' he declared, clapping his hands together and rubbing them, and blow me if he didn't lean forward and whisk the plates from under our noses. Off came the cutlery. Off came the candlestick. Away went the best tablecloth while Lilly and Samuel sat there staring at him. And he upended the table and fixed it there and then.

It was done in a trice, but all the same I could tell Lilly was none too impressed. She had a point. A cold fritter is not nice, after all.

When he had finished, Elijah righted the table in one swift movement and stood back with a flourish, looking at us all for applause.

Lilly rose stiffly and went to retrieve our supper.

Elijah looked at me, a little baffled. Had he not done a nice thing, for our friends who had been so good to us? Where was his congratulations?

That was Elijah.

I spent my wedding night, and every night for the next month, sharing a bed with Aunt Lilly, while Elijah went back to Gas Lane. Finally, in July, we were able to get the rental together and find our own house. We were lucky to get one in that area at all as East Cambridge had got mightily crowded in the eight years I'd been out on the farm. An old lady living at number twenty-two, just three doors down from Lilly and Samuel, passed away. The rental of the property should have passed back to the Corporation but the old lady's daughter was still officially on the books even though she'd moved in with a friend on Norfolk Street. The daughter was a friend of Aunt Lilly's and Aunt Lilly had had quite enough of me sleeping in her bed and her husband on the settee. She put a bit of pressure on, and number twenty-two was sub-let to us, furniture and all.

So Lijah and I had been married a month before we got our own bed. When we first closed the door of number twenty-two on everyone, the day we moved in, we stood and grinned at each other for a moment, before Elijah chased me shrieking up the stairs. We were so pleased with ourselves that what happened next was a bit noisy, if you get my drift.

*

It wasn't the first time we had lain together, mind. We couldn't wait that long. No, the first time was a few days after we were wed, at the Midsummer Fair.

The fair had come every June when I was girl and my mother and I would always go together – so there was no chance of me missing it my first summer back in the Garden of Eden. I pleaded with Elijah to take me but in a way that made it quite clear I would go with Lilly and Samuel if he didn't.

So one bright afternoon, we dressed up as much as we could and set off down Maids Causeway, along with most of East Cambridge.

It was a fine thing to be promenading with my new husband. We passed lots of folk who remembered me from my childhood – I daresay word had got around – and so many stopped to congratulate us that we felt quite the swells by the time we reached Midsummer Common.

Not far past the first displays there was a man in an apron doing a hog-roast: two hog-roasts, in fact, as one was turning on a spit and another was laid out on a carving table with an onion in its mouth and its legs pulled diagonal, as if it was running. The hog-roast man was sharpening his knives, about to commence the carve-up, and a queue had already formed.

I turned my head away, not wanting to take too close a look, for I was hungry already and the sign said a serving of hog-roast was two and six for gentlemen and a shilling for ladies. I glanced sideways at Elijah as we walked on, hoping he might ask me if I'd like some, but he was looking carefully ahead, and I gathered by that we could not afford it. I gave a small sigh, and looked around for some amusement that was cheap.

Luckily for us, there were plenty of amusements where it was nothing at all to stand and spectate. There was Catch-a-Pig, where the men all paid tuppence to chase a piglet around and if they caught it and slung it over their shoulder they could keep it. I didn't think a great deal of this, as I could remember being beaten for failing to catch one once, so it didn't seem all that amusing to me, and besides it was obvious the piglet had been greased with soap so nobody could get it. But we stood and watched for a while and pretty soon some fella fell in the mud and Elijah started roaring with laughter and I joined in and before we knew it the whole crowd was off. The young men started queuing up for the next go and I do think Elijah would have joined them if I had not prevented him.

What would a Midsummer Fair, or any fair for that matter, be without pigs?

Just past the apple-bobbing, I saw a large sign: TOBY, THE SAPIENT PIG.

Elijah didn't seem keen on taking a look. He frowned, as if there was something sinister in it, but I dragged him by the arm and we stood behind the first row watching and moving our heads from side to side to peer between the others.

Toby the Sapient Pig was a large white with black patches and one black ear. He was held in a sty with clean golden straw, around which had been strewn a number of volumes: *The Plays of William Shakespeare*, I spotted, and some foreign-sounding names I did not recognise from my small amount of schooling.

Toby stood amidst these, ignoring the crowd. A man stood next to him, in a cape and top hat, beaming proudly as if he was presenting his newborn child for our delectation. 'Ask me anything you like, ladies and gentleman!' he declared. 'Shortly I will allow you to question the Sapient Toby – as you can see, he is currently having a short repast.' The pig was eating a book.

'What's he eating?' a man called out from the crowd. The manner in which the question was asked did not ring of true curiosity, in my opinion.

'Plutarch,' responded the man in the cape. 'He is fond of the Ancients.'

'How was he discovered?' called another.

'Well, his first master . . .' the man began, and then began spilling some nonsense about how he had been sold as a piglet to a schoolmaster who had taught him all he knew.

Pretty soon the crowd grew restless and the man clearly decided it would be politic to let the pig show what he could do. At this point, he withdrew a pack of playing cards and there followed some game, which involved putting them down on the straw and letting the pig choose one with his trotter and some young woman in the audience affecting amazement and shouting, 'The very one I was thinking of!'

Meanwhile, a young boy went among us with a cap. I saw Elijah toss something in and was surprised he was contributing as he had a rather sour look on his face. 'Come on, Rosie,' he muttered, 'let's be off.'

We were turning away, when the man in the cape called out, 'Now, you look like a highly intelligent young miss, if I might say so.'

I glanced about. A woman next to me hissed, 'He means you!'

The people in front of us parted and I was ushered forward. I looked back at Elijah but he had crossed his arms with a mildly amused but still sour look on his face.

'Young lady! Young lady! You of the lustrous locks. My Toby has eyes to read but can also appreciate human beauty. Do please honour me by showing yourself to him . . .'

I hope he doesn't think I'm climbing in that sty, I thought. But no, he merely wanted me to stand in front of it while he scattered some pieces of card with letters painted on them in front of the pig. The pig snuffled in front of some of them and the man bent to the straw, picking up R, O, S and E.

He held them up, fanning them for the crowd to see. 'And what is your name, fair one?' he asked me with a small bow.

'Rose!' I said, looking round at the crowd, hoping that they would see by my genuine amazement that I was not in on the act.

A few people at the front clapped and I blushed as if they were applauding me rather than the pig. I looked for Elijah but could not see him.

The man thanked me and handed me a small posy and a piece of paper which had on it a poem that he said had been written by the pig himself.

I found Elijah when I worked my way out of the crowd. He was standing a few feet off, looking grumpy.

'How did you do it?' I asked him gaily.

'Do what?'

'Tell him my name.'

'I didn't do any such thing . . .'

'Elijah,' I said, 'you were in on the joke, weren't you? Don't tease me now. Look I got a poem and a flower for my trouble.'

I planted a kiss on his cheek – but he really did look quite annoyed.

'I tell you I didn't.' He brushed me off.

We stood in awkward silence for a moment. Then, all at once, his face brightened. He nodded. 'Be right back, Rosie. Just seen a fella I know.' And off he went.

So I was left holding my paper flower and my poem written by the pig.

I stood around for a bit, then I read the poem.

Of the crowds who the Sapient Toby have seen
Not one of them all disappointed have been;
But all to their friends have been proud to repeat
That a Visit to Toby indeed is a Treat.

TSP

Elijah is a queer one, I thought. He must have told the man my name and got me the flower and the poem so why did he not take credit for it?

I was still standing close to the crowd that was watching Toby, so I heard the boy with the cap shouting, 'Oi! Which of you mean bastards put a button in my cap?'

I decided to take a wander around, figuring that Elijah would be able to find me when he chose as long as I did not stray too far. It was sixpence to go inside the tent of the Menagerie and see the Elephant Ridden by a Valorous Maiden and of course I had no money on me – so the Steam Powered Rides were out of the question as well. I watched the Eel Dipping, for a bit, which was quite droll. Next to the eels was A Three Legged Cat in a cage but I thought that was horrible and didn't look. The novelty of hanging around on my own was beginning to wear off and I began to feel annoyed with Elijah. Why could he not have taken me along with him to see the man he knew? I was hungry.

By the time he returned, I was ready to be sharp with him, but before I could say a word, he lifted up one fist and shook it in the air. It made a rattling sound. I could tell he was pleased with himself.

'What's that?' I said.

He dropped whatever rattled into his pocket. Then, he showed me that both his hands were empty. Next, he clapped them together, shook his sleeves, then lifted one hand from the other to reveal a palm full of coins; some pennies, thre'penny and sixpenny bits – even some florins.

'Elijah!' I cried. 'Where did you get that from?'

He tapped the size of his nose. 'Never let it be said I don't know how to show my Rosie a good time . . .' He linked his arm with mine and turned me. 'Now, where was that hog-roast man?'

The hog was roasted so well his skin was as orange as Aunt Lilly's hair and hard and crispy as a sugar stick. As the butcher sliced into it, you could see the white fat slithering beneath its shell and the pale meat falling away. It came with a slab of bread as huge as half a loaf, and chunks of apple sauce so generous they slid off as you raised the whole to your mouth. I shrieked as I bit down on it.

Lijah had a man-size portion. It was almost as big as his face. As he bit into it he said, with his mouth full, 'There's good pigs and bad pigs, Rosie. And this here . . .' he was grinning '. . . is a very good pig indeed!'

When we had eaten enough for it to be manageable, we strode around with it. How I loved the indelicacy of eating outside, for all to see, in the open air; the soft meat and the crispness of the crackling and the sweet, sweet apple sauce. We never had hogs done like that on River Farm, I can tell you.

We spent the whole afternoon at the fair, and we saw almost everything, then stopped and sat down and drank cider with some friends of Elijah's, the pals he had made who had been at our wedding – George Muggleton, the monumental mason, and Albert Tanner, who was a cellarman at the malting house. I hadn't taken to them much but after a couple of glasses of cider I decided they and their lady friends were all right and there was no point in being snooty about people. The cider made me giggle.

As the light began to fade, we left them and took another promenade to see the lanterns lit. Then we got a ferry across the river, for no reason other than Elijah thought it would be a nice idea. We walked around the boathouses and across the common. There were loads of courting couples in the twilight and we went to a wooded bit up near the farm and Elijah had a good feel. To start off with I put him off. I thought we might be getting our house soon and I wanted our first time to be in our own married bed, not out of doors like people who are up to no good. It was getting chilly as well. But his kisses melted me – we had had so little time alone together they still had that power – so I let him put his hand up my skirt. I let him start on account of wanting to please him, then I let him continue on account of wanting to please myself.

The actualness of it was not as nice as the touching and the kisses – it hurt a bit, and made my legs feel wobbly – but he was kind and gentle afterwards. We sat and leaned against a tree trunk and he wrapped his arms around me to keep me warm and together we watched the stars pop out above us, and Elijah said, 'We're going to have as many babbies as there are stars in the sky, Rosie, you'll see.' And I watched the stars and thought of all the good things that lay ahead of us.

CHAPTER 9

I like to think that was the night my first child was conceived – my son, Daniel. I could be wrong about that, of course, as Elijah made sure we had one or two other opportunities before we moved into number twenty-two. I do so like the idea that my Daniel came into being inside me on that night, when Elijah held me in his arms beneath the stars. I suppose it could have just as easily have been the next time, when we did it awkwardly and sweatily, standing up in the stable behind Gas Lane, with Elijah's horse snorting and breathing next to us. I got my back bruised against the wooden wall.

My Daniel. How should I begin to describe that child? My first, my plumpest . . . the only one who never gave me a moment's worry. I think if any mother is honest they will admit they love the first in a way they cannot love the others, especially if that first is a boy. The first one cracks you open. With the first, your whole life goes topsy-turvy and nothing is ever the same again – for it is the first that turns you from an ordinary mortal into a mother. It is a coronation you never forget.

He was born in Paradise Street, the following March.

But before that, she arrived.

Elijah had not said much about his mother before we ran away together, nor after, for that matter. I knew he lived in his wagon with an older woman and man who I assumed were his mother and father. It was only when I started to talk about my mother dying, and how I never knew my real father, that he told me the story he had learned from his mother as a boy, about his father being the King of Russia. When I laughed, I saw I had offended him. He didn't think it funny at all.

I did think it a little odd that he didn't want to talk of his mother at all, or his life on the camp. I asked him once, in Paradise Street, was there no one he wanted from his old life at his wedding? He scratched his head and pulled a face. 'Well, it's not really the done thing where I come from,' was all he said. But surely he wanted his own mother? 'Well, I'm not sure she'll be all that pleased to be perfectly honest with you, Rosie . . .'

'Why not?' I asked, but I couldn't get a straight answer out of him. I didn't press him. To be honest, I liked the idea that we had jointly discarded our old lives.

He had a good way of silencing my curiosity in those early days. Upward, he would look, then down. 'Well, you might ask,' he would say, with a mock frown. Later, I was to find this phrase of his infuriating, but in the first few weeks of knowing him, it only added to his air of mystery and, anyhow, he often followed it with a kiss.

Those kisses – full of everything. He would hold my face, quite firmly, hands either side of my head, and pause for a moment, looking at me, long enough to let me know that I was his now, that he would not release me for the world. Then his face would move towards mine and I would close my eyes without even meaning to. And then it came . . . the meeting and the parting of the lips, his mouth first hard on mine, then soft, the grazing of our tongues together and the feel of his hands holding my face. The surrender of it . . . to be held firmly and kissed softly – is there any more a girl can ask for? They were hypnosis, those early kisses.

Why should I be curious about his mother?

I had been out to see Lilly. Her inflammation of the spine was bad and she had been in bed for a few days. It was past Christmas and I was too obviously with child to be out and about in the wider world, so visiting her was a nice excuse to get out of the house. The air was icy but I scarcely felt it – so huge was I my shawl could hardly cover me. I was like a great balloon as I floated down Paradise Street. People would jump into the street when they saw me coming, as if they were afraid that bumping against me might detach my moorings and send me sailing skywards.

I had left Elijah snoozing at home. He often snoozed after dinner if he had to be out late. I didn't like it much, but he brought money home with him so I could hardly complain. New horses would appear in the Gas Lane stables now and then – then disappear a few days later, but he never got rid of the horse we rode to Cambridge on. He said every man had to have one horse that was special.

He wouldn't let me near the horses once he knew I was carrying. He said it was bad luck. I didn't mind. By then, I was used to the fact that he was superstitious.

Lilly loved my pregnancy. It was the nearest she would ever get to having one herself, she said, so she wanted all the details, even the private stuff like how often I needed the privvy and how I craved potato. That afternoon, we'd had a long chat and it was getting gloomy by the time I ambled down Paradise Street. I expected that Elijah would have gone out, but when I opened the door he was standing in our little sitting room, and in front of him was a small, dark woman, in an old-fashioned mourning dress with a brooch at the neck. She looked a little comical, in fact, as she also had pointy, lace-up boots on her feet and a large hat with a drooping ostrich feather. Round her neck was a fox fur which, to my mind, looked as if it had been taken from the rest of the fox by an amateur, not necessarily a two-legged one. As I entered, she drew herself up to her full height, which was still a great deal shorter than me.

I looked at Elijah. He exhaled, then dropped himself down into his armchair. 'Well, Rosie, looks like we've got company.' He stared ahead.

The woman drew in her breath. She glanced me up and down, then picked up an old leather bag from the floor, lifted her skirts and turned to our staircase. I watched her ascend. What was this strange woman doing, going up our stairs?

Then I saw a huge carpet-bag on the floor. The penny dropped. I rushed over to Elijah. 'Elijah!' I hissed, bending a little so she should not hear me, 'that's not your mother?'

'Who else might it be, my love?' he said calmly.

'Elijah!' I said. 'What were you doing sitting yourself down? Haven't you been looking after her? Why didn't you fetch me at once from Lilly's?'

'She's only just this minute arrived,' Elijah replied irritably, waving a hand.

'Well have you offered her some tea?' I could not believe how ill mannered he was being, to his own mother.

'She's not in the mood for tea. She's had some bad news.'

'What news?'

'Her husband died. She'll be with us for a bit, all right? Now leave it be, Rosie.'

He was often gruff when he was upset, Lijah, but I had not fully learned that yet. Later I knew not to press him on anything that he might be feeling something about. 'But, here? She's staying here? Shouldn't we have a talk about it?'

'There'll be plenty of time for all that,' he huffed, rising from the chair. 'Mark my words.'

He strode over to the door and took his jacket and hat from the peg on the back.

'You're not going out?' I cried in dismay.

'Oh yes, I am.' He went to the mirror by the bottom of the stairs to check his hat was on straight.

I was bewildered. 'What am I to do with her?' I asked.

'Well I daresay you'll have plenty to talk about, you two women.'

I tried firmness. 'Elijah Smith, you cannot go out on one of your appointments when your mother has just arrived after not seeing you for months, and her husband dead, and, you can't . . .'

'I'm not off on an appointment,' he said, 'I'm off to The Bleeding Heart.'

'Elijah . . .'

'Oh stop beefing, woman. I'll be back later.' And he left.

We had a small settee that we had bought on the never-never not long after we'd moved in. I sank down onto it and knew I was about to cry. I wept often when I was carrying. I was bewildered by Lijah's behaviour. How could he be so rude to his own mother? It shocked me, that he was capable of treating someone like that. It was a side of him I'd not seen before. And what would I say to her? I would have to make some excuse for him. I could hardly say he had gone down the pub.

I was still sitting there in some disarray when I heard a light tread on the stair. Elijah's mother was making her way down, slowly. The stairs came straight into the sitting room so I was able to observe the last few steps of her descent. Her little booted feet were pressed sideways against each stair. She was holding up her skirts with one hand and clutching the rail tightly with the other, as if she had never used stairs before.

She stood before me. She had removed her hat and the fox fur and I could now take a close look at her old-fashioned mourning dress, which had pleats down the front and puff sleeves with lace, like on a child's dress. I was about to rise and offer her a cup of tea but something in her strange look kept me pinned to the settee. She was staring at me as if she was trying to see beyond my face, to what was inside, my secret thoughts.

Then she said, 'Ee's gone down the pub, I s'pose.' She had a thick Fenland accent.

Had she been eavesdropping on us? I am ashamed to say that more tears sprung to my eyes as I nodded. I felt humiliated, all of a sudden, as if it was my fault Elijah was off down The Bleeding Heart, as if she was judging me for being unable to keep my husband in the house.

Her eyes narrowed, became two pin-pricks, and I suddenly remembered the hostile stare she had given me the very first time I had seen Elijah sitting on the step of their wagon.

'You've married my son,' she said evenly, 'and you'll sup sorrow by the spoonful 'til the day you die.'

She went back up the stairs.

It was not what you'd call a good start, I suppose.

What was extraordinary to me was that the next day, Elijah and his mother behaved as if there had been nothing odd in either her sudden appearance or his reaction to it – as if it was quite normal for people to drop in and out of each other's lives with hardly a word.

She had not reappeared the previous evening and eventually I went to bed alone, presuming she would look after herself in the tiny box room next to ours. She had closed the door and, after her pronouncement, I was far too timid to knock on it to enquire if she needed anything.

Elijah returned some time in the night. He had been drinking ale, which always made him snore. I was finding it difficult to sleep, so lay awake most of the night, heaving myself from one side to the next every now and then when my position became uncomfortable. I finally dropped off not long before dawn, and within minutes was awoken by the sound of creaking on the stairs. I started awake – each of my pregnancies gave me wild nightmares and I frightened easily. My first reaction was to shake Elijah and tell him there was an intruder in the house, but then I remembered his mother. What on earth was she doing up at that hour?

In the morning, I left Elijah where he was, pulled my shawl over my nightdress and clambered carefully down the stairs. I slipped on Elijah's boots over my bed socks and let myself out the back door, shuffling down the path to the privvy. The night-soil man had been, thank God. He didn't always do his duty, and the smell out the backs of the houses if he missed our street was quite unbearable. I let myself into the privvy.

As I came out, I let the wooden door swing shut behind me. A blackbird was sitting on the bare twig of a nearby bush. The banging of the door made it take flight. I shuddered with cold and turned to shuffle back up the path – and then I got a right old fright.

Elijah's mother was squatting on her heels by our small vegetable patch. She was smoking a thin clay pipe and staring at me, puffing on the pipe by pursing and unpursing her lips in short, sharp movements but otherwise as motionless as a garden ornament.

I saw myself through her eyes – a huge woman in a nightie with wild red hair, her bed socks round her fat ankles and her husband's unlaced boots on her feet. I hurried back inside.

When the kettle was on the stove, I went back upstairs and dressed noisily, to wake Elijah. I was damned if I was breakfasting alone with his sprite of a mother.

It started that first day. After breakfast, the silence broken only by a casual remark about the weather or a horse, she got to her feet and picked up our dirty plates. I had only just sat down after serving us all, but I jumped to my feet instantly. 'Do sit down . . .' I hesitated over what to call her. I didn't know her name. 'Mother, please. I can do that.' At the word *mother*, I thought I saw her and Elijah exchange a glance.

Either way, she ignored me, taking the plates over to the sink and placing them in. Then she turned and cleared away our cups, including mine, which still had some tea in it.

'Had enough, Lijah?' she said.

'Yes, thank you,' he replied meekly. He stood.

'Right then,' she replied, as she began to unbutton her sleeves. 'You'd better be off, then, and let me and your wife here get on with our chores.'

I stared at him.

'Right you are,' he said, and turned away without meeting my gaze.

'I'll wash these things,' Elijah's mother said. 'Now, this is your bowl for dishes, isn't it?'

'It's my bowl for everything,' I said. We lived in a house scarcely wider than the wagon she was used to. Did she think I had a scullery or washroom?

She stared at me. 'You've buckets I can take outside when I do the laundry, I hope.'

The laundry?

'Yes, Mother, we have buckets, but you'll not be wanting to wring cloths outside in this weather.'

She drew breath, blew it out slowly through pursed lips, shook her head and turned back to the sink.

If it hadn't been for Lilly, I am not sure how I would have got through those first few weeks. Elijah's mother was the most peculiar person I had ever met. Her ways were beyond me. Each afternoon, I would escape to Lilly's bedside and tell her of the latest antic. 'And yesterday, she served up some potatoes and she had not put any cabbage in gravy on my plate and it took me all my courage to say something to her and do you know what she said?'

'Go on . . .'

'She snapped at me, *it's bad luck for a woman in your condition to eat anything green*. And that was it! I'm not allowed to eat cabbage in my own house.' I'd never liked cabbage much anyway, but that wasn't the point.

Lilly would be agog. Like any invalid, she was bored and it was rare entertainment for her, my stories of Elijah's mother.

'You'll never guess what now . . .' I said one afternoon as I dropped my bulk down onto the edge of Lilly's bed. The bed-springs squeaked in protest. It was nearly March and I felt in my bones that my baby would be coming soon.

'What?' Lilly said, as she took the plate of fried potatoes I had brought over for her. I had put another plate on top of it, to keep it warm.

'This is a great one, this is. Last night, we was all talking. Lijah was at home for once and we were seated at the table. I rose up to get a cup of water and my back twinged, as it does, and I gave a gasp. Well, Lijah's mother jumps to her feet and orders Lijah out of the room. He's about to go when I tell them both to sit down for heaven's sake as it's only my back, and Lijah's mother starts questioning me. Do I feel peculiar in any way? Have I had a sudden urge to scrub the floor or anything? No, I say firmly, my baby's not coming but I think it's only a day or two if they want to know the truth. When Lijah leaves the room, his mother says to me, all confidential, that she's sure it's soon too as my bump has dropped down lower, but I shouldn't really say such things in front of my husband as it was indecent to mention women's matters. Honestly, all I'd said was the baby was coming soon. It wasn't as if I went into any detail.' Lilly was forking fried potato into her mouth while she listened. A small piece had dropped onto her bed shawl. 'Anyway, that's not the end of it. This morning, I get up. She's up before me as usual. She always is, no matter what time I rise. Sometimes I think she gets up in the middle of the night and goes out for her smoke just to make sure she beats me to it. Anyway, she's downstairs this morning, and what is she doing?'

Lilly paused, fork halfway to her mouth.

'She is draping scarves over the mirrors.'

'What?'

'This is her latest. I'm not allowed to look at myself now.'

'Why not?'

'She said the baby might come any minute, and I might walk past a mirror holding the baby on my shoulder and the baby might look into the mirror and lose its soul into it, or something. Oh, God knows, Lilly, the woman is completely batty and Elijah never says a word to her and what am I supposed to do?'

'That big mirror that you've got over the settee, the one with the painted frame that looks like gilt?'

'It's covered with a black shawl with orange flowers on it, frame and all.'

Lilly frowned at the trials I was undergoing. 'You can always bring that mirror round here, if you like.'

There was one aspect of having Elijah's mother around which I have to confess was useful, apart from the work she did about the house. Elijah cut down on his drinking a bit.

It hadn't really bothered me that much at first. Well, most men like a drink or two, don't they? And growing up in East Cambridge I would have thought it a bit odd to have ended up with a man who didn't partake once in a while. I was even fond of the occasional cup of cider myself sometimes, when we first moved into our house, and as the evenings drew in we would sometimes sit down together and share a jug and I would read aloud to him from *Ally Sloper's Half Holiday*. He loved Ally Sloper. Most Frequently

Kicked Out Man in Europe. 'Only 'cos they've not met me yet!'
Elijah used to say, slapping his knee.

Then, as my pregnancy drew on, I realised I couldn't really drink
more than a cup without it making me feel sick and dizzy, but I still
sat with him and read aloud. I remember those evenings fondly.
And the baby hadn't put me off intimacy with him, not at all.

But as I got fatter and more awkward, and more tired, Elijah
started going out more and more and by the time his mother
showed up in our lives it was already causing a bit of strain
between us. But something became clear to me within a few days of
her arriving – he was a deal more afraid of her than he was of me.

Then, one evening, just after the mirrors were covered up by
Elijah's mother, Elijah and I had an unpleasant argument.

It was a Sunday night. He had been out drinking the night
before. At teatime, I asked him for the rent money, which was due
every Sunday. He hadn't got it.

Now, this had happened before, and Aunt Lilly's friend that had
the rental on the house had been very good about it, I might say. We
had never fallen more than a week or two behind before Elijah got
hold of it somehow, but even so it embarrassed me mightily as it
was a friend of Lilly's we were holding it back from, not some horrible Corporation man. I wouldn't have given two hoots about
being late on the rent to one of them.

Eventually, the knock came at the door and I went to it and there
stood Lilly's friend, Miss Riley, and I said how sorry I was and
how next week there'd be double, and she looked a little crestfallen, but then leaned in and said, 'Don't you worry, my dear,
you've got quite enough on your plate as it is.' She glanced behind
me, to where Elijah's mother was standing in the room.

I went back inside and said, 'Well I hope you're happy, Elijah.
That's Miss Riley's week ruined. She buys her groceries with the
rental from this place, you know.'

'I thought you said she lived with a friend,' said Elijah's mother, although I had not been addressing her.

'She does,' I replied, 'but that is hardly the point, Mother. We owe her that money fair and square and she's been good to us.'

'And made a pretty penny out of it. I can't believe what you pay her to live in this box.'

Oh, a box, was it? A box that was good enough for her, for weeks on end, and with no word whatsoever on how long she might be with us. I could not be rude to her but my blood was beginning to boil. So I turned on Elijah. 'I do think you might consider my feelings,' I said to him. 'You go off doing as you please but I deal with the womenfolk in this street and by tomorrow lunchtime everyone is going to know how we are taking advantage of Miss Riley.'

'Well, she should hold her tongue, then,' Elijah snarled. 'What right has she got to be telling everyone our business?'

She wouldn't, of course. She would tell Lilly, and Lilly would tell everyone else. He had a point, but that was not the point.

I've never been much good at arguing. It upsets me too easy. I say whatever comes into my head and make myself look foolish. 'They are friends of mine,' I said tremulously, 'and . . . and . . .'

I looked from one to the other and saw how they were united against me. And I saw, moreover, that they would always be united against me in any sort of argument; that as soon as I disagreed with one, the other would be with them, and I would never win. I knew I would cry if I was not careful, so I left the room.

As I clambered up the stairs, I heard Lijah's mother say, quite distinctly and with no effort to avoid me hearing, 'How do you stand it . . .'

Lijah came up to bed later. I pretended to be asleep but he put his arm around me from behind.

'Don't bother yourself so, Rosie . . .' he said in a low voice. 'You

know I'll get the money together by next week. I always do. You
get in such a lather. Loads of folk are late with the rent, my
chicken.'

'You're forgetting something,' I muttered bad temperedly. 'I used
to go rent collecting myself, remember? It isn't as easy as you think.
And if someone doesn't give you what they owe you it's dreadful
because you never know if you'll get it or not and you never know
if they're going to give you no end of trouble.'

He let go of me and lay on his back. 'You get in too much of a
worry about such stuff. You'll feel better later.' He meant, *when the
baby's come*.

Oh no, I thought. I'm going to be much worse then. For surely,
once we had a baby to worry about, being behind with the rent
would be ten times as bad? And anyway, I had had quite enough of
how anything wrong with me got put down to the fact I was carrying.

I lay on my back next to him for a moment, but I couldn't do it
for long. It didn't feel right. I rolled over on my side again, but
towards him this time.

'What did she mean, *how do you stand it*?'

'What?'

'What did your mother mean?'

'She ain't used to houses, that's all. It's a bit cooped up for her
here.'

Is that what she meant? I wondered to myself as, unusually for
me, I began to fall asleep.

The next morning was a Monday and I got up early after sleeping
quite well and checked and stoked the range. When it was firing up
nicely, I left the door open so the air could help the flames along
and I went out to the privvy. The garden was empty. As I came back
into the house, I listened for Lijah's mother moving about. All was
quiet upstairs, so I knew that she was still asleep. I took a deep

breath. How nice it was to have the house to myself for a few minutes.

The fire in the range was burning up, so I closed the door and started making Elijah's bacon and onion roll. I always rose extra early on a Monday morning and did it fresh, then we all had some. The rest of the week, his mother and I had bread while Elijah had a slice of the roll cold with his mug of tea. He always sliced it exactly so that there was enough to get him through to the following Sunday.

I chopped the bacon and onions and set them on to fry, then I began rolling out the suet. It was then that the words I had heard the night before came back to me. *How do you stand it?*

She wasn't talking about the house. What did Elijah think I was, some kind of fool?

How do you stand it?

Me, she meant. How do you stand *her?* And suddenly it came to me, the malice in those words. She was clever, that one. She knew better than to say outright, *your wife is awful*, for that would get Elijah's back up, and he might tell her to mind her own business. No, she was smarter than that.

How do you stand it? They were words to make him think how wonderful he was for putting up with me. The thought that I was something to be put up with would sneak in behind that other thought, but be planted in his head all the same.

It was a mean trick, to hide her dislike of me behind her love for Elijah. Mothers can do that – take any unkind thing they feel for another person and justify it to themselves by their love for their child. They can resent and resent, and twist their resentment into something noble. I've done it myself. When I coveted Mrs Herne's new hat in which she paraded up and down the street at Christmas, I thought to myself, *imagine her spending that on a new hat for herself when her child goes about in his dad's old shoes with newspaper stuffed into the toes. I'd never buy a hat like that when my child wanted for some-*

thing. So I went back into the house in a high dudgeon, congratu-lating myself on what a wonderful mother I was going to be to my yet-unborn baby, so much a better mother than Annie Herne. And it was only later when I calmed down that I admitted to myself that from what I'd seen of her she wasn't a bad mother at all and loved her little boy dearly. It was just that I wanted her hat.

How do you put up with it? My poor lamb, my dear Lijah, when you deserve so much better than the wife you've got and here am I, your mother, to tell you so and to love you so much more and so much better than your wife will ever be able to.

Hatred: a small word, but one that holds so many different feel-ings all tightly packaged up into two short, hard syllables. Envy and meanness and resentment and plain old misery – a whole load of stuff, but spin them all together and what do you come up with? Let's be plain speaking and call it by its name: hatred.

So, I thought, she hates me. I cried, of course. Bitter tears of self-pity ran down my cheeks and dropped freely from my face onto where the suet lay in a helpless lump on the rolling board. I had to stand still for a moment while I gathered myself, then wipe my face with my sleeve as my hands were sticky and I didn't want to reach inside my apron pocket for my handkerchief. Fortunately, Elijah liked his suet rolls well salted. I heaved a breath.

Well, Mrs Smith, I thought as I bent back to my task and pressed down on the rolling pin, *or whatever your name may be*. The suet bulged like flesh beneath my efforts. It was sticking, so I reached for the open bag of flour. *Well, what you have forgotten is that I am going to be a mother too, and your equal, and if hatred is what you want to bring into this house, then you shall have it back as large as you like.*

All my fierce thinking and kneading of the suet had distracted me and I had let the bacon and onions get too brown. I rescued them from the hot-plate and took the pan to the board, scattering them on top of the suet. Then I drizzled the cooking fat over the top and began rolling the whole thing up. It was then that it happened – a feeling inside me, like something tearing. Water rushed down my leg. I stared at the puddle on the floor. I took a deep breath, and stepped backwards. Then panic overcame me.

I hobbled quickly to the bottom of the stairs, and shouted up, in a voice high and hollow, '*Mother*!'

CHAPTER 10

And then came Daniel.

We got rid of Elijah double quick, of course. Clementina went for Mrs Dawson. Lilly got wind of it and rose from her sickbed to come over and Mrs Dawson brought her two nieces along as they were in training. Our tiny house was suddenly full of women – although I registered them all only dimly as I was pretty far gone by then.

Afterwards, I held him, my Daniel, upstairs in our bedroom, while the others busied themselves. One of the nieces brought in strong tea with lots of sugar and toast dripping in lard, and I ate and drank with one hand as I couldn't bear to put my baby down. I thought I would never put him down, ever, in my whole life.

Daniel. I stared at his shiny little cheeks, the smear of blood on one of his eyebrows, the slick of dark hair on his head. His eyes were clamped tight shut, like he was saying to us, *I've got a lot to get used to so you're all going to have to give me a bit of time*. 'It was you in there,' I whispered to him. 'All that time, I was walking around and I didn't know who was inside me. And all along it was you.'

When I had finished my tea and toast, the niece came back with a hairbrush and began to brush my hair firmly. 'Aunty says you're to tell me where to find a clean nightgown to put on you. We've to get you tidy, so we can let your husband come in.'

Husband . . .? Oh, yes, I thought, Elijah. I carried on gazing down at Daniel while I let Mrs Walton's niece pull at my hair. *I suppose I had better show you to your father, hadn't I, my little one?*

When I had been got ready, they all left me alone. Daniel still had his eyes clamped tight shut and I was still looking down at him, when I became aware of a shape in the doorway. I didn't lift my head, but whispered, 'Come in quietly, Elijah. He's asleep.'

I was the Queen of Paradise Street, for a while. No boys had been born on our street for some time, so he and I were fussed over something rotten. The stuff we got given – Mrs Herne bought a green lace bonnet from Peaks. It was the oddest thing you'd ever seen in your life, with a little tuft on top, like he was a pixie, but I could tell it cost a fortune. Mrs Walton made us rhubarb crumble twice a week for weeks on end – said I had to keep my strength up – and I'd quite liked rhubarb up 'til then but, after a while, the very smell made me feel ill and to this day if I smell rhubarb I come over a bit poorly. Every child in the street came round and begged to be allowed to take Daniel out in his pram. We belonged to everybody. I had never been so important, or cosseted. It was the best time of my life.

Then, one night, I was awoken. I had no idea what time it was, but I stirred to see my husband standing on my side of the bed. He had been out all day and evening and I had gone to bed early.

'Move over, Rosie,' he said, his voice slurry and affectionate.

Daniel was on my other side.

'I can't,' I said sleepily, 'the baby's . . .'

'Move the baby then!' His tone had changed completely. I sat up on my elbows.

I knew what he wanted, of course, and I didn't think it unreasonable as it had been several months and it was a side of our lives that had been quite important to us before. It came to me that I hadn't paid Elijah any attention at all since Daniel had been born. More than one woman in our street had whispered to me that I mustn't forget my husband's needs if I didn't want him to stray.

My head was in a fog. I had fed Daniel not an hour before and had been in one of those deep, drugged sleeps you get after feeding, but I roused myself and picked Daniel up. We didn't have a Moses basket for him yet; that was the one thing we hadn't been given. Elijah had said he would weave one and I was still waiting for it. I didn't want to put Daniel on the floor, so I opened the top drawer of the chest of drawers in the corner and laid him gently down among my underthings. He didn't stir.

I got back into bed, lay on my back and hitched up my nightie.

It wasn't that I didn't like it. It just felt wrong. When he touched me, I couldn't escape the thought that he was stealing something that belonged to Daniel. He was gentle enough, on account of it being my first time since, but I was still a bit out of sorts down there and could hardly feel him. He managed it, but I didn't get the feeling he enjoyed it all that much either.

Afterwards, he drew away from me and sat up. I rolled over and eased myself to the other side of the bed.

He came round his side after a moment or two, undressed himself properly, and got in. I picked Daniel up from the chest of drawers and put him back between us, and could not prevent myself from giving a satisfied sigh as I snuggled down next to him. Bless him for not stirring that whole time.

Maybe Elijah heard my sigh and understood it. Maybe he realised that, for the time being, he was something to be endured.

After a short silence between us, he said awkwardly, 'How's the little fella been today, then?'

'All right,' I said, drifting back towards sleep. My last thought was, well, at least you can't get pregnant when you're feeding a baby already.

Turned out, I was quite wrong about that.

Mehitable was born just before Christmas that year. Mehitable Smith. She was early; a tiny, scrawny thing, with folds of dark skin and a head of jet-black hair. She slipped out easy as anything but was a nightmare to feed – completely different from my Daniel. She was that restless on the breast, as if it made her uncomfortable in some way. She would toss and turn her head – while staying clamped on to me, mind – and kick her thin, little legs. It hurt me in a way that feeding Daniel never had. She was colicky as well. That was a trial. I thought it was only boys got the colic but I was soon put right about that.

Just after teatime it would start, the screaming, and it would go on for hours and hours, and the only thing that kept her quiet was feeding and that only worked for as long as she was actually doing it.

I thought it would never stop, the screaming. I couldn't think what I had done to produce such an unhappy baby. It drove us all near demented.

Well, I say all. What I mean is me and Mother and the poor, unfortunate neighbours at numbers twenty and twenty-four. Elijah was never there. Things were not going too well between me and him.

Elijah's mother had been gone for the whole of the summer – where to, I do not know – but she had taken off somewhere doing whatever it is her sort do in the summer. I wish I could say Elijah and I were happier with her gone but we weren't. He was twitchy and bad tempered the whole time she was away, and once I snapped at him, 'Oh for heaven's sake, why didn't you go off with your mother?' He gave me a look so dark it made me frightened.

Come the weather turning colder, she was back. Daniel was glad to see her. She spoiled him rotten. It was quite nice to have her around the first few days, helping out, and I thought maybe it will be all right this time. Then, she started. Why was Elijah out so much and coming home with so little lovah to show for it? *Lovah*? You know, cash. *Don't ask me, Mother, he's your son. I haven't a clue what he gets up to in the evening.* Was Daniel maybe getting a bit squinty? Had I been taking him out in the wind too much? Didn't I know it was bad for a baby's eyes? *Mother, Daniel's fine. He's the healthiest baby in the whole of Cambridge.* Was that Empers woman still getting poorly and taking to her bed? Her poor husband. *Actually, Mother, Lilly nearly died in July. Samuel was beside himself.*

I didn't say any of these things, and perhaps that was my mistake. I thought to myself, just let it all wash over, you know what she's like. So all the things I would have liked to have said to her piled up inside me, month after month. I would lie awake at night – bigly pregnant and unable to sleep, yet again – and I would rehearse in my head my smart retorts to all her snide remarks.

Of course, what I really wanted to say was, if you don't like it round here, Mother, then why don't you *ife*? Oh, I'd picked up a bit of their cant, right enough, even though they usually only talked it to each other when I was out of the room. I wasn't near as daft as they thought.

Then Mehitable came along, and everything went downhill from there.

I think, in my head, I thought I would be spoiled again when I had another baby. It was so short a time since Daniel I could still remember how everyone came around and how even Elijah would hold him and sing songs and tell me I was a clever Rosie to have produced such a handsome boy. What I didn't know was that, with baby number two, everybody just assumes you've done it once, you know the ropes, and what's the point of making a fuss of you? Which in my case was something of a disaster, as I needed far more help than I had ever done with Daniel.

Two weeks after she was born, I left them both with Elijah's mother and said I was going to walk to the street and back, just for a breath of fresh air, and to see the candles lit up in people's windows. It was nearly Christmas and I hadn't been out of the house in a fortnight. It was almost dark. I had just got to the end of the road and was turning to come back when I saw Mr Winfield pass on the other side of the street, on his way to his evening shift at the brewery, probably.

He raised a hand to me. 'Evening, Mrs Smith. Hoping for a Christmas baby, I expect?'

He went on his way and I waddled home with my spirits so low. All right, it was dark, and I was still huge and had a shawl on and he couldn't tell I'd had my baby already – but with Daniel the whole street knew the minute he was born. They almost hung bunting out the windows. With Mehitable, a lot of folk didn't even notice, let alone care, and that's the truth.

Then the colic started. They knew I'd had the baby then. Ha, that told them. Mehitable Smith made her presence felt loud and clear, then.

I should probably explain something about the children's names. It was not my doing. Turned out Elijah's mother had pretty firm ideas about that, like she did about everything else.

When Daniel was about four weeks old, she put him on her shoulder one day and said she was taking him out for a bit. I hated the way she used to tie him to her with a shawl – we had a perfectly good pram that we'd borrowed from the Field family, but she never used it. I had had a rough night feeding him, however, so I said okay. Elijah was out, as usual, so I thought I could get a bit of rest.

Little did I know what she had in mind. A couple of hours later, she's back, and she's telling me about how she thought it was going to rain on the way home but it didn't, then she adds, as relaxed about it as you like, 'Oh, by the way. I got him registered. I called him Adolphus.'

I stared at her in disbelief. I was sat on the settee, and she was standing picking bits of fluff off her hat. '*What?*'

'Adolphus. You was saying last night we've got to get him registered, it's the law, so I thought I might as well do it while I was out. There wasn't any queuing up or anything. I took him in and said I've come to get the baby registered. And they said, what's his name?'

From her tone of voice, I gathered that this question had surprised her.

'So I said Adolphus. Adolphus Smith.'

'*Adolphus!*'

She looked at me irritably. 'Yes, that's what I said, weren't it? Adolphus.'

For once, I could not restrain myself. 'What sort of name is that? For heaven's sake, Mother! How could you do that? What kind of name is that?'

She stopped picking fluff off her hat and her eyes narrowed. 'It's a perfectly good name, a very respectable name.'

'We've been calling him Daniel for weeks!'

'I know that,' she said crossly, 'what difference does that make? It doesn't matter what name you tell the registration folk, does it? You could tell them his name is Lemon Thyme. It's got nothing to do with anything, does it?'

Exasperated and shaking her head, she went into the kitchen.

When Mehitable was born, I stared down at her, but nothing came into my head. In truth, I had been convinced it was another boy. I'd been carrying low, exactly the same way as I was with Daniel. I was planning in my head how I would register this one myself and his name, in life and on paper, would be something nice and normal like Frederick or William or George.

I didn't have a single girl's name in my head. I suppose I should have named her after my own mother, but my mother always hated her name.

'What's your Christian name?' I asked Elijah's mother, as she busied herself at the foot of my bed, gathering the soiled sheets.

'Clementina,' she said without looking up. 'But most folk calls me Lem.'

Oh well, that's out, I thought.

I glanced back down at my poor, scrawny little girl. I wish I could say I felt overwhelmed with love and protectiveness, how I had with Daniel, but I felt nothing much – just a strange, dull emptiness inside.

Elijah's mother came and stood by the side of my bed and looked down at her too. There was a long silence as we stared at her, as if all three of us were, quite calmly, contemplating the difficulties that lay ahead.

'Mehitable,' Clementina said simply.

I turned my head away. 'All right.'

It upsets me to think about the next few years in Paradise Street. What came later was hard, but those years were hardest because they had started off so well, me and Elijah happy together and me full of what a good wife and mother I would be; and I was, to start off with, I swear I was.

It is hard, when a child is sick on you. It is hard not to blame yourself and then to blame the child, for you cannot bear the thought that if you'd done something different it would have been all right. That doctor that we got, eventually, I felt like he was blaming me. You never stop being wrong when you're a mother, I soon discovered.

Elijah started disappearing, for days on end sometimes. Daniel took it stoically enough, but Mehitable would cry and whine for her father something rotten. I remember one day, Mehitable had been crying and moaning all day. Elijah had been gone a couple of nights and we'd run out of everything. I had borrowed and borrowed from everyone in the street, and we had a reputation now, and even Lilly was getting fed up with it. I didn't even want to show my face outside that day, so ashamed was I, so Mehitable and I were cooped up together. Clementina was off somewhere. Daniel was old enough to go to school in the mornings.

At dinnertime, Daniel came trotting home. He came and found me in the kitchen. He must have only been five or six but he was the little man of the house, no doubt about that. In he came, crackling away. It was the vests I made him, out of brown paper. I had tried newspaper but the print came off on him and made him filthy, so crackly brown paper it was. That's how cold it was outside.

He had already been into our little parlour, the only room with a fire lit, where Mehitable was lying on the settee clutching a blanket and staring at the walls.

'Me and Mehitable need something hot to eat, Mam,' he said firmly, as he came in the kitchen.

I said, as gentle as I could, 'There a piece of bread each I've saved. It's a bit stale but it'll be okay, we can toast it. I've got a slice of brawn for you to share but there's nothing hot.' Brawn was the cheapest thing the butcher had that was edible. Elijah sometimes ate whips, but you can't feed children on cow's tails.

'Why don't we warm it up in the fire?' Daniel suggested.

I wasn't thinking straight. I said. 'All right. Use the spike.'

He took the toasting spike, found the slice of brawn in the cold box in the pantry and brought it in. Then he took it into the parlour room. I heard him say, 'Here you are, Billy. We're going to have hot brawn on toast.'

She always smiled for Daniel, did Mehitable. He was like a god to her.

There was a moment's silence, then a wail of despair from Mehitable. *In Lord's name what now?* I thought and went into the sitting room.

Daniel was sitting on his heels before the fire, holding the empty spike and looking disconsolate. Mehitable was sat next to him, her mouth open, howling.

'Sorry, Mam,' said Daniel.

The slice of brawn was in the fire. When Daniel had held the spike in the flames, the fat had melted straightaway, of course, and the brawn had fallen off among the coals. It was all I had for them. There was nothing else but stale bread in the house.

'Never mind, Daniel,' I said, thinking of how stupid it was of me to have let him do it. Mehitable was still screeching. You would've thought it was her on the end of the spike.

'Oh for God's sake, Billy, shut that wailing, will you?' I couldn't help myself from snapping at her. Daniel had been trying his best.

We all three of us looked into the fire, and I thought, *marrying Elijah Smith was the biggest mistake of my life.*

Later that afternoon, Clementina came home. Somehow she had got the wherewithal to buy us some giblets, so's we could make a broth. She was more helpful that way than her no-good son; I'll give her that.

I was feeling low, as low as low could be, but as she came in, I forced myself to rise from my chair and take the packet from her. A little blood was leaking at one corner. I unwrapped the giblets and put them in the colander, rinsing them under the tap. I left them to drain while I washed my hands and put the kettle on.

And then she started in on me. Were the children over at Mrs Herne's house, yet again?

Yes they were, I replied. Mrs Herne had three boys now and Daniel loved playing with them – he liked doing boy's games that he couldn't do with Mehitable.

Did I know that Mrs Herne felt so sorry for our two that she fed them?

I had always suspected as much as they didn't nag me for tea when they came home – I had been pretending to myself that I didn't know.

I let her rattle on at me while I tipped the giblets on to the chopping board. The butcher had already trimmed the crop, so I didn't have to worry about that. I took the short knife and cut the top off the heart. There was a small well of dark red blood inside, which I cleaned beneath the tap.

How did I know what Mrs Herne was feeding my children? Clementina went on . . .

I turned the liver. It was fresh and shiny, the colours shimmering on its surface. Behind me, Clementina had stopped going on about Mrs Herne. There was a moment's blissful silence. *Oh please just leave the room*, I prayed to myself, *please just go away and leave me in peace*.

Then she said, calmly and purposefully, 'Don't forget to cut out the bile.'

I slammed down the kitchen knife, leaned on my knuckles on the counter top and took a deep breath. 'Yes, thank you, Mother,' I said between gritted teeth. 'I think I know how to trim giblets by now . . .'

I still had my back to her, otherwise she might have seen the look on my face and realise she shouldn't push me further.

'Oh we are Miss La-di-da this afternoon,' she remarked casually. 'Well, it's a good job I know how to buy them, isn't it?'

I still had my back to her and managed to keep my voice light. 'You wouldn't need to be going down to Neave's for giblets if that son of yours brought a bit of money home once in a while.'

I knew that would needle her, criticism of her sainted boy.

'Lijah's been very busy lately.'

'Aye, yes, and he's been keeping the landlord of The Bleeding

Heart busy and all, all that pulling of pints he's been doing for Elijah. Rushed off his feet.'

I turned to face her. She had sat down at the table. She looked at me steadily. 'Bit full of airs and graces today, aren't we?'

'If it's airs and graces to want my children fed, instead of relying on other people's charity, then yes I am. My mother raised me all on her own and she never had to do that.'

At the mention of my mother, she made a *humphing* noise. 'Yes, well, I daresay your mother found ways to get the wherewithal to feed you, didn't she?'

I stared at her. She stared back. The kettle on the hot-plate began to whistle and I turned and removed it. I realised I was shaking. We were rushing headlong into something, this woman and I, and I knew something unpleasant was about to happen. I felt sick, and the palms of my hands were sweating, but I could not stop myself. Without either of us meaning to, we had crossed a line.

'What's that supposed to mean?' I asked, quite calmly, as I turned back to her.

She pulled one of her faces, turning down the corners of her mouth. 'Well, let's just say *I* knew who my father was.'

I was so astonished that she should raise this that I stared at her in disbelief, and when I spoke my voice was unsteady. 'It may be true,' I faltered, 'that I was born illegitimate, but as I understand it so was Elijah.'

'That's none of your business!' she snapped back, and closed her mouth firmly, glaring at me.

'It is my business when you start making unfair remarks about my mother and casting judgement on me,' I replied. 'Do you think it is easy to be a fatherless child? I assure you it is not. Indeed, it was one of the first topics of conversation between Elijah and I, that we had this in common.' I saw from her face that this remark hit home, that she did not like the thought that Elijah and I had something in common and that we had discussed it between ourselves, especially something that affected her so closely. And then I added something I had not intended to add, but in truth my head was spinning with her rudeness and I was a little too flush with having got one over on her. 'Although it is true that our stories differ in one respect, mine and Elijah's. *My* mother never lied to me.'

Her mouth had opened again, but only a little, to form a small, round 'o'. Her eyes were tiny and black as raisins. I knew that I had cut her to the quick. I should have had the sense not to press home my advantage, but all the small slights I had received since she had come to us were boiling up in me, and I could not prevent myself. How dare she sit there casting slurs on my mother, and me not able to say a word against her son who had all but deserted his family?

'And as far as I gather, you continue to lie to him. The King of Russia! Do you think you're the only one who told him stories? The rumours he's heard, and to this day he does not know who his father is, and have you never stopped to think what that might be like for him? He has children of his own now and still he does not know . . .' I was speaking fast, my words running away from me, spilling from me.

She raised one hand sharply and held it up flat, to silence me. I stopped, breathing hard, awaiting her response. But instead of speaking, she levered herself up from the chair slowly, pressing her knuckles against the tabletop to raise herself, as if she was infirm. She turned to leave the room.

I could not stand that she would answer me with silence. It was not right, not when I was making a fair point and had bested her in argument. 'I am talking of Elijah's feelings,' I insisted, my voice high and hollow with fury.

She had her back to me by then, and lifted her hand, again flat, then patted the air with it, as if to push away some invisible force that was pressing in on her. With the other hand, she reached out and grasped at the rail of the range, to steady herself. Then she walked slowly to the door.

I allowed her to reach the bottom of the stairs, then stepped after. Still she did not turn.

As she mounted the stairs, leaning on the banister, I called up after her, wildly, 'He's not stupid, you know! He's got a good enough idea! His father was a baker's boy by the name of Freeman, that's what he got told, although *you* may never have owned up to it! A baker's boy who fancied a bit of *gipsy* skirt, was he? I s'pose it was in a ditch somewhere . . . or . . . or maybe . . .' I had nearly used up all my strength, '. . . beneath a *hedge!*'

At that, she stopped on the stairs, bent almost double, but did not speak or turn. Then she continued up.

I stood at the bottom of the stairs, shaking. I felt such a sense of triumph and anger that I was almost alight with it. I burned.

Then, almost immediately, a feeling of wretchedness and shame washed over me. My knees almost gave. I thought of how, with these small houses, all the neighbours up and down the street had just heard me shout out how Elijah was got – and how they would all look at Clementina and me next time we went out of doors . . .

I turned and went back into the kitchen and put the kettle back on the hot-plate, not because I wanted to boil the water but because I had to do something ordinary. And my chest was heaving up and down, and, sure enough, the tears came. I thought of how, for the first time since her arrival, Clementina and I had argued openly, and how I had wounded her, how I had won. And I knew that the feeling should have given me great satisfaction but in truth it did not.

Clementina stayed in her room for the rest of that day. When the children arrived back from Mrs Herne's, the three of us ate our giblet soup together. Hungry as I was, I could not finish my bowl. It had no taste. Later, I put the children down, head to toe in my bed as Clementina had still not emerged from her room and there was not so much as a single sound coming from it. I found myself tiptoeing down the stairs afterwards.

I tidied and cleaned, swiftly and quietly, listening all the while for her door to creak open and wondering what on earth I could say to her when she emerged. I prayed that Elijah would come home that evening, so that I would not be alone with her, but he did not, and I retired to bed at my usual hour, pushing the children over gently as I climbed in, so as not to waken them.

Elijah had still not returned by the following morning, which was not unusual at that time. Daniel went off to school and Lilly came over and said would Mehitable like to come and sit in her shop and help her count the pennies? Lilly often had her in her shop in the mornings, out of pity, I suppose. Usually I couldn't wait to get rid of Mehitable so that I could get on with my chores undisturbed, but that morning I said, 'I am not sure, Lilly, Mehitable seems a bit chesty. Maybe she should stay at home.'

Well, of course Mehitable piped up, 'No, I'm not, Mum, I'm not chesty at all,' and gave a clear cough to prove it. Children always like to make liars of you, don't they? Mehitable loved going to Lilly's as there was usually a small treat in it for her if she was good.

Lilly gave me a straight look.

I sighed and said, 'All right then, but no spoiling her. She's gets spoiled quite enough as it is.'

So it happened that I was alone when Clementina finally emerged from her room. I had been laundering bed linen and it was flapping nicely on the line. It was warm and breezy outside and the sheets would dry quickly. I had just sat down for a minute, and was resolving that, whatever I said when she came down, I would not apologise. Or maybe I would apologise but make it quite clear that she had pushed me to it. Or perhaps I would just wait to see what she said, then take my cue from her.

As I was thinking this, I heard her step on the stairs. The back of my neck prickled with anxiety at the sound. I rose to face her. She came into the kitchen and said, 'Those sheets should be ironed while they've still got a bit of dampness in them. If you heat up the iron, I'll do it.'

Instead of all the speeches I had prepared in my head, I found myself saying. 'The stove is stoked. The iron'll heat in a minute.'

'Best go and fold them, then,' she said, and turned towards the back door.

I put the iron flat on the hot-plate and followed her out, meek as a lamb. While we folded the sheets, we talked quite normally of how the sky was darkening already and it was a good job I'd done them early and not waited until the afternoon. I could not believe how normal we were being, and even started to question in my own head whether the events of the previous day had really happened at all.

What is she thinking? I thought to myself as we took the folded sheets inside. Is she in inner turmoil, like me? She shows no sign of it. She was acting quite ordinary – much more ordinary, in fact, than she ordinarily did.

When we got back inside, she said, 'I'll do this. You get on, if you like.'

So I left her to it and went about my other tasks, a little humbled, I have to say, a little washed out and empty – and enormously relieved.

It's amazing we lasted as long as we did in that house. We staggered on for another year – and amidst all our difficulties another baby came, Bartholomew. He was small like Mehitable but healthy, thank God.

Then came the night when there was a knock at the door. Elijah was out, of course, so his mother answered. I was upstairs feeding the new baby but looked out the top floor window as the men left. They stalked off down Paradise Street in the dark, three big bulky fellas, and Elijah's mother ran after them and pleaded with them, and I thought, *that's it*. We've borrowed from friends and neighbours until we can't hold our heads up any more. We're weeks behind with the rent. And now he's brought the bailiffs down upon us.

A few days later, Elijah's mother sat me down and explained, quite gently, that the men were debt collectors and if we didn't leave that very night, they would be back tomorrow, take everything we owned and put us out on the street, in front of everybody. Elijah was going to come to the house after dark that night, to help us get away.

'Where's he been?' I said, dully, trying to summon the strength to be angry – but in truth the fight had long gone out of me by then.

'Sorting things out,' was all she would say. 'He's found somewhere we can all go. Friends of his.'

He had not come home to discuss it with me, needless to say. He and his mother had it all arranged. She knew more about the parlous state we were in than I did. Me, his wife, I counted for nothing. He had not even had the courage to come home himself and explain to me that his boozing and gambling had lost us our home.

'I'll go and pack,' I said. As I mounted the stairs, to parcel up what had not already been sold or pawned, I thought to myself, and to think I once craved a marble-top washstand from Peak's.

We crept out before dawn, skulking down Paradise Street like stray dogs who'd been starved and beaten. Elijah and Clementina both had heavy bundles and I had the bedding, which was lighter, but I was bent double all the same, bent double with shame. I could not believe my life had come to this. I prayed and prayed as we slid down the street that nobody we knew would be up and looking out of a window. I was finished in East Cambridge. I would never be able to come back after this.

As we reached the corner of Adam and Eve Street, Mehitable, who was just in front of me, tripped over a beer bottle left out on a step. It clattered and rolled with a jingly-jangly sound that echoed down the empty street. I gave her a sharp kick on the leg and hissed, *'Be careful, you clot.'*

Daniel was carrying Bartholomew and I heard him turn and mewl. *'Hurry up . . .'* I hissed, to all of them.

I did not begin to feel easier until we were well out of the Garden of Eden, past the narrow streets where I was born.

We were heading for the edge of town, to Stourbridge Common. Elijah said the friends who would help us out lived near there. Probably one of his drinking pals in some tumbledown cottage, I thought with foreboding.

But no. It was worse than that, much worse.

When he said *near* Stourbridge Common, what he actually meant was *on* it. I did not realise precisely where we were headed until we were walking up Garlic Row, past the Oyster House and on to the open grassland of the common.

There, ahead of us, were the dark shapes of tents and wagons just visible in the breaking dawn.

I stopped where I was, in the middle of the common, and put down the bundle of bedding. 'Oh Elijah,' I breathed, and my voice caught in my throat. 'Oh no.'

He turned, looked at me and scratched his head. The children stopped too, baffled.

Elijah grimaced, as if he was about to speak, but his mother cut in. 'Beggars can't be choosers,' she snapped. 'If we spend this night with something over our heads, even be it a bender tent, you should think yourself lucky.'

I glared at her. 'You may be used to this, Mother, but I am not,' I said sharply.

She glared back in response, but Elijah stepped in. 'Shut it you two, will you?'

Mehitable burst into tears.

'What's *wrong* with you?' I asked.

She shook her head, and sobbed. Clementina stepped forward and bent her head to the child, then lifted it and said, 'She's thirsty.'

'Well, we'll be there soon,' said Elijah. 'Come on, then.'

I picked up the bedding. I had no choice.

Elijah had given me the impression that he knew the folk we were visiting, but as we approached the first row of tents, I could see him stiffen and glance around, as if sizing the place up. Clementina strode ahead a little. Elijah dropped back to me and said, 'Keep your mouth shut to start off with, all right, Rosie?'

'What do you mean?' I said.

'Just keep it closed, all right?'

We walked forward in a line, and as we did so, a young woman emerged from the nearest tent. She saw us, and stared at us. Her skin was dark, even darker than Clementina's, and her cheeks were hollows, her hair black and straggly. She was wearing a huge man's shirt which came down to her knees but her legs and feet were bare. *What on earth have we come to*? I thought, shocked by the state of her and wanting nothing more than to snatch the children and run for it.

As we passed her, the young woman turned and shouted across the still quiet camp. I did not understand the words she used. They were full of *ushing* sounds.

Immediately, other figures emerged from other tents, in various states of undress, and came over to us quickly across the grass: men, women and children in a swarm. Within a moment or two, we were surrounded by a crowd that pressed in on us unsmilingly and prevented us from moving further into the camp. I looked from face to face, but still nobody spoke a word. I put my arms around Daniel and Mehitable and pulled them in close to me. Daniel was still holding Bartholomew. Mehitable clung to my legs. Still the people pressed forward, not smiling or speaking. We were effectively trapped. Lijah was separated from me a little and I looked to him for help but he just glared at me, and I understood from his glare that I must not speak.

Mehitable said, 'Mother . . .' in a whining, frightened voice and I took my arm from around her shoulders and clamped my hand over her mouth.

One boy was insolently close to me. He reached out a dark, dirty hand and plucked at the fabric of my sleeve. I shook the sleeve free, but he just pressed in closer and continued plucking. I felt someone else, behind me, tug at my skirt, and resolved that if Elijah did not intervene soon to save us I would shout out, whatever he had told me.

Just at the point when I thought I might suffocate with all this unwanted attention, a man emerged from the light-grey gloom and strode quickly towards us. He stopped a few feet away and the crowd fell back. He was looking at Elijah.

He was a tall man, barrel chested. He was wearing a shirt that was unbuttoned, despite the cold, and I could see that he was strongly built. He had a huge moustache that draped over his upper lip and hung down either side. He stared at Elijah very directly but ignored the rest of us.

Then Elijah started to speak, and I looked at him in amazement, for though I had heard him and Clementina use the odd peculiar word together, I had never heard anything like this – a proper language.

There were a few exchanges between Elijah and the man with a moustache, the crowd listening intently all the while. Then all at once, the man broke into a smile. At this, the crowd all smiled too, and the atmosphere changed completely – the people around us loosened, fell apart. Some returned to their tents or wagons – others began chatting among themselves. A couple of women came forward and gestured that we should walk with them.

As we were led towards the centre of the wagons, I realised that Clementina was not with us. Looking around, I saw her, heading off to another part of the camp, chatting in a lively fashion to a woman about the same age as herself. A young boy walking beside them was carrying her bag. It was the last we saw of Clementina for a couple of days.

I did my best to fit in, I really did. I'm not one for moaning when there's no point in it, and after my initial shock and a short period when I felt very gloomy, I saw that I had better get used to the idea of being a . . . a what? Lijah had told me, a long time ago, never to use *that word* in front of him. *Gipsy* was an insult, he told me – bad language. It was only *gorjers* who used the word *gipsy*. Travellers is what they called themselves and Travellers is what they were. Romanies. The People. I can't say as I really understood the difference myself at the time, but I understood well enough how the word *gipsy* got used as an insult. I'd heard the way my stepfather used it in the kitchen at the farmyard. 'Have those damn *gipsies* all paid up, Rose?' Or sometimes, 'Take a good look round the camp when you go down, Rose, and see if any of those *bloody gipos* have lifted my sharp spade. I can't find it anywhere,' when I knew for a fact that Henry had left the sharp spade in the yard.

I thought the Travelling folk who came to the harvest were a bit queer in their ways and I was a little scared of them, but they were always nice to me and the fact that my stepfather hated them was a pretty strong recommendation as far as I was concerned. And I did fall for one of them, after all.

Sometimes, when Elijah and I fought, he would try and use it against me, being a Travelling man. 'You've no idea, woman, when you've lived the life I've had . . .'

'Don't you use that as an excuse, Elijah. I wasn't exactly born with a silver spoon in my mouth, you know.'

I wouldn't have Elijah trying to make me feel bad on account of what a hard life he'd had – and I never blamed his bad behaviour on his being a Traveller. Elijah was Elijah, and if he'd been born a lord he'd have been exactly the same.

So what I'm saying is the problem with the Stourbridge Common lot was not on account of them being Travellers. It was on account of the fact that I wasn't, and they made sure I knew it.

I think the problem was I expected they would be like Mrs Boswell, who had always been so nice and kind to me back at River Farm. She would have explained things to me and I would have understood the life much quicker then. Mrs Boswell was a lady, whatever she called herself, and she always made me feel like a fine lady too. She respected me, and I respected her back. There was no one in the Stourbridge Common lot who was like her, I saw that the very next day.

The man who had spoken to Elijah when we arrived was a Cambridgeshire Smith, and I gathered some weeks later that he and Elijah had decided they were distant relations in some way. Bartley, his name was, or Bartle or something like that. Bartley Smith's wife was called Morselina, although I was never invited to be on first-name terms with her. She was a thin, suspicious-looking woman, and I knew as soon as I set eyes on her that she had decided not to like me.

I went over to their caravan the very first morning, with Elijah. We had gone to bed for a couple of hours after we first arrived, in a tent which someone else had been sleeping in that night, for the blankets were all mussed and the ground warm. Me and the children were so tired we thought nothing of it.

At full light, Lijah nudged me awake and, whispering that we should leave the children to carry on sleeping, told me to brush myself down and come with him.

I didn't want to leave the children. They had only that night left their home and all they knew behind. What if one of them woke and was afraid? Lijah told me not to be stupid. If the children woke up, they would be looked after by whoever was nearest to them; that was the way it worked in a camp.

It's not the way I work, I thought to myself as I brushed myself down and tried to make myself presentable.

It was a chilly morning and my bones ached. I had a terrible thirst and was dying for a cup of tea. How will I ever get through this day? I thought to myself as we made our way across the damp grass to the Smiths' wagon.

The whole family was up already and a fire lit. Bartley Smith and two other men were seated on upturned boxes. An elderly woman, older than Clementina, was squatting on the grass beside them. Morselina Smith was pouring tea into the row of tin mugs that sat on a tray on another upturned box.

Bartley Smith rose and greeted Elijah. He ignored me, and I should have taken the hint. Instead, I did what I would have done had we just arrived as guests at a house in Paradise Street. I sat myself down, and waited to be offered a cup of tea.

Morselina Smith straightened herself from pouring the tea and stared at me. I stared right back. She lifted the tray up and I half lifted a hand, expecting that I would be offered tea first, but she gave tea out to all the men, including Elijah, and then the old woman. There was no cup left for me, and I was left sitting like a fool with my empty hands in my lap, while they all drank noisily and nodded their appreciation.

I could have wept with disappointment. I had been up half the night and left my home with nothing but what I could carry. Was it too much to expect a little kindness from these people?

Elijah was glaring at me but I could not work out why.

Then he and the other men began to talk to each other in their strange language. I thought it most rude of them when they knew I could not understand.

So I had to sit there, in the damp and chill, with my shawl wrapped around me, while the men ignored me and drank their tea, and I could feel my cheeks growing pink with humiliation. Elijah had never behaved this rudely toward me in company before, whatever rows we may have had in private.

All this time, the old woman had been staring up at me keenly. Eventually, she rose from where she squatted and spoke to the men. Whatever she was saying, I knew it concerned me as she nodded in my direction when she spoke. The men took notice of *her*, all right. In fact, they all grinned from ear to ear. I gathered she had made some joke at my expense.

She came over to me, and grasped my upper arm. She was bent quite double with age and scarcely taller than I was seated. She had no teeth at all. She gestured some way distant.

I could not understand her, but rose anyway and looked pleadingly at Elijah, who suddenly became interested in the interior of his tin mug. I understood that he had completely deserted me, and I was to be left to sink or swim with these people on my own.

The old woman led me round the back of the caravan and across the grass to where a large group was gathered. As we neared, I saw it was all women and children, including Morselina Smith, who stood in the centre while several young girls were busy around the fire. She stared at me in an unfriendly manner as we approached and spoke to the other women, two of whom laughed openly.

'Where I come from,' I said firmly, my voice high, 'it is considered unkind to laugh at guests.' It was a stupid thing to say, but I could think of no better, and it certainly quietened them for a minute. Morselina Smith spoke to one of the young girls, who turned and came towards me with the largest tin mug I have ever seen, enamelled bright red and painted with a flower design. In it steamed hot, dark and, as I discovered to my bliss, heavily sweetened tea. I took the cup from the girl, carefully as the mug was so hot it was necessary to hold it precariously by both handle and rim. I looked down at her. She had a round, sweet face, and heavy black eyebrows. She smiled at me, warmly, and I was so grateful for her kindness that had I not been holding the tea I think I would have fallen on my knees and hugged and kissed her in front of everybody.

I sometimes wonder, did we get it the wrong way round? When Elijah and I first ran off together, it never occurred to me but to go to Paradise Street, to get back to where I had been happy before and where, I assumed, Elijah would be happy too. I've sometimes wondered, every now and then, whether we got it all wrong. Perhaps I should have just joined the Travellers at River Farm and gone off with them somewhere and let Mrs Boswell help me find my feet. I was still young and in love with Elijah then, and maybe I would have thrown myself into it a bit more. As it was, by the time we became Travellers, I had three children to look after, and I was worn out and my heart was heavy with the humiliation of our debts back in our settled lives.

Maybe it wouldn't have made any difference, anyway.

I didn't let Elijah near me the whole time we were Travellers. I told him I wasn't having any babies born beneath a hedge.

Morselina Smith never liked me. I had made a grave mistake in sitting and expecting her to serve me tea, that first morning. I realised that pretty quick.

Clementina said to me, when I saw her a couple of days later, 'I hear you've still got your la-di-da ways, then?' She had a grim but gratified smile on her face.

Somehow, I felt able to stand up to her then. 'Yes and I'm sure it gave you no end of pleasure to hear about that, didn't it, Mother?'

She looked at me, surprised I had spoken back at her. Then, unexpectedly, she smiled. 'You're learning, *rawnie*,' she said, nodding approvingly. 'You're learning.'

I was indeed. It was time to stand up for myself more often, from now on. Facts is facts, as my mother would have said. Like it or not, for the time being, I was a Traveller.

PART 3

1895–1914

Clementina

CHAPTER 11

We were on Stourbridge Common for the whole of the winter, waiting for springtime when the weather would be good enough for us to take to the highway on our own. It wasn't a bad winter, as winters go, but still not exactly the best time to be getting used to life on a Traveller camp.

It was hard on the children, and harder still on Rose. Morselina Smith took against Rose so bad that I found myself obliged to stick up for her and put the word around that anyone who had a problem with the *rawnie* had better come and see me. Well, she was mother to my grandchildren, after all. There was one incident I couldn't prevent, however, as I was off the site at the time. One of Morselina's gang, a thin woman, a Cooper, had a go at Rose one morning, over Mehitable tripping up a pail of milk or something – I never got the details. Anyhow, it ended with this Cooper woman squaring up to Rose and Rose, to her credit, squaring up back – and although she got a black eye for it, she got the respect for standing up to her and was quite thick with the Coopers after that.

Morselina Smith was another matter, mind. Morselina Smith always called Rose a stinking *gorjer* and a *grasni* and one hundred other names behind our backs – and my grandchildren were naught but filthy half 'n' halfs. Now, where have I heard that before, I thought? I had to tread a bit careful with that lot myself as although I was an Old One and due some respect I had been living in bricks that five year past and there was some who weren't shy of reminding me of it. Five years. Had I really been away from my old life, on and off, for five whole years? I'd never been good at the marking of time. If it wasn't for my grandchildren being born, I'm not sure I'd have noticed that the years were moving at all. To me, it seemed like last week or the one before when I had packed my old carpet-bag after Adolphus passed away, and set off for Cambridge.

It weren't easy to find Paradise Street, that first day. Manibel Heron's son had taken me down to Cambridge on his cart, letting me off in what he said was the area. He wanted to stay until I found the right house but I sent him off sharpish. I weren't sure what sort of state my Lijah would be in when I found him and I didn't want the Heron boy talking when he got back to the camp.

I asked around a good deal before it was pointed out to me: a long, narrow street, full of little houses all packed together. Children were running up and down playing with balls and skittles but it was a bit parky for the women to be standing around so I had a chance to take a good look. It was a poor neighbourhood. Boxes, those houses were, squat little things all tight against each other with no air in between. Just looking down that street made me come over all poorly.

I had been told a certain house, so stood across the street from it for a few minutes, looking to see if anyone came in or out. Nobody did, and I couldn't stand there all day as the children were staring at me something funny when they ran past. Probably aren't used to finery like I've got on, I thought to myself, glaring back at them.

After a while, I caught a glimpse of a woman passing an upstairs window. She glanced out briefly and I could see she was wearing a nightie and had bright orange hair – some old trollop still a-bed of an afternoon. That can't possibly be where my Lijah is living, I thought. I went into the tobacconists at the far end of the road and he told me which house and I knocked on the door and who should open it but my Lijah.

Well, we've never been the kind to fall into each other's arms. I'm not one for all that sentiment-type nonsense and so Elijah hasn't never been neither.

He looked down at me. 'Hello, Dei,' he said, nodding, and stepped back to let me in.

The door opened straight onto a little parlour. There was a settee and an armchair that didn't match. Above the fireplace was a large mirror with a wooden frame that had been painted golden, quite badly. It was not hanging completely straight and there was the brown speckling of mirror spoiling in one bottom corner. Such poor workmanship made me wince. I wondered what had become of my Lijah that he could put up with such an object in his home. He left our fine *vardo* for this? I thought to myself.

Perhaps a little of what I thought showed on my face, for when I looked at Lijah I can't say he seemed particularly overjoyed to see me.

'So, this is what you've been up to then,' I said, glancing round.

He was never one to beat about the bush, my Lijah. 'I'm wed now, Dei,' he said.

'Aye, so I heard . . .' I replied. No matter how old a man gets, he is still a boy when he faces his mother. I was quite gentle as I added, '. . . and I'm a widow now, son.'

He stared at me, then fell to scratching his ear, which was always his gesture when he felt bad about something. 'I'm right sorry to hear that,' he said eventually.

Then the door opened, and in it swept.

I took in right away that she was expecting. It shouldn't have shocked me but for some reason it still did.

We stood there for a moment, all three of us. Lijah had a slightly panic-stricken look in his eyes. I knew if there was any awkwardness about to happen, he would bolt. Maybe I had best leave them to it, I thought, so he could explain to her how things were. I picked up the skirts of my dress and headed up the stairs. At the top, there was a small wooden landing and a door left and right. I pushed at the door on the left and saw a bed with a green eider. So that was where they slept. In the other room, there was a wooden rail with things on and some crates. So, this is where I'll be stopping, I said to myself.

I had left my carpet-bag downstairs for Lijah to bring up. There was nothing for me to do but sit on one of the crates and wonder if they were laid end to end whether they would take a straw mattress. And I decided they would, right enough.

There was a little square window with no shutter, so I went and looked out of it. It looked out over the back – their tiny garden with a small shed for the doing of private things and, beyond, a narrow dirt alleyway. It was all so small out there it was like the houses that backed onto theirs were pushing in and I thought I shall never be able to breathe with others living so close. How do they stand it?

Below me must've been the sitting room, for I could hear raised voices coming up through the floorboards. I say raised but I mean lowered, for though it was clear they were having fierce words about something, they were whispering to each other. I would have been able to hear every word otherwise.

I tried not to hear but waited for Lijah to bring up my things.

His voice grew into a murmur, sometimes a growl. Hers stayed steady, and then rose.

Then, all at once, there was the slam of the back door.

I went to the window. Lijah had come out into the garden in a hurry, his jacket unbuttoned and his hat askew. He didn't even open the back gate but placed one hand atop the wall and jumped over it, then strode off down the back alley. *Now why has she made him go and do that?* I thought vexedly. He hasn't even brought my things up. I sat back down on the crate.

Downstairs, all was silent.

Well, I couldn't stay there all day and I was feeling I would like nothing more than a cup of tea and a bit of something to go with it after my journey. I was thinking maybe I should go and help her put the supper on, just to show how I wasn't there to take advantage or anything. Most women in her condition would be glad of a bit of help around the house, I thought, and I may be a small body but I've worked from dawn 'til dusk with my bony little fingers ever since I could walk and I'm not here to be waited on.

So there was nothing for it but to go downstairs and straighten things out with her.

I stood, and brushed down my skirt, and I thought how I was prepared to put my best foot forward here, to get off on the right footing like, and she'd be a right fool if she didn't realise it. Plain speaking was the thing. I came down the stairs slowly, clutching on to the rail, as I weren't used to them. And I was also feeling how I didn't want to startle her as I wasn't right sure what sort of state she would be in and when someone's going to have a baby you have to not-shock them, after all.

She was sank down on the settee but raised her head as I came down the stairs. Dordy, you've never seen such a sight. Her face was all red and puffy and tear streaked. She was clutching the edge of her petticoat in her hands. She let it fall but I do believe she had been wiping her eyes with it. Her hair was all hanging loose from where she had pinned it with fluffy feathers of it sticking up here and there and a strand across her face. She looked like she'd been dragged through a hedge backwards. Daft hayputh, I thought, feeling right sorry for her. She'll never keep him if she lets herself go.

She looked so fat and soft with her great big belly. She was not so much a-sitting on the settee as spread all over it.

She looked at me, all miserable like. 'He's gone down the pub, if you want to know,' she said, and I thought I saw something defiant in the set of her mouth.

Oh, of course he's gone down the pub, I thought to myself. What else is a man to do when his wife cries all over him? She's been married this year – has she not yet realised that much? And she married my Lijah to boot, who has always been trouble and always will be. What did she think she saw when he looked up at her from the step of our *vardo*? A halo floating over his head? A choir of winged angels a-singing in the background?

My husband, my Adolphus, was dead and I had nothing. And here she was with her husband and a baby coming and her little house – and me to help her out into the bargain. And she was crying because he was off down the pub? She had better get to grips with how things are, I thought. It won't do any good if she fools herself longer. I know my Lijah and I know he's only going to get worse in that way, not better, and his drinking is something she's going to have to live with. She'll have me and her babies for company, and when Lijah chooses to come and shine on us that's all well and good, but any girl who thinks her man will be the whole of her has got a nasty shock coming. She had better know now, so's she can get used to the idea and make the best of what she's got.

'You've married my son,' I said, as gentle as I could. 'He's not a bad type, but there are things about him you won't change, ever, and you'd better get used to it, or you'll sup sorrow by the spoonful 'til the day you die.'

She stared at me.

I spied my carpet-bag in the corner, so I went and picked it up. She did not move to help me. I turned and climbed the difficult stairs. I saw I would be sorting out the little box room all by myself.

*

I hated that house. How I stayed there as long as I did I will never know. I felt it was my duty, really, what with the babies coming thick and fast and Lijah's wife having no one to help her out but me. If she'd had her own mother around it wouldn't have been so bad, I suppose.

It took a bit of getting used to, her high-handed ways, and I kept saying to myself how's you can't expect a woman who's carrying to be in any way normal and I must make allowances. But nothing I did was good enough for her. If I washed dishes and put them away I would catch her moving them around from cupboard to cupboard afterwards. If I folded clothes, she refolded them. And I never had a word of thanks.

Where I come from, a woman of my age got looked after by her daughter-in-law, not the other way around.

And I knew she talked about me to the orange-haired trollop. I was horrified to discover they were friends, for it made me wonder what sort of background our young Miss Rose had come from, before she moved out to the farm. She'd enough airs and graces then, all right. I began to wonder if maybe her mother had been a woman of loose morals or some such and thought, I'd better keep a close eye on what goes on in this house.

When my first grandchild was born, my Adolphus Daniel, the midwife-woman who had helped him out gave him firstly to my daughter-in-law, as was right and proper. Then a few minutes later, Rose needed to sit up. And what did she do with her new babby? She handed him over, not to me or the midwife-woman, but to the orange-haired trollop, who was waiting in a chair by the bed. All I could do was stand in the corner of the room and watch. I was his flesh and blood, that little boy – and she gives him to some lazy tart who lives up the road. That was how she thanked me for everything I'd done.

I got acquainted with the boy in my own good time. He was as good as gold, that *bobum*. I couldn't believe how good he was when

I remembered what a perisher my Lijah had been as a boy. She didn't know she was born.

I blessed him, that boy, as soon as I got the chance. I waited 'til one night, when they were sound asleep and I heard him stir and I crept into their room and lifted him up. And I took him down to the garden, and I showed him the stars. It should have been done by his mother when he was but a few days old – but I was his Romany mother, I suppose, mother to the Traveller bit of him, and I held him up to the stars and I asked for breath and long life and good fortune for him and an unusual breeze blew and I knew he would be blessed all right. I lowered him, and sat, and put him on my knee. Lovely thick eyebrows, Daniel had, even when he was a baby.

The boy, the warm breeze, all asleep around me – it was as good as when I had my Lijah. Better, in fact. You can love them straight and simple when they're yours but not yours. I sang to him softly and my heart was so joyful it was like bells ringing. Oh, it was the greatest feeling I'd had in years.

There was much I didn't care for in daughter-in-law, as you may have gathered by now, but if there was one thing she was good at it was producing grandchildren. Aye, the babbies came thick and fast, those early years. They fair popped out of her.

Daniel may have been an easy little thing – but the next one was a different matter. Mehitable, dordy, she was a madam.

She came early, did Mehitable – slithered out, all thin and slimy. I took one look at her and knew some dark days lay ahead. It began almost as soon as she was born – the screaming. It was something chronic. I did not blame my daughter-in-law for not loving that child, oh no, for I could see how difficult it was to love a child that unhappy. There is, after all, only one thing we ask of our Little Ones – that they outlive us, and that they be happy with it. That is all our hopes and dreams, all wrapped up into one request. If some stranger came along and started making your child miserable, day in, day out, would you not hate them with all the passion in your heart? Yes, you would – and even when it's your child is making *itself* miserable, you can't helping hating it for doing it to itself, while still loving it at the same time. And that sets up a new kind of torment, inside. I watched my daughter-in-law hating and loving that sickly babby – and I was not surprised that often she would thrust her at me and say, 'Mother, you do something with her, she don't want me.'

I would take Mehitable off for a walk or out into the garden and she would maybe quieten down for a little bit. I suppose it must have seemed unfair to my daughter-in-law that I could calm her child but I couldn't really – she was just an unhappy baby, and that was that. The only difference was, I wasn't all tight about her being unhappy, like her mother was. I could accept Mehitable's unhappiness and think of it as part of her, not take it personal like. I loved her at one remove, without blaming myself for everything that was wrong with her.

Whatever I did, it never lasted long. And there were times when even my comforts had no effect. Mehitable's moaning was ghostly, sometimes. It was like she was not a human thing at all, and it could go on for hours and hours. I did everything I could for her. I sang the old songs to her, about the moon and the sun. I placed charms under the padding in her Moses basket. Nothing worked. She was beyond me, or anyone. It was like there was a devil in her. I even started to wonder if I should take her out into the country and find one of our people who could really help. I don't think my daughter-in-law would have minded, she was that desperate. I think we all went a little mad at that time – no wonder Lijah stayed out drinking so much. So would we all, if we'd had the choice.

She was an odd-looking thing, Mehitable. Dark eyes, straight dark hair. She put on hardly any weight as an infant and when you bathed her you could see her ribs sticking out funny, her chest heaving in and out as she bawled. (She hated being bathed as much as she hated anything.) Then when she was grow'd a bit to the age when she should've been walking, all she could do was haul herself up on the furniture and move along it, clutching on for dear life. Her legs were bent funny, bow-legged but more so. She'll never stop a pig in a passage, I used to think.

My daughter-in-law went on something awful to Lijah about getting a doctor for her but proper *gorjer* doctors cost a fortune. Oh, I ached to take that child out into the fields to lead a proper life.

When she got bigger, she could still hardly walk. She would stagger along, holding on to the furniture, her chest all puffed up and heaving, with her dark hair and dark eyes staring – it was like having our own baby blackbird. Our cripple. Our Mehitable.

The money was saved for a doctor, eventually. He came one afternoon and looked at her and stared at us like we'd done it to her on purpose. Rickets, it was called. It was on account of not getting the right food and we had to get liver inside her or her bones would set wrong and she would never be right even when she was grow'd. She would need braces on her legs anyway. I said to him, did that account for how she had always cried as a baby and he said, yes, it hurt their bones to have rickets.

After he had gone, my daughter-in-law and I were sitting in the little parlour. We had got Daniel to carry Mehitable outside. My daughter-in-law had her hand over her mouth, which I had learned was a sign she was not right happy.

'Well,' I said, 'when Lijah gets back we'd best tell him to be off down the butcher's with whatever he's got, find some way to feed that child up.'

My daughter-in-law stood up, looked at me with thunder in her eyes and said, 'Don't you mention Elijah's name to me. I don't even want to hear his name *spoken*.' Then off she went upstairs and slammed her bedroom door and would not come down the whole day and night.

When Lijah got back that evening, I told him about the doctor's visit, and he frowned. 'Well, there's lots of children don't eat proper,' he said after a while, 'but it don't make them bow-legged.'

'It's more than that, if you ask me,' I said. 'It's how she's cooped up here all day long. Because she can't walk proper she never goes anywhere, just lies around being sickly and miserable. I know your wife's got a house to run but she's got to get that child out and about more. You've got to make a little cart or something so's I can take her with me when I goes shopping. Just think of all the air going stale in this house. If she was out in a field, she'd grow strong enough, you'd see.'

He turned away without speaking, that habit of his.

'Nobody never had rickets when you was a boy,' I added.

'Oh yes, that's right, Mother,' he said, in a nasty-sounding voice, turning back to me. 'Nobody *never* got poorly, did they, and we *hall* had a right good time with enough to *heat* and nothing to do but sit round a campfire singing songs to *heach* other?'

I was shocked that he could be so ironical with me. 'What has got into you, Elijah Smith?' I asked. I knew what had got into him of course: the strong, black stuff, Audit Ale – evil, it was. They served it down the pubs on a Friday when everyone had just got paid and my Lijah drank it whether he'd been paid for anything or not.

He muttered something but I couldn't hear him properly. I let it go.

That house, that house. It was like the graves in the cemetery at Werrington. It was like we was dead people all packed up into little boxes. Night after night I would startle awake and lie in the dark thinking maybe I was dead and crammed into a box all on my own and I was going to lie there, underground, for all eternity. I would feel hot and clammy at the same time, and my breath so raggedy it would make my throat ache. When I got like that, the only thing that would calm me would be to go down to the garden: to sit in the night air and light my pipe and feel the cool smoke in my throat. I would look back at the house and think, how do they stand it?

Mehitable got to walk when she was older, and she only had to have a brace on one leg, which seeing as we had to borrow for it was a good thing. Things got a bit better for her, after that, and she was even able to hobble around after the other children in the street, in a fashion. I've seen some children be right horrible to cripples, but no one never said a thing to Mehitable. She was such a peculiar little thing. When she turned her smile on, it was like the sun after a storm, on account of it being so rare.

No, the other kids never bothered her. Maybe it was because their parents told them not to pick on the poor crippled girl from what was now the poorest family in the street – or maybe it was because they knew her big brother Dan would thump them if they tried. Mehitable being a cripple brought out the worst in my daughter-in-law and the best in my grandson. For Daniel learned from when he was very young that it was his job to care and look after a small thing what could not look after herself – and I think that kind of lesson gets stuck in you when you learn it young enough, for Daniel was the kind of boy who spent his whole life looking after other people and never thinking not once of himself.

Next was Bartholomew. Along he came, Barty-boy, and he was half his brother and half his sister: small and dark, but healthy with it. The third child – just the next thing, really. He had the good luck to be ignored a bit more often than the other two and it never seemed to harm him. Things went a bit bad for us, after he was born. It was probably a good thing he weren't paid much attention to, as I don't think it would have been the sort of attention he'd've liked.

Yes, things got bad all round, for a bit. After her third baby, my daughter-in-law went down with the melancholia. Sometimes, she wouldn't even leave the house. She started saying how all the neighbours hated us because we brought the down the tone of the street, which was naught but foolishness as that street was about as low as you could get before any of us set foot in it. Once, when Rose was crying about how hard her life was I pressed her and she owned up to having borrowed money from the Empers and how she couldn't face them as she couldn't pay it back. Well, that explains a lot, I thought – those askance looks I get from time to time. Lilly Empers was the key to that street. Cross her and you were finished.

The mirror went, with its ugly golden frame. Lijah's one suit that she had laboured over to make him, with a sewing machine she had rented for a shilling a week – that went, but only to the pawnbrokers. She managed to get it out so Lijah could wear it to get each of the children christened.

A dark time it was. I would have disappeared myself if it weren't for the grandchildren. Lijah was off as much as he could get away with – which didn't mean he brought any more *lovah* into the house, and the less he earned the more he drank, as far as I could tell. The money situation got a bit desperate. I took to a little dukkering, on the quiet like, without telling Lijah or his wife, and that brought in a few pennies from neighbours who were sworn to secrecy with the reasoning that if rumours of my extraordinary powers got out, there would be queues that stretched as far as the common. But there was days when there was no food in that house and things between Lijah and Rose got pretty chronic.

Then came the incident that really put the lid on it.

It was September. Time for the farmers to get their corn in, if they haven't already. But not where we was living.

*

Lijah was out. He'd been out all evening, on one of his benders, no doubt. Sometimes he didn't come home at all but went and slept in the Gas Lane stable with Kit the Second, which was the best thing, often enough.

It was late. The children were asleep upstairs. Daniel slept across the foot of his parents' bed and Mehitable and I slept toe-to-tail on my straw mattress. The new babby was in a Moses basket on top of the chest of drawers in Rose and Lijah's room. That house was far too small now there were three Little Ones as well as three of us.

Barty-boy was restless that night and my daughter-in-law had just gone up to see to him. I was cleaning, wiping all the surfaces in their little parlour with a damp cloth as we'd had a bit of autumn sunshine earlier in the day and I'd thought they looked a bit dusty. It was dark, though, and I couldn't really see what I was doing by lamplight. I had just about had enough and was thinking of going up myself.

There came a knock at the door.

I knew straightaway that it was not a good knock. A good knock is light, a little apologetic, even. Someone who means you well is worried that they might be disturbing you, and they communicate that with a light tap-tapping, with little breaks in between – merry tapping, like a dance.

This was three knocks, more bangs than knocks, in fact. They were done with a closed fist.

I went quickly to the door, the cloth still in my hand.

Three men stood on the doorstep. The light was dim but I could see them quite clearly. One, the biggest one, had mounted the step and the other two were pressed in behind him. They were rough-looking types, around my age, working men with flat caps on their heads and leather waistcoats beneath their jackets.

The one in front said to me, 'We want to speak with Smith.'

I knew I had to think quickly. Lijah might be back any minute. I took care to look each one of them in the face, long enough so's he knew I would remember him another time.

'My son is away on business,' I said, eventually.

What the first one said next was shocking. I don't like to repeat his actual words. 'You *eff*ing pikey,' he said, his face contorted. 'I want your son out here now or I'll come in and get 'im.'

One of the others put a hand on his arm. 'Bert,' he said, 'there's no need to be rough with the lady. He might not be here.'

'Don't be daft,' Bert replied, shaking his arm free. 'He's here, all right.'

I stood back. 'Come in, gentlemen, if you don't believe me. You are welcome to search the house. I just ask that you don't disturb the children what are sleeping upstairs.' Such an invitation would have been understood as a clear refusal where I come from. No *Romani chal* would ever enter another's *vardo* uninvited, however strong his grievance.

The first one stepped up – but the second held him back.

'He's not here, Bert.'

I waited for a minute. It seemed at first that 'Bert', whoever he was, was persuaded and they might leave. Then he shook his head, and pushed past me. The others followed him in.

'May I ask . . .' I began, but I was interrupted by a sound from above. Bartholomew had started to cry and Rose was moving around her bedroom. Her door opened and she called down. For once in her life, she said the right thing. 'So he's back, is he?'

The men glanced at each other. Bartholomew's crying rose in pitch.

'My daughter-in-law has retired for the night and will not be decently dressed,' I said, 'but I am perfectly prepared to call her down if you wish, gentlemen.' Then, for good measure I added, 'She has probably finished feeding the baby by now.'

I went to the bottom of the stairs and called up, 'There are three men here to see Elijah.'

Rose came to the landing, holding Bartholomew on her shoulder. 'Oh Lord,' she said, 'what's he gone and done now?'

I turned back to speak to the men but they had already left, leaving the door open. I went after them, closing the door behind me as I went. They had hurried off down the street and I was forced to run after them in the dark. When I caught up with them, they turned. I could see that Bert was still angry, not in control of himself, so I addressed my question to him. He was most likely to give me an answer, however indelicately put.

'Excuse me, but you must tell me. What has my son done? Is it money? Does he owe you money?'

One of the others replied. 'He does not, missus. It's a deal worse than that.'

Worse? 'Why have you come looking for him, then?'

The third, the one who had not spoken yet, answered me. He had a piping voice and dry, gingery hair, like my daughter-in-law's. 'He beat up our father. He punched him good and hard, even though he did nothing to him. He set upon him outside The Bleeding Heart. There's witnesses.'

'I am sorry, gentlemen,' I said firmly. 'But you must be mistaken. My son would do many things but he would never set upon an old man, never in his life. Why, that would be a wicked thing.' I knew for a fact my Lijah had never had a fight with any man but was his equal.

They could see my opinion was not feigned and I reckon that must have softened them a little, for they glanced at each other.

'Is your son Elijah Smith, the *gipsy* what deals in horses at Gas Lane?' said the second.

'Aye, he is, but he's not capable of . . .'

'Well, I tell you he is,' insisted Bert, angry again. 'There were three or four folks witnessed it. It was one of his own friends pulled him off.'

'What happened?'

The one with the piping voice said, 'Our Dad was drinking in The Bleeding Heart. He's an old fella and doesn't have his shop any more. Anyway, he gets chatting to the *gipsy*. The next thing, the *gipsy* flew at him and dragged him outside and started hitting him.'

I could not believe this story. What could an old man have said that was so insulting to Lijah?

'He must've been provoked.'

'He was not, missus. The others followed them out and broke it up. I asked Fred what happened, and Fred said he'd asked the *gipsy* what was up, and the *gipsy* pointed at my father lying on the ground and said, his name, that's what's up.'

'What is his name?'

'George Rawson. He's our father.'

The name meant nothing to me. I was bewildered. All I could think about was how I could stop these three men from tracking down my Lijah and beating him to a pulp. They must've been to Gas Lane already, so that meant he wasn't there. With any luck, he would have taken himself off somewhere for a few days.

'Gentlemen,' I said, 'I am most distressed to hear this story. I promise you, when my son reappears, I will send him to you at once with his explanation.'

'I bet!' Bert spat viciously onto the pavement.

The second one pulled at his jacket. 'Come on, Herbert, there's no point in being bad to the missus. It wasn't her beat up Dad.'

As Bert was pulled away by his brothers, he called back over his shoulder to me, 'You make sure your son knows I'm looking for him, missus. Rawson's my name an' all . . .' He jabbed a finger at his brothers, each in turn. '. . . and his, and his. You make sure he knows!'

We had been talking quietly enough up 'til then, but at that shout, one or two folk came to their doorsteps to see what was going on. Another black mark against us.

*

It was four days before I had any sign of Lijah. I knew he would go to Gas Lane sooner or later, to make sure the horse was all right. I had been feeding Kit myself and walking him round the yard so's he didn't get stale. I left my mark in chalk on the stable wall and drew a picture of a box and a line through it, so's he knew not to come home.

When I went back the next day, Lijah's mark was beside mine.

Two days later, when I went, Lijah himself emerged from behind a straw bale. He looked terrible – a week's stubble on his cheek, his face grey. I'd never seen him look so bad.

'Have you been eating?' I asked him.

He shook his head. 'Nor drinking, neither,' he said grimly.

'Well that's one good thing,' I huffed, and went to tend to Kit.

Lijah sat down and watched me. 'So, they've been to the house, then?' he said, philosophically.

'Aye,' I rubbed Kit down ferociously. 'This horse needs some proper exercise.'

'Does Rose know?'

'She does not, but she's frantic wondering where on earth you are.'

'I didn't mean to hurt the old fella that bad. I just wanted to learn him, that's all.'

I stopped rubbing down Kit. 'How bad did you hurt him, Lijah?'

'Bad enough. He'll be all right.'

'His sons seem to think it was bad enough, and there's three of them and they're big fellas.'

'I know. I know them. I seen them in there.'

'If you was going to have a fight, then why did you pick a family like that, for heaven's sake?' He did not answer me. I turned to face him. 'Them sort of *gorjers*, they don't fight clean, you should know that by now. You can't box one of them fair and square like another *Romani chal*. They don't work like that.'

He had closed his eyes and leaned back against the stable wall. 'I know that, Dei, don't go on . . .'

'Then what were you thinking of?'

'It was men's business, Dei.'

'Don't give me that. It's my business now you've brought those men to our house. They stepped inside, Lijah. They came over the threshold, into our home. If any man had offered me that insult on the Fens, my Adolphus would have dealt with him fast enough.'

He jumped to his feet. 'That was what I *was* doing! Give me credit for once, will you, Dei? You bloody women never give me any credit, do you?'

I was facing him. 'Are you going to tell me or not?'

He sat down again. 'Only if.'

'What?'

'Swear you won't never tell Rose.'

Well, that was easy enough. There were a whole lot of things I was never going to tell her anyway so I didn't see how one more made a difference either way.

'Course I won't.'

'Swear.'

'I swear it now get on and tell me, will you?'

Lijah looked at the floor and mumbled. 'He paid for the church bells to be rung.'

'Who did?'

'Rose's dad. Her real dad. Old Man Rawson. He told me. He boasted about it. He boasted about how her mother was, well, *little tart*, was the words he used, if you must know. And how he'd paid for the church bells to be rung when Rose and I was wed. When he knew who I was, that's what he said.'

I stared at him.

'I'd been nodding to this old fella in the pub for upwards of a year. Never knew'd who he was 'til the other night. Then we got chatting and he worked out who I was, and off he went. It was like he was boasting about how he'd bought us our wedding, as if he was some rich fella and we were nothing and he could buy us any time he liked. He never gave nothing to Rose in her whole life, not even his name. He'd had a few, like, must've done. And he laughed like he thought I should be laughing too and called her mother a good little tart and asked if her daughter had taken after her and that's when I hit him.'

I sat down next to him. What was I going to do with my son?

I still had straw in my hands from wiping down Kit. I let it fall. 'We've got to leave, you know,' I said, brushing some small strands from my sleeve. 'As soon as they get wind of you back in Paradise Street, they'll be back. I know their sort. They don't give up.'

'I know that, Dei.'

I gestured towards Kit the Second. 'How much do you think you'll get for that horse?'

He rubbed his chin. 'Not sure. I won't be able to sell it round here. I might on the other side of the city. It's not a bad horse.'

'Well, you'd better do it tonight. Leave word for me here tomorrow. I'll start working out what we can take with us.'

I stood. I felt better, now there was stuff to do. It was always the same, moving on. Whatever reason you had to do it for, there was a rightness about it, so whatever sadness you felt there was a goodness inside too.

'What about Rose?' he said.

'I've told her they were debt collectors,' I said. 'We're that behind with the rent. She's had enough. She'll go.'

I leaned against Kit the Second and put the palm of my hand on his nose, by way of saying goodbye.

CHAPTER 12

We stopped on Stourbridge Common for the whole of that winter, but as soon as the weather got good enough the following spring, we took off on our own with a cart and a bender tent. Lijah scraped together the wherewithal for a grinding barrow and him and me would go round a village while Rose went door-to-door with the children. Lijah sharpened knives and I dukkered or sold stuff out of a basket. I liked doing that, flattering the housewives while we stood together on the doorstep and watched Lijah at work. I liked seeing the sparks fly off the knives as he worked at them and hearing the *shk-shk* sound of the blade against the spinning-stone. Each sound meant a few more pennies. Each turn of that stone took us a few more inches away from going hungry.

People weren't always bad to us, neither. In one village, we met a vicar on the High Street who crossed the road to speak to us. I am always wary of vicars, with good reason, you might say, but this one had spotted me and said he was having a Meat Tea for Old Folks that afternoon and would I like to go along?

Well, it was a right laugh. I ate 'til I was stuffed. Then we sat back, all us Old Folks, and the vicar showed us Lanternslides of Foreign Parts. As I left, he blessed me, and gave me a packet of tea, which he pressed into my hands with many kind words about how *Members of Your Race*, as he put it, were always welcome in his church. I decided I quite liked vicars, after that. I began to see the point of them.

The children grew. Daniel was a fine boy – Bartholomew a mischief. Mehitable . . . she stayed a singular child.

She was my only granddaughter, at that time, so I made sure to teach her a little of what I knew. I taught her how to curtsey so her calliper showed and she looked brave for trying. I taught her how to hold a lady's palm and trace the lines on it with the very tip of her finger. 'You must touch a lady softer than she's ever been touched before,' I said to her. 'You must hold the hand firmly, but touch softly. That way, a person feels protected, cared for, coaxed. You must never hurry it, my chicken. Hold a person's hand properly and they'll pay you the going rate, whatever you claim to see lying ahead of them. For a moment, they have been concentrated on – and that's what they are paying you for. They are paying you for being curious about them.'

I never met a happy *gorjer* who believed in all that nonsense.

And what lay ahead for us? Well, it has never been my way to look towards the future. That sort of thinking is brooding. Brooding leads to badness. When you have a cooking pot to fill, then you have to be doing, not thinking. So, if you had said to me at that time, where do you think you all might be in a couple of years hence? I would've shrugged. Same way I shrugged when Lijah and I was harguing one day and he said, you've got to realise such and such, Dei, it's the twentieth century now, you know. I can't say as I'd noticed that the century we had slipped into was a great deal different from the last.

What I am trying to say is, I didn't know whether or not we was going to carry on living on the road – we were at that time, and that was it. But I did know that it was hard and that after a while I was not altogether happy about it. At first, it had been good to be back where we belonged. But after while, I found myself thinking sometimes that a solid ceiling above you is quite pleasant when the rain is that sharp rain like pointy needles.

In truth, it was just like always. I wasn't at all sure where I belonged.

It's horrible, that feeling, the knowing-you-are-different. That knowledge – that there is a wrongness or a badness or a not-fitting-in-ness that is inside and around you the whole time. In Paradise Street, it was easy. I was an outsider because I was one of the People, a Romany woman and proud of it. But now I was back among others of my kind and it turned out it was not so simple at all. There was still something not quite right with me – something lost, or taken. *You can be pushed in the mud any time, you know.* That little voice spoke to me, all too often. It had never gone away.

I think I knew, as a result, that this being back on the road was not a permanent thing, that it was only a matter of time.

We joined back up with the Smiths and the Coopers come the wintertimes. You can't really manage on your own when the weather is bad, not when you have Young 'Uns. You need to be with others who can help you through the dark and cold and wetness of it. We all came off the road in a big group, from November through to March. There wasn't much work in the district, though.

That year, it was just after the first frosts and the parsnips were in and there was a misunderstanding with the landowner and he told us we had to *ife* by the end of the week. Well, that would have been all right but it had been raining solid for a month and we weren't ready for it. The landowner wouldn't listen to reason, though, and sent the gavvers in – so off we all set with things not stowed properly and it pouring with rain and our cart going, humpitty-humpitty down the rutted lane on account of one of the wheels being askew.

We had only got a mile down the road when Lijah pulled up and said we had better all walk otherwise we might lose an axle. Then him and Rose had words about the children having to walk in the rain. I must admit, they did look like a trio of poor mites as they stood there, all sorry and wet while their mother and father shouted at each other and the rain pelted down.

Mehitable had grown into a tall, lanky girl, still skinny as any-thing and still with a calliper and a bad limp, still the unluckiest mite of all. She'd had a cold that week – she was prone to them on account of her weak chest, and was constantly sniffing and blow-ing into her hanky. The nose was going bright red with it, and the skin round it cracking. When Lijah and Rose had finished holler-ing at each other, the boys went over and helped their father with the cart, so Mehitable was left standing on her own beneath the tree with the water dripping on her from above, and she did look like the most miserable little sparrow.

When the men had finished their men-jobs with the wheel, I said to Lijah, 'Let Billy ride up with you. She's poorly. The boys can push and I'll lead the horse.'

He looked at Mehitable, with her shoulders all hunched up and said, 'Rose can lead the horse. You stay on that side and shout if we veer off that verge.' Then he helped Mehitable up onto the cart.

We set off again, slowly. The other carts and the *vardos* had gone on ahead. They had long since disappeared round the bend but we knew where they were headed.

If we didn't catch up soon, someone would head back to find us and I did find myself thinking that if it was the Coopers I might get offered a lift in their *vardo*. *I'm getting a bit old for this traipsing in the rain*, I thought to myself, a bit grumpy like. I've been doing it since I was a *biti chai* and I'm ready to sit down in front of a fire and not have to spend the evening cleaning mud off everything I own.

Thinking of all the times I'd walked down a lane in the rain, it came to me: the time just after Lijah was born, when we set off in bad weather, just like this, and my mother got taken from us and killed. I have always done my best not to think of that time. But the rain came down – and it came to me how my mother and I had sheltered beneath a tree, like Mehitable had done just then, and how the farmer had come by and spat at us for no reason. And a feeling of dread and gloom came over me and I found myself raising my face and looking around to make sure we were all together and no one was coming after us. There was Lijah, on the cart, huddled down with a blanket over his head to keep the worst of the wet off, the reins drawn tightly in. Mehitable was sat on the edge of the cart sideways, facing out with her legs dangling over – Lijah said he wanted her on that side for balance. She was holding on with just one hand as the other was clutching her shawl round her head. The hand she was holding on with was white with the cold, the knuckles raw.

Rose was at the front, leading the horse and stumbling in the mud. At the back, the two boys were one at each corner, ready to push when needed. Daniel was a big, strong lad, by then. Barty was only a little thing but wiry like my Lijah. Above us, the sky was gathered tight and grey, the clouds all packed in. The rain pelted and the branches of the trees bent and shook above us. The brown mud gave beneath my feet with each step I took. It was as if time had slowed right down, as if we had been making our way down this wretched, sodden lane for all eternity.

Then, time became even slower.

I saw it all happen, just before it happened. A picture came into my head, but I was so slow in my thoughts I was powerless to do anything about it.

We was trudging. The wheel beside me was turning slowly, with an ancient, creaky sound. The rain came down. All was slippery. *Folk slip, go under*, I thought, and shook my head to push the thought away: the lane, the rain – the sight of two gavvers banging on the side of our *vardo* as I came back from the stream and the hollow feeling inside as I ran towards them, baby Lijah clutched on my chest. There was an almighty cracking sound from the other side of the cart and Rose's head whipped round. Lijah looked that way too, then leaned to one side. The boys at the back called out.

'Dadus!' cried Bartholomew.

'It's going, Dad!' shouted Daniel.

'Push!' bellowed Lijah back at them, over his shoulder, and cracked the whip over the horse. Rose shouted something else, above their shouts, her hand up. I was looking toward her and only saw sideways – Mehitable's arm, wheeling up in the air. Then she tumbled, just dropping down from the cart, like a blackbird swooping for something on the ground. The cart lurched forward. There was a cry in my throat that could not find release. Instead, it came from Mehitable, as if my fear found voice in her, as the wheel of the cart pushed her down into the mud.

Then, too late, came the panic, the busyness of trying to do something. Lijah jumped down from the cart. Rose ran around from the front, pushing Lijah out of her way to get to her daughter. I was nearest and there first, already calm enough to think, the ground was soft and gave, that will have saved her.

She had struck her head as well, somehow, but it can't have been that bad as she was screaming fit to burst, and Rose was beside her, holding her on her lap and screaming too. They were both of them covered in mud. And I heard myself saying, babbling, 'It was my fault. It was my fault, Lijah.' And he gave me a glance as if to say, *last thing we need right now is you going daft.*

He sent Daniel off to run ahead and find the others. Barty helped us lift Mehitable out of the mud and onto the verge, in the shelter of a bush. And we all wept and the rain came down and I was on my knees in the mud with my hand pressed against my chest thinking, *but it was my fault. I made it happen by thinking of my Dei and the rain and the tread-wheel. Bad things follow me.*

As if she had not had enough pain already. As if she hadn't already had her fill. I think that is how come Mehitable wanted to leave us. She knew how unfair it was that such an accident should happen to her, of all people. She couldn't take any more.

The Cooper lads came back with Daniel and we got Mehitable onto a cart. Rose and Daniel went with her into the next town, where they found her a doctor. They brought her back later that day, one foot a huge ball of bandage. It was broken in different places, Rose said, but the leg was saved by the calliper. It was that iron thing what had tormented her all her life, what stopped the rest of the leg from being mashed. She had a poultice on her forehead, too, but the doctor had said the head wasn't serious.

But then, when she was laid up, a fever set in, and we all of us knew how serious that was. We couldn't find any infection in the foot and we burned leaves in a dish but still the fever worsened. It all came back to me, as horribly clear as if it was the day before – it was just the same; taking Dei to Huntingdon Common when we got her out of the House of Correction; her pain and fever; her slipping away, just slipping from me like something I had been clumsy and dropped out of sheer carelessness.

I started preparing in my mind for losing my only grand-daughter.

*

We stayed in the clearing for a fortnight. There was the Coopers with us, and some Kentish Scamps they were related to who stayed behind as well and were right good to us, taking charge of the mending of our cart.

We had been there three nights and Mehitable's fever was at its height. Lijah and I were sat outside the bender tent, smoking. Rose was inside with Mehitable.

Lijah and I had not spoken much since the accident.

After a moment or two, he said quietly, 'Why did you say it was your fault, Dei, when Billy fell off the cart?'

How can you explain that sort of thing to a son when he is grow'd? Grow'd he may be, but he's still your boy and you want to protect him from realness.

'I saw it about to happen,' I said. 'I had a bad feeling and got a picture in my head. I should've shouted.'

He looked at the cigarette he was smoking, one of his own rolled-up things with a few shreds of 'baccy and lot of dried leaves. 'It weren't your fault, Dei,' he said, with a long sigh. 'It were mine. I was too busy looking at the other side and thinking about how it was going down. That's how come I made the horse go forward.' Of course, it was all our stupid faults for letting her sit on the edge of the cart in the first place.

Ghosts, I thought. I felt the ghost of my own Dei, broke on the tread-wheel. I felt it as strongly as if she was squatting on the damp grass beside us. I knew she'd long forgiven me for my part in her death – but she didn't want to let go, neither. She was lonely. *You can't have Mehitable*, I whispered to her, in my heart. *Not yet. We've need of her.*

The ghosts of dead children are the worst sort, of course, the most evil, that is, for they are the ones who went wrongly, before their time. They are the ones who haunt the living with the most fierceness. I would walk through a whole field of adult demons in the dark before I crossed the path of one ghost-child in broad daylight.

I knew that if Mehitable died she would haunt us, and it would not be nice.

'Lijah,' I said, 'I've been thinking.'

'Aye,' he said, still staring at his roll-up, not bothering to relight it.

'Let's settle for a bit,' I said. 'For the children's sake. They've schooling to catch up on. They've missed a good few years what with one thing and another. And Billy's never really been strong enough for all this. Let's go to that village, the one where the old mush offered you that dyke work. The boys could do some too.'

Lijah was quiet. 'Well you weren't too keen on house-dwelling, as I remember,' he replied eventually.

There wasn't much I could say to that. 'Rose would be pleased,' I said, after a while.

'Sutton,' he said. 'It was called Sutton. I wasn't keen on that mush, he was only paying by the chain. It was handy for Ely, though.'

Daniel approached us, over the clearing. He was holding an enamelled dish in his hands. 'Ida Scamp brewed us a basin for Billy,' he said, as he came near. There was a cloth over it, to keep the vapours in. I tossed my head to indicate he should take it straight in, before it lost its goodness. He bent into the tent.

Lijah and I were silent while Daniel was in there, just smoking and waiting for him to come back out.

He emerged, after a while. Lijah and I both looked at him. His face was downcast, which meant she was no better.

'Take that dish back,' I said.

Mehitable is going to die, I thought. She is going to die and haunt us for all eternity.

You do not get to keep a person when they are a ghost. You only get to keep what was bad of them, what you and they resent. A ghost is not made up of nice memories – it is made up of all the horrible things that have happened to a person, all the things you want to forget.

I had not thought of it in years, but as Elijah and I squatted on the grass outside that tent where Mehitable lay trying to die, the story of the Ghost Pig came into my mind.

It happened not far from a village called Kennyhill, on Mildenhall Fen, east of Ely. As a result, I will never go east of Ely again in all my born puff.

I say Mildenhall but actually the place we was stopped near was more on Burnt Fen.

Burnt Fen was an evil place. It looked like it sounded. The black peat earth was hard work and of course it was our men hired to dig it. They said after dark you got spirits coming out of the earth and it wasn't safe to walk abroad, although my Dadus said that was a load of foolishness. There were gases in the earth that came out when you did the digging.

Maybe that accounts for how the Ghost Pig appeared to us that one black night. We were all pretty spooked, even before then. It's when you're spooked that the Evil Ones know they can come and get you. There is something in your mind that lets them in.

There were fifty or so of us in that camp. It was before the time of the big camp which we joined later – it was only Smiths and I was so little that I can hardly remember it, so I think I was probably only just big enough to join in the work with the other children. All us children, and some of the mothers, was employed at stone picking on this big estate, the same one that the men were digging peat for. Stone picking was filthy work, and poorly paid. We only did it when there was no other work to be had. We would form a line across the bottom of a fallow field, first thing in the morning when the cold still shuddered our bones. As the grey light of dawn revealed the black earth to us, we would move forward, taking care not to break the line, either bending or on our hands and knees. The soil had to be looked at and felt through, so's we could pick out any stones and the field could be dug over without breaking the ploughs or harrows. Any stones we found, we dropped into the cloth bags we had tied round our necks.

It was horrible work, especially when it had been wet. We would move so slowly – you wouldn't believe how long it would take to get across a field. It had to be done with great care for the landowner's man came and inspected the field afterwards and if he bent and picked up so much as a pebble we would none of us get paid until we'd done the field again. I remember pushing my hands into the muddy earth and hating the way it blackened my fingernails. To get them clean again, you had to soak them in frozen stream water until you thought you'd scream with pain. I can remember how it was a relief when you filled the bag round your neck with stones because although it hurt your neck, at least it was an excuse to stand up and walk back to the edge of the field to empty your bag, and that was lovely for your back. You could-n't take too long about it, mind, as the whole line had to stop until you got back to your place. I can remember most is how my knees used to go bright red with the cold. Later, they would crack, and my Dei would have to rub oil in them.

I hated that work, as you can probably tell. We hated the work, and the landowner hated us. I'm not sure what sort of farmer he was as he wasn't a regular sort with crops and cows. We couldn't rightly work out what he grow'd. He was a wealthy man, that much was certain, and it seemed a bit like he was playing at being a farmer as his house was not a low farmhouse but a tall thing with fancy drapings at the windows, and he was always dressed up to the nines himself and riding fine mares, not proper farm horses.

He had a pig, and the pig was his pride and joy. My Dadus was one of the men picked to go and get our wages as he had a way of dealing with *gorjers*. He said this landowner had been quite pleasant one day and taken them outside and shown us his prize sow in a spotless pen. There were ribbons pinned to the gate of the fen. She had won lots of prizes, apparently. She was huge.

But relations between us and the landowner went bad not long after that. The men finished their digging after a week or so and they asked if they could be put on to helping with the stone picking. The quicker all our jobs were finished, the quicker we could move on and get other work. Well, the landowner refused. Women and children got paid less, of course, and it was cheaper for him to have us finish the job than let the men help. This meant we had the choice of stopping on Burnt Fen with the men not getting paid for anything, or moving on and losing what little us children would earn.

After news of this got back, there was some discussion of whether the men sent to talk to the landowner had handled it right. One of the men had the bright idea of sending a couple of children up to the big house, to explain the problem politely. The smallest, sweetest boys were chosen, and dressed up nice, and were sent off with smiles as they looked like little angels.

The landowner set his dogs on them. One of them got bit.

I have never seen such dark looks as there were on the men that night, and the darkest of all was on the face of the man who'd had the idea in the first place.

Well, I don't know all the details, of course, but I suppose what happened was that some of the men decided that the boys being bit on purpose could not go unanswered. So they planned to *drav* the *bawlo* – to poison his prize pig.

Now, there were several reasons why you might poison a pig, which was a serious business and not done often. Mostly it was done not to kill it or anything, but to make it poorly so that it could be bought cheap. Or sometimes it was done so that others could go along and fix it up and get in a farmer's good books. It could only be done by people who knew what they were doing, mind, as the weight of the pig was important when working out what to give it.

A couple of days after the deed was done, some of our men went along to the farm on some pretext or other. They was hoping that the landowner would complain to them how his pig was poorly. Then they would fix the pig up, and we would get right back in the landowner's good books and, as a result, get what was right out of him. So four of our men went off: Caleb Smith and his brother Absalom and two of Caleb's sons.

Maybe they was clumsy in the way they enquired after the pig's health. Anyroad, the landowner didn't beat about the bush. He marched them straight out to the sty. The pig was lying stone dead on its side. Whoever had given it the *drav* had overestimated just how big that sow was, and killed it.

When the landowner had shown them his dead pig, he took a whistle out of his pocket and blew on it. At that, a whole load of *gorjer* men ran out from a barn holding sticks. They beat our men black and blue, beat them into the ground. Caleb Smith came back with a lump on his head the size of a hen's egg and his brother Absalom had his jaw broken. One of the *gorjers* had jumped on his face when he was on the ground. He never spoke proper after that and his food had to be mushed up with a fork. His mouth never worked proper again.

Well, when the men got back from the beating, the women wept and howled, and begged them to leave that place, which they had always said was an evil place and they would now put the say out around our People just how evil it was so none of Us would ever come and dig the landowner's black earth again. But the men had their pride, of course, and did not want to leave without hurting the farmer back. Some were all for going and torching the farmer's barns but he would be expecting that, my Dadus said, and there would be nothing but another beating in it.

Then Caleb said, he had heard one of the men who beat on

them say how the pig was good for nothing and would have to be buried by the duck pond and they were lucky they weren't made to do it with their own bare hands. This set the men thinking. The least we could do, one of them said, was to have that pig. The *gorjers* wouldn't dare use it for anything, not with poison in it. But we knew precisely what it had had and we could still make use of it all right. The least we could do was dig up that pig and roast it fair when the wind would carry the smell of it across the fields to the landowner's house, and he would know we were feasting on his prize animal. We hadn't had any meat inside us for a good long while, that winter, so this revenge would be killing two birds with one stone, as they say. It was a right clever plan.

So, a night or two later, a group went over to the duck pond carrying spades. The pond was a little away from the farm itself and so they hoped would not be guarded, and it wasn't. They searched until they found some freshly turned earth. It was a large patch, a few feet away from the pond. My Dadus was in that group, and I heard him tell Dei when they got back later, that they was just raising their spades, when one of them said he saw the earth move a bit, rise and fall. They were doing the digging by moonlight, of course, so nobody could be sure of anything, but they stopped and had a discussion about whether the pig could still be alive in there. My Dadus said it was just the gases in the earth. But the fella who had seen the rise and fall said no, it wasn't a quick movement, like gas escaping, it was more like something breathing in there. Caleb Smith's eldest son what had been beaten was there with them, and he swore that there was no way the pig was still alive. He had seen it in its pen and it was dead as dead could be.

The more they stood there talking about it, the more they was getting a bit spooked. Then they heard a dog barking in the distance and wondered if maybe it was the landowner come to investigate – and that was a good enough excuse to leave it for the time being.

My Dadus was not in the next night's party on account of having stumbled on the way back and hurt his ankle. So Jabez Smith, Absalom's son, went in his place.

The next night it was black as black but windy so they reckoned that the clouds would clear from the moon by the time they got there. They crept to the same place and found . . . a big hole in the ground. They stood around it for a little while, shaking their heads in bafflement. That pig had been in the ground not the night before, they were sure of it. They had a bit of an argument about whether it was the same place but they were sure it was.

Then, one of them said, a cold feeling came over them all, all of them at once, a feeling of such overwhelming badness that they began to shiver. They all looked around in the dark – and then one of them saw it, a few feet away . . . It was white, just like it had been in life. It's eyes were glowing red. It was breathing through its nostrils and staring at them. It came towards them, just floating over the hole, and they turned and fled.

There was no more argument about whether we stayed in that place after that. The camp was packed up and ready to go before sunrise.

Looking back, now I am grow'd, I do not know if I fully believe this story. For maybe someone else had got there before them and dug up the pig – it was a valuable pig after all. Perhaps some gorjer neighbour who had helped the farmer bury it had decided to go back later and have it for himself. But the men swore they saw the ghost of the pig coming at them, after his revenge for having been poisoned.

Word got about, as it does, and after that, the Ghost Pig became the thing that mothers frightened their children with, across the whole of the Fens. I remember my own mother, when I got lost one day and didn't come back until after dark, taking me by the arm and leading me to the copse nearby. She was shaking with anger, she was that relieved I was back.

'Do you know what's in there?' she said, pointing into the still, dark trees, at the blackness in between. 'Do you know what walks round here?' I shook my head. *'The Ghost Pig!'* she exclaimed. 'And he *eats* children like you what get lost in the woods. Do you understand?'

Maybe it was just a story to make us behave, but my father believed it. He would go quiet when he talked about it.

Looking back now, I think I know what the Ghost Pig was – it wasn't the pig itself, not really. It was evil in the landowner and his friends. It was all the *gorjer* evil in all the *gorjer* world that got together and stamped on Absalom Smith's face when he was beaten and lying on the ground. That was what got the men so spooked. It was the bad things that are waiting for a person when all they are trying to do is a live a life – and it was the badness of having poisoned the pig in the first place. It was sort of like the realness of life that lies in wait for you and jumps out. That is why it was so frightening, for all of us. When you are a Traveller, you are never allowed to forget that whatever you have might be taken away from you at any minute. And all you have to do is one wrong thing – and I'm not saying we never did no wrong things – one wrong thing, and you get punished and punished far worser than the thing you did. That's what it's like being one of us. And the Ghost Pig is always out there, to remind you, in the dark or even in the daytime. Everybody has their own Ghost Pig, in my opinion. It follows you, even when you're not thinking about it. It never goes away.

I am usually good at forgetting. *Mi Deari Duvvel* forbid it should be otherwise. It was because I forgot-to-forget that Mehitable fell from the cart, that day, in the lane in the rain. I learned my lesson, after that. I reckon we all did. As soon as she was well again, I vowed I wasn't going to be tempting the *mullas*, the ghosts, no more, with the Travelling and the remembering and the wanting to live like I once had. We all of us get born into a stone cradle but some of us have the sense to climb out of it.

Mehitable pulled through. We went to Sutton. And I never forgot-to-forget again, not once.

CHAPTER 13

I still had a few mixed feelings about going to the village, mind, for my only experience of houses had been a cottage in a graveyard and a box in a street in Cambridge which came to much the same thing, in my opinion. That was house-dwelling for you, I thought. We took the cart and bender tent and stopped at Mepal, then Elijah and Rose went on foot into Sutton to scout around for somewhere. I was left behind to keep an eye on the children – so we all said to each other – but in actual fact it was because I looked a bit too much like what I was. Rose and Lijah could pass for *gorjers* easy enough.

They came back with the news of having found not one but two little places, right on the outskirts of Sutton. Lijah had taken some dyke digging work for a month and even got a note from the old mush so's the landlord would let us off the down payment. The places were empty and needed a bit of work, but if we didn't mind that we could move in right away.

That's how easy it was to become a family of house-dwellers again.

My place was tiny. It had a little parlour with a kitchen alcove and a bedroom upstairs. After going up and down the stairs a few times, I worked out that if I used the settee for sleeping then I didn't need to go upstairs at all, which was a thing I'd never liked. I would be right next to the door. None of that sweating and trappedness like I had felt in my box room in Paradise Street. Suddenly, it seemed like not-such-a-bad little place. I would be close to the others but still able to come and go as I pleased and keep it as clean as I liked.

After Lijah and Rose had settled me in, they went next door with the children to sort out their place and I sat on the step – my step – with the door open. I looked up at the sky and felt as chuffed as a puppy with its first own bone. My little place – close enough to the others to keep an eye, like, but with my own door handles and cooking pots and feather duster. My own. I wasn't going to be odd-one-out no more – you need other people around you to make you that. From now on, it was going to be just me.

And there was something else which amazed me, 'til I got used to it. For the first time in my life, I had the lektiv. *Helectricity* was the proper word for it, Lijah told me. They'd had it Cambridge before we left there, but it had not come to Paradise Street, nor anywhere near. They put it in the theatres and people would go and see plays not to watch the actors on the stage but to sit and stare at the lights. As a consequence, I had always thought of it as a rich person's thing and could not believe I was going to have it in my own little home.

Lijah stood me in my sitting room and flicked the switch up and down, to show me how to use it. The light came through the wires, he said. After he'd gone, I did the same thing myself, on and off, for a good long while, until the old man over the road came across and said, was I trying to signal that I needed help?

Lijah got himself some steady work, just like he promised. He did the dyke work for a while, and then he went back to being a pack-man. Being on the edge of a village was good for that. He had a shed to keep his stuff in, and a few shops to buy extras, but was near to the paths across the Fens and the outlying farms. The walking everywhere was good for him, I reckon – and he was good at chatting to the farmers' wives what were lonely and didn't get to speak to many people. I think him being a bit older helped, like, as he was a charming old-ish man now which is quite a different prospect to a charming young man. People weren't so wary of him.

After a year or so, he got the wherewithal to go back to dealing with the horses. We got ourselves another Kit. I'm not sure which Kit it would've been by then. Kit the Fourth, probably. He wasn't as nice as the First Kit, what had been my favourite, but he was sweeter than the Third. Lijah would go out with Kit of an evening, pulling the cart, and go and buy a horse off a fella. The deal would take ten minutes, then they would shake hands on it and go and spend the next three hours in the pub. After they had finished celebrating the deal, Lijah would take the horse he had just bought – some old nag, ripe for doing up – and tie it to the back of the cart. Then he would climb up into the cart, pull a blanket over himself and say to Kit, 'Come on, Kit, take us home.'

Kit would plod home in the dark with Lijah sound asleep in back of the cart. When Kit got to our cottages, he would stamp about a bit. As I always slept with the door open and slept lightly, I could easy hear Kit a-stamping and the jangle of the harness what was hanging loose. So I would get up, release Kit from the shafts and take him and the new horse to the little stables Lijah had at the side of his place.

When the horses were settled, I would take a look under the blanket to make sure that Lijah was actually in the cart, then leave him to sleep it off and go back to bed.

Sometimes, as I turned, I would glance up at their cottage. Rose never came down, either to check he was all right or to upbraid him for being drunk. I think she had found a way of letting it not matter no more. They were paying their rent, and the children was fed.

They still had their ups and downs, did Rose and Lijah, but I suppose they must have been getting on a bit better as, to my surprise, I got two more grandchildren out of it. Fenella was born one springtime. Scarlet, the last of my grandchildren, popped out during an April storm which brought down the Elder tree in my back yard but led to an early hot spell.

Oh, we all loved those girls – especially Fenella. She was a fashion-plate, that child. Even when she was little. She could wear a hand-knitted cardy like it was a velvet gown. 'Mami . . .' she would say, sidling up to me when I was stitching a stocking or mending a tear in something. 'Mami, do you have any pearl buttons in your box?'

'You know right well I do, my acorn,' I would say, 'for you've been into it looking, haven't you?' She wouldn't've got away with that with her mother. Her mother would have gone crazed if Fenella had been in *her* sewing box, and well she knew it.

Funnily enough, I wouldn't have been too chuffed if any of the other girls had been into mine, but Fenella had a habit of charming things out of people. Curly hair she had – soft brown curls. The men were going to go doo-lally over her when she was older, everybody said. And they were right.

'It's just, I've lost a button . . .' she would say, looking down at her cardi, a cable-knit I'd done myself, with wooden buttons.

I would see the tail of thread hanging off and think, *lost . . .* Really?

I liked to tease that Little One a bit. 'Well, *biti mouse,* I suppose I could spare just one of my pearl buttons if you was good.'

Her face would be a picture of horror. 'But Mami, then they won't match!'

She was the only child in her village school with pearl buttons on a cable-knit cardi, I'm quite sure of that.

There was a special thing that Fenella and Scarlet both loved in the village, and that was Mayladyin'. We all had our own time of year, I suppose. In January, the boys had Plough Monday with the plough they carried round all decorated, and their lanterns. They got ale and cakes for their trouble. Even the old ladies like me had Goodnin' Day, for widows only, when we got given packets of tea or sugar. I would-n't go round with the other widows as I thought it was undignified, but someone always left tea and sugar on my doorstep anyway. I wasn't too proud to take it in and drink it, I might say. Shortest day of the year, Goodnin' Day. One year, I thought about getting one of the children to write a note on a bit of paper, for me to stick on my door. 'It's nearly Christmas so blow the tea and sugar, how about a bit of brandy and some 'baccy for my pipe?' I never did it as I wasn't sure I could rely upon the villagers to see the humorous side.

The girls had Mayladyin', when they was allowed to dress up dolls and take them door to door, and get pennies for them.

Well, my Fenella, she was determined to have the prettiest doll in the village – dordy, yes, the preparations took weeks. A lace bonnet, she had to have, and little boots made of real leather cut from an old piece her dad had. Nearly ruined my fingers stitching them tiny boots. The evenings she spent round at my place, sorting it out. Scarlet was only just big enough to join in and luckily she was easily pleased with something that was a lot less effort. As long as it was pink, she didn't care.

One Saturday, I was at home. It was the first of May in a couple of days. There came the sound of clogs on my path and I thought, here comes Fenella, after something else for her May Lady. But very quickly I realised it wasn't Fenella's step. Fenella tripped along – skipped everywhere, that child – this step had a drag to it. It was Billy, as we called her. My Mehitable.

Billy was almost a young lady, then. She had stayed short and thin but had straightened out nicely, although she still wore a calliper and had something of a limp. She never had much to say for herself, but would often come round and sit with me, for no reason. She and her mother did not get on, and it seemed to be getting worse rather than better as she came into an age when she might be grow'd.

How bad things were between Rose and her daughter got more obvious when the other two girls came along, for the other two were so much more what daughters are meant to be.

'Mami,' she said, as she stepped through my open door, 'how are you today?'

'I'm all well and good, Billy,' I said, 'I'm just dandy. What brings you here? Aren't you supposed to be cooking food for that donkey?'

Lijah had bought a donkey the week before. It was a mangy old thing with holes in its pelt and half its teeth fall'd out. When I saw it, I asked Lijah if someone had paid him to take it. He said almost. He was going to fix it up and sell it but in the meantime it needed all its food cooking for it, as it couldn't eat a raw carrot or a turnip if its life depended on it.

Rose had gone berserk. 'Don't you think I've got enough to do?' she said.

So Billy got the job of cooking the donkey its food. She got all the jobs that no one else wanted, on account of how there were a lot of jobs she couldn't do with that leg of hers.

Billy's face darkened a little. 'I've got a pig's head and some sour bread boiling out back.'

'I was wondering what that stink was,' I said, as we moved toward the kitchen alcove bit and seated ourselves at the little table.

'Everyone else has gone out and left me to it. It'll need boiling more than an hour.'

'Don't you let it dry out or your mother will go something mental.'

'Don't I know it . . .'

'*Mehitable* . . .' She knew the warning tone in my voice. It doesn't do to let children speak ill of their parents, even when they're absolutely right.

She looked down at the tablecloth and plucked at it with one hand. There was something to be got-to-the-bottom-of here, I saw.

'If you're after getting away from the stink, then you've not gone very far, have you?'

'I've something to ask you, Mami.'

'Go on,' I said. I rose from my seat and took a step to the cupboard. I had some oaty biscuits in a tin and no grandchild of mine ever visited my house and went away without a little something in their stomach.

I put the tin on the table. 'Do you want some milk to go with?'

'No thanks, Mami.'

'Have you had your milk today?' Billy hated milk. You had to squeeze it down her.

'Mum made me, at breakfast.'

'Well quite right, too. Have you washed your hands lately?'

'Just before I came over.'

'So what is it you're after, *chai*?' I took an oaty biscuit myself. They have to be cooked in ovens, them biscuits, so I'd never had them as a child. I had a fierce liking for them, as a result and cooked them several times a week. I was mad about them.

Billy reached into her pocket and brought out a doll. It was a small thing but nicely turned out with a little skirt and bodice made of blue cotton. I recognised an old blouse of Rose's. Billy had snipped up some brown wool for hair and put it into long bunches and tied it with thread.

'I don't know what to do for shoes,' she said. 'Fenella's doing boots, so I can't do those. I'd like shiny black shoes but she's too small for anything stiff. Have you got a piece of anything that will do it?'

I took the doll and looked at it. A feeling of sadness came over me, like a cool wind blowing. I said quietly, 'Does your mother know about this?'

Her face darkened again. She took the doll back and held it in her lap. 'Well, Mami, what do *you* think . . .' she mumbled.

'*Mehitable* . . .'

She looked up sharply. 'She'll let me go if you say so. Oh please, Mami. Tell her it would be a good idea. I could keep an eye on Scarlet.'

I stared at her. I had a hollow feeling inside, a caving in, for all at once it had come to me how hard her life still was. Rose had never let Billy go Mayladyin', ever. She said it wasn't right for a child with a calliper to go dragging it around the village – it looked too much like begging. I'd agreed with her at the time and never thought more of it. And then Fenella comes along and she's such a pretty, sunny girl. And when she's big enough she rushes home from school one day all excited because she's going a Mayladyin' for the first time with her friends . . . and it never occurs to any of us to say no to Fenella. For Fenella is a proud, cheerful child, and Mayladyin' doesn't look like begging when she does it – no, it looks like a game that gets her a few pennies, that's all.

So off Fenella and Scarlet go, each year, and it never occurs to nobody that Billy might be sitting there and dying to go herself. Why did she never speak up before?

'Billy,' I said gently. 'Don't you think you're a bit old for all that? Mayladyin's for little girls. You're a young lady, you know. Why, I can't believe how fast you've grow'd.'

She looked at me, crestfallen. I hated to be the one to disappoint her but I knew if I didn't, then her mother would be a lot more blunt about it.

'Come on, now,' I said. 'What are you? Fourteen? Fifteen? Most girls your age were wed with babbies when I was young.'

'I'm thirteen, Mami.'

'Oh well, even so . . .' I pushed the biscuit tin towards her. 'Here, take another to have on the way home.'

She shook her head, then stood. She looked at the little doll, then let it drop on to my kitchen table. 'You have it, Mami. Maybe you can fix it up as a present for Scarlet some time. She hasn't seen it yet. You could make it look nice.'

I wanted to say, *it won't always be this bad, you know, Billy. Some day, you might have a real piece of luck and then you won't always feel like the nice things in life happen to other people.* I couldn't say that, of course, as I didn't know if it were true.

At the door, she turned. 'Mum wouldn't have let me anyway, would she?' she said, and the bitterness in her voice was as clear as church bells ringing.

I shook my head.

She went back to the pig's head that was stinking out the back yard.

Not long after that, Mehitable took my advice and started to become a young lady. That didn't improve relations with her mother any. Rose had a bit of difficulty in recognising that her first three were getting grown up, I reckon. Daniel left school and started his apprenticeship. Mehitable cut her hair short and made herself blouses on her mother's sewing machine – she was all for getting herself a position as a maid in a big house, if she could find anyone who would take her with that leg of hers. Bartholomew was still at school but played truant like the devil and took beer with his breakfast, just like his dad. You didn't need to look at the palm of his hand to see which way he was going. Barty-boy, my Barty-boy, what can I say of him? What he was like as a boy is all wiped out by what came later. Broke his mother's heart.

Fenella grew into a beauty. The boys would fight each other to carry her things for her. She was a fashion-plate.

Scarlet, tough as old boots. My baby.

I still liked my little place. I had got it just how I wanted. I didn't miss being on the road at all, although I never closed my front door unless it was really freezing. What I loved most was waking in the night and having that strange moment you have when you wake unexpectedly, the odd not-knowingness of where you are – or even who you are. Then it comes to you. *My name is Clementina Lee, widow, and I am living in a little house on the edge of a village called Sutton-in-the-Isle, west of Ely.* And I would think, *the strangeness of ending up here. During all the things that were happening to me in all the years previous. Here was waiting for me, all along.*

I would shift in my bed, turn my head and open my eyes, gazing through my open door from where I lay, at the whole expanse of *here* out there. The dark outside, the whole of the Fens stretching, lying flat and quiet . . . *This is what it must be like to be the King of Russia*, I sometimes thought, *as if the world was only made for you to inhabit it, and all the other people in it are different parts of you.* If it was a clear night, I could lie and watch the stars.

Sometimes I would just drift off back to sleep, all calm and quiet, thinking about the stars. And sometimes I would rise from my bed and pull on my boots and shawl and go outside. Some nights I would sit on my doorstep and smoke a pipe, but on others I would go for a little walk in the darkness, just a little wander around, not because I needed to particularly but because it was right nice to do it, maybe to pretend I was the King of Russia, or maybe for no reason at all.

It was on one of those nights, on one of my walks, that I had a strange encounter with my son. I had woken before dawn, as usual. It was pitch black outside – it must've been a cloudy night for it was completely starless and I could hardly see a thing. Nights like that were good. You felt the ground beneath your feet more better when it was all you had to go on.

I stood on my step for a minute, closed my eyes and breathed in deep, as I liked to do. Glory be to *Mi Duvvel*, I thought. The air feels good inside your lungs when it isn't shared with *gorjers*.

Having the air to myself. That was why I went out at night.

I turned up the lane, to do my usual circuit of the village. There was something right pleasant about going round the houses when all else was asleep. Sometimes there'd be a workman out and about and it always annoyed me terrible if I bumped into one of them – like they was interfering with me. I would never greet them, and I daresay word had got round the village that I was a queer old boot, which suited me just fine. It kept fools away and was good for business.

What I liked most was how even though the sky seemed pitch dark, the shapes of the trees would be even darker against it. It reminded me there were lots of different sorts of darkness in the world and that was a good thing. It meant that however much you knew, there was always something else beyond – and if there isn't anything beyond, then what would be the point?

Within a few paces, I would pass Lijah's cottage, and I always glanced that way, of course. That night, before I even neared it, I knew my Lijah was up and about. I could see the glow of a little flame. I spotted it as I came down my step. He was sitting on his doorstep, lighting his pipe.

The flame went out – if I'd walked by a minute later I wouldn't have known he was there.

The shape of him became him as I got close.

I didn't speak or anything. I just came and squatted down next to him, and wished I had my pipe with me too.

There was a long silence between us, while we both looked out at the dark.

'Thing is,' he said after a while. 'I haven't forgotten how she was.'

I said nothing.

'Might be a bit easier if I did, like.'

There was another long silence.

'Like when we went to the fair, just after we was wed. We walked around together, and I could see the other fellas looking at her, and then looking at me, for none of them had her on their arm, but I did.'

A wave of honesty came over me, and I wanted to cry out, but it's never been right for you, Lijah. What did you have to go off and marry a *gorjer* girl for? *When gorjers' merripen and Romani chals' merripen ven kitanee, kerk kosto merripen see*, you should know that. Why didn't you stick with your own kind, for heaven's sake?

And you might not have your five fine grandchildren then, missus. What of that? Mrs Pure Adolphus Lee, Clementina Smith as was, Little Lemmy – let's wish the done undone, shall we? Let's wish you hadn't taken that journey in the mud – you wouldn't even have your Lijah then.

Fortunately, I am quite good at ignoring the voices in my head when they talk inconvenient.

It didn't matter what the truth of it was, really, for I knew I could never say anything to him against his Rosie. He had fallen for her, good and proper, all those years ago back on the farm, and whatever his faults had been as a husband I was certain no other girl had turned his head since. She was his Rosie, pure and simple, and it wasn't my place to interfere. All I could do was keep my mouth shut.

'And there was one time when she was holding Dan and talking to him soft, when he was little, and he was holding on to her hair with his fists. She looked right fine that day.'

He would never have spoken like this in the daylight. It was like he was saying it to the darkness, like I wasn't there at all.

He tapped his pipe against the step. 'She don't like me, Dei. She used to, but she don't any more. Hasn't done for years.'

I suppose that was the moment I could have said something, but

I was that worried of saying the wrong thing that I didn't speak at all.

'This 'baccy's a bit damp,' he said. He had pushed it down with his finger and was trying to relight it. I rose from the step.

The warning signs were there, looking back.

I can remember, in East Cambridge, sitting of an evening, on one of the few evenings when Lijah chose to grace us with his presence. He would bring home news-sheets, sometimes, that he had lifted from somewhere, and he would give them to Rose and say, 'Go on, Rosie, read to us. Read to us about the S'ara desert.' I do believe he would have gone there himself to see what it was all about if he knew where it was.

And then there was that time me and him took little Scarlet out blackberry picking.

It was right warm that day. I can't remember what the others were up to but it was just the three of us. We were standing next to the hedgerow at the far end of the lane, just where it petered out into a fallow field. It was a hot day. I was gathering the berries from the top of the bush and Lijah was helping Scarlet collect them from the bottom branches, the ones she could reach.

Lijah had his favourite stick, the old, gnarled one that was worn dark and smooth. He was holding back the lower branches so that Scarlet could reach some of the blackberries inside the bush without pricking her fat little arms. He was being right good about it, as he would have done with any of the girls (not the boys, mind you) for he was pretending how he hadn't spotted the best clusters.

I was having to lean over them to pick mine, and was feeling a little cross on account of how it was taking a long time and I had jobs to do back home.

'Have a look in there, petal,' Lijah said to Scarlet. 'I can't see anything. I don't think there is anything in there.'

Scarlet bent and peered into the bush, then cried gleefully, 'Yes, there is, Dad! I can see them!'

'No!' he replied, in mock astonishment. 'There's no blackberries in there . . . never in a million years.'

Scarlet reached in and pulled out a few blackberries, already squashy in her hot little fist and not much use for anything but jam, they were that mashed. She held them up to me, with a look of triumph. 'Look what Dad and I have founded, Mami!'

She was that proud of herself. 'Well done, Scarlet. That's wonderful, that is,' I said. 'Now you put them in this tin here and I think we'd best be off home.'

On the way back they walked ahead a little, holding hands. I trailed behind with the half-full tin. The sun was beating down that day and I had on my dress that was a bit tight around the arms and on the itchy side.

I heard Scarlet say to Lijah, 'Dad, where did you get that stick from?'

'Ah,' he said, and I did not need to see his face to know the expression on it, 'well you might ask . . .'

Behind them, I rolled my eyes.

'This stick, this here stick? I got this stick in the S'ara Desert!'

Scarlet's voice was full of wonder. 'Did you really, Dad? When was that, Dad?'

'Lijah . . .' I muttered from behind, but he took no notice of me.

'Why, Little One, that was when I went off to war, before you was born. I was off a-fighting against the Boers what was trying to steal Africa from us . . .'

The signs were there. I should've known what was coming.

We had been living in the village for some years then and was well established, if you know what I mean. What I mean is, I don't think there was anyone who took against us, in particular, and I had got quite friendly with some of the other Old Folks. There were a few

Old Folks lived in our row as there was several little places like mine too small for anything but widows or widowers. At the far end of the row was Mrs Canning, quite a posh *rawnie* fallen on hard times. Her father had owned a jeweller's shop, she told me once. She didn't have any side to her, though, considering she was used to being quite high up in life. She was just a poor old *pivli rawnie* like the rest of us now.

She and me shared a smoke sometimes, sitting on her step if the weather was fine. She was much more up to date with what was going on in the world than me, was Edie Canning. She read the local paper, every week.

Sometimes I would say to her, 'So, what's up with the world, then?' and she would tell me how they were going to stop opening the library in Ely on Saturday afternoons and it was a disgrace as that was the only time the working men could get there and improve themselves. Last Thursday, Robert Cooter from Windmill Lane had chased his wife down the street with a rolling pin. Now there was a man who needed improving.

It was Edie Canning told me about the *Bell-jums*. They were a brave people, she said, but extremely small. She had met one, once. They wore tall hats to try and make themselves look bigger but not so's it would fool you. They ate nothing but bread and ham.

The Germans, they was different, mind. They were big fellas, and they ate twice as much as the Bell-jums and they had a hundred different sorts of cheeses. They were very cruel to their animals. When a horse got lame, they would beat it to death and then leave it to rot by the side of the road. Edie Canning's nephew had been to Germany and seen it happening with his own eyes.

I was shocked when she told me that. I thought the Germans probably had what was coming to them, if that's the sort of folk they were.

*

It seemed to me that all my life I had been able to not-think about the world. Lijah said to me once, 'Have you never wanted to go and see the sights of London, Dei?' and I said, 'What for? I've been to Thetford.' The Fens were world enough for me. They stretched as far as the eye could see, which is quite far enough to my way of thinking.

What I didn't realise was that if you don't go out and visit the world, it doesn't matter. Sooner or later, the world comes to visit you.

When the War started, a lot of the local lads rushed off, of course – the young ones, the ones who couldn't wait to get out of the village. But a fair few of the older men held back. The men who had children knew what leaving those children might mean. The high-ups knew it too. When they had killed off the first lot of volunteers, they brought in the Bachelor Bill, as it was called, and that used up the rest of the unmarried ones pretty sharpish, so it was only a matter of time before they started on the husbands.

I would like to tell you that it was then that my Lijah got forced into it, against his better judgement – but you'll have worked out by now that *better* and *judgement* were words that were not often joined together when Lijah was around.

No, Lijah went all of his own accord. He told me later that he volunteered because he thought that if he waited any longer then the army would fill up and they wouldn't let him in.

I was in their kitchen when he came back, that day. He hadn't told nobody what he was planning, of course.

Rose and I were standing by the range. She had just said, 'This coal we're using is brittle. I don't think it is Northamptonshire coal like the fella said.'

I was about to reply, when Lijah appeared at the back door. He stood there, framed in the light. In his hands, he was holding a piece of paper. He held it out for us to see, proudly, like it was a rabbit he'd just caught, or a bouquet of roses. I couldn't read what was written on the paper but I could see his mark at the bottom.

Rose took a step towards him.

'What is it?' I asked her, although I had a sinking feeling I could guess.

'Oh Elijah . . .' she said despairingly. 'Could you not have talked this through with your own wife first?'

Elijah frowned. 'They're paying a shilling a day,' he said. 'You get bread and kippers for breakfast when you're training. Square-bashing, they call it.'

'You don't like kippers,' I said.

Then, he glanced over his shoulder, and tossed his head. Side-stepping neatly, already the military man, he moved to make space in the doorway.

Something terrible happened. Into the space Lijah had left, stepped Daniel. And he was holding the same piece of paper as his father.

Rose gave a small cry, then clapped both hands to her mouth. I thought she might collapse and was ready for it. Instead, she just looked from one of them to the other, and her gaze burned.

Daniel realised straight up he should not do the proud bit and avoided her gaze. He glanced at his Dad, then down at the step. 'Mum, don't take on . . .' he said. I think it was the only time I ever heard him come close to arguing with her.

Lijah was looking deflated now. 'Oh don't make such a fuss, woman,' he growled at Rose, although she had not spoken another word. 'Everyone's at it. We thought you'd be proud of us.'

We? I knew the real source of Rose's anger. If Lijah wanted to go and get himself killed in Foreign Lands that was one thing – but he was taking her best son with him. Daniel was nineteen years old and had never been away from his mother. He was apprenticed to a sign-writer in Haddenham but still came home every night. He had turned down a chance to be a bricklayer in Whittlesey because it would have meant moving away from home.

'It won't be that bad,' muttered Lijah. 'Crikey the trouble we get in round here, it'll be a nice rest, won't it, Dan?' He nudged his son with his elbow.

He looked at me then, and grinned, expecting me to appreciate his levity. 'I think you had better go off somewhere for a bit, the both of you,' I said quietly.

Lijah glanced at me, a little surprised, for I hadn't taken him to task on anything he'd done for a while. Daniel turned immediately and went back down the path. After a moment, Lijah followed his son.

When they had gone, Rose sat on an upright chair and took her hanky from her pocket. She did not cry, though her face was twisted. 'Oh Clementina,' she said, 'what are we going to do?'

'I don't know,' I said and for once, I didn't.

PART 4

1914–1929

Rose

CHAPTER 14

There was before the War, and there was after. It was like a door suddenly appeared in all our lives. You could go through it both ways, if you tried hard enough. If you really concentrated, you could think back to how it was before. The hardships you'd had seemed like adventures, looking back – rough, but liveable through. No one died, back then.

They did, of course. People died all the time. It just didn't feel like it, before.

Then there was after. After was a different land. So many men gone, just disappeared, and nobody supposed to scream that no, they weren't proud their best boy had vanished into thin air because they'd give up honour and all place in society to have him back, even if it was just a body to bury.

I went to church every Sunday when the War was on. I'd never been much of a churchgoer before, but during the War the whole village seemed to go. I suppose we all needed it in a way we hadn't before. Some of us might have gone for the right reasons, to pray for king and country and for the victory of our noble cause – but I reckon most people went for the same reason I did: to make their bargain with God. Send him back to me, just send him back, and I will do *this* or *this* or *this*. There wasn't a thing we wouldn't have offered.

Plenty of the people who went already knew their prayers would not be answered. I remember one Sunday, about a year before it ended. The church full, as usual. Clementina had come with me, and the girls. We were late, again as usual, and sat near the back.

The very front pew belonged to the Demoine family, who were the nearest we had to lords of the manor as they owned Middleton House a few miles out of the village. Sir James and Lady Demoine had been blessed with but one child, Charles, twenty-two years old when he was killed. He received the Military Cross posthumously, we later heard, after leading an attack on a German tank battalion.

This particular Sunday, Sir James and his wife were there, sat at the front as was their due, all alone in the family pew – childless now. They had had their son late and were getting on in years. It crossed my mind to wonder what would happen to the Demoine name and Middleton House when they passed on. Perhaps it would all end with them. It was not long after their boy had been killed, so I imagine there were quite a few people in church that day who were thinking the same as me. I wondered if the Demoines were aware of us staring at their backs and whether they were grateful for or hated our pity.

It was during the sermon. The vicar was saying something about Jesus' noble sacrifice on the cross. He hadn't even mentioned the War yet. Suddenly, in full view of everybody, Lady Demoine got to her feet. She raised her hand and pointed at the vicar and in a trembling voice, she shouted, 'Liar! Liar!' The words rang out, as clear as anything, echoing around the church, up to the rafters.

I was on the end of our pew, so could see her quite clearly. She was shaking from head to foot – I could see it in the arm that was pointing. I could not see her face but I could hear the hatred in her voice.

Nobody knew what to do. We all just sat there, even her husband who was gazing up at her. He couldn't have looked more shocked if the statue of the Virgin Mary in the alcove next to them had spoken.

Lady Demoine was breathing in great, heaving breaths. Her shoulders went up and down with the effort and the arm sank a little. Then she seemed to recover her strength.

'Liar! Liar!' she repeated, with an amazing amount of venom, still pointing at the vicar.

Her husband came to his senses at last, got to his feet and ushered his wife out of the pew. She made it to the end before she collapsed, weeping hysterically in great, howling cries. Her knees were gone and her husband had to hold her up and half drag her down the aisle. Not a soul moved to help him. They were the only people of quality in the whole church and it wouldn't have been seemly for anyone else to lay hands on her. There was nothing we could do except stare straight ahead.

Normally, if a person of such standing had made an exhibit of themselves in that way, it would have been the talk of the village for weeks, but none of us mentioned it as we filed out at the end of the service. I saw a couple of men shake their heads in bafflement but the women knew – they knew why the vicar's fine words had raged her so, and why she'd shouted *liar*. What woman hasn't wanted to do that at the whole world at least once in her life?

*

We had been living in the village nearly fifteen years by then. Fifteen years. When you stay in one place, time goes more quickly, for some reason. Well, the days don't go quickly – they drag and drag – but the years? They fly past.

There comes a point when you stop trying to fill the holes in your life. What a great relief that is.

Our cottage was right on the edge of the village, with a big vegetable patch at the back that looked out over the Fens; just empty farmland, stretching away from us, like a great ocean. Every afternoon, you could watch the slant of the sun.

It was right for us – a decent roof over our heads but a little bit separate from the *gorjers* in the rest of the village. I had come to feel our differentness, as a family, and to be happy that we weren't slap bang in the middle of the village with everybody watching and judging us the whole time the way it had been when we lived in East Cambridge. We had been judged on Stourbridge Common, too, mind you. The judging never stops when you're neither one thing nor another – I had learned that by then. In East Cambridge my kids got picked on for being *gipsies* and on the road they got picked on for being *half 'n' halfs*. So from now on I wasn't making any allowances for anybody, any more. We was us, and anyone who didn't like it could *ife*.

The cottage was pretty small – especially once we had five children in it. Clementina had her own little place in a neighbouring row of one-up, one-downs. I think they had been almshouses, once. Her vegetable patch was on a slight rise, so she had a better view than us. We had a ditch at the back and a damp problem in the kitchen. Right opposite us was the Forage Works and when they opened the chaff cylinders a cloud of foul vapours would drift across the street. But in comparison with living cheek-by-jowl with Clementina, it was sheer heaven.

When Scarlet was old enough to go to school, I started taking in more sewing. I was fast and brought in a good little bit – and for the first time in my life I didn't have to go pleading to Elijah to keep food in the cupboards. Elijah was still drinking sometimes and the horse business went up and down but between the two of us, we managed. We was settled.

I'm not saying we were well off or anything, or that I didn't sometimes look at Elijah and curse the day he'd smiled up at me from the step of his *vardo*. Things always went a bit bad for us after each child was born, for some reason. He always wanted to disappear a bit then and of course that was the time I most objected to it.

We had a rum patch not long after Scarlet was born, I remember. She came out a wee bit early and needed a lot of feeding up. Elijah hadn't done a deal on a horse for a while and the hawking was not so good, so he'd taken on a bit of rod peeling. Tuppence ha'penny a bundle, he got. He hated piece work and always came home in a foul temper saying they were trying to cheat him somehow or other. Sometimes, when he'd been paid, he took what little he'd earned and went straight down The Toll House. They had regular dice games at The Toll House, and there wasn't a woman in Sutton unprepared to swallow those dice whole if she got the chance.

They always started the same, our arguments. He would come in looking all sheepish and boyish, and try to be affectionate – 'Ah, my Rosie . . .' That's how I knew for sure he was drunk. Then, when I pushed him off, or asked him where his earnings was, he would start off with a bit of humour. 'Oh, I've not *lost* the money, Rosie. I've just lent it to him 'til we play again!'

Ta-da!

I didn't respond to the humour any more than I did the affection. It was all as thin as the ice on a puddle.

'You're a drunken fool, Elijah Smith, and when your children want feeding tomorrow are you going to make jokes to them, then?'

We weren't exactly starving at that time, not like we'd been in Cambridge, but I liked to remind him we once had been and that it was his fault. That was when it would turn nasty.

'Is it any wonder I'm off down the pub when all I get here is . . .' On and on.

When you've been married more than a decade, then all arguments are the same arguments, really. The exact wording changes now and then, that's all.

It always ended the same way, with me going upstairs for the spare blanket and dumping it on the settee.

Scarlet woke me at dawn, that particular day, wanting a feed. When I'd sorted her out, I put her on my shoulder and took her downstairs. Elijah was out flat. I pulled the blanket off him and told him in no uncertain terms to take himself upstairs before the children got down. Then I set to, lighting the fires and getting breakfast ready.

They all pounded down: Daniel all excited like he was each morning. He was fourteen and would be finishing school soon and starting his apprenticeship. He couldn't wait. Mehitable – well, she was always surly of a morning. She wanted to finish school too but I wouldn't let her just yet. Fenella had only just started and I would need Mehitable to take her and look after her a bit. Bartholomew was eight and would be going to school for a while yet but I didn't trust him to keep an eye on his little sister for more than a minute.

There was the clamour and clatter of feeding them all and shouting at them to get their coats and shoes on, then they were gone.

Elijah didn't come down all morning. I went and did my shopping with Scarlet and came back and there was still no sign of him. Mid-afternoon, Scarlet was in her pram in the garden and I was shaking a mat out over the ditch at the back, when I looked up and saw him at our bedroom window, staring down at me. I knew that sullen stare. I knew what it meant, right enough.

I went straight to our little stable. Kit had his head bent in his straw. He raised and shook it. 'Never you mind, Kit,' I said to him, as I lifted his harness down from the wall.

Elijah was downstairs by the time I got back to the house. His pack was all bundled up and he was pulling on his boots.

Do we really have to go through all this? I thought wearily.

'You're not going nowhere,' I said to him, arms folded. 'Not on that horse, anyway.'

'I'll walk, then!' he spat at me, without looking up from where he was tying his laces.

'Stagger, more like,' I spat back as I stepped past him into the house.

'You'll be sorry,' he said, as he rose and hefted his pack on to his back, 'when you get word I've found myself a nice little fancy piece and am comfy settled down in the Garden of Eden! You'll be sorry, then!'

That got my attention all right. But by the time I'd turned, he'd strode off down the path.

When she first moved into her cottage, Clementina used a brick to prop open her door. She said she couldn't sleep otherwise. Recently, she had acquired a conch shell, a huge, gleaming thing it was. Lijah must have got it for her somewhere, when he was out hawking. I always think it's a bit strange how those things are supposed to be natural. The pink bit inside looks all wrong. For some reason, I had taken an instant dislike to this particular conch shell and it always annoyed me.

As I stepped up her path that afternoon, I glanced down at the conch shell, and felt cross, about everything in my life, really – her included. After all these years I was used to her peculiarities and sometimes we got along all right for months, before something made me suddenly annoyed with her again.

She was sitting in her little kitchen, next to her table, on an upright chair. As I entered, she looked up without surprise.

'What do you want?' Only Clementina could make such a simple question sound so scornful.

I wasn't in the mood to beat about the bush.

'He's gone,' I said, and sat down on the other chair, even though she had not invited me to.

She drew on her little clay pipe and puffed out extravagantly. She knew I hated smoking and did not allow it in my own home.

'He's always going,' she said lightly.

'No,' I said firmly, bending forward to lean weight on my words. 'He's *gone*.'

She paused in the act of raising the pipe again and looked at me keenly. I knew she was working out how serious it was. She frowned slightly. There was a smoke-filled silence that hung in the air. I had to make her understand.

'He's gone,' I repeated, 'and he isn't coming back. I hid Kit's harness and he just put his boots on and said I could do what I liked, he'd *walk* to Cambridge if he had to.'

When I mentioned Cambridge, she knew how serious it was. If he got to East Cambridge, back to his old pals there and his old drinking habits, she knew that would be it. We'd never see him again.

Her gaze didn't leave my face for a second. 'What time did he go?'

'About an hour ago. Scarlet was screaming to be fed. She's asleep now. I had to put some potatoes on to boil before I came over. The others will be back soon.'

'What are you cooking with the potatoes?'

'Mrs Piggot gave me some goose fat and I've a bit of cured ham and an onion. Why?'

'Go and fry the onion. He won't be back before tea but you'd better save him some.'

I rose, mightily annoyed. Was that the best she could do? She put one finger in her mouth, then damped down the pipe with it, before laying it carefully on the table between us. Then she folded her hands in her lap. She looked down at them, composing herself, then looked back up at me, as if surprised I hadn't gone yet.

'Go on,' she said.

At the door, I turned.

She lifted her chin, jutting it in the direction of the path behind me. 'Go on,' she said softly. 'Go home to that babby and make the tea. I'll get him back.'

She looked down at her lap again, and closed her eyes.

I've never been a superstitious person, never. I'm not even that religious, although my mother was, and drilled it into me. Getting married in a church was more to do with wanting it to be proper in my head than doing it in the sight of God. The War was not yet upon us, at that time, and I hadn't been to church in years.

I believe there is a God, of course, and I've prayed often enough, in the bad times. But He and I don't really have a close relationship, on account of how I always feel I am complaining about my lot and asking Him what I've done to deserve Elijah. I think God probably has better things to do than concern Himself with me.

My mother believed in God, and tea-leaves, and in not walking under ladders, as if it was all one and the same.

I know what people say about Travelling folk, but I also know that Travelling folk have to make a living just like anybody else and it does them no harm whatsoever to let people believe they have special powers. I always thought there was something a bit funny about Clementina but she had never tried to show off, and I knew when she did fortunes in East Cambridge it was just to earn a bob. So I've no real reason to think she did anything special that day. I'm just saying what happened.

Elijah was home before nightfall, exhausted. There was a strange unease about him. He wouldn't at me look me properly. I thought his hangover had kicked in good and proper and sent him up to bed. I had saved him some tea, just like Clementina told me to, but he said he didn't want anything.

Once the children were asleep, I went in to him to check he was all right, expecting to find him lying spread-eagled on his back, fully clothed and snoring.

Instead, he had undressed himself and got into bed, but was sitting up leaning against the headboard, fully awake and staring straight ahead of him.

I had Scarlet on my shoulder. She was fretful that evening. She was still too little to sleep in the big bed with her sisters and was in a Moses basket Elijah had weaved which sat on top of the dresser in our room. I put her down into it, but she kicked her covers off and began to cry in that funny, sneezy little way she had.

'Can I look at her?' asked Elijah.

I turned to him, surprised. He had never taken much interest in any of the children when they were tiny. He liked them more when they could do things.

I lifted Scarlet out of the Moses basket and carried her over to him. He raised his legs so that I could lay her on them, with her head supported on his knees and her little swaddled feet pointing down. I sat on the edge of the bed so I could look at him looking at her.

Her woollen bonnet had fallen back as I laid her down. He stared at her, then said. 'What's wrong with the skin on her head. Why's it all flaky?'

'It's cradle-cap,' I said. 'None of the others had it so I don't know why she has. She'll grow out of it. Your mum has given me some oil to put on it at night.'

At the mention of his mother, he looked up sharply and said, 'When did she do that?'

'Last week.'

He looked down again at the baby. 'She's got a nose like yours, but eyes like mine,' he said thoughtfully.

You've actually noticed something about your new baby, I thought. I wanted to say it out loud but knew he would thrust her back at me if I did. I didn't want to break the spell.

A wave of tiredness came over me. I had been on my feet all day. It's always a mistake to sit down at the end of the day. You never want to get up.

'I've got to finish downstairs before I can come up,' I said. 'Do you want to keep her? I'll be done that much quicker.'

He didn't look up from his examination of his new daughter. 'Aye. All right.'

I didn't question him that night. I could tell it wasn't right. But in the morning when the children had all piled off to school, he didn't pull his boots on and leave the house as I expected him to, but sat in his armchair, sipping his tea. I went upstairs to feed Scarlet and change her, then took her out to the yard and put her in the pram, with the cat-net over her, so she could have a good bawl and get some fresh air in her lungs. Then I went back inside.

Elijah was still sitting in his armchair. I went over and took his empty mug from him, then, with this new quietness of his, felt bold enough to ask, 'What happened, Elijah?'

He didn't look at me, just stroked his chin. 'I was walking down the lane. I was in open country, just striding along like.' He paused. 'My feet went.'

'What do you mean?'

'What do you think I mean?' he snapped, a little of the old Elijah returning. 'I mean what I say. My legs went. I fell down.'

I'm not surprised with what you'd drunk, I thought to myself.

'I lay there, then started back. Took me hours. I couldn't walk until I got . . .' He stopped there and tried a half-smile but it wasn't at all convincing. Whatever it had been, it had frightened him half to death.

I thought of him crawling back to Sutton on his hands and knees. I confess the thought gave me no little pleasure.

He went out later, and I knew he'd gone to see his mother.

Like I said, I'm not a superstitious person by nature. But from that time, I felt a bit more kindly towards Clementina. I don't know whether she got Elijah back for us or not, but I knew for certain she had tried to, and I knew that she would do it again if needs be. It was like when she'd helped deliver my two last babies. I never doubted when she pulled those babies out, that she was fighting to bring them out safe and sound.

Her conch shell still annoyed me, mind you. I still felt cross every time I looked at it.

From then on, Elijah seemed a bit more happy in himself. After that night when he had so nearly left us for good, then come back and sat in bed and stared at his new baby girl – well, things changed for Elijah after that, I think. It was like he had made his mind up about something, in that bit of time he spent staring at Scarlet. I think when he sat in bed and looked at her, he was realising that if he'd disppeared off to Cambridge like he was intending, he might never have seen her again, might never have even looked properly at her in his whole life. And even a man like Elijah knew the wrongness of that. Something raw happened to him, then. Scarlet was his kitten, after that, his little mouse, his acorn. There wasn't a word for *little* or *precious* that he didn't lavish on that child.

He was soft on all the girls, even Mehitable. Bit tougher on the boys, mind. Overstepped the mark once or twice with them.

For a long time, I thought I was just no good with girls. Daniel was so easy, and Bartholomew was a little terror but of course he worshipped the ground his big brother walked on, so they were off together all the time. Mehitable was the one who clung to me, and the one I couldn't deal with. Other women said to me, a mother always loves the boys best, so I just thought, well, maybe that's it. Maybe I wasn't meant to have a daughter.

Then along came Fenella and Scarlet, and I didn't have any problem with them, and I loved them with a lightness I didn't know existed. I remember how I would plait Fenella's hair when she was little – she had such beautiful hair – it was a pleasure to dress it up. And I would sing to her while I did it, and think, I can't wait until this one's grown up so we can talk about things and I can lend her my best coat with the collar and show her how to do her powder and hitch a stocking without tearing it. All those things I had never shared with my own mother, and I was going to make up for that with Fenella. Peculiar, in a way – she was such a lovely little girl, and yet I couldn't wait for her to be a grown woman.

And it was then that things between me and Mehitable really went downhill, for I realised it wasn't that I couldn't love a daughter. I just couldn't love *her*.

If I'd been that bad a mother to her, then someone would've spoke to me about it, wouldn't they? Clementina or Elijah or even Dan – one of them would have said, *aren't you a bit hard on our Billy?*

There was one day: I think I was pregnant with Fenella at the time, so Mehitable must have been about seven or eight. She wasn't at school that day. She had had a stomach-ache in the morning. Well, of course, as soon as the boys had gone off, her stomach-ache seemed to get better right away, so I said to her, 'Don't think you're lounging around here all day while I work my fingers off,' and gave her a list of chores.

Elijah rose late – he'd had a few the night before. He ate breakfast quickly as he said he had to get all the way over to Horseley Fen and go and see a farmer about a pony. I was complaining to him about Mehitable pretending to be poorly, just to get off school, and how I was going to give her what for if she didn't help me that day. He went a bit quiet.

I left him to finish his mug of tea and took a load of laundry out to the line. I had washed it the previous afternoon but then rain had swept in across field and I hadn't been able to dry it. It had sat wet all night long and needed putting out as soon as possible.

It was a cold morning, still, with damp in the air but a glimmer of pale sun coming through and I thought, as I pegged my laundry out, that if the rain would just hold off 'til lunchtime I'd be all right.

I went back inside and cleared the breakfast things. Mehitable was clunking around upstairs.

I was just in the hallway, dusting in the cold light, when Elijah came through from the kitchen. He walked past me, opened the front door and put his pack down on the step. He walked past me again to get something from the back. While he was gone, Mehitable came down and limped over to the shoe-box under the stairs. She pulled out the brown lace-ups she had just inherited from Dan, sat down on the step and began to pull them on.

'Where do you think you're going?' I asked her. She hadn't even started her chores.

She looked up at me, in that half sly, half scared way she had, her small, dark eyes giving me a glance, then looked down again and concentrated on tying her laces. She muttered something.

I couldn't bear it when she muttered. It was a form of insolence, however much she may pretend it wasn't.

'Speak up, Billy, for heaven's sake.'

'I said, I'm going with Dad.'

'You're doing no such thing, my girl.' What did she think her
father did each day? Went off on a little country walk for the fun
of it? Lay in the long grass and looked at the sky? 'Your father has
selling to do and you've to clean the upstairs before you think of
going anywhere.'

'But . . .'

'I said you're not going.'

'She is.' Lijah strode back into the hallway, rubbing his hands
on his trousers. I looked at him in astonishment, but he strode on
past me to the front door, ruffled Mehitable's hair, then picked up
his boots from where he'd left them ready and sat down on the
step, next to her.

She smiled at him, and it cut me to pieces, that smile.

'What do you mean, she's going with you? She's work to do,
and so have you.'

Lijah ignored me. He finished his laces, rose and hefted his
pack on to his back. 'There's our lunch on that shelf, Billy,' he said
to her. 'Do you think you can carry that?' He gestured to where I
had put some bread and cheese and a bottle of beer into a tea-cloth
and tied it all together.

'Yes, Dad,' she replied, and ran to get it.

'Lijah!' I said, as they turned to go. 'Mehitable has her chores
and you need to set out at a fair pace, you can't just take a child
with a leg like hers off gallivanting round the countryside.' He'd
never taken one of the children across the Fens with him before,
not even Dan, who could have kept up with him.

Mehitable had already limped off down the lane at an impressive pace. Lijah paused on the step and looked down at the
ground. He spoke quietly, almost to himself. 'She's off school, isn't

she? And I'm not leaving her, not with the mood you're in.' He pulled his hanky from his pocket, blew his nose and stuffed the hanky back in. 'She'll only get mistreated.'

He was gone.

I remember standing and staring at the open doorway, at the rectangle of white light they had left behind.

CHAPTER 15

Then came the Great War. Daniel was eighteen years old when it broke out – on the threshold of everything.

As a man, I would say he was very similar to how he was as a boy. I never heard him raise his voice to argue with anyone, despite the fact that he was big enough to knock any man or woman flat, if he'd wanted. He had a large-featured face – took after my side of the family, right enough – big ears, he had, with very long ear-lobes, wide shoulders. I suppose he was everybody's idea of a strapping soldier lad. Elijah told me, when they went to sign up, the Recruiting Officer had looked up at Daniel and nodded with satisfaction. 'Aye, you'll do,' he said.

Elijah repeated that remark to me with a flourish, as if I'd be pleased and proud.

I would hazard a guess that it was a bit more difficult for Elijah to volunteer – he was nobody's idea of a strapping soldier lad, after all. No, he was everyone's idea of a small, wiry hawker, and a middle-aged one at that. He lied about his age, I suppose – and

I suppose by that stage they were starting to get not too particular.

A year after Elijah and Daniel went, Bartholomew joined up as well, as soon as he could pass for old enough. I had steeled myself for it. Once his dad and big brother were in, I knew it was only a matter of time before he joined up too. He and his father both had to lie to get in, one to make himself younger, the other older. It was only my Daniel who went to do his bit legitimate.

After it was over and the men came back – some of them, that is – it was common for the wives and mothers to talk, when they met in the street or at market, of how changed their menfolk were. Mrs Hinkin's husband had nightmares every night and tried to strangle her once, she told me. Mrs Mott's son twitched all the time.

Often I felt, having known the men before, that they came back not changed, but more so. It was like the war gave them licence to be what they had always been. The loud ones became louder, the quiet ones silent. Mrs Mott's son was always the nervy type – and Eli Hinkin had come close to murdering his wife on many an occasion, I was sure, long before the War got to him.

Alice Mott said to me, once, when we was stood in the queue at Bell's the baker's, 'Has your Elijah ever talked about what they did over there?'

I shook my head. 'He did tell me once about a charge they did to frighten the Hun. Scattered like geese, he said.'

Alice Mott was silent for a bit. We moved forward in the queue. 'My Benjamin can't abide dirt,' she said quietly. 'He won't go out and about in the fields, or even the garden sometimes. If it's raining, he stays indoors. I said to him, you've stood up to the guns of Germany my boy, you're not telling me you're frightened of a bit of water.'

My turn had come. 'Three cob loaves please, Mr Bell,' I said, and he turned to wrap them in paper. 'Was it muddy over there, then?' I asked Alice Mott.

'I think so,' she said, thoughtfully, 'from what he said.'

I don't think the men had any idea how dreadful it was for us who were left behind. I know they had a terrible time, some of them – you could see it in their faces – but in our own way we went through things as terrible, in our imaginings, I mean. There wasn't a minute of a single day when I didn't think to myself: what is happening to them, *right now*. I knew that if I ever got the news that one of them was gone, then I would cast my mind back to the day when it had happened, and I would run through that day, and I would think to myself, *as I shook out that pillowcase, was my Daniel running towards his death? As I collected the eggs, brushing straw from them as I laid them in the basket, was he lying on the ground, the life draining away from him?*

Not gas, I used to think, as I went about my daily business. Please let none of them be gassed. I could not bear the thought of one of them choking.

It was a week before Easter that I got the telegram. Bartholomew had joined up two months previous and just been sent to the front. Elijah and Daniel had been in the thick of things for a year. I was weeding the front garden and saw him cycle up the lane, bald Mr Carter with the squinty eye. He had his head down, as if to prevent the wind from buffeting him. I felt quite calm as I watched him dismount, lean his bike against our gatepost and, head still down, walk up our path. The minute he appeared, it seemed inevitable.

Which one is it? I thought to myself as I watched him approach. He hadn't looked up yet. He hadn't yet composed his face into the look that he must have acquired by then, as he handed the telegram over. It was clutched in his hand.

I don't need to read it, I thought. We all know the words of those telegrams off by heart by now. I just want to know, which one of them is it?

Mr Carter made his way steadily towards me, still not looking up.

I prayed and prayed that it would be Elijah.

I am not ashamed to admit that. I knew that if he had taken our sons off to war and got one of them killed, I would never, never forgive him. It would be finished between me and him, for ever. He might as well stay in France.

And then, another thought, as clear as water, *if my Daniel is dead, I do not want to go on living myself. He is the only thing in my life that has never been spoiled by anything. The only thing that is completely pure and good.*

At last, Mr Carter looked up. We were quite close by then, so he gave a small start at the sight of me standing there staring at him, waiting. I watched as he struggled to compose his face. He could not quite achieve the expression he wanted, and so settled for a meaningless grin. Without speaking, he extended the hand that was holding the telegram.

I stepped forward, over some withered tulip stems, and approached him. I think at this point we may have exchanged a few words.

I took the telegram and he handed me a small book and a pencil to sign for it. When he had retrieved them, he bid me good day and turned. He took care not to hurry back to his bike, for that would have been unseemly. He walked slowly down my path.

He righted his bicycle and mounted it, wobbling a little as he turned. Only in that action did he betray his haste, for the normal thing to do would have been to turn the bicycle before he mounted it. I watched Mr Carter cycle down the lane. He did not look back.

I stood in my front garden, holding the telegram, and I did not move. All at once, I felt as if I had all the time in the world. It was the middle of the day and the girls were out. Mehitable was at her

cleaning job at Sampson's. Scarlet and Fenella had gone with
Clementina to the Thursday market in Ely. I was quite alone and
felt a strange sense of peace. It was as if everything that had happened in my life had been leading up to that moment. Once I had
opened the telegram, then that would be it, the rest of my life
would begin. So there was no hurry, then, not if I had the rest of my
life.

I looked at the sky for a bit, then I walked back inside, closing the
door gently behind me. I went into the kitchen, put the telegram on
the table in front of me and sat down. *Which one of them is it?* I
opened it, to find out.

My eyes passed over the *regret to inform you* and travelled
quickly to the words I needed to see, the name.

Adolphus Daniel Smith. Missing presumed dead. It was my
Dan.

I never managed to grow sundance in that front garden. We got
given a nice big plant, by someone, but I stuck it in the wrong
place. The problem was the beech tree, which stood by the gate.
Not only did it keep the sun off, but the greedy roots sucked up all
the water from the earth and the poor thing wilted from thirst,
went quite green. That was why it wouldn't ever take. Later, when
we moved to Peterborough, I grew a lovely sundance in the back
garden there without any difficulty.

A week after Easter, we got another telegram. Adolphus Smith had
been found in a field hospital, where he and some other casualties
had been taken in error. When he came home on leave, he showed
me where some shrapnel had grazed his chest and gone through a
muscle on his upper arm. He had also broken a toe.

They should have been demobbed together, all three of them, but
there was a bit of a problem with Bartholomew. He went Absent

Without Leave towards the end of it. Then, to get himself out of trouble, he joined up again under another name. So he ended up in a different regiment from his brother and his dad.

So Elijah and Daniel came back in January and it was near March before Bartholomew made it back, and then it was under his assumed name. John Hastings, he was calling himself, and Elijah said to me how I mustn't mention to anyone that he was back as the police might come for him.

It didn't stop the three of them all going down The Tollhouse to get *motto*, the first night he was back. They sang as they came back down the lane, their voices ringing in the black of night, and I lay in bed listening to them and thought, for once, that it was the sweetest chorus. Three male voices, belting out some not-too-polite army song, and they all belonged to me. They were all back.

Within a month, however, I started to hear different voices.

The first time it happened, we were sound asleep upstairs. Our bedroom looked out over the back so I was used to field noises like foxes or owls, but that night I was suddenly awoken by the most terrible howling sound. I sat up in bed. My first thought was that the dog had got free of his kennel and was caught in one of the rabbit snares. Elijah had a series of snares all set round the veg-etable patch.

I was throwing my shawl round my shoulders when the sound came again – and this time, it froze my blood, for this time I recog-nised it as human.

Lijah had awoken too. He caught hold of my arm. 'Rosie . . .'

'What is it?'

'Rosie . . .'

I shook him free and went to our window, lifting the curtain gently aside with one finger.

Below our window, in the moonlight, I could see him. He was no more than a dark shape, moving restlessly to and fro, but there was enough light for me to make out that it was Bartholomew.

'What is he doing?' I said. Elijah had not left the bed.

'Leave him be,' he replied, flatly.

'What is he doing? He hasn't even got a coat on.' All I could make out was that Bartholomew was hunched over and swinging his arms back and forth, as if he was threshing. 'We should go down to him,' I said. 'He might hurt himself.'

'Leave him,' Elijah said, and his voice was rough and insistent. I glanced back at the bed and saw that Elijah had lain down again.

I stood by the window for a long time, watching my son below, not knowing what to do. If he had not been making that strange noise, then I would have gone down and guided him back into the house. But the noise frightened me. I knew that wherever Bartholomew was, it was not in the back garden at Sutton. Perhaps Elijah was right. The best thing was to leave him.

I watched the dark shape, its restless movements. It was one of my children, down there.

How little I know of you, or what has happened to you, I thought.

I assumed it would get better, but in fact it got worse, much worse. I began to realise that Bartholomew had not come back.

He drank all the time. He'd always been a drinker, like his dad, but when he came back from the war, it wasn't just in the evenings. It started from the minute he got up in morning, and it stopped only when he collapsed unconscious somewhere – in his bed, on the settee, sometimes in the yard. Elijah would not let me say a word to him, and even Daniel said I should let him be. He couldn't work or anything as officially he was still Absent Without Leave from the army and we were all trying to work out what was to be done about that.

One night, we were seated for an early supper. It was not often we were a group at table at that time, but Clementina had cooked a ham and brought it over. I had done the veg, and it was a strange old tea as it was like we were having Sunday lunch in the middle of the week.

It was more than a year since the war had finished. Lijah was hawking again. Daniel had gone back to his apprenticeship, which Slaker & Son had kept open for him. Mehitable had moved up to a big house outside Yaxley. She had started off as a live-in maid but was now full housekeeper. Scarlet was due to join her in a month, as a scullery girl. I didn't like the thought of Scarlet taking her first position so far away when she was still so young, but Mehitable said the lady of the house was the kindest person she'd ever known and was paying for her to get her leg looked at by a man brought all the way from London. Fenella was turning out to be a fine seamstress – I was right proud of what she could do. She had been offered a job in a cloak and gown workshop in Peterborough, and we were discussing it.

Daniel had just said, 'Mr Slaker has been talking of moving to Peterborough, Mum. I think it would be good, don't you think? I could keep an eye on Fenella, then.'

Fenella shot him a look, as if to say the last thing she needed was her big brother keeping an eye.

'You're fifteen years old,' I said to Fenella. 'You're not going.'

'Scarlet's going to Yaxley and she's younger than me.'

Scarlet stuck her tongue out at Fenella, triumphantly, and I picked up a spoon and gave her a sharp rap across the knuckles.

'That's different,' I said. 'It's live-in, and Billy will look after her. You'll have to find lodgings.'

'You could come to Yaxley with me instead!' Scarlet said brightly, and the withering look from Fenella said that she saw herself as something a bit better than a scullery girl.

Good on you, girl, I thought. Although I was objecting, I had in the back of my mind that I would probably let her go to Peterborough, if Daniel was going as well. There wasn't much in Sutton for a girl like Fenella – and certainly no young men fit for her when she was older. They were all gone now. I didn't want her spending the rest of her life in a village surrounded by empty fields. She deserved a chance at somewhere bigger and better.

Clementina was serving up – she could carve as good as any man. Elijah was at the head of the table, a bit morose as he often was when we got together. Bartholomew was seated at the far end and through the whole of this conversation, he was muttering to himself. I could see his lips moving restlessly as he stared straight ahead.

'Why don't we all move to Peterborough?' Clementina said, as she speared a fat pink slice of ham and stuck it on the top plate of the pile in front of her. I picked the plate up and handed it to Fenella, who passed it down to Bartholomew at the far end. She put it down in front of him.

'What do we want to do that for?' said Elijah, frowning.

'Well, why not?' Clementina said, doling out more ham, 'You've been saying for ages you've had enough of Sutton.'

'Oh, has he?' I murmured, but they took no notice of me. 'Well, I suppose it would be nice to be with Dan and Nelly,' I added.

Fenella's face lit up as she realised I was agreeing to her going.

'And it wouldn't be so far for the girls to come and visit,' added Clementina, meaning Scarlet and Mehitable.

At that point, Bartholomew raised an arm, lowered it swiftly, and then rushed it backwards across the table in a great sweeping motion. His plate with its slice of ham went flying across the room and smashed against the wall. Fenella, who was closest to him, let out a shriek of surprise and pushed herself back from the table as her own plate skidded off and landed on the floor. The pots of relish in front of them toppled and Bartholomew's mug of ale spewed its contents over the tablecloth.

We all froze. Bartholomew was on his feet and staring off into

the middle distance. He gave a strange chortle, as if he found something amusing but couldn't quite catch his breath.

'Conducts sales of furniture and effects!' he shouted, before
adding softly, 'and valuations of the same.'

I looked at Elijah, but he was looking down at the table.

'Conducts sales of live AND DEAD farming stock!' Bartholomew
called out, then simpered, 'and valuations of the same.'

The rest of us stared at him.

'Conducts sales of houses, lands, reversionary interest and life
policies!' Bartholomew stood up straight and proud, like a town
mayor. He crouched down and brought his hands together, wig-
gling his fingers. He spoke in a squeaky little voice, like a mouse,
'and valuations of the same.'

'Elijah, do something,' I said, but Elijah did not move.

Bartholomew's voice took on a posh accent. 'Conducts sales of
growing crops including grass.' He stood upright, lifted his finger
up and clicked his heels together, then shouted, 'AND VALUA-
TIONS OF THE SAME!'

There was a dead silence. We all waited to see what
Bartholomew would do next. He looked around, then scratched his
head. He looked down at the table and reached out a hand to pick
up his mug of ale, then seemed surprised to see it on its side on the
table. He turned, nonchalantly, stuck his hands in his pockets, bent
his knees once, then strolled out of the room.

When he had gone, Fenella stretched out a hand and gently
righted the two pots of relish. Daniel rose to his feet and retrieved
Fenella's plate, then went and picked up the pieces of
Bartholomew's broken one. They made small chinking sounds in
the silence as he gathered them up.

In all this time, Elijah had not moved. Clementina and I were still
standing.

'He's your *son* . . .' I said to Elijah, and I heard the tremble in my
own voice and realised my eyes were brimming with tears.

Elijah did not respond.

'Elijah!' I said, more sharply, 'I said he's . . .' I could not finish.

Clementina put down the carving knife and spike and came round to my side of the table. She placed a hand gently on my arm. 'Go into the kitchen and get yourself a drink of water,' she said. 'I'll clear up a bit, and serve up.'

He disappeared the following spring, did Bartholomew. Fenella's cloak and gown job had fallen through and she was terrible disappointed, but that summer she got another offer, and I let her take it. Daniel had already moved to Peterborough with Slaker & Son. Scarlet joined Mehitable. So that was it. My children were gone, and the house that had always seemed too small was suddenly as cavernous as a grain store.

We stayed on in Sutton another two years. I suppose a small part of me was wondering if Bartholomew might come back. Elijah even went down to London for a few weeks and made enquiries about him – Bartholomew had talked of London, apparently. He said there were some rum old areas there now and a lot of fellas sleeping rough in the parks. When he told me that I got a bit upset. He didn't go into the details. We even wrote to some of the hospitals where they put the tommies who had gone wrong in the head, but there was no trace of Bartholomew under either of the names we had. Elijah was worried he'd do time in prison if we found him, on account of his desertion, but I didn't care. I just wanted to know where he was.

You get used to pain like that. It's like backache. You don't like it, but you forget what life was like without it.

We made our plans to move to Peterborough. Peterborough was the coming place, Elijah said. He went up there to visit and came back quite enthusiastic. It all looked big and new, he said. There were five different railway stations. There was a huge cathedral in the market square that made Ely marketplace look quite pokey. He started to talk about getting a market stall together, selling kitchen goods. Maybe if Scarlet and Mehitable got tired of domestic service, they could help him out.

I began to pack up our things and work out what we could take and what we should leave for the local auctioneer to sell off. Elijah brought the leaflet home so I could look at it. *Mr M. Beezley, Auctioneer and Land Agent*, it said at the top, *conducts sales of furniture and effects, and valuations of the same.*

CHAPTER 16

I haven't hated Elijah, whatever he may think. If I have hated anything, it is the gap between what he is and what I wanted him to be. When he and I first met, I thought he would make my whole life right. But, of course, it wasn't his fault that my whole life was wrong in the first place.

Maybe that is all love is; a need, a wanting. Maybe you never love in the first place unless there is a hole in your life that needs filling. You meet someone, and you put on to them the ability to fill that hole, and you call it love – and when they only fill it a little bit, or not at all, you are angry with them. Then they get confused.

Men have to speak in code. Why did my mother never mention this to me? Maybe she meant to tell me when I was older, only she never got the chance. Men can't say things outright. It's not in them. Like Horace, on River Farm. Horace slapped me across the face and drove me to run off with Elijah, and I am quite certain that when I went, he thought me ungrateful. I am sure he believed that he cared for me and was offering me the world, in his own fashion, and how could I not realise his feelings for me? Horace had never known a minute's kindness in his whole life. All he had ever seen of men and women was the way that his father had treated his wives. It was probably Horace's idea of courtship, to bully and threaten. When I ran off, I am sure he was wounded and bewildered.

But there is right and wrong, that's what the men forget. They think that because they don't *mean* the bad things they do, then those bad things shouldn't hurt us. But a slap stings however it is meant.

A few days before our move to Peterborough, Clementina and I went to Ely market for the last time. Most of our furniture was sold – there was only the clothes to pack. Elijah had gone on ahead and was finding us a place to rent. He would come back for us with a cart, at the weekend.

We went to Ely market that day to sell rather than buy. Clementina had made a pile of things and put them in a crate: crockery and cooking pots we no longer wanted, and a few clothes. We would probably be in temporary lodgings when we first got to Peterborough, so there was no point in carting round a load of stuff. There was something satisfying about getting rid of things, even things which would have to be replaced once we found our new home.

We went early, so that Clementina could talk to the stall-holders as they were setting up. I was buying one or two things: eggs, as our laying hens had been sold the week before, and some green thread that I needed to finish off my last sewing job, the mending of a best suit for Mr Clifford, wheelwright.

I knew Clementina's tasks would take longer than mine, so I lingered at the thread stall, chatting to the Misses Oakley who ran it. They had some new gold lace in, in a beautiful filigree design, which they said had been made in London by the same firm that supplied blouses to the ladies-in-waiting of Queen Mary herself. I fingered it covetously, for I had been doing very ordinary jobs of late, and I thought of how it was high time one of my girls got engaged to be married so I could show them what I could do.

I had put down my basket – a large one Elijah had made for me. As I bent to pick it up, I winced. I had eaten porridge for breakfast and it always caused me digestive difficulties.

'Are you quite well there, Mrs Smith?' one of the Misses Oakley said to me, as she handed the green thread to me in a paper bag.

'Why, yes,' I said, surprised at the concern on her face. Odd she should say that, I thought, as only this morning, on the carrier-cart, a neighbour had told me I was losing weight and looking peaky with it. Well, if moving house makes me a little thinner then that's no bad thing, I thought. There's enough on me to spare a bit, after all. It was true, I had been off my food of late.

After I had bought the few other bits and bobs we needed, I still had time to spare, so I went round the back of the Corn Exchange. A fishmonger and his boy were skinning eels by the water-pump, throwing the skins against the cobbles to reveal the grey, jelly-flesh beneath. Just past them, another boy was leaning against the wall with one leg bent, playing a mouth organ. *Why Was I Born?* I think it was, but he was playing it so badly it was hard to tell.

Behind the Corn Exchange was a little tea shop. Come late morning, it got hectic as lots of folk would pile in there for tea and a bun after the shopping was done, but as it was still early I managed to get a seat in the window and enjoy the feeling that my errands were achieved. Clementina would be a little while yet, so I could take as long as I wanted. I watched the folk going past – all that hurrying – and listened to the boy with his tuneless mouth organ and felt the sweet ache of time going by. It's a symptom of getting on in years, I thought, allowing yourself to enjoy small moments of nothing in particular. My bun was fresh that morning and had candied peel inside but it was too big and I couldn't finish it.

I hefted my basket and left the tea shop. I thought I might as well

take a wander down the High Street and back before I went up
Bray Lane. I still had plenty of time. Although my basket was half
empty, the size of it was awkward and as the pavement was busy,
I kept having to lift it in front of me so folk could get past. I didn't
want it bumped when I had eggs in it. A light rain began falling.
My shoes were hurting as well. I had got no more than halfway
down the street when I decided to turn back.

If I had done so one second sooner, I would not have seen him.

Just before I turned back, I looked ahead, up the street, and there
he was. He was standing on the pavement, facing me, holding a fob
and key and staring in my direction. He was wearing a new suit of
dark grey wool. His shirt collar stood up stiff and white above the
lapels, and he had a satin cravat at his throat, golden coloured like
the lace I had been fingering. Very smart he looked, but aged,
though.

As I approached, weaving through the people between us, he
took his hat off and bowed to me. I saw that his hair was very thin
on top, and what little of it remained was pure snow white.

'Hello, William,' I said.

He straightened and looked at me. 'Rose . . .' he said.

I didn't want to talk to him. I just wanted to stare, to take him in.
He was both changed beyond all recognition and not changed – so
smart, so much older, but still the same thin figure, the pale features. It was nearly thirty years since we had last set eyes upon one
another.

I knew that if I did not speak, the situation would become awkward. 'William,' I said, 'what brings you to Ely?'

He gestured at the door before him. I saw, etched on the glass,
Childer & Watson, Chartered Accountants. I opened my mouth in surprise. 'Why, William . . .'

At this, he gave a half-smile. 'Yes, it would appear I was never
quite cut from the right cloth to be a farmer.'

Oh, I wanted to know everything. How had all this come about?

How had he got away from the farm and become an accountant, of all things? I would never have thought it of him in a million years. I wanted to sit him down in a coffee house and hold his hands and get him to tell me everything. What of Horace, and Henry? His father must be long dead by now . . . Had Horace ever managed to persuade anyone to marry him?

I had noticed the gold wedding ring on his finger. 'And you have a family?'

His half-smile became rigid. 'Yes. I married while I was still training. We had three sons. My youngest will be joining me in the office, soon. The eldest two were killed in France.'

'I am sorry to hear that, William.' Now I knew what had aged him, what had balded and whitened him and given him that strained look.

There was a brief silence, which I felt obliged to fill. 'I have five now, all grown up, of course.' What could I tell him about my children? That Daniel was doing well for himself and talking of setting up his own little business in Peterborough; that Mehitable and I no longer spoke to each other since she broke off her engagement with the chimney sweep and I told her she was getting on a bit and should have grabbed him while she got the chance; that Bartholomew had disappeared to London and broken my heart; that Fenella was the handsomest girl alive and everybody's favourite – and Scarlet, so much her own person, despite being the youngest – the strongest of them all, perhaps . . .

Instead I said, stupidly, 'My husband and my two boys served in France but they came back safe and sound, thank the Lord.' I suppose I wanted him to know that our family had done their bit too, but it came out all wrong. It sounded as though I was bragging that *mine* had survived.

'And how is Mr Smith?' The question sounded so absurdly formal, that I could not help giving a small laugh. How was Elijah? Same as ever – how else would he be?

William smiled back. We held each other's gazes and our stares were full, brimming.

He dropped his gaze and turned back to his door. 'My clerk will be waiting,' he murmured, unconvincingly.

'Of course,' I said, looking down and brushing at my skirt with my free hand, suddenly aware of what a smart, upstanding gentleman William was these days, and how I was no more than an ageing village housewife with a basket over her arm.

Before I let him go, though, there was something I wanted to ask him, and the years of not seeing each other made me bold. This was the last time I would ever come to Ely market, after all. I knew I would never see him again and gathered all my courage.

'William, I am sorry to ask you this . . .'

He looked back at me, his expression a little alarmed. He was frightened I was about to embarrass him.

I spoke hastily. 'You will think me foolish after all these years, but did you ever receive my letter telling you I was to be wed? It's just I've always wondered . . .'

'Yes, Rose, I did. I am sorry . . .' He looked down.

What was he sorry for? For not having had the courage to defy his father and come to the church to give me away? But he had paid for the church bells to be rung. That was enough for me, more than enough. Kind thoughts of William and his affection for me had cheered me many a time over the years, I realised. Even though his feelings for me had never come to anything, the thought that someone had regarded me softly at the most difficult time in my life had sustained me on many a black night. I wanted him to know how much his gesture had meant to me.

'William,' I said. 'When I came out of the church on my wedding day and heard the bells ringing, it was the happiest moment of my life. I still cherish the sound of those bells in my head.'

He looked up at me, his face closed and tense. I could not decipher his thoughts. 'I am glad to hear that, Rose,' he said.

'Now, if you will excuse me . . .' He bowed to me again, and lifted the key.

'Goodbye, William,' I said. 'Please give my regards to your wife. I wish you both well.'

'Goodbye, Rose.'

I walked back down the High Street, my head full of thoughts. It was only as I reached the market place again that it came to me. *Oh William*, I thought. *You loved me, didn't you? Loved me properly, I mean.* I thought back to the time on the farm – it seemed like such an age ago, and it was: another century, before the children, before the War that took so many of our children. Our generation has this great chasm in our lives, I thought, a chasm that has swallowed so much of what is dear to us. How can any of us clamber down and up its sides to get back to the past? But William had loved me. I was sure of that.

What if William had made his intentions clear to me at the time? Would I have loved him back? Married him, perhaps? Would I now be his wife, living in a smart town house somewhere in Ely, brushing fluff from the shoulders of my husband's smart new suit before he set off for work each morning? Then, after I had kissed him and waved him off from the doorstep, would I return inside and close the door, check that the maid was clearing the breakfast table, then go upstairs to my room and sit at my dresser, to spend my morning as I always did, staring at pictures of my two lost sons . . .?

You can't pick and choose, after all. If you want somebody else's life, you've got to take the whole of it. It isn't like plucking only the ripe cherries off a tree and leaving the ones you don't like the look of.

As I passed the market, I glanced around to see if I could spot Clementina, but if she was there, she was lost in the crowds. I decided to go on up Bray Lane and wait for her at our usual place. There were benches by the roadside where the carrier-carts pulled up and the rain had stopped. An omnibus service had started up on market days, but it was three times the cost of the carrier-cart and I couldn't abide the horrid smell of it.

It wouldn't have made any difference, I thought. Even if William had told me he loved me on the farm, I still would have run off with Elijah. At that time, I would have thought that marrying William would have tethered me to River Farm as surely as marrying Horace would have done.

The benches were all full when I got there and I had to stand, but pretty soon a carrier-cart going the other way rumbled into place and several women clambered up, so I was able to get a seat on the bench. A younger woman moved over for me as I sat down, and I thought how old I must seem to her.

There is no point in being wistful, I thought to myself. Yes, I would love to be married to William and live in a town house and have a maid – but would I swap my five healthy children for his dead two? He loved me, that's all that matters. I can hold on to that thought. He loved me, all those years ago, and he paid for the church bells to be rung as I came out into the sun.

My digestive system really was bothering me that day – it was the first day I began to think there was maybe something that needed sorting out. I'd better brew myself some mint leaves in hot water when I get home, I thought.

I suppose if it hadn't been for the move to Peterborough, I might have gone to the doctor sooner. As it was, it took us more than a year to settle – we had four different addresses in that time, due to Elijah taking a while to sort out a bit of regular income. Then there was the new house to establish – the new routine of just Elijah and me. Clementina had her own little place again. And there were the girls to be visited – and Fenella's engagement to her Tom. Fenella was married not three months when Mehitable upped and did it too, and gave me my first grandchild all within the space of a year.

So, what with one thing and another, I put up with the digestive problems for a good few years and got quite thin for the first time in my life, before I finally went along to Doctor Dodds and let him lie me down and press at my stomach with a frown upon his face. These things have a way of taking their course, so I doubt it would have made much difference if I'd gone before.

CHAPTER 17

The world shrinks. That is what it is like, being ill. As getting out and about becomes more difficult, you lose the edges of the world, and then the things you are losing get nearer and nearer, closer to home. First you can no longer go on long journeys – then you can't go down the market square to Elijah's stall carrying his sandwiches wrapped in brown paper. Sooner or later, you can't even go to the end of your road for fresh bread to make the sandwiches with – Elijah has to do that himself. Then, getting out of bed gets more and more difficult so you lose the downstairs of the house – garden, hallway, kitchen, parlour – and then, when you are bedbound, you lose even your own bedroom, for you can see it from beneath your eider but it is like you are looking at it through a glass.

The glass is made of pain. Sometimes the pain thickens, becomes opaque. Then you can't see anything. At others, it is there, but almost see-through – you get so used to it you forget what it was like to see the world properly, not through the glass of pain.

People arrive, from the rest of the world. Mostly, they were just visitors from my own home, one of the family, but once in a while it was someone from a far-flung land, like the vicar from the local church. He didn't stay long. He was a young fella, embarrassed by old people and death and dying, I could tell. He went bright red when I asked him about the afterlife. I felt so sorry for him I pretended I was tired, so he had an excuse to leave.

It was not long after his visit that some odd things started to make their way into my room. Lijah struggled all the way up our narrow stairs with a old washstand, God knows why. He must have got it from one of the general stores he visited, or the marketplace. I heard him huffing and puffing and clunking up the staircase, as if he was trying to lug a camel. The door banged back, and in he came, all on his own, and without a word, started edging this thing across the carpet. It had a marble top, and shelves beneath, so it must have weighed a ton. When it was in place, flush against he wall, he went out and came back in with a cloth and some bleach and set to scrubbing the marble.

All he said was, 'The only thing that brings marble back to itself is a bit of bleach, you know. Bleach and elbow grease.'

I thought, *he should be wearing gloves for that job*, but it was one of those days when talking was bit tricky.

Other items of furniture followed, with a day or so interval in between; a mahogony chiffonier, a walnutwood whatnot with a plate glass back. The following week, engravings and chromos started going up on the wall. Lijah's hammering the nails was so loud it felt like he was knocking them into my forehead. A cane seat with a velvet cushion materialised next to the wardrobe one afternoon, while I was asleep. I believe the final item was a Brussels-pile bordered carpet, but I might have started to lose track by then. The room was so full I felt I was floating on a sea of furniture. My visitors could hardly get in the door.

*

The girls did most of the looking-after of me, the girls and Clementina. Daniel visited, of course, but neither he nor Elijah were comfortable sitting with me for too long. The girls always had things to do; move me over to slip a sheet from under me, or coax me to eat something. The men had no such function and without those things to do for me, they didn't really know what to do with themselves.

Elijah only sat down once. I think he thought I was asleep. I was, sort of, but woke with the weight of him sitting down on the edge of my bed, and the feel of his hand resting on mine.

I opened my eyes, and he moved his hand away.

'Shall I tell one of the girls to come up?' he said.

I nodded slowly. I was thirsty. 'Are they both here?' I asked. My voice was getting hoarse, whispery.

Fenella and Scarlet were taking it in turns to come round to look after me. Fenella had her own family now, and Scarlet was still working, but somehow they were managing it between them. There was always one of them there, however early I woke each morning, so I suppose they must have been sleeping on the sofa. Elijah was either in the spare room, or sometimes sleeping at Clementina's house which was just round the corner from ours.

'Aye,' he replied.

There was a pause.

'They're good girls,' I said quietly.

'They all are,' he said, quietly back.

Neither of us needed to say any more. Mehitable had not visited me since I became bed-ridden, not once. She sent a card. *Get Well Soon*. It had a line drawing of sweet peas on the front, filled in with coloured pencil. I had accepted that I was going to die without seeing Bartholomew again, he had been lost to us many years before, but Mehitable lived less than three miles away, over at Dogsthorpe.

'Ask Scarlet if I can have some fresh water,' I said to Elijah, and he nodded, then rose.

While he was gone, a strange thought came to me – and I don't know why I should have thought it then, after all those years. The pig. Toby, the Sapient Pig. It came to me how it was done. I had thought that Elijah must've somehow told the man my name, so that he could make the pig spell it. But he hadn't, of course, no more than he had paid for the church bells to be rung on the day we was wed. All Elijah had done was spoke my name, just before, and the woman next to us had heard and somehow signalled to the fella who had owned the pig.

Why did I want to believe, at the time, that it was him? What did it matter?

Then I began to think about Mehitable. I thought of all the times she and I had fallen out, when she was a child, and I thought of the sly look in her eyes and how close I had come to beating that child and how I had congratulated myself on not doing it. Considering what I had put up from Elijah, I thought how I had really done quite a good job – five children raised on nothing? I had worked my fingers to the bone for years and years.

I never hit that child – well, they all got a smack on the bottom when they were naughty, of course, and I used the spoon on their arms in the kitchen, once in a while. But I never, ever beat her properly, not like I got beaten by my stepfather. I pushed her around a bit a few times, but she was so wilful and difficult – I don't think anyone has the right to judge me unless they've had a child as wilful and difficult as she was.

A dark feeling that I cannot describe came over me.

I thought of the fantasies I used to have, as a child, of the kind of wedding I would have: the man who would be my husband; the home I would live in – somehow they never went away, not even when I married Elijah in front of his drinking pals, in a pawned hat.

Even when we crept like thieves down Paradise Street, sneaking off because we couldn't pay the rent, a part of me was still thinking how I would make the house all nice once I had all the things I coveted.

Being ill gives you plenty of time to think, so I thought some more. I thought about how strange it is that you can walk around knowing life is one way but still holding on to your belief that it is really, somehow, else. I suppose the trick is never to put the two pictures of your life together, never try to make them fit. It is not wise to think about how things really are, for there is always this yawning chasm between how our lives are and how we want them to be, a great, big black hole, big enough to fall into and disappear for ever.

All my life, I have congratulated myself on being a good person. And in comparison with some around me, mentioning no names but a certain son and his mother come to mind, I have been. But I saw, as I lay there thinking about Mehitable, that I have only been good in comparison to the bad that was done to me – my mother dying on me when I was young and my stepfather's unkindness to me, Elijah and his drinking. How wrong I had got it, all those years. That badness around me may have made me look good, in my own eyes, but it didn't mean I *was* good. It gave me excuses, that was all, when I passed on a little of the badness to others. When I was unkind to Mehitable, I was thinking in the back of my head, that my unkindness to her was as nothing compared to the big unkindness my mother did to me by dying on me.

All this time, I thought, I have walked around and thought of myself as a nice person, and I haven't been, at all.

Scarlet came up with a glass of water and my pills. She sat by my bed for a bit, in silence, then she said, 'Dad's gone round the corner to see Gran.'

I didn't reply. She looked at me. 'How was Dad?'

'Oh well, you know your Dad.'

She moved as if to leave, and without intending to, I found myself reaching out a hand and grasping her arm. She looked a little surprised and then sat down again, looking at me expectantly. Scarlet, such an uncomplicated child: broad, beaming face, solid and straightforward. I saw a lot of me in her, or how I would have liked to have been, if I'm honest.

She wasn't a child, of course, she was of age, that year. I had a feeling she might be married soon. Daniel had a friend he was thinking of going into business with. He had been to tea round at ours a little more than was necessary if he was nothing but a friend of Daniel's. I had seen looks between him and Scarlet.

She sat on the bed, just looking at me, saying nothing, just waiting. She always knew the right thing to do, that one.

'I wasn't a bad mother, was I?' I said to her, simply, looking intently at her face.

Her look of surprise was instant, and unforced. 'Oh no, of course you weren't, Mum, what a silly thing to say. The way you looked after us . . . You were the best mum in the world.'

I held on to her hand and squeezed it. 'Thank you, love.'

She frowned, glanced round all the stuff jammed into the room, looked back at me and said, 'What was Dad saying to you?'

'Nothing, oh nothing, I just, sometimes I wonder, you know. Sometimes I feel bad. When I think of how I was. I meant well, but sometimes it didn't always come out like that with you children. Always telling you off, and such, I feel bad about it.'

'Dad has no right to come in here making you feel bad.' Her face was agitated. She snapped at her father a lot, did that one, took his devotion to her quite for granted.

'Scarlet, I want to see Mehitable.' The sentence came out of nowhere. I was almost surprised to hear it myself – I hadn't been planning to say it.

Her indignation faltered. Her face closed. She hesitated.

I knew it was up to me to insist. Suddenly, I wondered if I had the energy for it. 'Scarlet, there's things Mehitable and I need to discuss. Before.'

'I won't have you talking like that.' The indignation was forced, this time.

'Please, will you speak to her for me. I know it's not an easy thing.'

She rose from her chair and began tucking the candlewick bedspread firmly underneath the mattress. 'I'll speak to her. I can't promise.'

'Thank you, love.'

I think Scarlet did more than speak to her – I think she insisted, for Mehitable came to me a few days later but so unwillingly it must have taken a prod with a red-hot poker to do it. The door to my room opened and in she came, sidling around the door but staying close to it, the way a cat does – ready to bolt at any moment.

She managed a thin smile. I tried to heave myself up, winced and fell back. She came over to help me, so we touched each other before we said so much as a word. As she lifted me and propped a pillow up behind my head, I felt what I always felt with her, that she was bracing herself for any closeness to me, in the same way she might brace herself against a cold wind in her face.

She smoothed my bedspread, then fetched the upright chair that was in the corner next to the wardrobe, the one the doctor used.

She placed the chair carefully at an angle, so she could sit facing me, then undid the top three buttons of her cardigan and pulled off her neckscarf. I daresay she found the room hot. I was keeping the windows closed as I felt cold so much of the time, even though the sun streamed through and in normal times I would have had every window in the house flung open on such warm days.

We did not speak, and the moment passed when we could have started off with a bit of small talk. *How's that boy of yours?* I could have said, or, *What's the news over in Dogsthorpe, then?* But the moment for that slid away from us, like a ball rolling downhill, and the silence became so long there was no pretending this would be a normal little chat.

I watched her in the upright chair. There she sat, my difficult grown-up daughter, fiddling with the scarf she had just removed, passing the fine fabric through a hole she had made with her thumb and forefinger. She reminded me of my mother, suddenly, with her sleek dark hair and her thin manner. Odd that she should be growing like my mother when I was never like her myself – that was a likeness that had skipped a generation entirely.

Mehitable – in her thirties now, older than my mother was when she died.

I let the silence go on too long, I suppose. I could feel her not wanting to be there, a feeling as solid as the oak wardrobe in the corner of the room. The not wanting grew with each passing second. I wondered if Scarlet had begged her to come. Maybe Scarlet and Fenella had done it together, like a pair of pincers.

'*Just go and see her, will you?*'

'*She's dying.*'

'*You'll be sorry later, if you don't.*'

I could imagine the whole scene.

It came to me that as I had summonsed her, it was up to me to speak first.

'Do you know why I wanted to see you?' I said, eventually, and saw her wince. She glanced away, then sighed.

'I've an idea,' she said eventually. Her voice was cold.

I thought back to when I used to smack her sometimes, when she was little, and how it wasn't that I wanted to hurt her, but the anger inside me used to build up, and she would just crouch down and take it and never even cry.

Pain began to blossom inside me, somewhere down in the pit of the stomach. I cursed that it came at that moment for I knew I wouldn't have long before I started to perspire. Soon after that, conversation would become impossible.

'I can't die until you say you've forgiven me.' There. It was out.

Her face was small and dark and set, and even then I could see what I had found so difficult in her as a child, that she would never reveal anything, that I could never work out what she was thinking.

She could have said, *for what*? Then I would have said, *for the fact that I wasn't very kind to you when you was little, when you was poorly*. Then we both would have understood that it was all right to talk not directly about things. Then the talk could have moved on quickly to being ordinary.

But instead, she said, 'Why d'you do it, Mum? Why were you like that with me all the time? You weren't with the others.' She was looking at me.

I had not expected this, this challenge from her. The pain began to radiate out, to travel up through my chest cavity and to my limbs. I would have to ask her to fetch one of the others, soon.

'I don't know,' I said, breathing hard. 'I do know that if you'd stood up to me, just once, I'd have stopped, but you just took it and took it, whatever I gave you. I never understood what you were about.'

'I was a child, Mum.'

'I know.'

My sight began to blur. The shape of her sitting in the chair wavered, became diagonal.

'I forgive you, Mum.' Her voice sounded distant.

I tried to arch my back slightly, as if I could lift myself away from the pain, but I knew it was no use.

'Do you really?' I could hear the wincing in my voice. I had to finish soon, 'or are you just saying that?'

'I do,' she said quickly. 'Mum, shall I get Scarlet or Fenella?' Her voice was high pitched with anxiety.

I nodded. The movement sent small rockets of pain up the back of my head. 'Get Scarlet.'

She left hurriedly. I closed my eyes and thought, I didn't even ask her about that boy of hers.

Scarlet came quickly, with the pills and a glass of tepid water. She sat by me and stroked my hand while the pills did their work, oh so slowly, and made the pain a dull, bearable ache, instead of a fire. Afterwards, she left and I dozed for a while.

Later, there was a light knock at the door. It opened, and Clementina came in. She was carrying a small tray with a china plate and a glass of milk. She set them both on the bedside table. On the plate was four pieces of bread cut into neat triangles and spread thickly with butter.

'I've brought you some supper,' she said.

My head felt as if it was stuffed with cotton wool. With Clementina's help, I managed to raise myself slightly. She plumped up the pillows behind me, then sat down on the upright chair and handed me the glass.

The milk was ice cold. It slipped right down. For the first time in a week, I drained it all. Clementina noted it as she took the glass from me.

She handed me the china plate. It was one of my favourites, a very old one from when Elijah and I were first married, with gilt edging, faded now, and yellow rosebuds. I looked down at it. The pieces of bread had been neatly arranged, overlapping each other.

'I haven't seen this plate in years,' I said, 'where d'you find it?'

'Billy made your supper,' Clementina replied. 'She found the plate at the back of the dresser.'

I lifted one of the pieces of bread and took a small bite, then put it back on the plate. Swallowing was very uncomfortable.

'Why didn't she bring it up herself?'

'She had to get back. You were asleep.'

There was a long silence between us. It came to me that Clementina, my mother-in-law, was the one member of my family I could rely on to tell me the truth.

'I've not got long, have I?' I asked her, looking her directly in the face.

She shook her head.

'What did Mehitable say when she came downstairs?'

For the first time ever, I saw hesitation in Clementina's eyes.

'Tell me,' I said quickly. 'Don't give me any guff. You, of all people . . .'

'She said you asked for her forgiveness and she gave it.'

'And?'

'Scarlet said did you mean it, and she said yes.'

'And what else?'

'Rose . . .' Clementina said. I thought how strange it was to hear her use my name, how we had known each other all these decades but hardly ever used each other's names.

I gathered all the little strength I had left. 'Clementina,' I said, 'I've never asked you anything my whole life, but I'm asking it now. I want you to tell me honestly what my daughter said when she got downstairs. What you've got to realise is that, however bad it was, if I don't know then I'll wonder and wonder and that is far worse and I think I've a right to know so I can get it straight in my head before I go.' It was the longest speech I had made for some weeks and it exhausted me. Towards the end of it, my voice was so hoarse she had to lean towards me to catch my words.

She stared at me, then said, 'Scarlet asked her did you mean it, and she said yes, then she said, I've forgiven her but don't go expecting me to put flowers on her grave every Sunday, I've forgiven her and that's it, I'm done with it.'

The pain returned anew, a long, slow wash of it, like the tide coming in. I closed my eyes and exhaled. When I opened them, Clementina was leaning forward to take the plate. 'She made you a nice supper,' she said quietly. 'She dug out that plate because she knew you liked it, and washed it too, and she went and opened a new bottle of milk from the larder so you'd get the cream of it cold.'

'Thank you,' I said.

After that, dying got a bit easier for a few days. The doctor visited every morning. Dan, Fenella and Scarlet popped in and out. Fenella liked to read to me from the paper and I didn't have the heart to tell her I wasn't interested as I knew it pleased her to be doing something for me. Whenever I got worried that she needed a break, I would say, 'I think I'll have a little sleep now.'

Fenella, always the beautiful one. She had taken to wearing her hair back off her face. It suited her but made her look older. I was worried how Tom and the girls would be managing without her but she never mentioned it.

I wasn't frightened in the times they left me alone. There is something wonderful about letting your mind wander around a bit, let it float free. Once you are released from spending all day, every day, worrying about what there is for supper and how you are going to keep the house clean – it's amazing how much time you have to think of other things. I found myself wondering, is this what it is like being a fine lady, a Lady Something, or a Dame or Baroness – or a Princess, even? Do they lie around, wondering what to think about? Of course, if you are such a person, then you do not even know that you have nothing to think about. You think thinking about nothing is being busy.

All sorts of odd things came in and out of my head. I remembered things I did not know were still inside me somewhere. I remembered how, in the bad days at Paradise Street, I had been so desperate for money that I had looked into Clementina's purse one day, when she was out walking Bartholomew up and down the road to get him to sleep. She had left her purse, a small velvet thing, with a drawstring, on the shelf by the door. I had gone to it and emptied it into my hands and had been disappointed to find nothing but a few farthings. Then I felt it, squeezed it in my hand, and realised there must be another pocket or a torn lining inside, as I could feel something hard.

I turned the purse inside out. There, it was, a secret little pocket, with a flap, stitched into the lining. I got quite excited at that point, for it came to me that Elijah's mother was just the sort of mad old lady who might have gold sovereigns hidden in a box under her bed. Maybe she's secretly wealthy, I thought. Her type often are. The coin I could feel was about the right size for a sovereign.

With a bit of fiddling, I managed to extract it, and then, of course, I was sorely disappointed. It was just a sixpence, one of the old sort, with the Queen's hair up in a bun and her looking like a younger woman – later, they made her look much older. Why on earth is she keeping an old sixpence buried secretively in her purse? I thought to myself. It was smaller than a sovereign, of course. I had let my imagination run away with me.

I had only just returned the coin to its secret pouch and replaced the purse on the shelf, when the door opened and in came Clementina, Bartholomew asleep on her shoulder.

I swear she guessed what I had been doing, for she gave me a look so poisonous that I turned and fled upstairs.

There were only a few occasions when Elijah and I were able to be alone together on River Farm, so it's not surprising they've stuck in my mind. There was one in particular . . . It was the only time we were able to be together for a few hours at a stretch. I can't remember the excuse I gave back on the farm, how I managed it.

May. Is there a better month? The sky is never brighter the whole year than it is in May. We had been lying on a bank of some sort, looking at the sky. There were woods behind us and nobody about. It was like we had the whole world to ourselves. I remember how we kissed, our carelessness. *Nobody knows where I am. Nobody can find me, lost in this man's kisses.* We did some talking as well, and some staring at the sky, and then a bit more kissing. I asked him how he learned to kiss so well and he got a bit funny with me, not liking to own up that he'd kissed a few other gorjer lasses, I bet, for that was one skill he certainly hadn't picked up among his own.

The grass around us was long and dry – the sun hot.

After a while, he jumped to his feet. He stood upright before me. I lifted a hand to shield my eyes from the sun, so I could look up at him.

'I'm tired of courting,' he declared. 'Let's box!'

I sat up. 'Box?'

'Aye, boxing. "Tis great sport and there's nothing better to watch than two fellas who know what they're about.' He was rolling up his sleeves. Then he reached out and pulled me up from the bank. He squared up to me. 'Come on, Rosie,' he nodded, 'you're a fair-sized lass. Let's see what you're made of.'

I thought he was mad, of course. But we circled for a while, and he made a few feigning jabs at me, with me shrieking 'Elijah!' in alarm, each time. Then, I do believe I managed to land one on him, for I was a good few inches taller. My fist glanced the side of his nose and he threw his face back in an exaggerated fashion. I stopped and dropped my hands, aghast I might have hurt him, and he took advantage of my dismay to throw himself upon me and push me backwards so I landed, winded and gasping, back on the bank.

I was panting. I could feel his weight upon me – a sweet weight, a weight that owned and claimed me, a weight that said, *I'll not release you for the world.*

He was silent for a while, still lying on me, using one hand to prop his face up, resting the elbow on the ground beside my head, and the other hand to stroke my hair back where I had gone a little sweaty at the temples.

'Why Elijah Smith,' I murmured, feeling him shift a little, 'I do believe you have told me an outright lie. You're not tired of courting at all.'

I lay on my deathbed and thought of this, and I forgave Elijah everything. I must tell him when he comes up, I thought, that I forgive him everything.

Later, there was a light tap at the door – and Clementina came in. She hovered at the door for a moment, and I could tell she was trying to work out whether I was asleep or not. Silly woman, I thought, of course I'm not asleep. After a moment, she came forward and rested two of her fingers gently against my neck. Then she stood up.

I opened my eyes. How had I seen her, before, if my eyes had been closed? My head is playing funny tricks with me, I thought.

Clementina was staring down at me. Her face was serious. Was something wrong?

'The children want to come up, to say their goodbyes,' she said quietly. 'Have you got enough puff for it?'

I nodded.

In they came, one by one: Dan, Fenella, Scarlet, in that order. Only Scarlet managed not to cry, and it was a great relief to me, for I felt as though I had not one ounce of strength left in me, and I could not bear one minute more of anybody else's grief. We held each other's hands in silence for a while, then talked a little, then we had a little more silence, and the silence was lovely.

'Shall I send Dad up?' she asked gently, after a while.

'No,' I said, 'I don't want your dad. I want your gran.'

She didn't seem surprised but then, all through her life, Scarlet rarely was.

When Clementina returned to me, it was as if she had aged

while she had been waiting downstairs. Slowly she came, clutching at the door handle with her bony fingers, leaning on her stick. She sat down on the upright chair and looked at me, with those piercing black eyes of hers, and suddenly, I would have given a wild laugh if I had been able, for I realised I now had licence to say whatever I liked to her, after all these years.

'Well, Mother,' I said, 'you said I'd sup sorrow until the day I died, and you were right.'

She nodded, and to my astonishment, I saw that her eyes were rimmed with tears.

'You're not going to let me down, are you, Mother?' I said, although my voice had suddenly become a strange whisper, hoarse but high. An odd calm had come over me.

Clementina looked at me, then sniffed loudly. 'What am I going to do?' she said, and her voice was practical as always.

'Oh, you'll manage . . .' I whispered, and a cloudiness descended upon me. My sight of her became misty, then was enveloped in white. *I am going where none of you can reach me*, I thought and I felt unfrightened and lucid and at peace.

PART 5

1929–1949

Clementina

CHAPTER 18

We buried Rose in Eastfield Cemetery. It was a slow procession from the church – fitting it was, for it gave us all time to prepare ourselves for the bit that came next, the most awful bit, the putting of her in the ground. Lijah led the procession, with Dan next to him. The three girls walked behind, arms linked. I was walking behind them but could tell they were all crying. Fenella started them off – sobbing brokenly by the heave of her shoulders. Scarlet was shaking her head a little and breathing hard. Mehitable was motionless as she walked but I knew that tears would be streaming down her face, nonetheless. Mehitable. Who knew what was going on in her head? Scarlet and Fenella would recover in their own good time – but Mehitable had a double load of grief to deal with, mourning her mother and the mother she would have rather had.

I watched their backs as they walked and thought, how many different ways there are of crying, as many ways as there are unhappy people in the world.

And then we came to it: *ashes to ashes, dust to dust* . . . the swing

and sway of the words, the waving of the vicar's arm, the bluster-
ing breeze and the sobbing of the three daughters. Rose's coffin was
lowered. How dreadful, I thought, as it descended – how dreadful
to be shut up in a box and put in a hole in the ground and have the
earth cover you over, and to be stuck in there in the cold and dark,
all alone, for all eternity. You can't burn people no more, Lijah told
me. You can't get away with it. So we've all got to go in a hole in the
ground, whether we like it or not.

Afterwards, we all stood around for a bit, as you do. The vicar
spoke quietly to Lijah at one end of the grave then started moving
around the company. Lijah was left alone, looking down into the
hole where they had put his Rosie, forlorn as a boy. I was standing
a little way off, watching him. I waited for one of his children to
approach him and comfort him, but none of them did. They were
all talking to each other, or the other mourners. After a moment or
two, I went up to Lijah and put my hand on his arm.

'Come on, Lijah,' I said gently. 'It's time to go back to the house.'

He did not move. He was staring down at the grave.

'Come on, love,' I said.

He raised his head, and shook it slightly. 'Well,' he said, awkwardly, 'she's got a bit of peace now, I suppose.' He lifted the
corners of his mouth in a grimace, shrugged and made a *humphing*
sound. Then he scratched his ear, and stuck his hands in his pockets. I squeezed his arm.

As we turned to go, I saw that the girls were standing at the far
end of the grave, all looking towards us. They turned and walked
off down the path, after Dan.

The wake was in Rose and Lijah's house in Buckle Street. Once we
got inside the door, the girls moved into action. Mehitable brewed
up some large pots of tea – Mrs Loveridge had borrowed three
enormous teapots from the Legion. Scarlet and Fenella set to with
the sandwiches. Lijah and Dan and the other men went to the

parlour for a smoke. The neighbours were all in, of course, and the
women saw to the handing out of the sandwiches and cake and
everyone talked quietly and bustled about as they do at these
things. I did my best to help out and make a bit of conversation
with folk but it's not really my strong point, idle chat. I was pleased
when folk started to give their condolences and drift off. Dan
stayed by the door to see them out. 'Are there many men left in the
parlour?' I asked Scarlet as she came out balancing a pile of empty
cups and saucers.

'Not many,' she said. 'With any luck we can all get off soon.' She
bustled past me, into the kitchen. Oh we can, can we? I thought.

I felt a sudden need for a bit of air. Dan was still at the front door
ushering folk out, so I went out the back. I went and stood in the
middle of the garden and took a few long, deep breaths

Those terraces had long, thin gardens and low walls, so you
could look right down over everybody else's garden. Washing was
strung up, here and there. Pigeons were cooing in their coop at the
end of number forty-two. It was an ordinary day; washing,
pigeons, empty sky. I looked up at the sky and thought it had never
seemed emptier.

I waited until I thought everyone but family would be gone
before I went back inside. The clearer-uppers were still there. Mrs
Lane and her daughter who was grown-up but retarded were
washing plates and cups in the kitchen. Sally Loveridge was emp-
tying ash trays into a tin can. I looked around for the girls but
couldn't see them. I peered in at the parlour. Lijah was sat on a
straight-backed chair with Mr Lane and his sons around him. They
were still sipping tea. The air was white with cigarette smoke. They
weren't saying much to each other, the men. I backed out and
closed the door behind me.

I wondered what had happened to the children.

As I closed the parlour door, I heard footsteps on the stairs. They
were all descending – Daniel first, with a few papers in his hand,

then Mehitable, Scarlet and Fenella. Scarlet had some of Rose's old dresses over her arm.

Daniel glanced at me, and nodded, 'All right, Gran,' he said. 'Thanks for helping out this afternoon.' He went out of the front door.

It was only as Fenella, the last, was passing me, that it dawned on me they were all leaving. I caught her by the arm.

'Where are you lot off to?' I said, and I had a bit of difficulty keeping the sharpness from my tone.

Fenella looked a little embarrassed. She could never tell a lie, that one. 'Well, Gran, it's sort of wrapping up now, isn't it? You've got lots of help to clear up. Billy has to get back and we thought we'd walk her round. I hope you don't mind.'

Scarlet turned back. She came up close, so she could speak without being overheard. The door to the kitchen was stood wide open.

'Look, I'm sorry, Gran,' she said. 'But we just need to get off, okay? We'll see you and Dad tomorrow. We've done our bit for now. We stayed until everyone went.'

I stared at her. I lowered my voice as much as I could. 'What do you mean *stayed until everyone went?* What's your father supposed to do this evening, stare at the wallpaper?' I hissed, and I could feel my gaze blazing.

Scarlet lowered her voice still further. 'We've said goodbye to Dad, he's fine about it. He's got you, all right? He's got you. Now we need a bit of time to ourselves. She was *our mother*, all right?'

'There's still her things to be sorted.'

'That's what we were doing. Dan's got the paperwork. I've taken some dresses and Fenella will have the brooch. Billy don't want anything. The rest can just be disposed of now *please* . . .' I saw she was close to tears, 'just let us go, will you?'

She took Fenella by the arm and marched her towards the door. Fenella looked back and gave a weak smile. 'Bye then, Gran,' she said. They closed the door gently behind them.

Sally Loveridge came out of the kitchen. She had been waiting until our little exchange was over. She was holding a stack of clean plates. She gave me an ingratiating smile. 'Now,' she said, 'do you want me to stack these in the kitchen or take them through?' She indicated the parlour door with her head.

Put them on yer 'ead and dance the fandango for all I care, I thought. *Loving it, aren't you? Being so good and noble.*

'Kitchen'll be fine,' I said, then forced myself to add, 'thank you.' She went back inside.

Upstairs, in Rose and Lijah's bedroom, I manoeuvred my way around all the extra furniture and opened the wardrobe. Rose's house-coat was still there and a few old dresses, along with a couple of skirts and blouses. They had left the shoes – she always had very big feet, did Rose. I thought, there's probably some large woman out there who'd be glad of them but I'm blowed if I know her.

In the chest of drawers there was underthings and some fine stockings – they would all have to be disposed of in the proper manner. I laid out a clean sheet on their bed, and began piling everything else onto it. That night, when the house was empty but for me and Lijah, I could parcel it all up, then I would take it out to the garden.

No, I thought, not the garden. The neighbours. No, I will go and find a field, somewhere, and I will do what is right by Rose out in the open, without anyone watching, just her and me. I will set a match to all that is left of her, and say the right words in my head. She should be blessed on her way in the proper manner by someone, after all.

We do right by the dead in the hope that the living will one day do right by us.

A few weeks after we buried Rose, Lijah moved into my little house in Wellington Street, not far from the Corporation Depot. Well, there wasn't any point in him hanging around his and Rose's house, kicking his heels.

It's a strange thing, to be an old lady and have your son living with you when he is an old man too. You do not see the oldness in your own child. You look at him and see the boy who used to whimper in his sleep. And you can't help treating him like the boy who used to whimper in his sleep an' all – which doesn't go down so well sometimes when's he middle-aged and balding.

It was like we had returned to what we was before. Lijah had lived with me for the first twenty years of his life, on and off – and then there was a break in our arrangement when he went off and married and had five children – and then he came back to live with me for another twenty years. I do sometimes wonder if my life has been a bit peculiar.

It saddens me to relate this, but despite the fact that we had been a large family, once, it came pretty clear to me that now it was just me and Lijah. Scarlet and Fenella came round the day after Rose's wake, to help me brush the carpets what needed a good going over after a load of feet had been tramping on them. We cleaned the curtains too, tried to get the smoke out of them.

But as soon as their jobs were done, they made their excuses again and left. Billy came at the weekend and brought some steak and kidney with dumplings on top for us to heat up on Sunday. She didn't stay long either. Oh, they all did their bit, I'm not saying they didn't. But their bit was all they did. When I decided that Lijah should move back in with me, they all came and helped us pack stuff up and carried it round, and I had baked biscuits and cakes so we could all sit crammed round my little kitchen table for the rest of the afternoon and drink tea and eat 'til we were stuffed. And how long did they stay? Half an hour. There was a fruit cake didn't even get broken into.

Bright and cheery, they were with us. All full of helpfulness and not sharing anything. Lijah was too grief stricken to notice, but I noticed, all right.

One day, some weeks after Lijah had moved in with me, I decided to take the initiative and call by Daniel's sign-writing business. He was busy, which maybe accounts for how he was a little off with me. We were stood in his yard and he had just had a load of work in. One of the big breweries was opening up a string of pubs across the county, all with the same name. The idea was, Daniel explained, that wherever you went, you would be able to find a Crown & Anchor, and they would be all the same inside so you would get comfortable with them being all the same. And after a while, you wouldn't want to go nowhere different, as it being not-the-same would make you *un*comfortable. There was something about this that seemed not-right to me, although I'm not sure I can really put it into words.

So, he had a big job on that day. He had a row of signs constructed – must've been more than twenty of them, and three men going from one to the other. One was doing the background, another the anchor and another the crown. The lettering was done by Daniel himself as he wouldn't let nobody else near that.

We stood in his yard, and I said to him, 'Well, it's quite the little factory you've got here now I've come to find out what's up with you lot and why you're all being so off with me and your father.'

There was a pause. His voice went a bit careful. 'We all appreciate you looking after Dad,' he paused again. 'Don't think we don't.'

'So in other words, now he's moved in with me, you think that lets you off the hook.'

Daniel gave me a sideways glance. 'That's not the way it is, Gran. I don't think that's right fair, if you don't mind me saying so.'

'So why don't you come round more often?'

He took a deep breath. 'We was round only last weekend, Gran, and Scarlet dropped by after work on Wednesday, she told me.'

I couldn't find the words for it. It wasn't that they weren't coming to see us, it was that they were being dutiful and no more, and I wanted more.

'Gran, I don't want to be inhospitable or anything, but the lads are waiting for me to tell them what to do.'

Ah yes, the big businessman now, I thought bitterly. He hadn't even taken me into his office and offered me a cup of tea. I could have come up with a smart retort but I didn't have the heart for it, that day. I turned away.

As I walked off down the road, I could feel Daniel watching me go. I hoped his conscience was pricking him a bit. I even felt a little tearful and sorry for myself. I thought, *I didn't realise when we lost Rose we were losing the children as well. How has this happened?* I didn't turn around.

I bought myself a canary. Lijah had been promising me one ever since we'd moved up to Peterborough but there must have been a drastic canary shortage or something as he kept telling me he couldn't find the right one. 'I'm not fussed,' I kept saying to him. 'Anything yellow with a pair of wings will do.' In the end, I gave up on him and went out and got it myself from the market. Trouble was, I put it in the parlour and the chimney in there was not too efficient – not bad enough to pay for a sweep but blocked enough to make sure a bit of smoke and soot came in the room. Sooner or later, that yellow canary looked more like a blackbird. I couldn't let it out to hop around, even with the door closed. It would have made a right mess.

I liked talking to it, though. 'Good morning, *meero chiriclo,*' I'd say. '*Sar shin meero rawnie?*'

If he had been himself, Lijah would have made sarcastic remarks about my canary. But instead, he sat in the parlour in silence and watched me talk to it.

He hadn't done much since he'd moved in with me. Not even gone off down the pub. Sometimes he said, 'I'm off for a little walk now, Dei,' and I knew he was going to go and sit by Rose's grave. We didn't have much *lovah* at that time and it still only had a wooden cross on it. Before the funeral, Daniel had offered to pay for a piece of granite but Lijah got quite sharp with him and said nobody was paying for his wife's gravestone but himself. Still stubborn, even in his grief.

I never said it to him but that was the real reason I persuaded him to move in with me at Wellington Street, to save the rent on the Buckle Street house. I had a little money put by, but he would have to pull his socks up and get back to his market stall sooner or later.

He did, eventually, of course. Perhaps that is the most painful bit of losing someone, the bit when you realise that your life is going to carry on. It's painful, of course, because it makes you think that others will do that after you have gone, too, and none of us likes to think that, do we? The weeks turned into months, and Lijah went back to his market stall and his dealing and we saw the others from time to time but it was like we saw them through a fog. I put up with it and put up with it, thinking it would change but it didn't, it got worse, whatever *it* was, and in the end, I thought, I'm not prepared to just sit by while this family dissolves around me just because Lijah and me haven't got to the bottom of what's going on.

Scarlet. She was the answer to it. I knew that right enough. Scarlet had loved her mother fierce-like, in the way that youngest children do. I also knew she was the only one who would be honest with me if I tackled her head on. Mehitable and Fenella would have been scared of upsetting me, but not Scarlet, oh no. And she was the only one who didn't have a family of her own yet, so by rights she was the one who should have been looking after her father now he was a widower. So, it was her I decided to tackle.

Scarlet. She was a match for me any day.

I went round one Saturday afternoon. Scarlet was lodging with a Miss Cowley who worked in the same office as her. I waited at the end of Bishop's Road, sitting on a bench by the Recreation Ground, until I saw Miss Cowley go out. I wanted to talk to Scarlet in private.

I knocked on the door with the end of my walking stick. Scarlet opened it quickly, as if she had been passing when she heard me knock. It was two steps up to the door and being on the short side as I was, I was at something of a disadvantage as I looked up at her. She didn't seem at all surprised, standing there, and I felt as if I was suddenly seeing her for what she was, a large woman, broad of face, not pretty exactly but quite handsome, hair in careful waves – but for that hair, the image of her mother.

'Hello, Gran,' she said, moving back to allow me to step up.

'Scarlet,' I said, nodding to her.

She hovered for a moment while I put down my stick and unbuttoned my coat, which is a right fiddly job for me these days. Then she turned to the kitchen, to put the kettle on.

As soon as we was sat in the parlour with a cup of tea, I started. 'I've not come here to muck about,' I said, pushing my cup away from me. 'I've come here to find something out and find out straight.'

She had a dry sort of expression on her face. 'What might that be, Mami?' She was the only one of my grandchildren who still called me Mami, sometimes. It was her way of getting on my good side, I suppose, but it wasn't going to put me off, not that afternoon.

'Why are you lot being so off with me and your father? You come round and you can't wait to get out the door as soon as you've set foot inside it. It's breaking his heart.'

'Has he got a heart to break? That's news to me.' She took a sip of tea.

'Don't be insolent, my girl. Remember who you're talking to.'

At that, she had the grace to glance down, but still a bit mutinous-like.

'He's got five children, he's entitled to be close to at least one of them.' It was a strange sort of logic, I suppose, but it made sense to me. 'And the man's been widowed this past year. Do you not think he could do with a bit of comforting from his own daughters?'

At that, her head shot up. 'Five children, well, yes, Gran, you're right. Let's take them one by one shall we? One: Daniel. Well I can't speak for Daniel, all I can say is I'm not sure whether he really feels like he's got a father seeing as he has had to be father to us all since he could nearly stand up. I saw Dad give him a back-hander that knocked him across the room once, when he was pissed, so we'll leave Daniel out of it, shall we?'

I was shocked she should use such language in front of me.

'Two: Billy. Well now, Billy was always closest to him out of all of us but she's having quite a hard time at home at the moment and could do without any extra bother. Three: Bartholomew. Oh no, there's no point in doing Bartholomew is there, as none of us have heard from him in years and why not? Because he's just like his father.'

'I can count, you know. You don't need to go on.' I hadn't expected this. This was horrible.

'Four: Fenella. Nellie's too good natured to hold grudges but she tends to agree with me on most things and she does on this, so there.'

She stopped. I saw a look of hesitation in her eyes. I couldn't help but let my voice be a bit dry sounding. 'Well, that leaves one we've not yet accounted for, don't it?'

She took a deep breath. 'Five. Five is me.' She looked me right in the eye. 'You were the only one with Mum when she died, Gran. What did you say to her?'

I thought that a mighty peculiar question. 'I told you. I said, whatever will we all do without you? And she smiled at me, and then she just went to sleep. I fetched you all straightaway, soon as I realised. Don't tell me you don't believe me, in the name of heaven, *mi biti chai*, what reason would I have to tell you else?' This was all getting far too deep for me.

'Why didn't she want Dad?'

'What do you mean?'

'When we all went up to see her that morning. I was last up. I said, do you want Dad, and she didn't. Why didn't she want to see her own husband?'

'How on earth should I know?'

At that, she looked defeated. She stopped, took another sip of tea, and sighed. Her broad shoulders sagged. 'I'll tell you why not. Because he only made things worse, that's why not. She was dying. She deserved a little peace, for once.'

She wasn't making a right lot of sense, I must say. 'Scarletina,' I said gently, my nickname for her. 'They were married a long time, your mum and dad, and I think maybe when you've been together that long maybe you're just not that important to each other any more. Maybe she'd said all she needed to say to him.'

Her eyes narrowed, and I sensed we were about to get to the marrow of things. 'Aye, and what had he said to her?'

I looked at her.

'He told her she'd been a rotten mother, that's what he did. He went in there and accused her of the worst thing he could think of, a week before she died, when he took in all those stupid bits of furniture that he'd insisted she should have when she couldn't even get up to use them. She was dying, and she should've been allowed to die in peace, and instead he went in and told her how useless she'd been with our Billy and Lord knows what else as well.'

I could not believe it. 'No, Scarlet, you must've got it wrong.'

She rose from her seat, her gaze firm. 'I've not got it wrong,

Gran, I've not at all. She pleaded with me, after he'd gone. You should have seen how agitated she was, desperate to see Billy. You were there that day when Billy went up, so you know all about it. After everything our father did when we were growing up. And when his wife was dying he went in there and accused her of all sorts and she died tormenting herself with everything she'd done wrong.'

I rose too. 'Don't you dare say that of your father. Your father loved you like anything! He thought the sun shone out of your plump backside when you was a baby! He doted on you!'

She crashed her fists against her forehead. 'You're not listening to me, Gran! *Listen* to me! I know he loved us, that doesn't mean he was any good at it, does it?'

I couldn't believe she could disrespect her own father so. 'So, you lot think you've had it hard, do you? You don't know what hunger is. You've know idea how little we had when he was growing up. Compared with the life he had, you lot lived like royalty. At least you had a roof over your heads . . . most of the time.'

She turned away from me, and spoke over her shoulder, her voice ringing with feeling. 'You're still not understanding me, Gran. I can forgive him not knowing any better. But I can't forgive him going into Mum when she was dying and taking away her peace of mind. Even if he didn't mean to do it, it was wicked. It was just as wicked for him not meaning it.'

I saw that I was wasting my time. Lijah's children would have to be reconciled to Lijah in their own good time. There was nothing more I could do.

It took me some time to raise myself from my chair. My knees had started to hurt bad when I got up and down.

Scarlet picked up my stick from where it rested against the table and handed it to me. Then she took my arm and helped me to the door. 'Do you want me to walk you back?' she asked.

'I'm not quite that far gone yet,' I said. 'Will be one day, mind.'

We made a slow journey to the hallway, and she lifted my coat and hat from the peg. I rested my stick against the wall, and put my things on. She wrapped my scarf once around my neck and then she tried to do my coat buttons for me, as if I was a child. I batted her fingers away. I still find it odd that I can't straighten my hands no more. I look at these strange, twisted things on the ends of my arms, like tree roots with their lines and lumps, and I think, are these really my hands?

Scarlet watched me while I fiddled with the buttons. I daresay it took a deal longer than it would have done if I had let her help.

'You and Mum didn't really like each other all that much, did you?' she said. She said it quite gently, just stating the fact, without any accusation.

I stopped what I was doing and looked at her. 'Your mum and I were close as close can be for thirty years,' I said. 'I don't know what to do now she's not here.'

She turned to open the front door.

As I stepped out into the bitter cold, I remembered a conversation I once had with Rose. We were mangling some laundry. It was February and freezing and we were out in the yard at Sutton. I was turning the handle and she was pulling the laundry out the other side – it was sheets, so it needed two of us. We always did the sheets together.

She was doing the bit I hated. I hated gathering heavy, wet cloth when it was cold. Your fingers would redden and freeze in a minute.

I sneezed.

Rose said, 'You've not got an ague there, have you?'

I shrugged.

'You want to watch it,' she said, as she pulled the sheet through. 'It was the Fen ague that killed my mother. It can carry you off in a trice.'

She had never raised the subject of her mother with me before. 'Was that when you was on the farm?' I asked her, lifting the next sheet from the tin tub.

'It was. It was the farm that killed her, for sure. We didn't have those sorts of agues in East Cambridge.'

All at once, I thought of my little Dei, broken on the tread-wheel in Huntington House of Correction. 'I lost my mother when I was young, too,' I said, as I pushed the edge of the sheet between the rollers 'til it caught. 'I'd just had Lijah.'

'What took her?' Rose asked. She had folded the sheet and was rubbing her hands together against the cold. The chill wind lifted her hair around her face as I looked at her. I wondered what she would think if I told her the whole story, about us being arrested and accused by the farmer and his *prosecutrix* and hard labour and cannon balls.

Well, what would any *gorjer* think if you told them a story of a *gipsy* that had died in prison?

'Same as yours,' I said, and took a deep breath as I pushed the mangle handle to its full height, always tricky for me as being on the small side it's hard for me to put my weight into it. 'An ague.'

'Well, like I said,' Rose said, as she grasped the emerging sheet from her side and began to pull, 'you want to watch it.'

Her sleeves were rolled up and the muscles on her forearms bulged as she pulled the sheet. She pursed her lips with the effort, frowning.

She was as strong as an ox, that girl. It never once occurred to me I might outlive her.

As I walked away from Scarlet's house I thought, if I could take Rose out of that box in Eastfield Cemetery and put myself in there instead, I'd do it in a trice. Lijah, Daniel, Mehitable, Fenella and Scarlet – all of them grieving away over Rose, all broken apart over it and unable to comfort each other. I loved them all, every sodding stubborn one of them, and would bring Rose back in a minute, if I could.

There are some people who are like threads in a knitted jumper – pull them out, and the whole garment starts to unravel, and you realise too late that you've pulled out the one bit of thread what was holding the whole thing together. Strange, when it looked like all the other bits of thread.

CHAPTER 19

The odd thing about living as long as I have, is, you get so used to the idea of dying that it stops being real. You start to think you never will.

I've been expecting to die for decades. I thought I would when I was poorly, when we were stopped on Stourbridge Common. I had stomach-pains fit to bust after some young *grasni* from the next *vardo* gave me a stew with the wrong leaves in it. Kale is for cows, I told her – that's how come they eat it.

Then, when we were in Sutton, I had the *noomonia*, and that was a fair one for carrying off the old ladies like me. Then Rose died, and her being a generation down from me meant it felt all wrong. Surely it was my turn, not hers?

So I keep waiting, but it doesn't happen. And now I've got to the point where I can't get my head around dying at all. There've been too many false alarms.

*

I thought I had better try and take the subject seriously for a change. So, one evening, when Lijah and I were sat in the kitchen after supper, I tried to bring it up. It must have been a year or two after we lost Rose – or maybe it was longer than that.

It annoyed Lijah that I always wanted to sit in the kitchen of an evening. 'That's what we've got a sitting room for, Dei,' he would say, 'to sit in, you know.'

And I would say back, 'The parlour's for guests.'

And he would say, 'We never have any guests, Dei,'

And I would say, 'Well, whose fault is that?'

And that would be an end to it.

Anyroad, we were sat in the kitchen, both with mugs of tea in front of us, mine lovely and dark, and I thought it was time I took dying seriously.

'Lijah,' I said, 'I've decided it's time I took dying seriously.'

'Righto, Mum,' he said, and took a sip of tea.

I had a sudden urge to make him promise to burn me, with all my things, like we did in the old days on the road. That would give him what you might call a bit of a dilemma, as I don't reckon it's legal these days.

'I've thought about what I want, after,' I said.

'After what?'

'After I'm dead, you fool, what d'you think I'm on about?'

He would have rolled his eyes at the ceiling if he'd thought he could get away with it.

'I want to motor, so I do. I've never been in a motor car.'

'Haven't you?' He looked a bit surprised.

'Never in all my born puff.'

He scratched his head. 'Well I'm sure I can manage that, Dei.'

'I want a nice shiny black one, like all the posh folk have. And I want to motor nice and slow, all the way up Eastfield Avenue, so slow that folk have plenty of time to stop and stare and wonder who's in there.'

'All right, then,' he nodded.

'Apart from that, it's up to you,' I said, shrugging. 'It'll be your business when I'm gone, nobody else's. I'm not fussed about having crowds of people or one of those daft get-togethers where nobody says what they're thinking. Can't stand all that nonsense. You can put me in the hole with your own bare hands if you like.' Lijah frowned a little, as if he was trying to get his head around the idea of me actually dying, me not being here any more. 'But I do like the idea of a big shiny motor, so I do.'

There wasn't any one point when I realised things had got a bit better between us and the children. I just realised they had, bit by bit, as the years passed. But I'm not sure Lijah was ever close to them like he should have been. I don't know what you have to do to make that sort of thing happen between a mother or father and children what are grow'd. Maybe it's too late by then, too late for the sorting out of stuff. They do it in the moving pictures, I'm told. I've never been to the cinema myself but they say that on stage, when the piano plays, it's like lanternslides only the people can move about. They have writing at the bottom that says what the people are saying, and they are saying things like, 'You've never loved me, have you?' and the fella replies, 'No I haven't, but only because I lost my first fiancée in a tragic drowning accident.' After that, they come to an understanding.

People don't have those sorts of conversations where I come from. Leastways they didn't on the Fens, nor in East Cambridge, nor in Sutton – and especially not in the little brick houses of Peterborough. No, in all the places I've ever been, they come round for a cup of tea and they keep their private thoughts to themselves. They drink tea by the gallon, so they do, as enough of it might wash away the secret things what have got buried in the secret insides of themselves.

Except sometimes, in the dark. That's the time when you think about ghosts, and dead pigs and whether stories really happened the way you remember them or whether you are just a bit mad in the head and it would be better if someone shut you up so you won't do no harm to nobody.

We had a routine in the mornings, did Lijah and I. We were always up at first light. I would come down and light the fires and brew tea, then take my cup outside for a bit of a smoke in the fresh air. It was the only time the gas tower looked pretty, in the morning light. You couldn't see it from the back garden, so I liked to take my tea and my pipe out to the front step, even if I needed a shawl round my shoulders. A few folk would be about – people always greeted you right politely first thing in the morning on account of how the day hadn't been able to upset them yet. I would squat down on the step and chew on my pipe and sip my tea and as the dawn rose, the gas tower would glow – this huge orange cylinder, looming over the houses, like a big bucket of answers.

Lijah was usually up by the time I went back inside. Quite often, he'd have had his tea and a slice of bacon and onion roll and be getting himself ready for the outside world. He would sit in on a kitchen stool with his comb and his cap on the table in front of him. He was quite bald by then but for a small piece of hair that grew at the back of his head, which he had managed to grow as long as long could be, like a China-man. He oiled this, so he did, by dipping the comb in one of my saucers. Then he would wind the strand of hair round his head, until it stopped on his forehead, when he would fashion a kiss-curl out of the end of it. With his cap on top, it looked almost normal.

When we were Travellers, no decent mother would ever let her child fix his hair inside, nor use a saucer to do it. Sometimes, I watched him do this and wondered what we had come to.

'All right, Dei,' he said, when he had finished. He would rise up and pat his waistcoat pockets. 'It's off to the market for me.'

Mehitable and Scarlet had market stalls right next to each other, by then, selling woollens and hats and gloves. Fenella helped them out sometimes but she was a bit busy with her girls. Mehitable was renting her stall from a fella called Thompson and went down there every morning while her boy was at school. She didn't like Lijah going down the market when Thompson was around, on account of how Lijah might forget and start rokkering to her in Rummanus. That would be the end of it, then. She needed the bit of money on account of how the no-good she had married had upped and left her to raise her boy on her own. Always unlucky, Mehitable.

'Off to *dik* the big wide world, *amaro chavo*?' I would say to Lijah, as he set off.

'*Avali*, I am that, Dei,' he always replied.

I had a nasty moment, the other day. It was like I sort of woke up, and I was in the middle of the parlour. Thing was, I couldn't remember why I was there. And for a moment, I didn't even know where 'there' was. I looked around me for a bit. There was an empty birdcage hanging in one corner, from a standard lamp with the bulb and shade removed. There was a carriage clock on the mantel. Beneath me was carpet, in a swirly pattern. When I moved my toes inside my soft house-boots, I could see the knuckle of them bulge upwards, rising above the carpet like small sea-monsters. It was like these things were the pieces of a jigsaw puzzle that suddenly rearranged themselves into the right order and it came to me that I was in the parlour of my own little house.

For the life of me, I could not remember what I was doing in the middle of the parlour, or how I had got to be there.

Once, my father sent me to get him something from a market. And he gave me some pennies to buy myself a pie. I was stood in front of the pie stall and I must have looked like a poor, starving child or some such, as the stall-holder called out to me, 'Hey, come here, girlie.' I saw that in his hands he was holding a piece of brown paper, and there was a heap of broken pastry on it. I realised that he had been watching me while I was staring at his pies.

I had only been staring at them as I was wondering what sort of pie to choose but he must've thought I had no money for a pie. He was a giving me a broken one for free.

I took it, even though I was too embarrassed to thank him properly, and turned away and ate it, and it tasted every bit as good as a not-broken one, I must say. Having got it for nothing didn't spoil the flavour of it, neither.

As I'd got myself a free pie, I walked around the fair for a bit, wondering what to spend my pennies on.

I bought myself a little bird. The lady put it in a brown paper bag. I could feel its wings a-fluttering inside. It was a pretty feeling. On the way home, I stopped on a bridge and decided to take a peek at it, but when I opened the bag, the bird flew right away.

Just like my black canary.

I met a madman once, a real one. It was in a field. He came back with me to the camp and he frightened everybody but I liked him and fed him and gave him jobs to do. But as he was a real madman, we had to give him back. Some men came and got him. I wasn't there when they took him. Dei told me about it later. I think. No, I saw him. So I did.

There's going to be another war, apparently. It's the Germans again, still up to their old tricks. We didn't beat them good enough last time, so we've got to do it all over again. When Lijah told me about it, I got right agitated and made him promise not to go off, and he said, 'Dei, I'm in my sixties. They wouldn't have me in the army even to polish their boots.'

After a while I said, 'Was my grandson killed in the war?'

'No, Dei,' said Lijah. 'The boys came back safe and sound. We all did. We was lucky.'

'Well, where did he go, then?' I meant Bartholomew, my Barty-boy, the little terror.

Lijah knew who I meant, right enough. He sighed. 'Bartholomew was not right in the head after the war, and he went off to London and no one knows where he is, now.'

I frowned, just trying to get the pieces right in my head. 'And what about Daniel?'

'Daniel owns his own sign-writing business. He's done very nicely for himself. Got fellas working for him, now and a girl what's almost grow'd. We saw them Sunday.'

'Oh,' I said,' that's right.' Daniel's wife had served us lamb. She had put a little dish in front of me and shouted in my left ear, 'That's mint sauce, that is, Grandmother!' Snooty little cow.

This next war wasn't like the last one. In the last one, people just disappeared. Men marched off and some of them came back injured or not right in the head like Bartholomew – and some didn't come back at all. But it all happened somewhere else a long way away as I remember, not here.

This new war came here a bit more. They tried to set fire to the cathedral by the marketplace, did the Germans, although we put it out in time. Some people broke shop windows and said you shouldn't work at Werners.

It made things ugly, this war. If you didn't have curtains on your windows then you had to paint them with green paint and put up strips of sticky brown paper all over them to make your house so ugly the Germans couldn't be bothered to bomb it. Lijah said you couldn't get a horse for love nor money.

I get confused sometimes. Sometimes I wonder who I am telling my story to, for it is like I am telling a story over and over in my head. And sometimes it feels like I'm there, right back in it, and I lose myself, and then at other times it's just remembering, like any other old fool.

Sometimes, it's like there's someone listening. I found myself wondering the other day about who that someone might be, and I pictured a girl, who's waiting for me somewhere, and maybe she's someone else or maybe she's only me, the old me that used to exist and is still there underneath the layers of everything. Then, when I think this girl is me, I feel as though I am talking to her and warning her of who she's going to become, except she's not really listening, of course, as she's too flipping stubborn.

There are many things I don't believe in, but I do believe in ghosts. How could I not when I saw *Bafedo Bawlo*, the Ghost Pig, with my own very eyes? Sometimes I think I'm talking to a ghost but it is not the ghost of a dead person, oh no, as that would be an evil thing and it would drive me quite mad. No, it is like the ghost of someone not yet born. They are not evil. They are thin and pale and wispy, like made-up ghosts in the picture-books my grandchildren used to have – pretty little things, like dandelion fluff, not like real ghosts at all.

Lijah said to me once, when we were sitting together at the kitchen table after supper, smoking in silence, 'Dei, for what are you always muttering and talking to yourself these days? Are you going mad on me, or what?'

And I replied, 'I talk to myself, my son, as it's the only way I get a decent answer.'

Well, he might've been an Old Fella by then but he still needed slapping down once in a while.

It was when I went to buy tobacco that I saw it, the Ghost Pig, right here on a street in Peterborough, with my very own eyes.

I was on my way to Phipps', the newsagents. You could get the 'baccy at the stationers as well, but old Phipps liked me, for some reason. Probably my girlish charm. Anyhow, when he'd taken my ration card and weighed a quarter ounce for me, he always added a few scraps more, before he twisted the paper.

I had just paid for my quarter and tucked the paper into the special pocket in my handbag, when he said, all casual like, 'I see that new pub's opening on Friday, they've got a notice up. Have you seen it?'

'Another?'

'Aye, for all the lads been demobbed, I reckon. Those boys need a pint when they get home.'

'Another.'

I knew which one he meant. It was on the corner with Star Road. Yet another public house, as if Peterborough wasn't stuffed full of them already. Well, that will be nice and convenient for my Lijah, I thought to myself. He'll be able to roll home, if he wants.

'Your son won the competition, didn't he?' said Phipps. 'They all had to stand up and tell a story, and he won it.'

A boy had barged into the shop and asked for something, rudely, cutting into our conversation. I was a bit confused as I thought he'd asked for a red apple but Phipps was turning and opening a jar that had some sweets on sticks. The boy was looking anxious. He was probably on his way to school and shouldn't have been in Phipps' at all.

'A competition d'you say?' I said, cocking my head as though I hadn't heard him right, although in fact my hearing is perfect and always has been. It's useful to pretend it ain't, sometimes.

'Yes, the competition, to give it a name.' The schoolboy was hopping from one foot to another, holding out his copper to pay, but Phipps was making a point of ignoring him, to teach him some manners. 'They had a night in there last month. Did he not tell you? I suppose the idea was, get everybody interested. They had to stand up and tell a story and whoever told the best story that gave the landlord the idea for the name for the new public house gets to drink the first official pint on Friday, and then free for the rest of the night.'

Lijah hadn't mentioned any of this to me, but that was no surprise. He knew I wouldn't approve, and I didn't, but I must admit to feeling a little chuffed at the thought of my Lijah winning something. Well, that's a first, I thought.

The bell tinkled as I pushed open the door to leave the shop. I was still standing on the step, pulling on my gloves, when the schoolboy came barging out behind me, nearly knocking me off the step. *Chavos* these days have no idea about respect. If he hadn't been so quick, I'd have given him a clip round the ear.

I thought I'd take a wander up to Star Road and have a look at that new public house, even though my house was in the opposite direction. I wasn't in any particular hurry to get home, that morning.

So I walked up, taking it slowly as I have to do these days, and stood on the corner of Star Road and Wellington Street.

They'd done the place up nice, I'll say that for them – new window frames and a brand new door with a shiny brass handle. A man was up a ladder in front of the door. He was a-fixing the sign, which was covered in sackcloth and swinging lightly in the wind.

I stood looking up at him, and he glanced down.

'All ready, are you?' I asked, just by way of making conversation.

'Aye,' he said. 'It's creaking a bit. But it'll be all right. It's new.'

'So I hear.' I said. 'Are you the landlord?' I thought maybe he might tell me a bit about the competition Lijah had won. I was right interested in the idea of Lijah winning something.

'Nope,' he said, 'I'm just fixing it. The boss is pleased with it, though. Fella over at Walton did the painting. It's a *gipsy* legend, you know.'

I felt a certain tightening in my chest. 'What's that, then?'

The street was mostly empty but for a few children still late to get to school. The men were all off at work and it was a bit early for the women to be setting out to do their shopping. I was only out and about because I still got up early as ever and liked going to get my 'baccy while it was quiet.

The man up the ladder didn't reply. He just removed the sack-cloth, to show me what he was fixing. He gave the sign a little push, to see if it would still creak.

The picture was of a snow-white pig with black patches and one black ear. It wasn't a normal pig, though, oh no. It was painted all fuzzy edged, and with light strokes so the background showed through a bit. It was staring out of the picture at me, and its eyes were glowing red. It was the Ghost Pig, sure enough. And it was living on the corner of my street.

I felt my chest tighten a little more, and my hand went to my throat. My blouse was buttoned up to my neck against the cold and I was overwhelmed with a desire to undo it. *Dadus, soskey were creminor kair'd? Chavi, that puvo-baulor might jib by halling lende . . .* The man looked down at me, his face creased in concern. There was a ringing in my ears. *Dadus, soskey were puvo-baulor kair'd? Chavi, that tute and mandi might jib by lelling lende.* My sight went a bit blurry. *Dadus, soskey were tu ta mandi kair'd? Chavi, that creminor might jib by halling mende.* The man looked back at his sign and gave it another little push with his finger. It swung silently, to and fro. I felt myself begin to swing as well, although whether it was up or down, I could not tell.

CHAPTER 20

Thomas Freeman was a slightly built boy, light on his feet he looked. There was an easiness about him. It's hard to put it into words. He just had an air of knowing what he was about, what lay ahead of him in life. His father owned the bakery in Werrington, and probably his father before him. Thomas was the third child but the eldest son, so he'd take over in his turn. Maybe it was knowing his future was secure made him such a simple, cheerful sort of person. There was nothing to worry about for Thomas Freeman, oh no.

We first got talking one spring afternoon. I knew who he was, of course, as we had been stopped on Werrington Green long enough for us to work out who most of the *gorjers* were. I hadn't spoken to any of the village boys up 'til then, of course – such a thing would have been unthinkable back in them days. Some of them would throw mud at our *vardos* when they went past, but only if my Dadus or Redeemus Grey weren't around. I had first seen Thomas Freeman with that group, but he didn't throw any mud himself, just carried on walking, with his hands in his pockets. He didn't say anything to the other boys and he didn't look at me.

After they had gone past, I thought about the thin, light-haired boy who hadn't thrown mud. The other boys he was with looked a lot tougher than him, but there seemed something strong about him all the same, perhaps because he hadn't felt the need to join in. I wondered who he was, and what his name was, but knew there was no way of finding out as the heavens would have opened if I'd asked a question about a *gorjer* boy.

The next I saw him was a few days later, when I was walking down the lane that led to Walton. I was looking for nettles. Dei had said they were thick down that particular lane. Thomas Freeman was on his way back from somewhere, with a bundle tucked under his arm.

I saw the *gorjer* boy with the light hair walking towards me and I did what any girl in my position would have done. I crossed over the lane, as you would if you'd spotted a dog you didn't like the look of.

As we drew level, he stopped where he was and watched me pass, then called after me, 'There's no need to avoid me, miss. I don't bite, you know.'

I just kept my head down and quickened my pace. Course you bite, I thought dismissively. You all bite.

But as I kept walking, I thought how his voice had sounded friendly and regretful, not harsh like most boys' voices. He had sounded a little sad that I wouldn't acknowledge him. And the whole time I was picking nettles, bending low to grasp the bottom of their stems, I thought of the sadness and kindliness in his voice, and resolved that next time I came across him, as long as no one else was around, I would be bold and speak with him.

The opportunity did not come for some weeks, and I had almost forgotten about him by then. I was walking down the same lane, around the same time of day. Looking back on it, I wonder if I had not done that on purpose a few times, on the chance that he had been on a regular errand before and I might see him again.

I was not yet at the place where we had passed each other before. I was still quite close to the village. But it was a quiet, sunlit afternoon and no one was around, and as I neared a long wooden gate that led into a farmer's field, I saw that he was sitting on top of it, and I knew at once that he was waiting on the off-chance I might pass, and that for the last few weeks we had both been trying to bump into one another, and both been disappointed, until now.

I glanced behind me, to make sure no one else was around. I thought, *he'd be in as much trouble as me if we were seen together*. He was from an upright *gorjer* family, after all, with a good trade. The last thing they would want is for their prized eldest son to be seen talking to a *gipsy* girl.

I had never met any of his family, of course, but the thought of how unpleasant they would be to me if they got the chance was what made me bold enough to speak to him. I stopped in front of the gate and looked up at him.

'Good afternoon,' he said politely.

'It is indeed,' I said, loving my boldness, loving the newness of it.

'What is your name?' he asked. 'Mine's Thomas Freeman,' he added quickly, with the air of someone who was prepared to go first.

'I know,' I replied, even though I did not until that moment. 'You're the baker's lad.'

He looked surprised. 'How do you know that?'

How do you think? I laughed to myself. Could it be something to do with the way you ride round the village on your dad's bike after school, selling loaves from the front basket?

'My name is . . . Edith,' I said. Edith sounded good, I thought. Nice and proper.

'Edith,' he repeated.

We looked at each other for a bit, then he shuffled along the top bar of the gate, to allow me to climb up and sit on it to but not to be too close to him. I clambered up, and there we sat, like two birds, both of us glancing this way and that down the lane so that, from our vantage point, we could see if anyone approached.

'Where are you off to, then?' he asked after a bit.

'Just walking,' I said.

'I am on my way back from visiting my aunt and her family in Gunthorpe. She's a seamstress there, but she's not been well recently.'

'I am sorry to hear that,' I replied.

We were in a strange position, for it was clear that neither of us wanted to jump down from the gate and go off while neither of us could think of a decent reason for staying there either. I did not know what was happening between us, if anything – but I knew I was enjoying it, right enough. It made me feel like I wasn't a little girl, right at that minute, that I was myself, and that that self was somehow and importantly different from the girl I had been a few minutes before. It was a new, clean feeling, like being able to fly – not that I have ever been able to fly, of course.

'Have you got any brothers and sisters?' he said.

'No,' I said, 'I did when I was little but they all died.'

'Oh,' he said.

'What about you?' I asked.

'Oh loads of them,' he said. 'I've got two big sisters, Emily and Jane. I'm the eldest boy but I've got three younger brothers, Samuel, William and George, and then there are two little girls as well. There's always been loads of us. It's quite good like that when you've got a shop. Don't you get lonely on your own?'

It was a stupid question, so I didn't bother to answer it. We were quiet for a bit, then he said, 'I've never spoken to a *gipsy* before.'

There wasn't much I could say to that.

'Would you mind if I asked you a question?' he said politely.

I looked at him, the sun on his hair.

Without waiting for me to reply, he said, 'Is it true you all have your own secret language? I studied Latin at school but I never got the hang of it.'

'Well you can understand me, right enough,' I replied warily.

'I know,' he said, 'but I remember having a secret language with my brother when we were children, only we forgot it after a while, and I just wondered how you remember it, if you've never wrote it down.'

I confess this question flummoxed me a bit, so I said. 'I'll answer yours if you answer a question of mine after.'

'All right, Edith.'

'Well,' I said, 'the truth of the matter is, we can speak the same language as animals, you know, horses and dogs and foxes all understand each other, and so do we. We don't need to write it down, it's just in us, and that's the way it is. It isn't something we think about, you know, no more than you do, but we know ourselves to be greater than you for we understand you, but you will never understand us.'

The length of this speech surprised him, for he stared at me the whole while, impressed. 'So do you . . .'

'It's my turn now, I believe.'

'All right. Go on, then. Ask me anything.'

I tried to think of all the things I had ever wondered about the way *gorjers* live, all the things I had been curious about, but nothing came to mind, and out of nowhere, the words came, 'Would you like to kiss me, Thomas Freeman?'

The look on his face was one of such joy and astonishment that I could not stop myself grinning from ear to ear. He smiled and leaned towards me. I leaned forward too, and then gave him a sharp shove in the chest with one hand. He obliged me by tipping backwards, legs going right over, and landing on his side in the field.

I looked down at him over my shoulder and laughed. 'I didn't say you *could*, you know, I just asked if you wanted to!'

I jumped off my side of the gate and ran down the path, full of glee at my own wit, and happy as anything because I now knew for certain that a boy wanted to kiss me and I had never known that in my whole life before.

I had got no more than a few yards back towards the village when I looked ahead, then stopped dead on the path. Ahead of me, in the distance, was a dark, solid figure, right in the middle of the lane. He was some way off, but I knew from the size of him and the silhouette of his hat, that it was Redeemus Grey. He was standing stock still, so must have been staring along the path and seen me.

I glanced behind me and saw Thomas clambering over the gate. I looked back and realised that Redeemus Grey must be able to see him as well. What must it look like, me running down the lane, dishevelled and laughing, and a *gorjer* boy clambering the gate after me? My insides felt soft with fear, for I knew what a strict man Redeemus Grey was and how he'd be bound to tell my father what he'd seen and then I'd catch it. Mr Grey was terribly moral that way. He once took one of his own girls to the middle of the green and beat her with a stick in front of everybody because he'd caught her looking at a *gorjer* boy, never mind talking to one. There was no chance one of his girls would ever step out of line. They'd stay as pure as driven snow until he had them safely married off.

I gestured to Thomas, waving him back with my hand. His face creased in concern, and then he understood my gesture, turned and walked the other way. When I looked back toward the village, Redeemus Grey had also turned and gone – probably straight to tell my father.

Now I'm for it, I thought, and the thought quite wiped out my happiness at having pulled a trick on Thomas.

*

I walked back to the village as slowly as I had ever done, know-ing I had to go straight back to the green but wanting to delay the dread moment for as long as possible. As I came up Church Street, the vicar was leaving the churchyard, pulling the gate shut behind him. He glanced at me and I nodded politely, walking on.

But blow me if I hadn't gone more than a few paces when I realised he was hurrying after me and falling into step beside me. I kept my head down and walked quickly, for although he was a vicar, he was still a man and I thought, dordy, the reputation I'm going to get if I'm seen talking to two of them in one afternoon.

'Good afternoon, my child,' said the vicar, as we walked. 'Are you walking up to the green? Do you mind if I walk a few paces along with you?'

I kept my head down but nodded.

'Slow your pace a little, my child. I am not quite as young as you, remember.'

There was a little admonishment in his tone, so I unwillingly slowed my pace but still kept looking at the ground.

'I have seen you, of course, but do not know your name.'

'Emily, sir,' I said quietly.

'Emily,' he said. We walked a few paces in silence. Then he said, 'Forgive me for asking, Emily, but how old are you?'

'I do not know, sir,' I said.

'And have you had any schooling?' he asked next.

'No, sir,' I replied.

What was the point of this? We were approaching the green, so I stopped and faced him.

'Is there anything I can help you with, sir?' I asked boldly.

He looked down at me, a gaze of concern in his handsome face. He was a tall man with a shock of white hair and deep-set, brown eyes. He was concerned, yes, but also a little amused by me, I thought. I felt like a little rabbit before him. The feeling was not entirely unpleasurable. *Dordy, dordy, what is it with me this afternoon*, I thought, *am I giving off a scent or something?*

'Child, forgive me but I'll not keep you long. I just wanted to ask, are you happy with your degraded condition?'

I looked at him straight. Had *he* seen me talking with Thomas Freeman as well? 'What do you mean, sir?'

'I mean,' he lifted a hand towards the green, 'your road-side habits. Have you never wondered what it might be like to be a Christian girl, to live in a house and sleep in a bed and work and rest as the Lord intended?'

Oh, so that was it. Conversion. We had come across it many times before.

'I can't say as I have, sir.' Sometimes, it was worth encouraging them. You got presents if you baptised a baby, for instance. There were some Travelling families who did quite well going from parish to parish, finding God in each of them, and getting all ten of their children baptised every time.

'What if you were to take a position in a house, say, as a scullery maid? There are many advantages to such positions. Why, my own housekeeper is always saying she would well reward the right scullery girl if only she could find her.'

Is it my soul you're after or my working skills? I thought. At the time, it did not occur to me to think he might be after something else as well. I had met so few men, apart from our immediate group, that I had yet to learn that that is what they are all after, most of the time.

Oh Dei and Dadus, why did you keep me so protected? Why did I not know what happened if you gave a man any sort of encouragement, and that sometimes it could happen whether you encouraged him or not?

'Thank you, sir, but my mother is waiting for me.' I bobbed a little curtsey. I could think of no other way to be rid of him.

He leaned forward and laid a hand on my shoulder. 'Well, young lady, don't forget what I have said. Should you ever choose to live a different sort of life, then ways and means are open to you so to do.'

His hand was large, his grip firm. I knew nothing about men, but I knew this man felt he had the right to put his hand on my shoulder, and that I would be wise to keep my distance from him, however kindly he might seem.

I was troubled as I walked back to the camp, for my head was full of the encounters I had had that afternoon. I could not entirely distinguish between them: Thomas Freeman's smile and gentle voice, the vicar's hand upon my shoulder – the way my body felt warm and strange at night sometimes, a different body from the one I was used to. I wanted to be different, and was terrified of it. I could not name the feelings I had. But I felt as though I was on the verge of seeing the whole world in a new way, and although it was a frightening feeling, it was joyful as well.

My father was outside our *vardo*, whittling a stick. I looked at him warily as I approached. Redeemus Grey would surely have spoken to him straightaway. But Dadus looked at me and nodded in his normal, half-distracted manner, and I thought, maybe Redeemus Grey is not quite as hard a man as I have always thought him to be. Maybe he's decided to let me off – or maybe he just had other things on his mind.

That night, I lay on the grass between my Dei and Dadus – the weather was so fine, we were all sleeping outside, which was a thing that pleased me greatly at the time in my life when I was young, and safe. I loved stirring in the night, wakening a little, in that half-dreamy way. I loved lying on my back and looking up at the night sky, whether cloudy or star-lit, the whole of the eternity up there, opened up to me by the darkness, and me open to it too but safe between my parents. That night, I lay awake for ages with my arms flung above my head, as if to stretch out and show the all-of-me to the night sky, as if the very moon could swoop down and carry me high, high, high . . .

By the end of the week, a summer rain set in. It drizzled steadily through the next few days and the world went back to being damp and difficult, as it always does when it rains. The men and boys in our group started a good solid job on that Monday, up at Lowlands Farm. They were to build a new cow shed for the farmer, and clear some of his yards, and he wanted it done quickly so even the small boys were at it. Us girls were taking it in turns to go across the fields to the farm to take the men their victuals. They were out there from dawn 'til dusk, so it took several trips each day.

Come the Wednesday, it was my turn to do the to-ing and fro-ing, and what with helping with the preparation, that was most of my day occupied. Mid-morning, my mother prepared a basket of bread and cheese and sent me across the fields with it weighing heavily on my arm and my feet slipping on the wet grass. Before I left, she said that when I got back I was to put potatoes on the embers as she and Lena Grey were going out for eggs and she wanted the potatoes started.

A fine, warm drizzle fell as I crossed the fields. I was not really thinking about Thomas or the vicar that day. There is something about a change in weather that can make a week seem like a long time ago.

As I was approaching Lowlands Farm, I saw Redeemus Grey walking out of the yard. He saw me, and changed course to meet me on my way.

We met, and faced each other. There was a look on his face I didn't at all like, an angry look. I thought how he had spotted me talking with Thomas the previous week and wished that, if he was going to tell on me to my Dadus, he would do it quick and get it over with. Perhaps he was resenting me because he hadn't told yet, and would feel better when he had got me in trouble.

He held out one of his hands to take the basket. He was a large man, Redeemus Grey, with a huge round stomach and those fat lips that always look like they're inside out. 'That's for us, then.' He nodded at the basket.

I held it out reluctantly. I would have liked to have seen my Dadus and give it to him, not that there was any reason why I shouldn't give it to Redeemus Grey.

'I was on my way back to get something,' he said, 'Maybe I should give this to your father and walk back with you, eh?'

'I could fetch it for you, if you like,' I said hastily.

'All right, then,' he said, nodding. 'We need the trowel from my toolbox. Your father's got one but it's not as big as mine. We need mine.'

'I'll get it for you and be right back,' I said, and turned.

As I crossed the field, on the way back to the village, I congratulated myself on having avoided walking back with him, without ever asking myself why the thought of it made me so uncomfortable – or why, if he needed a trowel, he hadn't just sent one of the boys back to get it. Even if I had thought about it, I suppose I would have just assumed that he was disapproving of my friendship with Thomas Freeman and holding it against me. I don't think I would have put two and two together.

Between the fields and the village was a wide copse. The farmer used it for breeding game, I think. You didn't have to go through it to get back to Werrington, you could skirt round the edge. There was a narrow path between it and the hedgerow what bordered the field. It was as I passed down this path, skirting the corner of the copse that he stepped out, blocking my path.

He must have run like a hare to cut me off, as it would have taken him a few minutes longer to enter the copse at the top and cut through it to the edge of the field. He didn't have the basket with him, so must have stowed it somewhere.

I came to a halt, right in front of him. I felt sick and frightened inside of myself right away, even though I told myself it was just fat old Redeemus Grey and what was there to worry about, as he was nothing more than a man I didn't like much on account of his unpleasant appearance and manner with me.

There was a look on his face, a hateful look. I was beginning to realise I had seen that look on several occasions before.

Neither of us spoke for a while. I didn't speak because as long as we didn't say anything to each other then I could fool myself that there was nothing to worry about, that this was just one of those meaningless things that happens from time to time, instead of a disaster. I don't know why he remained silent. Enjoying himself, I suppose.

Eventually, I went to step round him. He moved to one side, blocking my path. I stopped, and tried the other way. I stopped again, took a deep breath, then turned on my heel to sprint back to the field, back to my father. That was a mistake, for it galvanised him into action, and later I was to wonder if maybe I could have talked my way out of it with promises. He caught me by the hair and pulled me backwards. The other hand came round my face to cover my mouth and pull me in close to him while he growled, 'You bite me and it'll be the worse for you.' I was trying to call out but could hardly make a sound and my heart was thumping loud in my ribcage as he dragged me into the copse, behind the bushes, and threw me down. He stood over me for a minute and I knew I had to talk fast. 'My mother'll be expecting me back, Mr Grey, she'll come looking for me in a minute, I'll be in trouble . . .' I got no further, for he was unbuttoning himself, and then he bent and pulled me into a sitting position. What he did then was a thing so awful I am ashamed to name it, for I did not even know it could be done. And while he did it, I began to choke and weep and he was talking to me saying, 'You'll not get the pleasure of them thin little boys that you'll get from me . . .'

and his voice was full of hatred, hatred spilling from him, salty like pig fat but thick as tar.

At first, when he made that strange sound, I though maybe he was dying and I'd be able to get away and he'd be found in the woods a few days later and nobody would ever know that it was me that killed him. He released my hair and stepped back a step or two, and that was when I turned on all fours and gagged into the wet leaves, spittle dropping down, my insides heaving.

I should have jumped up and run then – I could have got away if I'd run at that point. But I was so sick and frightened and shaking from head to foot, and I thought that was it. I even thought he might say sorry.

He was still standing over me and looking down at me. Maybe someone will come by, I thought. He'll have to move sharpish, then. Then I can hide in the bushes and sort myself out a bit before I go home. If I brushed the leaves off my skirts maybe I could make myself presentable. No one need know.

'I've seen you,' he said again, and his voice was just as vicious as before. 'I've seen you walking down the lane. Like it, do you? Walking past me like that, thinking all I can do is stare at it? Enjoyed yourself, have you, flaunting yourself to the *gorjer* boys 'cause you know they're too feeble to do anything about it? Didn't reckon on me, though, did you? I've heard you laughing, I've crept up on you when you've been behind the hedge, laughing to each other. I know what goes on in your filthy heads. My girls are just the same.' My head was swimming. What was he on about? His girls? He had been spying on us when we went to do our business, behind the hedge? Then I became more and more afraid, for I could tell that it wasn't over, that it had been going on for ages and I hadn't even known it. I didn't even like his girls. They were strange and sullen and I hardly even spoke to them if I could help it. And I thought of his wife and how quiet and bent she always seemed and how he had always been like just an ordinary man that we didn't like much and not this fat lump of hatred.

I glanced up at him. His breeches were still unfastened, and he was touching himself between his thumb and fingers. I looked away. I was sick with fear.

'Let's show you how it's really done then, shall we?' he said. And he knelt behind me and rested the flat of one thick, fat hand on my back to keep me bended. The other hand flung up my skirts, and then there was pain, just pain, and my face was in the dirt, and I was crying again and counting the seconds until it stopped and praying that no one came by to see me in such a low position, being done to as if I was nothing, and knowing I would always be nothing from now on because he was showing me how nothing I was.

When it was over, he lay on top of me. I was collapsed on the ground. His chest was over my face and I could hardly breath. There was a buckle or something sticking in my cheek. My other cheek was in the mud. He began to stroke my hair. 'So now you know, my little love,' he said, and his voice wasn't hateful any more. 'Now you know what all the fuss is about. You'll get to like it soon enough.' He rolled off me. I couldn't move. He did up his breeches, then stuck one of his hands in his pocket. 'Open your mouth,' he said.

All the fight had gone out of me then. I just remember thinking, please let him go away soon, then I can go back to the *vardo*. More than anything, I wanted to be in the *vardo* under a blanket like when I had the scarlet fever and Dei came and put wet rags on my forehead and sang to me.

'Here.'

I raised myself carefully on one elbow. My hair stuck to the mud on the ground and I had to free it with the other hand. He was holding a sixpence. He popped it onto my tongue, then closed my mouth by pushing at my chin. 'That's for keeping your mouth shut. You can buy yourself a bit of lace with that. I like lace on a girl.'

I gagged again and spat the coin into my hand. I sat looking at it on my palm.

He must have taken this for defiance, as he bent down and grabbed a handful of my hair and brought his face close to mine. His voice was low and filled with hate again. 'And if you speak a word of this out loud, I'll tell them all how you walked the length of Walton Lane with the baker's boy, laughing and talking with him, and went behind the hedge with him, and maybe I'll tell them how you sold yourself to me for the price of sixpence and they'll all know you for what you are then, won't they?'

Then he was gone.

I stood, unsteadily, and tried to brush some of the mud from my apron.

Going down to the stream was no good. I knew there wasn't enough water in the whole of the Great Ouse to wash away what had happened to me. And then I did something for which I have never forgiven myself. I put the coin in my apron pocket.

It might have all been different if my Dei had been at the *vardo* when I got back. Threats or no threats I could never have kept it from her if she had seen me in the state I was in. But she'd gone out for eggs. I was met on the green by Melinda Grey, Redeemus Grey's eldest, who took a long, hard look at me and pulled me into their *vardo*. Three of the young 'uns were in there and she tossed her head at them to go. 'What happened to her?' one of them said on the way out and Melinda snapped, 'She fell down in the spinney, now go and fix that fire unless you want a smack on the head.'

She tried to pull my things off me but my apron bow was too neat for her. I had to do it myself. When she saw the mud on my knees she stared for a moment before saying in a low, disgusted voice, 'Look at the state of you. Bundle it all up, for God's sake. You'll have to launder it straight off, all of it. I'll give you ours to mix in with it. It's your turn anyhow.' As I pulled my skirt down, I saw there was blood on the inside of it, and it was then I gave way. *He stabbed me*, I thought in terror. *I'll bleed to death*. I gave a low sob.

Melinda Grey took hold of my shoulders. 'Shut it, okay? Your Mam and mine will be back soon so you've got to pull yourself together.' She threw some of her sister's clothes at me. 'Put those on, then come down. If your Dei asks, say you came on early so I gave you some of my things to wear, helped you out.' She left the *vardo*.

I got dressed as quick as possible. I hated the idea that I was in *his vardo*, the place where he slept. My legs were still unsteady but I made it down the steps and Melinda was waiting with the tin bucket and a slab of grey soap. She handed them to me, then said, 'Wait here.'

While I waited, the three young 'uns sat in a row on the ground, staring at me. They know, I thought. Perhaps everyone will know when they look at me. I am different, now.

Melinda came back with a bundle of their underthings. Me and their two eldest girls and my cousin always took it in turns with the things the men and boys shouldn't see. 'Here,' she said. 'Orlanda has been on, so you'll have to scrub hers with a rock.'

There was something satisfied in her tone. I saw how it was, how now I would be washing underthings with a purpose and knowing it to be more than just another chore, like they'd been doing. I was one of them now.

'Go on,' Melinda said, 'and fix your hair while you're about it.'

It was only when I was down by the stream, on all fours, that I unfolded my dirty apron and found the sixpence. I looked at it. It was an old one, with the Queen a young woman with her hair up. I turned it over, staring at it, as if I'd never seen a sixpence before. On the other side was a coronet of leaves and the crown nestling atop of them, as if it was waiting there to be put on her head so's she would know she'd lost her youngness now and had to be Queen, whether she liked it or not.

I could have thrown the sixpence into the stream there and then I suppose, but there wasn't any point. It was far too late for that.

When a man doesn't want to leave you alone, there's nothing you can do about it. Too late, I realised that the only way out of my predicament would have been to have told Dei or Dadus straight-away, not have cleaned myself up. For once I had cleaned myself up, then I had been a party to the hiding of it, and then I was more afraid of being found out than I was afraid of Redeemus Grey. I wanted it to stop happening, but even more I wanted it to never have happened in the first place, and if my mother or father found out, then that would be impossible.

It was only a matter of time, and sure enough, that summer, I realised something was wrong. I started to feel peculiar. I got dugs, for a start, what I had never had before, being as flat as a pancake, like my Dei. And I felt exhausted all the time – not tired, normal tired, but completely done in, as if even walking to the end of the road was like crossing the whole of Cambridgeshire. I felt like that all day long. And then, as autumn came along, there was the unmistakeable swelling of my belly, low down, not soft like when you go to fat, but hard. I couldn't argue with that.

I was terrified. I didn't know what to say to Dei and Dadus. Luckily for me, my Dei was no fool. Nothing like that was going to get past her. She'd had her suspicions for a while before she took me up on it.

It was the only time she ever hit me. She said to me, 'Whose is it? Is it that baker's boy that you've been seen with?' I had not spoken to Thomas Freeman since what had happened with Redeemus Grey. I had avoided Walton Lane, and on the two occasions I had seen him in the village, I had run in the opposite direction.

I didn't know what to say to her, so I stayed mute. She took my silence for a yes, I suppose, and her small hand came swinging from nowhere and slapped me full across the face. It stung like anything, but I didn't move. I knew by then that I was going have to live with my mistakes.

She stared at me for a moment, then all at once, we both burst into tears. She took me in her arms and I sobbed like a baby and so did she, holding me so tight I thought she'd squeeze the life from me.

One of the best moments of my life was the moment we watched the others pull off Werrington Green. We had already moved into the cottage in the graveyard by then. We were not on speaking terms but happened to be walking along Church Road, all three of us, the morning they set off. They stayed stony faced, the lot of them, as they passed. Even my cousins who I had always got on well with. As their two *vardos* rattled by, I felt a huge weight lifting off and away from me at the thought that, with any luck, I would never set eyes on Redeemus Grey again.

The three of us stood in the street for a minute or two, then Dadus put his hand on my shoulder and said, 'Smiths should stick with other Smiths, I've always thought as much. When we want to move off, we'll go and join the Whittlesey lot.'

It was winter by then. Dei said, 'I thought I've told you to keep that shawl over your head. You've got to keep warm now, you know.'

One day, Dei said to me, 'If I go off to the marketstede tomorrow, I'll be gone all day. Can you manage?'

'Course I can, Dei,' I replied.

'Look after your Dadus, then.'

Dadus was out tending to the horse in the morning. I stayed in the cottage and did some knitting. He came back to get some water and talk about how it was time that horse had something more than chaff and mangold and he would have to go over to Gunthorpe the next day for linseed cake. Then he went out again.

As he left, I said, 'I'll do fried bread for tea when you get back, Dadus.' He nodded. He knew I always did it nice and crispy. We both liked it that way.

The trouble with the way I fry bread is, I like to shake it around a bit, and then you get fat spots all over the range. You have to give the range a good clean after I've been frying bread.

So the next thing I knew, I was outside in the cold and dark and the wind was howling fit to burst, as though there were ghosts in the trees a-shrieking for my child. It was the kind of evening that might have frightened me, under other circumstances, but I had something else on my mind.

I crawled a few yards, then the pain came again, and I had to stop and bend double. Behind our cottage was a large gravestone that had fallen over. I was heading for it. I don't know why. It was like the gravestone was a door floating down a wild river and I had to get to it or drown.

I made it to the gravestone. I grasped the sides. Beneath me would be the name of the person who was buried there, if I could read it. Above me, the wind was tossing the tops of the trees back and forth, back and forth – I could just see in the pitch dark, when I looked up. I think I was howling by then. There was no moon. The pain came again and I stopped thinking about anything else.

I was still on my knees, but as soon as I felt my baby slip from me, I rolled on one side quickly, to reach down for it and pull it up. I don't remember thinking I needed to do it – I don't recall saying to myself, *you must get that babby on your warm chest as soon as possible*. It was like my arms made their own decision, for there was a rawness about me, a hunger that dulled all pain. I scarcely noticed the strange slipperiness of this little thing what I was lifting to me.

The only light was the yellow glimmer from the cottage window, where we had tacked up an old blanket. The blanket had holes in it, and it was like there were small gold stars, gleaming but distant, shining down on me and my child. I could only just make out his face, screwed up and dark and furious – heavy browed, even then, annoyed at having been pushed into the world. *A baby . . . it's a baby . . .* I said to myself, over and over, as I held him. I could not have stopped myself from gazing at him for the world.

I huddled down on the rough gravestone, parted my blouse, and put him on me straightaway. He had not uttered a sound, but I knew he was all right as soon as his mouth fixed on me – the strangeness and discomfort of that tugging – and the feeling, too, that there was nothing more right than this. Whatever else might be wrong with the world was made right by just this.

I was still getting after-pains – my Dei explained later about how you had to get rid of all the stuff that came with him. *I hope she's back from market soon*, I thought, as I fed my newborn son. *There's no way I will be able to stand up until she comes to help me.* My legs were numb and shuddery. At that moment, I couldn't imagine ever walking again.

So I lay in the cold and dark and waited for my Dei. And I stroked Lijah's slimy little head and thought to myself. *This is it, now. It has happened. He is all I need, now, and all I will ever ask of him is one thing – that he outlives me.*

I saw then, how simple and straightforward the rest of my life would be. It would not matter what befell me and my baby. As long as he lived, that would be enough.

The storm died after a while and the wind dropped right down. The night became calm. When the carrier-cart eventually came up Church Street, I could hear the turning of its wheels. 'Dei!' I called out, long before she would have been able to hear me.

'*Dei!*'

I was surprised to hear how tiny my voice sounded, for I was as proud as a lion. I could not wait for her to come and discover me – us. '*Dei!*'

It would be a minute or two before she came. The cart would

have to pull up by the church. Then the driver would have to help her unload the things she had bought. Then she would have to pay him and open the cemetery gate and make her way down the path with her bundles. How sweet that little space of time was, when I could enjoy the thought of how much I was going to surprise her.

Even if Dei went into the cottage, the first thing she would say to Dadus would be, 'Where's our Lem?'

'You're going to meet my mother in a minute, *biti* boy,' I whispered to Lijah. The sweetness of that moment: the scattered handful of golden stars on the ragged blanket across our cottage window; the roughness of the gravestone beneath me; the small pains and the bitter cold; the knowledge that my Dei was coming; and the whispered bargain I was making with my son. *Live for ever, Lijah Smith. Tiny boy of mine, and mine alone. Never die.*

EPILOGUE

Peterborough – 1960

The colours of a wet spring day are green and grey. Mehitable Thompson thinks this as the hearse pulls into Eastfield Cemetery.

It is a mid-week morning, April. It has been raining for a month. The air is heavy with moisture and the ground pliant underfoot – easy work for the gravedigger. Mehitable thinks of earth as she steps down from the car and stands waiting as her father's coffin is pulled from the hearse; earth made heavy with rain, thick and dark, easy to break apart in great clods. She likes to plant her daffs on wet days like this one – but autumn has a different feel, of course.

Today, despite the drizzle and the cloudy skies, there is no doubting it is spring. The daffodils are dying off but a few tulip stems are splayed apart in bunches either side of the cemetery gates, their wide leaves whitening. It is damp but not that cold. None of them need their dark, heavy coats.

Scarlet steps down from the car behind Mehitable. She pauses to remove her woollen hat and smooth her hair back over her wide brow. She catches Mehitable watching her and smiles her broad, beautiful smile. Mehitable thinks, Scarlet, the baby of our family, in her fifties already. How old does that make me? That's the way it is with funerals. We all move up a step, one step closer to our turn. They'll start taking them out my pen pretty soon.

My father, Elijah Smith, is dead, Mehitable thinks to herself as they gather round the grave, *and the wet, dark earth is waiting*. He died in the spring.

The vicar says his piece. They gather round to bow their heads and drop handfuls of soil down onto Lijah's coffin. At a respectful distance, two young men wait to fill the rest of the hole after their departure. Nobody cries, although Dan's expression has an unnatural stiffness to it. Mehitable feels comforted by the rituals, glad of them. *Dad is where he should be. Maybe this time, for once, he will stay put.*

Her father has been living with them these last few years, ever since his own mother died – she sometimes feels he went from child to invalid in one fell swoop. It will be strange to have her house back, after all these years. They have got so used to Lijah's presence; his silences, his smell. At least I won't have to cook any more of those dreadful suet rolls, she thinks. He loved his suet, did her Dad.

His room won't take much clearing out. She has already looked: a few shirts, they can go to Barnados; a few bits of junk in the top drawer of the chest of drawers, one or two photos, his pipe, three handkerchiefs, two pairs of braces and a silk neckerchief. Under his bed were two pairs of shoes, a large stone from the garden and some yellowing newspapers.

She glances round the graveside group. Her husband stands slight apart, still shy even though he has known everyone for years. She sometimes feels he has never quite got over being her second husband. He has got to go to a meeting over at Ailsworth afterwards and she can feel his gentle impatience with proceedings. He catches her looking at him and smiles. She smiles back. Jim Thompson. Sometimes, she still cannot believe her luck. Jim winks.

She winks back. He was fond of Lijah, she knows, but, like her, is not inclined to be sentimental about his passing.

Her son Harry has come in his own car and he has brought Dan's wife Ida, their daughter Sally, and Sally's husband. Scarlet's two girls came in a car behind them, and they have brought poor Fenella's two with them. Tom, Fenella's widower, is poorly and couldn't make it. There are also a few of Lijah's old drinking pals from The Ghost Pig. It's a respectable turnout. They are all going back to Scarlet's house afterwards, although Mehitable suspects the drinking pals will melt away to toast Lijah's health in their own fashion.

Dan, herself and Scarlet; three children out of five. You should have the whole set at your funeral. But no one has heard of Bartholomew in decades and Fenella, poor old Nellie, lies beneath the earth a few yards away, eleven years dead. A car struck her as she crossed Cowgate one evening with her husband Tom. They never caught the driver.

No one should have to outlive a child, Mehitable thinks, no matter what they've done. Lijah lost a daughter within months of losing his mother – small wonder he got old soon after that.

Looking around the group, Mehitable feels warmly towards them all. For all their histories, they are all there, together, and there seems something fine about that. Everyone looks philosophical, rather than miserable. It is a *had-a-good-innings* sort of funeral, after all; a spring funeral, grey and green – hopeful.

After the internment, they stand around, talking quietly. Then, with no one in particular suggesting it is time to leave, they turn and walk down the path towards the cars. Scarlet comes up to Mehitable, reaches out and slips an arm through hers, drawing her in close. Then, as if a little embarrassed by the gesture, she says, 'Still cold, in't it? For April. I'm glad he went in the spring. I think he would have liked that. He liked things green and new.'

Mehitable sighs. Then she stops, slips her arm from Scarlet's and says without looking at her. 'I think I want to go and see Mum.'

Scarlet looks at her older sister. 'You sure?'

Mehitable shrugs. 'Well I don't think I'll be coming back here much so it's now or never.'

'Shall I come with you?'

'If you like.'

Dan is walking ahead with Ida and Sally. Scarlet calls after them. 'Dan, we're going to see Mum. We'll catch you up.'

Dan raises the flat of his hand in acknowledgement.

The two sisters turn and link arms again, more firmly this time, a mutual gesture. They stride briskly back down the path. Mehitable thinks, nice to have Scarlet to myself for a bit.

The path reaches a crossroad. They both stop and look around. It is a large cemetery. The graves stretch in all directions.

'I found Gran's conch shell in our garden shed last week,' Scarlet says. 'I didn't even know we'd got it. Do you remember that conch shell?'

'I remember the canary.'

'What happened to the canary?'

'It's this way, isn't it?' Mehitable points to the right.

Scarlet shakes her head, 'Don't think so. She'll be in the old bit.'

Mehitable frowns.

Scarlet adds, gently, 'We're talking over thirty years, Billy. It's a long time ago.'

A long time ago: the worlds held captured in that phrase. Mehitable closes her eyes briefly, clutching Scarlet's arm for support.

She can feel Scarlet's concerned gaze upon her. She opens her eyes and straightens herself.

'Come on, then,' she says.

They find it quickly: a large headstone, facing the path. They stand staring at it for some time. Mehitable looks up and sees that they are being watched by a pair of pigeons sitting on the branch of a nearby tree. The pigeons look down at her. One of them cocks its head on one side.

'Do you know something,' says Scarlet, in a well-blow-me kind of voice. 'I'd completely forgotten that Gran was in there with her.'

'Yes, well . . .' Mehitable says, a small laugh in her voice.

Their father had turned up on her doorstep one day, and when she had opened the door, he had looked up at her and said, 'I buried your Gran last week.' That was the first they knew about it. Scarlet had refused to talk to him for six months. *This time he's gone too far*, she'd said. She had a point.

Then came Fenella's death, the awfulness of it, and for a while after that, nothing else had mattered.

'Is it quite right, do you think?' Scarlet says. 'Them being in together. I mean, shouldn't Mum be in with Dad?'

'I don't know, really.'

'Well, either way, it's a bit late now,' Scarlet adds.

They stare at the gravestone. In its inscription, Clementina and Rose's positions are reversed. Rose is on top. *In Loving Memory* the curved lettering reads, then in impressive capitals, *ROSIE SMITH*.

Scarlet nudges Mehitable. 'Her name was Rose, not *Rosie*. Now that definitely isn't right. You should have your proper name on your gravestone, shouldn't you?'

'I don't know when he had the gravestone put up,' says Mehitable. Then she reads the rest of the inscription out loud. As she does, she is unable to keep her voice from sounding dry. '*A loving wife, a mother dear, a faithful friend lies resting here.*'

Scarlet ignores the sarcasm. 'That's nice,' she says firmly.

Underneath, in smaller letters, is inscribed, *also of CLEMENTINA LEE.*

'Well, Mum's on top of her at last,' murmurs Mehitable.

'I should think the two of them are pretty much mixed up together by now,' says Scarlet. 'Have we time to go and see Nellie?'

'We should catch up with Dan, really. Nellie's all right.' I want to feel more, thinks Mehitable. All these years, I've made such a big deal about not coming here; you'd think I'd feel something more than this.

She draws her coat tighter around her, even though she isn't cold. *It doesn't feel like anything to do with us,* she thinks, staring down at the grave. *It feels like it's more to do with Mum and Gran together. It doesn't matter whether we're here or not.*

Scarlet glances over her shoulder. Mehitable follows her gaze and sees that the others have nearly reached the gate.

And there's Dad all on his own over there, and Fenella waiting for her Tom, and none of us above ground matter to them – I'm glad I don't believe in ghosts, she thinks. *If our lot could climb out of these graves at night there would be some good old family rows going on in Eastfield Cemetery while the rest of them were trying to sleep.*

Scarlet says, 'I'll leave you here for a bit, shall I?'

Mehitable replies quickly, 'No, I'm coming,' but Scarlet has stepped away. Still, Mehitable cannot move.

A picture of herself comes into her head. She was walking home from school one day, alone. It was lunchtime and she should have been going back into her class. A girl two years older than herself had pushed her over in the playground. Daniel wasn't there that day or he would have dealt with it. She was alone, with the jeering, and she had got right up and walked out of school.

She remembered walking home, through Sutton, crying all the way, with mud on her dress, feeling nothing but a raw need to be at home.

How old was I? Not small, surely, if it was Sutton. Old enough.

She had walked back to the cottage, but when she got there, she had known how angry her mother would be and was too frightened to go inside. She had stopped crying by then and knew she would be in trouble for having walked out of school in the middle of the day. She didn't know what to do, so she sat on the front step and waited. She had left her cardigan behind at school and was cold. After a while, she began to shiver.

Eventually, her mother had opened the front door, on her way out on some errand. She had started at the sight of Mehitable, shivering and muddy, on the step. Then she had sighed, wearily, stared down at her and said, 'What do *you* want?'

Mehitable stares at her mother's grave. I never have to come here again, she thinks to herself. This is the last time I will dwell on it. She turns away.

As she and Scarlet walk briskly down the path, she thinks, funny how there is this huge wall between the living and the dead – and funny that I should think it funny. I could have stood at the side of Mum's grave and cursed her for all eternity, or wept and forgiven her everything, and none of it would have made any difference. She can't hear me, and the words just echo back. When you look at a grave it's about as significant as looking down into a puddle. All you see is yourself, peering back up.

Maybe, one day, someone will come and look at my grave, maybe somebody I don't even know, and all they will see is themselves peering back, but they won't know that. They will think it's me. She finds the idea heartening. I will be thought about. Someone will wonder what it felt like to be me. And that is how we live on, in other people's heads, in their thinking things about us, even if they get it wrong.

It's a nice thought, she thinks, that nobody can know us, that we are thought about but safe, secret. She pulls Scarlet in close and smiles at her. Scarlet smiles back. As they approach the gate, she sees that Dan, their brother, is waiting for them. He holds out his arms.

Fires in the Dark

Louise Doughty

1927, rural Bohemia: a son is born to Joesf, leader of a company of Coppersmith gypsies. The son is Yenko, the prince of his tribe, treasured and protected from the growing hardships and restrictions imposed on his people. But his childhood world is soon overwhelmed by the Great Depression of the 1930s, the rise of Nazism and the calamity of the Second World War. Interned in a camp, Yenko faces the hardest decision of his life, to escape alone or stay and risk perishing with his family.

'An epic novel...absorbing, shocking, hopeful' *Mail on Sunday*

ISBN-13: 978-1-47113-758-7
£7.99

Honey-Dew

Louise Doughty

A brutal murder punctures the tranquility
of a rural idyll: a middle-aged couple are
found stabbed to death; their teenaged
daughter is missing.
'Where is Gemma?' demands the headline
of the Rutland Record. Alison, chief
reporter, endeavours to unravel the truth
and in doing so must confront the shadows
of her own, shocking past and the
bleakness at the heart of the prettiest of
English Country Counties.

'A darkly comic and disturbing reminder
of the messiness of real life, and of
people's ability to absorb the most
startling events – even murder'
Independent

ISBN-13: 978-1-47113-682-5
£7.99

Dance With Me

Louise Doughty

A man dies a week after re-writing his will. In it, he has left everything he owns to a woman he has known for only three weeks. As Bet investigates Peter's past, she discovers that her ex-lover was not all that he seemed...

In a crumbling office block, another woman has a different sort of ghost to confront. Iris runs her own business but strange things keep happening. Her phone rings and there's no one there. Somebody taps at her door. In the basement, something unpleasant is lurking....

'If you haven't got the Louise Doughty habit, get it now. She's the tops' *Evening Standard*

ISBN-13: 978-1-47113-681-8
£7.99

Crazy Paving

Louise Doughty

Against a rising tide of commuter mayhem, three women struggle in to work. Caught up in the chaos on the streets – and in the equally savage battle surrounding their boss's extortion racket – Annette, Joan and Helly are forced to ditch everything for an offensive of their own, only to find the cruelest circumstances can make heroines of us all.

'Like Dickens with a one-day Travelcard'
Observer

ISBN-13: 978-1-47113-683-2
£7.99